The Vulcan stood still as if too shocked to move.

Kirk stepped forward, doing his best to look alarmed and contrite. "Okay, so I started a fight when this alien hit me, but—"

Gilfillan gave Kirk a firm push on his shoulder to get him and his companion started toward the SCIS car.

Kirk tried to twist away, protesting. "That guy tried to put something in my pocket and I pushed it away."

But the agents weren't listening and the Vulcan was not resisting.

The inside of the car's back passenger compartment was uncomfortable and covered with a seamless coating of an easy-to-disinfect nanofilm to which nothing would stick—except the lingering odors from a hundred other prisoners. Kirk grimaced at the smell as he was thumped back in his seat and the restraints closed over him. He turned to look at the alien still cuffed to his wrist. The Vulcan stared straight ahead, his posture ramrod stiff.

Kirk frowned, leaned back, and closed his eyes as the car took off. "Well, this is going to be fun," he said.

The Vulcan offered no response.

Kirk sighed. This was going to be a longer night than he had planned. He might as well make the best of it.

"Jim Kirk," he said.

"Spock."

OTHER BOOKS BY WILLIAM SHATNER

with Judith & Garfield Reeves-Stevens

Star Trek: Totality
Captain's Peril
Captain's Blood
Captain's Glory

Star Trek: The Mirror Universe Saga
Spectre
Dark Victory
Preserver

Star Trek: Odyssey
The Ashes of Eden
The Return
Avenger

with Chris Kreski
Get a Life!

with Chip Walter
Star Trek: I'm Working on That

STAR TREK®
ACADEMY

COLLISION COURSE

WILLIAM SHATNER

WITH JUDITH & GARFIELD REEVES-STEVENS

BASED ON *STAR TREK*
CREATED BY GENE RODDENBERRY

Pocket Books
New York   London   Toronto   Sydney

Pocket Books
A Division of Simon & Schuster, Inc.
1230 Avenue of the Americas
New York, NY 10020

This book is a work of fiction. Names, characters, places, and incidents either are products of the authors' imagination or are used fictitiously. Any resemblance to actual events or locales or persons, living or dead, is entirely coincidental.

First Pocket Books paperback edition November 2008

POCKET and colophon are registered trademarks of Simon & Schuster, Inc.

For information about special discounts for bulk purchases, please contact Simon & Schuster Special Sales at 1-800-456-6798 or business@simonandschuster.com.

Cover design by John Vairo Jr.; cover art by James Wang

Manufactured in the United States of America

10 9 8 7 6 5 4 3 2 1

ISBN-13: 978-1-4165-0397-2
ISBN-10:   1-4165-0397-8

To

Grant
Eric
Kaya
Willow
Natasha

They, too, are the future.

I'd like to acknowledge the contributions
of all who have added their own unique vision to
Star Trek. The series went on the air in 1966, and since
then many individuals have used their talents to shape
the legends that became the worlds and history of the
Federation and beyond.

Among the first—
John Black
Gene Coon
Harlan Ellison
D.C. Fontana
Sam Peeples
Theodore Sturgeon
Barry Trivers

Every writer who contributes to the tapestry that is *Star
Trek* weaves their own thread that adds to the warp and
woof of the epic begun by Gene Roddenberry.

My thanks to them all.

The plot, story lines, and historical narrative presented in *Star Trek: Academy—Collision Course* constitute an imaginative work deriving solely from the author's unique personal vision.

I have always found some hope for myself in the fact that the Enterprise *crew could be so humanly fallible and yet be some of those greater things, too.*

—GENE RODDENBERRY

1

That first night in San Francisco when it all began was cool and gray and thick with fog. Soft billows of it drifted over the Academy, causing its tall locked gates to phase in and out of visibility for the teenager dressed in black, lost in the shadows across Pacific Street.

His name was Jim Kirk, and he was seventeen years old, plus five months. There was no fear in him, and there hadn't been for three years.

From the safety of a dense bank of juniper, Kirk studied the Academy's Presidio Gate with disdain for what it represented, and with growing confidence for what was to come, based on what he *didn't* see. Blue-white floodlights played over the old stonework, revealing the slow tumble of the evening fog as it flowed unobstructed through ironwork. Beyond, low streetlamps picked out the curving path of Presidio Boulevard, their halos fading with distance into the night and the glowing mist that enshrouded the Academy's vast campus.

Just as he'd expected, there were no signs of guards or other watchers. After all, this was a perfect world. How could Starfleet even conceive of someone like Kirk doing what he planned to do this night?

"This is such a bad idea," Elissa Corso whispered.

Kirk turned to his girlfriend and grinned to reassure her. As far as he was concerned, this was the best idea he had had in weeks. But there was just enough fog-filtered light falling through the branches to reveal the worry in her eyes.

"Elissa, there's no one there."

"Not at the gate."

"So we'll be fine."

Elissa frowned, not convinced. Kirk took her hand. "Look, they've got no right to go after you, and you know it. Their system's at fault." He held up his homemade override, a jury-rigged homebrew concoction of transtator filaments mounted inside an old tourist translation device. To the untrained eye, it was little more than a dented metal tube, not much larger than a finger. But Kirk had been bashing transtator kits since he was four. The old dented tube had a few surprises inside.

Elissa reached out for the override. "No—you'll set off an alarm or something."

Kirk teasingly held the device behind his back, hoping to bring her just close enough for him to steal a kiss.

Elissa refused to play, but Kirk knew he'd won. She couldn't resist his smile. Never had been able to. Her eyes were bright now, forgiving.

She slapped a hand against his chest. "What am I going to do about you?"

"Love me. What else?"

Elissa rolled her eyes, and laughed because he was right.

He kissed her and she didn't pull back.

"Hsst! Jimmy!" It was Sam; his timing, as always, awful.

Kirk waved one hand dismissively, used the other to sweep Elissa closer, not releasing her. Until a hand clamped on his shoulder.

"Give it a rest," Kirk's brother said. "I found one."

George Samuel Kirk was four years older, his sandy hair was longer, and he was thicker in the middle, running to fat. But tonight, clad in the same type of dark jacket, jeans, and boots that Kirk wore, most people would have a hard time telling the brothers apart, their resemblance was that strong, each his father's son.

Kirk reluctantly freed Elissa, who was by this time satisfactorily breathless, dizzy. "Okay . . . show me."

Sam held up a palm-size bicorder, the kind of commercial sensor anyone could purchase in a corner shop—and the kind Kirk excelled at modifying. The device's small screen displayed a quantum interference grid that looked like a random scattering of lurid purple sand. But Kirk saw in it what he needed to see—a repeating pattern.

"Good one, Sam." Kirk turned to Elissa. "What did I tell you? When you think you live in a perfect world, you get sloppy."

Elissa only sighed, mercifully forgoing her usual protest to Sam. For some reason she'd been unable to explain to Kirk, his older brother made her nervous. Though Kirk always stood by Sam in public, privately he thought he understood what bothered Elissa. But tonight, if she'd decided to be cooperative, despite her misgivings and Sam's involvement, then Kirk certainly wasn't going to disagree. After all, everything he was about to do was for her.

At Kirk's signal, the three of them turned away from Pacific Street and the Presidio Gate to the Academy and moved quietly back through the juniper bushes to the overflow visitor's lot. This early in August, with regular classes still three weeks away and only plebes going through indoctrination at the Academy, almost all the vehicle slots were empty. Almost.

In a lot capable of holding two hundred vehicles, there were fifteen parked overnight. Three were rental groundcars anyone could access with a currency card; four were robotic transports likely waiting until normal business hours to make their automated deliveries. The eight other vehicles were the reason Kirk was here.

They were Starfleet staff cars—compact, aerodynamically sleek vehicles designed to carry four to six personnel on official business. A few had Academy markings, the rest had fleet designations. All of them—white, of course—gleamed in the lot floodlights. White was the color of truth and purity and all the other self-righteous qualities Starfleet claimed to stand for. But Kirk wasn't fooled. "Which one?" he asked.

Sam led the way. "Fifth one. It's got a K-series navigation interface."

Kirk walked past the other vehicles with the bicorder, feeling no concern about being detected in this lot. The surrounding foliage blocked any view from the streets, and the simple sensor repeater he'd set up on their arrival continued to send out an unchanging signal to the lot's surrounding security sensors, reassuring the monitoring computers that nothing was on the move here.

Kirk focused the bicorder on the K-series vehicle. It was a heavy-duty version of a civilian Sky Rover with four ground wheels instead of landing skids. He couldn't tell how many antigrav plates it had—they were out of sight on the vehicle's underside. But all he would need for his demonstration was one.

He waved Elissa over, showed her the quantum interference grid again. "Here's the problem," he told her. "The car's controller is protected by a Starfleet encryption key. Quantum entanglement algorithms. More possible code combinations than there're elementary particles in the universe. Unbreakable, right?"

"So I've been told." Elissa kept looking around as if she didn't trust his assurances about the sensor repeater. In contrast, Sam stood ready, waiting, his silence and stance conveying complete faith in his younger brother's technical prowess.

"Smoke and mirrors," Kirk said. "Maybe that's what they use on starships—those things are untouchable. But on the small stuff like these cars—*and* the security lockouts at the Academy—look how the complexity of the key has been scaled down. There's a repeating pattern in there. See it?"

Elissa nodded.

"Ten million possible combinations, tops," Kirk said. He

held up his override. "This'll sort through all of them in under five seconds."

Elissa looked at him askance. "If you figured it out, don't you think someone at Starfleet might have, too? Built in some safeguards?"

"You spent a year at the Academy and you still don't understand these people."

Elissa began to object, but Kirk acted quickly to cut off the argument he was sure she was about to make. "What it comes down to is this: If Starfleet is so damned perfect, then why are they accusing an innocent person of breaking into the lab?"

His girlfriend's eyes flashed with indignation.

"Did you steal the dilithium?" Kirk pressed on.

He could see her control herself with difficulty. "You know I didn't."

"Okay. So all I'm saying is, their system screwed up and this is why." With dramatic flair, he pointed his override at the staff car, pressed a single blue switch. "Watch."

Two small control lights flickered on the side of the override, changing from amber to red in a blur. A few moments later, less than the five seconds Kirk had predicted, the staff car's interior lights switched on and the door locks clicked.

Kirk gave Elissa a quick "I told you so" smile and she grudgingly nodded.

Sam was more enthusiastic, gave his little brother a punch on the shoulder. "Jim-*mee!*"

"Thank you, thank you," Kirk said to an imaginary cheering crowd. "And for my encore . . ." He pressed the blue switch twice and instantly the staff car's power cells activated and its suspension rose a few centimeters, ready to be driven.

"So much for Starfleet security measures," Kirk said.

He enjoyed Elissa's change of expression as she finally realized that everything he had been telling her the past two weeks was right.

She looked from the waiting staff car to the override. "It's really that easy?"

"It helps if you're a genius," Kirk said.

"And modest," Sam added with a laugh.

"Can I show the override to my conduct adviser?"

"That's the whole idea. You're innocent and this is the proof."

Elissa launched herself at Kirk and wrapped both arms around him in gratitude. "Thank you!"

Kirk winked at Sam, but Sam wasn't paying attention to his brother's sweet moment of victory. Instead, he was looking across the almost empty lot.

"Sam . . . ?" Kirk began.

That was when the floodlights brightened and an amplified voice blared, *"You! Stay where you are!"*

Elissa jerked away from Kirk. "You said we'd be safe! I believed you!"

Kirk saw three dark figures running across the lot toward them, palmlights slashing through the fog. It didn't matter, though. He'd already done what he'd set out to do. "We're still okay. They can't catch us." He turned in the opposite direction. "Let's go!"

But from the opposite direction, two more figures ran at them, rapid footfalls like an approaching avalanche.

"Oh, crap," Sam said.

Elissa was furious. "That's it. I'm expelled."

But Kirk refused to admit defeat. He never would. He grabbed Elissa by the shoulder. "I said I'd help you and I will!"

"How, genius?"

Kirk aimed the override at the activated staff car, jammed his thumb on the blue switch. The doors slid open. "Get in!" He pushed Elissa into the back seat of the car. His brother stopped him before he could jump into the driver's seat. "I'll drive!"

Kirk quickly moved Sam aside. "You get picked up again, they'll cancel probation, remember?"

Kirk slipped into the driver's seat, Sam beside him. Behind them, Elissa stared out through the rear windshield, pulsing halos in her hair where the flashing palmlights played over her.

"*Get outta the car!*" the amplified voice boomed.

"Seat belts," Kirk commanded, then punched the control to close the doors as the car lurched forward, tires squealing.

Now shafts of light flashed through the staff car's front windshield as Kirk swerved around the first three figures who'd charged them.

Sam turned in his seat as they sped past. "One of them's on a communicator!"

Kirk swiftly checked the console navigation screen. "Ten blocks . . . see that overpass . . . we can dump the car there, grab a magtrain." He glanced back at Elissa. "Then hit Chinatown for some pizza. Is that a plan or what?"

An even more powerful light blazed through the back window. "Apparently not," Elissa said.

The staff car's emergency-alert speakers blared to life. "*Unauthorized vehicle, this is San Francisco Protective Services. Pull over at once!*"

Elissa slapped the back of Kirk's seat for emphasis. "Do what they say. Now. Don't make this any worse for me."

"I made a promise," Kirk insisted. His hand moved to flip three red switches on the console.

Elissa leaned forward, panicked, knowing what the switches were for. "No!"

"Oh, yessss," Kirk said. Then he pulled back on the steering yoke and the staff car soared into the air, leaving the SFPS patrol car on the road.

Sam whistled. "You have any idea what you're doing, Jimmy boy?"

Kirk savored the thrum of the car's Casimir emitters as it climbed over the fog-smeared lights of San Francisco. "Always," he answered.

He banked into the night, punching through the fog layer until the stars suddenly filled the night sky above him. And for all the adrenaline and excitement of the moment, for all the thrill of flying, the glimpse of stars inexplicably swept him with regret.

"Always," he said again, shaking off the odd feeling, then whooped with the sheer joy of free flight as he barrel-rolled the car and dove back into the sheltering fog, turning his back on the stars once more.

Just as he had three years ago.

2

There was no logic to it, but as he made his way down the steep and narrow street to the waterfront, the Vulcan felt that everyone he passed was watching him.

His name was Spock, and as time was measured on Earth he was just older than nineteen years. By other Earth standards, he was painfully thin, though that was a matter of genes, not choice. Vulcan was a desert world, and life there had adapted to extreme conditions and limited resources.

But then, in addition to being a child of Vulcan, his father's world, he was also a child of this world, his mother's.

A human might have hated that accident of chance and circumstance that had brought so much confusion and heartache to his childhood. But Spock had risen above such petty emotions because he had realized that, with his Vulcan abilities, he could will himself to be whatever he chose to be.

Thus, he had chosen to be Vulcan and only Vulcan: His intellect and force of will could easily overcome any weakness of the flesh brought on by his human heritage. So he walked the streets of this city as a stranger, though his black cloak and long black hair reduced him to only a shadow in the atmospheric haze, indistinguishable from other pedestrians in the night.

And yet, Spock still couldn't shake the feeling that every human stared at him as he passed and judged him out of place.

At the waterfront, the fog bank was even thicker, but there were more lights from the shops and restaurants and streetlamps. The entire area seemed to shimmer.

Groundcars hummed slowly along the narrow street, guided by sensors and not their fallible drivers. The overhead traffic made little more sound than the muffled rush of distant ocean breezes, only the occasional running light visible as a rapid, approaching glow, here for a moment, then gone.

Spock was reminded of the vision-obscuring sandstorms of home, though eerily no winds battered him. After eight months of living in the Vulcan diplomatic compound in San Francisco, the Earth city's weather patterns still eluded him.

He turned right at the corner, the water on his left, and made his way along the broad pedestrian walkway, his destination in sight: a food and entertainment emporium, its demarcation a red glow pulsing in the mist.

At fifty meters, Spock could decipher the holographic letters above the entrance: THE GARDEN OF VENUS. The outlines of humanoid female bodies without clothing faded in and out of the floating letters. One silhouette had a blue cast to it, and antennae, as if to indicate that Andorian females waited inside with the others. Spock experienced a flash of contempt for humans and their appetites, but suppressed it at once. He was certainly not affected by the images, nor drawn by them. Logic had brought him here tonight and no other reason.

The first set of doors opened automatically, and a warm gust of air engulfed him, carrying with it the scents of alien spices. Alien to Earth, at least. His sensitive hearing next detected an almost subliminal acoustic signal, the intermixed sounds of heavy breathing set in time to a cardiac rhythm. Spock's heartbeat was much faster than the human pattern that was playing. With scornful amusement, he noted the supposedly erotic soundscape was actually relaxing to a Vulcan, then quickly suppressed that emotion, too.

He walked purposefully into the entrance, each of his steps along the corridor precisely measured.

As he neared a second set of doors, where a short line of

patrons stood waiting by a greeter, Spock reminded himself to concentrate, to ignore the flickering wall displays of dancing females, their images no longer silhouettes. Vulcans could not be distracted, so neither could he.

"I need some ID, kid."

Spock blinked in surprise. He abruptly realized he was next in line and that he *had* been distracted by the graphic wall displays.

He reached inside his cloak, his hand brushing past the IDIC medallion he wore, then withdrew the ID case he had prepared for such a challenge.

The greeter was a tall human, thickly muscular, garbed in a formal black suit, white shirt, and small black neck brooch. He thumbed Spock's ID case, read the data display that slipped up from it, sneered as he handed it back. "Vulcan, huh?"

Spock's expression didn't change, but inwardly he concluded the greeter was somehow visually impaired. How else to explain he hadn't realized Spock wasn't human?

"Have fun, kid."

Spock couldn't help himself. "Vulcans do not have 'fun.' I am on a field trip to research human mating patterns and—"

The human cut him off. "Yeah, right. You're also holding up the line."

Spock set aside his no-longer-necessary, carefully constructed cover story. A pity, since he had spent days perfecting it. Annoyed with himself for feeling regret, and then again for feeling annoyed, he tugged his cloak tight and entered the main room.

The sudden shock to all his senses made him pause until the next people to be admitted pushed past him, making him stumble.

How could any sentient being come to such a confusing environment by choice? Music blared with a thought-disturbing beat. Insufficient lighting escaped small glowing red orbs on each table. On elevated platforms around the multilevel expanse, females writhed in a manner that the crowd of gaping humans obviously regarded as erotic, stimulating. Not that he was stimulated.

A flotilla of servers wove their way through the excited customers, guiding antigrav trays with food and drink—mostly drink, Spock observed—from table to table, with a constant clattering of glassware and a cacophony of conversations, each trying and failing to rise above the music.

Spock resolutely recited a Surakian mantra of calm, and sensation by sensation closed down his senses to the chaos here. His teachers had told him that, in time, that ability would become second nature. Perplexingly, they had told him that when he had been eight, and he still hadn't reached the required level of proficiency.

Then, remembering his instructions, Spock swept his gaze along the outermost ring of tables, each inset into a secluded alcove on the upper level that ringed the room. As he had been told, his contact was waiting at the eighteenth table alone. He made his way there, consciously avoiding looking at the dancers, though he couldn't help noticing that one wore artificial ear pieces to make herself look Vulcan. She wore nothing else. Spock was appalled. Sometimes, humans were little more than animals.

"You're late," his contact said. She also was human, perhaps twenty-five years old, Spock deduced, with butterfly make-up that could only be described as extravagant, and, he decided, unnecessary. Her features were quite regular, what humans would call attractive. Confusingly, even though the words the young human spoke were an admonition, she smiled warmly as she said them.

Spock knew better than to make excuses. The Vulcan term was *kaiidth*. What was, was. He got down to business.

"Do you have my money?"

The young woman laughed and leaned forward, patting the banquette beside her. Spock's eyes reflexively dropped for an instant from her face to the unfastened opening of her top garment that had yawned further open with her movement. When his eyes met hers again, she seemed even more amused.

He sat down on the edge of the banquette, as far from her as he could, assailed by her cloying perfume, heavily laced with pheromones. He doubted any human male could resist her sexual appeal, and though such enticements were, of course, not an issue with him, Spock regretted not bringing his nasal filters, if only to cut the impact of the twenty-seven different aromatics that made up the main notes of her scent. Like any Vulcan's, his sense of smell was exquisitely sensitive.

"I'm Dala," the young woman said. She held out her hand.

Spock recognized the gesture, but declined to reciprocate. He had decided to act with utmost seriousness tonight. "I am Spock."

Dala's eyes sparkled in the warm light from the iridescent orb on their table. She didn't withdraw her hand. "I don't bite."

Spock was taken aback. "Why would you?"

Dala sighed and lifted her drink, a concoction of three separate liqueurs that formed distinct vertical ribbons of color: red, blue, and yellow. When she sipped from it, the colors mixed, then separated again when she replaced the glass on the table. "You've never done this before, have you?"

"On the contrary." Spock wondered if Dala believed him, but was unable to read her smile. It was quite unlike his mother's.

"I have your money. Do you have the item?"

"Show me," Spock said.

The young woman idly ran one finger down her throat. "I could, but that's not how this works."

Spock's gaze automatically followed her finger's journey, down to . . .

He cleared his throat—irritation from the perfume, he knew—then removed a small, linen-wrapped object from his cloak. He placed it on the table, but did not let go. He wondered if he should try to analyze the dynamics of this unsettling meeting as if it were a chess game, but he had difficulty picturing the pieces on the board.

Dala, however, nodded her satisfaction with his action and, in turn, put a credit wafer on the table by her drink. Stripes of colored light filtered by that drink fell across it. "Now you show me."

Spock pulled back the wrapping to reveal a red clay figurine, small enough to fit in the palm of even Dala's hand. It was a crude, squat representation of a Vulcan *seleth* warrior, wearing a traditional tripartite helmet and holding a stylized *lirpa* to his chest.

"May I?" Dala asked.

Spock looked at the credit wafer. She slid it across the smooth tablecloth. When he reached for it, she at last took his hand and lightly ran her fingers over his.

Spock froze, spoke hoarsely. "You may inspect the artifact."

"With pleasure."

Dala released his hand to take the figurine, but Spock did not pick up the wafer. He ran mantra after mantra through his mind, telling himself he was a Vulcan. But at his core, at least half of it, he was also a nineteen-year-old human male, and from that perspective this young woman was, at the very least, an undeniable distraction.

Only when Dala ran a thin, pen-sized sensor over the figurine did Spock collect himself enough to check the balance on the wafer. Six thousand credits, as agreed.

The young woman coolly read out the small data display the sensor projected on the tablecloth. "Three thousand years. Definitely pre-Enlightenment."

"Vulcans do not lie," Spock said firmly. He had practiced saying that for days. Deception was very new to him.

Dala turned her attention from the figurine to him. "This is very valuable, Spock. I'm sure you could be in a great deal of trouble when they find it's been stolen."

"I have taken measures. The curators will think it has been misplaced."

"What measures?"

"That is not your concern."

"It is. I'd like to do this again. With you."

"That would be satisfactory." Spock felt pride at the steadiness of his voice, then just as quickly irritation with his pride.

Dala slid closer to him, stopping close enough to remain out of contact, just. Spock could feel the heat of her.

"Do I make you nervous?"

"The state of being nervous is an emotional response."

Spock's eyes widened as Dala's finger lightly touched his cheek. "And Vulcans have no emotions, is that true?" she whispered in his ear. Her breath was warm and . . .

Spock struggled to stare straight ahead. "That is not completely accurate. Rather, we do not allow emotions to control our actions."

"I see." Dala's finger parted his hair to reveal his pointed ear. She made a sound in her throat that to Spock sounded like a *sehlat* purring. "How sweet. What a shame you keep them covered up."

Spock's tenuous control collapsed. Defensively, he turned to face her, then jerked back sharply. Her face was a finger's width from his. Spock's chest constricted until he thought he would pass out.

"Your behavior is not appropriate."

But to his horror, not even his attempted emulation of his father's implacable tone affected his aggressor. Dala only leaned closer, inhaled as if savoring a fine bouquet. "Oh, I haven't even begun to be inappropriate . . ."

"We should be discussing our business arrangements."

"That's what I'm doing," Dala said with a terrifying smile. "Let's talk about all the different ways I can pay you for what you can do for me."

Spock swallowed hard. He'd run out of banquette. Another few centimeters, and he'd be on the floor. Surely there was a logical way out of this exceedingly unfortunate turn of events, but just for this moment, his grasp on logic felt exceedingly uncertain.

3

"I got it all worked out," Kirk said, then pushed down on the controls.

From the back seat, he heard Elissa gasp as the staff car suddenly dropped a dozen meters into an eastbound airlane.

Beside him, his older brother braced his arms on the forward console. "This'll be good," Sam muttered.

Kirk kept checking the nav screen—still no sign of renewed pursuit. He grinned and shot a quick glance back at Elissa.

"Eyes front!" she shouted. "Front!"

A slow transport had seemingly appeared out of nowhere.

Kirk effortlessly banked around it, then began to descend along a merge airlane marked by a holographic grid projected on the front windscreen. "Listen up, kids. The overpass is two klicks ahead. I'll pull in, park, and we scatter."

Sam nodded agreement, but Elissa wasn't buying it. "Are you out of your mind? Our DNA's on every surface in the car."

Kirk didn't see her problem. "Look, it's not like we've committed a crime."

Elissa grabbed his shoulders and shook him before letting go. "We *stole* a Starfleet staff car!"

"So we're giving it back, no damage, no trouble. They don't bother with DNA investigations for that."

"How do you know?"

Sam looked back at her. "He's never been picked up before."

"Before?! He's done this *before*?"

Kirk shrugged. "I had to make sure the override worked."

Before Elissa could grab Kirk again, a brilliant white light blinded all of them and a loudspeaker voice thundered like a pronouncement from Olympus. *"Unauthorized vehicle, you are being monitored by satellite control. Land at the next service apron."*

Elissa slumped back in defeat. "Well, that's it for me . . ."

Kirk and Sam exchanged a look. "Satellite control," Sam said. "They got us coming and going."

"They've got the car," Kirk corrected him. "They don't have us." Then he twisted the controls hard enough to set off the stability alarms and automatically tighten the seat restraints as the car spun left into an oncoming airlane, breaking free of the pursuing searchlight.

At once, the car's interior was again plunged into darkness interrupted only by the strobing running lights of the other traffic flying straight for them, the hum of each vehicle's emitters pulsing high then low as they rushed past.

"Hold on!" Kirk shouted as he dropped the staff car nose down again, out of the airlane and into nothing but gray. The pinging of the ground proximity alarm, faster and louder with each second, changed abruptly to a high-pitched squeal a heartbeat before he straightened the car out with a bone-jarring bang.

On a side street, late-night pedestrians scrambled out of harm's way as the staff car skidded along the street, its forward air scoop scraping the polystone surface in a spray of sparks.

The car spun around halfway, sliding backward, then lurched to a stop under a streetlamp. While it was still rocking, the tires rotated ninety degrees so the vehicle could slip sideways into a legal parking spot.

Kirk slapped at the restraint controls and punched the button that opened all four doors. "Pizza's on me!"

The instant the seat restraints unfastened, Kirk, Sam, and Elissa were out the doors and on their feet in the once quiet street, staring up at the glowing fog overhead.

"They overshot us," Sam exulted.

Kirk fumbled in his jacket pocket for his override. "They won't turn back until they come to an exit lane." The authorities were so predictable. He checked the override's status display. "No damage." He showed the display to a relieved Elissa. "They probably won't even write up a report."

Kirk glanced down the street, saw a red holographic sign beckoning. "That place should be packed. Let's go."

But before he could use the override to lock the car, Sam took him aside. "It'll also be the first place they look."

"If they look," Kirk said.

Sam turned his back to Elissa, dropped his voice. "You can talk your way out of anything. But your girlfriend . . . ?" He shook his head.

Reluctantly, Kirk admitted Sam was right. "Change of plans. Elissa, you and Sam take off. I'll dump the car back at the overpass where the satellites can't—"

"No." Sam shoved the override back into Kirk's pocket. "You're good, but I know what I'm doing. There's an old garage I can park it in, then take a tunnel to a train station. No satellite tracking, and Elissa's back for curfew."

Elissa's face brightened and she reached for Kirk's hand to pull him away from the car and Sam.

Kirk hesitated. "If they catch you . . ."

"They won't. Go." Sam slapped his brother on the shoulder.

Kirk made up his mind. He tugged the override from his pocket, used it to start up the staff car again. "Stay under the speed limit, and on the ground."

"No arguments. Go have fun."

Sam slipped back into the car.

Hand in hand, Kirk and Elissa began walking down the narrow street toward the sign. Elissa started to look back as the staff car came to life, but Kirk nudged her on. "Hey, we're just two pedestrians on a date. No interest in cars."

Elissa complied but squeezed his hand, hard. "A date. You sure know how to show a girl a good time."

Letters flickered through wisps of red-tinged fog.

"It's about to get better," Kirk said.

The sign read: **THE GARDEN OF VENUS**.

4

Kirk had four IDs in his pockets and pulled out the one that said he was twenty and old enough to enter the club.

The burly, tuxedo-clad greeter eyed Kirk. "Twenty? On what planet?"

Kirk replied to the challenge with a good-natured smile. "I get this all the time. You probably think I look fifteen, right? Check my place of birth. New City on Menzel V. High-gravity world. We're all short for our age."

The greeter read the fine print on the ID display, frowning. "I've never had an underage kid *not* argue with me before."

Kirk maintained his easy smile. "You still haven't. I'm not underage."

The man looked at Elissa, then back to Kirk again.

"She's twenty-two," Kirk said helpfully. "You could call the embassy." He patted his jacket. "I've got a communicator someplace . . ."

Elissa followed Kirk's cue and looked just as unconcerned as he did.

"Do you have a telomere scanner?" she asked the man.

Kirk nodded. "That'll confirm our ages." He held up his thumb. "Blood or skin sample?"

It was late. The line behind Kirk and Elissa was getting longer.

The greeter made his decision. He pushed the ID case back into Kirk's hand. "Have a nice stay on Earth." He stepped aside and waved them in.

Elissa took one look at the writhing dancers and then fixed

her gaze resolutely straight ahead. "Well, this is one for the diary."

Kirk took in everything, the dancers no more nor less interesting than the ever-changing mix of alien spices, pulsing music, and warm enticing light. He had never been in a place like it—at least, not one so large. "Just keep your clothes on and we'll be fine," he teased.

"You do see what these people are doing, don't you?"

Kirk glanced at the tables as they passed them. At most, couples were huddled intimately close in the soft red light of table orbs, kissing, embracing, oblivious to the fact they were in public view. The remainder of the tables were little different, except they hosted more than pairs.

"C'mon," Kirk said. "They're young. In love."

"They're creepy."

Kirk pointed to the side. "Here's a free one."

Elissa sat down quickly, hunched forward, elbows on the small table. Kirk sat beside her, as closely as the other couples, wrapped his arm around her. She shrugged him off. "Don't. Not here."

"Elissa, we have to fit in."

Elissa grimaced, but not with passion. She leaned her head on Kirk's shoulder. "You are in such trouble with me."

Kirk was still filled with the exhilaration of his flight and, even more exciting, the knowledge that his override had proven Starfleet's ineptitude. "It's worth it," he said, and nuzzled her soft brown hair. It smelled wonderful.

That was too much for Elissa. She pulled back, stared at Kirk.

"What?" he asked innocently.

"You lied your way in here awfully easily."

"It wasn't a lie. That guy knew I wasn't twenty."

"He let you in."

" 'Cause he could tell I wasn't the kind to cause trouble."

Elissa snorted. "You."

"Sometimes I think you have the wrong idea about me."

"Lucky for me, I probably do."

"Yet here we are."

Elissa shook her head, her expression suddenly grave. "What're you going to do with your life, Jim?"

"Before you kill me? Get you back to the Academy by curfew."

"Not good enough. Try again."

Kirk suddenly swept Elissa into his arms and kissed her thoroughly, as if they were still alone in the bushes by the parking lot.

She broke free, indignant. "I'm serious!"

"So am I," Kirk said. "We gotta make this look good." He repeated his action and prolonged it till she understood, then released her.

"What did you see?" Elissa's voice was unsteady.

Kirk's condition was no better, but he mustered enough composure to nod at something over Elissa's shoulder. "Check out the dancers."

Elissa shifted in her chair, eyes darting from one scandalous dancer to the next on the raised pedestals as if trying her best not to actually see them. Then Kirk saw her eyes widen. She turned back to him, aware now of what he'd noted: two harsh-faced men in gray suits and cloth caps—clothing that was clearly a uniform of some kind. One of them was holding up a glowing ID for a server who spoke with them, her antigrav tray of drinks floating beside her.

Elissa's lips brushed Kirk's ear. "They don't look like protectors," she whispered. Her behavior, though protective camouflage, was not without effect on Kirk. He forced himself to concentrate on a new plan. "Maybe private security from the lot?"

"Wouldn't they be tracking the car?"

Kirk didn't voice his own worst-possible-case scenario—that Sam had been caught and these two security agents had backtracked his accomplices here. Backtracking was the only reasonable possibility. His brother would never give him up.

"Elissa, I can handle these two." Kirk bent his head to kiss the nape of her neck, marveling at the smoothness of her skin. "You've got to get back to Archer Hall."

Elissa closed, then opened her eyes with a sigh. "Understood. If they're looking for a couple, it's safer if we're not together."

Kirk scanned the room. The two agents, unsmiling, had split up and were walking the perimeter of the club, eyes moving from patron to patron like high-intensity sensors. Elissa saw them, too. She turned to Kirk, unsure if she should move or not.

Kirk edged her out. "Don't hurry. If they notice you . . . I'll distract them." He nodded imperceptibly to a set of doors at the back that he guessed led to an outdoor seating area overlooking the bay. "Go out that way."

Elissa stood, eyes downcast. "I don't like leaving you alone."

"I'll call tomorrow at lunch. We can set up a meeting with your adviser."

Elissa suddenly leaned down and kissed him. "Be careful."

Kirk slouched in his chair. He waved over a server, using the opportunity to watch the progress of the agents. They were getting closer to him. "Go. Go!"

Elissa walked away without looking back.

Kirk had no intention of being careful.

For Elissa and Sam, he had to win.

5

Spock had seen the men in gray as soon as they entered the Garden of Venus, and had immediately sunk back on the banquette beside Dala.

"Now that's more like it," she said, and reached out to playfully stroke his thigh.

Spock felt his heart race and hated the sensation and what it signified to him: not a physical response to Dala's unwanted touch, of course, but an acknowledgment of the danger the men in gray represented.

"Those two," Spock said, indicating the new arrivals. He waited until Dala had seen them. "Consular agents."

Dala removed her hand from his leg. Spock's relief was immediate. "They followed you?"

"Unlikely. But I should not be found here."

"If this was a setup . . ."

Spock recognized the mixture of human emotions in Dala's expression—anger tinged by apprehension—but he was ready, having rehearsed this part.

"I assure you, I am in even more danger than you." He rose to his feet, to bring this disquieting meeting to an end. "I will go. They have no reason to suspect you. And the next time we meet, *I* will choose the venue."

Dala's expression shifted disagreeably from one of apprehension to sly knowing. "A more private one. I'd like that."

Spock pulled his cloak shut, as if sealing himself in an environmental suit. "Madam, good evening."

Dala's dark eyes sparked with amusement. "My pleasure. And maybe next time, yours, too." She blew him a kiss.

Spock could not suppress his shudder, and as he walked away his sensitive hearing caught her throaty laugh.

He shook off his discomfiture and quickly pinpointed the two agents, separated now, each patrolling the outside edges of the club's huge room. The solution to avoiding their detection was obvious: He would cross through the middle of the room, between them.

Gratified by the logic of the situation, Spock went down the few steps to the main floor and began walking purposefully toward the doors he had entered through. With each step, he also berated himself for feeling gratified. His human side had been vulnerable to the human female and her pheromonic perfume—more unwelcome evidence of his particular genetic weakness.

He was almost at the entrance, close to freedom. His work here at an end. His plan, as he had predicted, now perfectly in play.

Even as Kirk automatically flirted with the attractive server who had brought him a glassless column of distilled lunar water, he kept his attention on Elissa.

She was walking toward the back too quickly, head down—the picture of someone who didn't want to be noticed, which, of course, made everyone notice her. Including one of the men in gray.

Kirk thanked the server, waved a credit wafer over the payment sensor on her tray, and tapped it twice to add a generous tip.

"Nice," the server said, and meant it, hovering to see if Kirk was open to more expensive transactions. But Kirk had already dropped her from his mind and the server moved on. He was busy visualizing the layout of the club like a chessboard whose primary pieces were Elissa, the security agents, and himself. Somehow, he had to set up an immediate diversionary tactic to upset his opponents' attack on his queen.

It was time to sacrifice a pawn.

Fortunately, there was one headed his way.

Kirk held his column of water without conscious awareness of the spongy sensation of the low-powered force field that kept it in place, and silently counted out the timing of his target's footsteps.

Then, at just the right moment, he commenced Plan A. He extended his foot and—

The sullen youth with long black hair awkwardly sprawled onto Kirk's table before righting himself.

Kirk instantly leapt to his feet. "Hey, watch where you're going!"

For the briefest of moments, Kirk's pawn looked flustered, but his response was brittle and, unfortunately, under control. "You deliberately attempted to trip me."

Kirk commenced Plan B. He threw the column of water at the teenager's long, narrow face and the force field sparkled off, drenching his dark hair and clothing. The youth stared down at his sodden cloak, up at Kirk, down at his cloak again, but did nothing else, as if he were in shock. The nearby patrons who had paused for an expectant instant returned, disappointed, to their other pursuits.

Now Kirk noticed that one of the security agents had obviously signaled the other, because both were converging on Elissa.

Kirk couldn't believe his bad luck. A few hundred people in this club and he'd picked the only one who was unused to bar fights.

Kirk commenced Plan C.

He swung his fist at the teenager's jaw.

Then it was Kirk's turn for shock because in a move too fast to see, the youth *caught* his fist mid-swing.

Kirk put his full weight into pushing his fist forward, but without seeming to expend the slightest effort, the skinny teenager slowly forced it down and to the side.

"You are behaving in a most illogical manner."

Amazingly, the kid wasn't even breathing hard. Yet.

"You're right. My mistake." Kirk let his arm go limp.

And as soon as he felt the grip on him loosen, Kirk charged forward, punching the teenager in the stomach at the same time as he delivered an upward head butt.

Kirk's stomach punch was deflected and his head butt only struck a shoulder, but as he and his pawn flew backward into another table, he finally heard the sounds of chaos. Some of the more boisterous patrons were flinging themselves enthusiastically into fights of their own. Others were scattering, heading for the exit.

For the moment, though, Kirk was on his back, his reluctant accomplice pinning him with one hand to the floor. "What are you trying to accomplish?" the teenager asked calmly over the din. He flipped his soaked hair out of his eyes.

Kirk had run out of plans so he resorted to the truth. "Those two guys in gray are after my girlfriend—they're security agents. I needed a distraction."

Kirk's erstwhile prey gave him a withering look. "The 'agents' are from the Vulcan Embassy. They are after *me*."

Sure enough, Kirk saw pointed ears through the youth's flattened hair. "Five hundred people in this joint and I pick the one Vulcanian . . ."

"Vulcan," the Vulcan said.

Kirk realized the crowd had stopped yelling and the music had stopped. Instead, he and the Vulcanian—*Vulcan*—were surrounded by an unmoving wall of official-looking legs.

Kirk looked up to see the two men in gray, their cloth caps

covering their ears. With them was the club greeter in the black tuxedo, and four protectors, blue-clad officers of San Francisco Protective Services.

"You done now?" the heavyset greeter asked him.

"Looks that way," Kirk said with a smile. If all these officers of the law were gathered here, the odds were better than good that his diversion had worked and that Elissa was already halfway back to the Academy.

A protector motioned for the Vulcan to release him.

Kirk swiftly calculated the odds of getting out of this particular entanglement, developed his strategy on the fly. He sat up from the floor, held up his hand to the Vulcan. "Hey, buddy . . . no hard feelings?"

Reflexively, as Kirk had anticipated, the young Vulcan helped pull him to his feet. Kirk stumbled against him. "Whoa . . . sorry. You're a lot stronger than you look."

"Vulcan is a high-gravity world and my species has evolved myostatin inhibitors to enhance—"

Kirk interrupted what threatened to be a biology lecture. "Okay. That's great." He turned to the club greeter, held up his credit wafer. "For the mix-up. I'll pay for the damage."

As the greeter sneered at Kirk unpleasantly, a protector took the wafer.

"Yes, you will," the officer said. "But not the way you think."

Kirk felt powerful hands grab his upper arms as two protectors frog-marched him toward the main doors. "Let's take this outside," one said.

The two Vulcans from the embassy took up position on either side of the young Vulcan and encouraged him to go in the same direction.

The Vulcan appeared unperturbed by his capture, and, for himself, Kirk didn't care what happened next.

Whatever it was, it couldn't be worse than seeing a cloud of vaporized blood puff from the back of Edith Zaglada as the eight-year-old girl ran for—

Kirk shook his head, forcing the familiar blur of horror from his mind.

All that mattered here and now was Elissa. One way or another, she could use what he'd done tonight to prove her innocence.

He'd outsmarted Starfleet.

He just didn't care about anything else.

6

Almost a century earlier, when the first dish-shaped component had been assembled 35,900 kilometers above the Pacific within perpetual line of sight to San Francisco and Starfleet Headquarters, the facility had been named for a heroic admiral who had successfully held back overwhelming Romulan forces at a beleaguered colony world.

But just as nation-based armed conflict had long been relegated to Earth's distant history, the success of the United Federation of Planets promised to bring the same fate to interstellar wars. So the orbiting structure had grown, with segment after segment added over the years, until it had become an immense white blossom of duranium plating and sublime technology, unarmed, a major hub of Starfleet's vast network of logistical supply.

The admiral's statue remained in an alcove near the main transporter complex to greet each arrival if they cared to look. But with the drumbeats of war so faded, and the primary mission of Starfleet now, more than ever, one of exploration, the facility's once-heroic name had been simplified, so that now throughout the fleet it was simply called Spacedock. Its main purpose was to offer protected berths for starships in port for replenishment, and a warren of corridors and cramped little offices to serve the intricate bureaucracy that enabled an interstellar fleet to function.

One of those collections of small offices on a seldom-visited level in the first and largest level of the facility bore a simple sign, a few of its letters scratched. It was called the

Department of General Services, a footnote to a footnote in Starfleet's organizational charts, of no particular importance.

In terms of spycraft, the DGS, perhaps one of the most important units of Starfleet, was hiding in plain sight.

Eugene Mallory was fifty standard years old, but looked older. Even in this enlightened age, stress took its toll. While the Federation and Starfleet ably maintained the peace and well-being of hundreds of worlds united in common cause, there were those individuals whose task it was to look beyond the safe borders, to the frontier, and into the unknown. And if there was one thing all explorers knew, the unknown was often dangerous, sometimes deadly.

It was the job of Mallory and the DGS to see that the unknown dangers of the frontier never took the Federation by surprise.

Ten years in the job and his once dark hair was white. But even he had never seen images like those on his subspace communications screen right now.

In the foreground was a Starfleet Security captain, still in adaptive armor scorched by weapons fire. His grime-streaked face was distraught and deeply troubled, and not just for the twelve comrades in arms he'd lost in a firefight three relative hours ago. That battle had taken place on Helstrom III. It was a frontier colony planet, where a thousand humans had banded together to create a peaceful new world, and then were taken captive, held hostage, by a savage, hostile force.

The captain was just finishing his report with words hard to come by. From time to time, the image and sound shimmered with subspace interference.

"We couldn't determine the enemy's communication protocols . . . couldn't tell how they were getting their orders . . ."

Mallory asked the obvious question. "Are you certain the attackers *were* receiving orders?"

The captain thought that over, wiped his face. "You mean, they were just left here to . . . to commit suicide like this?"

Mallory sighed. "No. No. They likely thought reinforcements were on their way. They didn't know it was a last stand."

The captain's eyes flickered, and Mallory felt sure the battle he had just fought was replaying itself in his mind. "They wouldn't surrender . . ."

Mallory understood what was left unsaid, but what the Federation faced was greater than this one small skirmish. "You and your team saved the hostages, Captain. You saved the colony."

"This isn't why we're out here, Mallory. This isn't who we are."

The captain moved back and away from the imager to reveal the bodies of the enemy, laid out respectfully by the captain's medical corpsmen.

The youngest of the dead was eight, the eldest no more than twelve.

Each enemy soldier, each corpse, a human child.

"You saved the hostages," Mallory repeated firmly, though he knew it was little comfort. But anguish and remorse were the traits of Starfleet and the Federation, not those of this new enemy attacking the frontier.

More than twice a hundred light-years away, the captain nodded his agreement, the gesture contradicted by his grim expression. "Alpha Team out."

The screen went blank.

Mallory rocked back in his chair and thought of demons— humans who would send their young to commit such atrocities.

The captain's words seemed to echo in his office: *This isn't who we are.*

His deskscreen beeped.

Thankful for the distraction, he tapped the accept button. "Mallory."

His aide replied from the outer office. *"Sir, a Starfleet staff car was stolen in San Francisco and the protectors have the thieves in custody."*

Mallory considered the surreal statement with a sigh. "Sally . . . you're telling me this why?"

"According to SCIS, the thieves stole the car with the same security override technique that was used to steal that dilithium from the Academy two weeks ago. The investigators think there's a chance the ones who stole the car and the ones who stole the dilithium are the same, and they said you'd want to know."

Mallory had read the analysis of how the dilithium had been stolen. "Whoever hit the Academy isn't stupid enough to get picked up stealing a car." Still, he found a stylus and turned on his padd. "But give me the details."

He began to jot down Sally's notes.

In his experience, details could lead anywhere.

7

Sam Kirk welcomed the fog and the night. The soft, dark blanket kept the world away. Kept everything else beyond the immediate moment indistinct and unthreatening. At some level, not that he'd ever admit it to anyone, that's what he needed most: protection from a world he didn't understand and didn't want to.

Unfortunately, the price of such security meant lying to the person who'd always protected him best—his brother.

So he maneuvered the stolen car, not his first by any means, through the older sections of the city where he and others like him knew that the old power grids and cables interfered with the sensors of the all-seeing protective satellites whirling past overhead. The electronic shadows he navigated were almost as good as the sheltering cloak of fog and night, because he could pass through undetected and unnoticed, the way he passed through life.

At the main dock, he carefully parked the car between two warehouses, well away from the blue-white spotlights that marked the pathway for the automated cargo handlers that rolled back and forth along the pier. Even in the twenty-third century, it was more energy efficient to ship bulk raw materials and large industrial components by sea. The squat machines loading and unloading the automated ocean freighters didn't require the pier lights. But they helped keep the handful of human stevedores out of danger as they worked.

And where there were lights there were shadows, and those had become Sam's home.

He stayed in the car for a few minutes, watching, checking, looking for any minute change in the pattern of the robotic handlers' actions. Then he opened the window, drew in the rich scent of the sea, listened for human footsteps . . . Nothing.

The moment he judged it was safe, he snapped open his communicator. "Call the office," he said quietly.

Almost at once, an artificial voice answered. *"Our offices are closed. Please call again."*

"I've got a fast delivery to make," Sam said. The code word "delivery" could stand for almost anything. But the code word "fast" had only one meaning—whatever was being delivered, it was Starfleet issue.

"We'll be available to accept deliveries on the sixteenth." The artificial voice clicked off and the call ended.

Keeping its running lights off, Sam started the car again and eased out into the cargo path, putting himself directly between two massive handlers on the search for new containers.

At dock sixteen, a security light shone over a towering section of seamless gray hull. Sam turned off the cargo path and drove steadily forward, into the *Pacific Rome*, not bothering to slow when the car's proximity alarm chimed.

A moment later, the car's windshield rippled with multiplied light and he was through the holographic projection and inside the freighter's cavernous cargo hold.

The welcoming committee was waiting. Seven of them. Each with a laser rifle almost as big as the small figure who held it, each aiming at Sam.

Sam pressed the door control, and when the door had fully opened, only then did he slowly step out of the vehicle, hands held in the clear.

An amplified voice echoed over the buzzing and grinding noises of power tools working on other deliveries that had preceded Sam's. *"He's okay. Get started on the car."*

Sam hurriedly stepped back as the children, most around ten or so, swarmed into the stolen Starfleet staff car. He watched it lurch across the metal deck plating toward a mechanic's bay where two teenagers with industrial 'plasers stood ready to begin disassembling the prize.

Then Sam's heart jumped a beat as a soft voice spoke behind him. "That's a pretty little thing."

Sam fought down his nervousness. He hadn't heard a single footfall. "Hey, Griff."

Griffyn was Sam's age, just out of his teen years, but that was all he and Sam had in common. Griffyn was tall and lean, and wore drab, utilitarian clothes more suited to deep-space freighters than Earth, with pockets everywhere and a hand laser on his belt. He'd told Sam he was running this operation for "other interests," and who those interests were, Sam didn't know or care to know. He didn't like coming here—even more, he detested himself for *needing* to come here. But Earth had long ago eradicated the conditions that fueled easy crime. The only large-scale organizations that remained were invariably from off-world, and most often from outside the Federation. Sam didn't require any more detail than that.

Griffyn now ignored him as he usually did, his attention focused instead on the newly arrived car. One body panel was already off it, clattering on the deck. "How the hell did *you* manage to steal a fleet car?"

"Security override," Sam bluffed. "Nonessential vehicles have a reduced encryption set. Ten million possible keys, tops."

Griffyn hooked his thumbs in his gunbelt and turned to study Sam.

He nodded toward the car. "How many emitters?"

"Four."

"Let's hope they're working. Looks banged up." Griffyn smiled at Sam, as if daring him to continue lying.

Sam capitulated quickly. Any conversation with Griffyn was a minefield. He'd never been able to find a pattern to what set the guy off. Probably no one could.

"Jimmy was driving. Did a fancy dive and hard landing."

Now Griffyn looked at him with eyes that were ice blue and unreadable. "Your little brother. He figured out the override."

"Yeah. He's good at stuff like that. Always building things."

"So you used some kind of override that got you into the car, let you drive it, but you still ended up being chased."

Sam looked down at the deck, couldn't hold Griffyn's gaze. "When Jimmy was driving, yeah. But . . . you should've seen him. He got away from the protectors, then the *satellites*." Sam chanced looking up to judge Griffyn's actual mood and failed. "All I had to do was drive here through the sensor shadows."

"So . . . not a lot of risk for you. Easy job."

Sam felt sick, knew what Griffyn was going to do. But it was too late. "Naw. Not really, I guess."

Griffyn scratched his cheek, then reached into his leather jacket, pulled out a credit wafer. "So this should cover it."

Sam took the wafer, squeezed it to read the balance. It was worse than he thought. "Two hundred . . . ?"

"Problem?"

Sam was desperate enough to plead. "Griff, it's worth at least a thousand. It's Starfleet!"

But Griffyn didn't even acknowledge Sam's foolhardy attempt at argument. He'd turned his attention back to the staff car, by now a picked-over carcass with only one seat remaining bolted in place, all mechanisms exposed and being disassembled.

"It's worth ten thousand to me," he said offhandedly.

Sam's mind reeled at the thought of what ten thousand credits could buy him out of.

Griffyn laughed as two of his followers swore at each other when a crackling gout of sparks sprayed up from one of the emitter conduits. He cupped his hands to his mouth to shout over the noise of the hold. "Hey, idiots! Cut the current *before* you 'plase it!"

The young teenager in charge of the disassembly crew waved back in acknowledgment, then cuffed the boy who'd done the damage. The child took the blow like a beaten dog, without fighting back.

Sam understood. There was no way to win with Griffyn in charge.

But still . . . two hundred credits for something worth ten thousand?

"So what do you say, Griff? I really need the credits." As soon as he'd spoken, Sam knew he'd messed up again. Never reveal a weakness. That's what his brother was always telling him. And in a negotiation, never let the other side know what you really want. Jimmy was always reading books about strategy and tactics and famous battles, but Sam had never been able to remember and act upon his brother's lessons, no matter how many times he heard them.

Griffyn's pale eyes were cold. "I pay for labor, I get paid for parts. You don't know who to sell the parts to. And you sure as hell didn't invest a lot of labor to get me the car. I figure what you did is worth . . . oh, let's say, a cee-wafer. So the way I look at it, giving you two cees, I'm being generous. How would you look at it, Georgie?"

Griffyn had deliberately and tauntingly used the name that Sam had left behind when he fled the family farm and the unwanted life that George Joseph Kirk had mapped out for his older son. Sam's brother and his new friends called him by his middle name, the one that was his alone.

Sam grasped at the last straw left to him. "How about . . . maybe something for Jimmy? For what he did?"

"You're still negotiating with me?"

Sam's pulse fluttered. Would Griffyn take back the credit wafer?

Griffyn stuck his lower lip out, thoughtful. "Tell you what. You bring Jimmy by and . . . I *will* take care of him. He's a talented kid. Made an override to boost fleet goods. I could use him."

Sam took in the scene in the cargo hold, the huge chamber stacked with disassembled vehicles and stolen freight and armed children willing to do anything for their leader. For all that he despised himself for his weakness and his fear, Sam had his limits. He would never—*ever*—do anything to bring Jimmy into this life.

He shook his head. "This isn't for him."

Griffyn looked into Sam's soul, testing him. Pulled out another credit wafer. "Are you sure? From what you've told me, I don't think your brother's found his calling. So maybe I can help."

Sam shook his head again.

Griffyn's only reply was to squeeze the credit wafer he held out so Sam could read the balance. Then he placed it in Sam's hand.

One thousand credits.

"It's not for the car," Griffyn said. "It's an advance. For arranging an introduction."

Sam stared at him, frozen. The thousand-credit wafer burned into his flesh.

Griffyn leaned forward, made it clear.

"Either give me all my credits back, or bring your brother to me. Your call. What's it going to be, Georgie?"

Sam already knew his answer.

8

On the far side of the Garden of Venus, there was a parking lot, and it was there that the official vehicles had gathered: three from the San Francisco Protective Services and one unmarked car with diplomatic codes on its ID plates.

Kirk and the Vulcan, joined at the wrist by a pair of inductance cuffs, stood by one of the SFPS cars. No one was paying attention to them, but both were aware that alarms would shriek if either of them moved more than two meters from the car.

Kirk raised his left hand, forcing the Vulcan's right hand up as well. He eyed the glowing blue stripes that pulsed around the metal bands encircling each of their wrists. "Don't suppose you know any good Vulcanian tricks for getting out of these."

"Vulcan," his companion said. "And an escape attempt would be illogical."

"But it might be fun."

The Vulcan stared at Kirk and Kirk finally had to grin at the young alien's expression of total incomprehension.

"Kidding," Kirk said. "But really, do you *want* to go to prison?"

The Vulcan blinked. "Earth has no prisons."

"You really aren't from around here, are you?"

"Do I *look* like I am 'from around here'?"

Kirk gave him the once-over. "That wrap of yours hasn't been in style for a couple of centuries, but with all that hair covering your ears, yeah, you could be one of us."

Kirk watched as the Vulcan seemed to shudder at his

assessment, but then again, who really knew how alien minds saw things?

"Anyway," Kirk continued, "Central Bureau of Penology, Stockholm. You've heard of Stockholm?"

"Founded in the thirteenth century of Earth's Common Era. Population of 3,487,612 as of the census of 2348. Home of the Karolinska Institute which decides the winners of your Nobel and Zee-Magnees Prizes."

"Wow. I can't believe you know that."

"You mentioned a Central Bureau of Penology."

"Right." Kirk studied him a moment longer, wondering if there was some attempt at alien humor here. "Mostly, it runs all the off-world prisons. You get it? They ship prisoners off-world so they can say, 'No prisons here on Earth.' But they do have this big detention facility there. For retraining, rehabilitation."

"Logical."

"That's a big thing for you, huh?"

"Rehabilitation?"

Kirk rolled his eyes. "Logic."

"Logic is the basis of modern Vulcan society."

Kirk waited expectantly.

The Vulcan gave him a questioning look. "You disagree?"

"No. I just wasn't sure you could give an answer that short."

"I could expand upon it."

"I have no doubt."

The alien's shoulders moved in what looked like a shrug, but he didn't say anything else.

Not wishing to encourage his fellow detainee to change his mind, Kirk shifted his attention to the four SFPS officers who appeared to be in heated discussion with the two Vulcan consular agents by the next car, about ten meters away and out of earshot. The way they kept gesturing at the two apprehended youths, it didn't look good.

"You ever been in trouble like this before?" Kirk asked. He kept his gaze on the adults, trying to read their intentions.

"I am not in trouble now."

Kirk laughed. "Really? How do you define trouble on your planet?"

"They are interested only in the person or persons who apparently stole a Starfleet staff car. Since I did not steal a Starfleet staff car, I am not a person of interest."

Kirk gave the Vulcan a sideways glance. "How do you know about the staff car?"

"That is what they are discussing."

"You can hear what they're saying?"

His companion regarded the group of officers, human and Vulcan. "The ranking SFPS officer claims that at least two, and possibly three young people are responsible for the staff car theft."

"Well, those ears are definitely good for something."

"Furthermore," the Vulcan said as if Kirk hadn't spoken, "Agent Kest, the senior of the two consular agents, makes the point that there is no logical motive for me to steal a staff car. He also states that I have diplomatic immunity, so any attempt to charge me with any crime is moot."

"Moot," Kirk said. "So if that's such a logical argument, why haven't the SFPS let you go?"

"I have found humans to be argumentative."

Kirk couldn't resist. "No, we're not."

"Yes, you . . ." The Vulcan hesitated, raised an eyebrow. "Kidding?"

"You catch on fast," Kirk smiled approvingly.

From the dense fog above, a landing searchlight produced a glowing cone that played over the parking lot until it locked onto an empty patch of pavement. Slowly, another Starfleet car descended into view.

It was different from the one Kirk had used for his demonstration. This new vehicle was dark blue with a red pinstripe and arrow running its length, as if someone thought it was a starship. On the aft fuselage, stark white letters spelled out the bad news: Starfleet Criminal Investigative Service. Kirk had never seen one of their cars before. If anyone had asked, he would've said they were responsible for starbase security. He hadn't even known they operated on Earth.

Kirk watched as two formidable women in civilian clothes got out of the car, looked over at him with expressions as blank as the Vulcan agents', then joined the SFPS officers and consular agents.

"Any idea what *they're* saying?" Kirk asked.

"Not a great deal. It seems they want to search us."

Kirk brightened. *Finally*, something was going right.

The two SCIS agents were leading the others toward the two teenagers. Kirk stood up, straightened his jacket, prompting another brief tug-of-war with his fellow prisoner.

"Evening," the senior woman said. She and her partner each held up their official IDs and switched them on—Special Agents Gilfillan and Rickard.

"Ma'am," Kirk said with a warm smile of utmost sincerity. "I'm sure hoping Starfleet can clear up this mess and—"

"Save it, mister," Gilfillan said. She nodded at her partner, who opened the case of the tricorder she carried over her shoulder and pulled its sensor wand from her jacket. Kirk had read the manuals and dreamed about what he could accomplish with one.

The Vulcan cleared his throat. "In the interests of efficiency, I must inform you that I am protected by full diplomatic immunity."

"Good for you," Rickard said without conviction. She aimed the sensor wand at Kirk, then the alien, made adjustments to the tricorder's main unit, then took a second set of readings. Kirk couldn't see the device's display screen, but he found himself relaxing, confident of what it would show.

Sure enough, Rickard shared her readings with her boss.

Kirk liked the fact that Special Agent Gilfillan didn't look surprised.

She walked up to the Vulcan, made him shift uncomfortably as she patted down his cloak, then reached into an interior pocket.

"I have diplomatic immunity," he insisted.

"Not for this," the agent said. She held in her hand a currency wafer and the override device Kirk had slipped into the pocket of the alien's cloak when he had pretended to stumble after the fight.

The agent squeezed the card, whistled appreciatively, showed it to her partner. "Six thousand."

"That is mine," the Vulcan said.

Gilfillan held up the small cylindrical device. "How about this?"

"I have never seen that before."

The agent showed it to Kirk. Kirk shrugged. "What is it? Some kind of alien gadget or something?"

The senior agent stared hard at the Vulcan as Rickard took further tricorder readings of the device. "It's a quantum-code transmitter designed to override Starfleet security lockouts. It's also illegal."

The alien's eyes widened for an instant before he caught himself and brought his face back to a neutral expression. "I am protected by—"

"Diplomatic immunity. So I've heard. But that only applies to local laws." She pointed to the two equally unexpressive consular agents. "Your friends'll tell you. Immunity does not extend to Starfleet's Uniform Code of Justice. And this is now a Starfleet matter." She stepped to one side and pointed to the SCIS car. "Let's go."

The Vulcan stood still, as if too shocked to move.

Kirk stepped forward, doing his best to look alarmed and contrite. "Okay, so I started a fight when this alien hit me, but—"

The junior agent held up her sensor wand. "Stow it, kid. Your DNA is all over that thing, too. So give it a rest."

Gilfillan gave Kirk a firm push on his shoulder to get him and his companion started toward the SCIS car.

Kirk protested. "That guy tried to put something in my pocket and I pushed it away."

But the agents weren't listening and the Vulcan was not resisting.

The inside of the car's back passenger compartment was uncomfortable and covered with a seamless coating of an easy-to-disinfect nanofilm to which nothing would stick— except the lingering odors from a hundred other prisoners. Kirk grimaced at the smell as he was thumped back in his seat and the restraints closed over him. He turned to look at the alien still cuffed to his wrist. The Vulcan stared straight ahead, his posture ramrod stiff.

Kirk frowned, leaned back, and closed his eyes as the car took off. "Well, this *is* going to be fun," he said.

The Vulcan offered no response.

Kirk sighed. This was going to be a longer night than he had planned. He might as well make the best of it.

"Jim Kirk," he said.

"Spock."

And that was that.

9

By the dawn of the warp era, the great military academies of the past were long gone. Annapolis. West Point. Colorado Springs. All early victims of the third world war. But their traditions lived on in San Francisco, one of the few major cities in North America to escape significant damage in that awful cataclysm and the long night of the post-atomic horror that followed.

More than anything else, the city's miraculous survival made it a beacon of hope in the years following Cochrane's discovery of warp drive and his first contact with the Vulcans. No debates were held and no votes taken—it had simply seemed natural and inevitable that the great city should become the planet's de facto capital, first as the home of Starfleet Command, and then of the United Federation of Planets itself. When, concurrent with the founding of the Federation, Starfleet decided to create a facility to train its officers separately from its enlisted personnel, there was no question but that San Francisco would be that facility's home, as well.

Strictly speaking, though, Starfleet Academy was not a military institution, any more than Starfleet was a military organization. But the unforgiving hazards of space travel, the discipline required for long missions on fragile ships, and the training necessary to rationally face the unknown at any moment, drew on skills and lessons that had been honed over centuries by warriors. Risk was risk whether faced on a battlefield or on a voyage of exploration, and risk, after all, was Starfleet's business. The challenge of facing that risk was what called humanity's best and brightest to the hallowed halls and gleaming labs of the Academy.

Eighty-eight years earlier, Captain Jonathan Archer himself had presided over the ceremony in which the Academy's main dormitory building was named in his honor, and Archer Hall was definitely a product of that simpler time. It still had doors that swung on hinges, windows that could open and shut, and a temperature-control system that sometimes seemed to the shivering midshipmen to be from an even earlier time, when their ancestors built fires in caves.

But Elissa Corso found nothing to complain about in the venerable old building. Like all the other mids who had taken the tests, jumped through the bureaucratic hoops, enlisted the support of politicians and serving members of the fleet to write letters of recommendation, she would have been happy to camp beside an active volcano for the privilege of attending the Academy. There was nothing in her life that was as important as achieving that goal.

Until she had met Jim Kirk.

He was smart, he was charming, undeniably attractive, and despite his cynicism for the Academy and Starfleet, he had supported her throughout the final semester of her first year, never complaining when she needed a weekend alone to focus on her coursework, always willing to help her review her studies. Sometimes, it seemed to Elissa that her boyfriend knew more than her instructors about certain subjects, and she would tease him by saying he should be attending the Academy instead of her. But he'd just tease her back in that cocky way of his or stop their conversation altogether, usually with a stolen kiss.

Elissa checked her midshipman uniform in the mirror hanging on her closet door, scolding herself for being such an easy mark. What was it about that guy, anyway? She was nineteen years old, a rational, independent adult—almost—who had demonstrated the unique talent, skills, and drive required to gain admittance to the toughest and most sought-after educational institution in the Federation. But when it came to Jim and that sunny smile of his . . .

"You're acting like an idiot," she told her reflection.

But her flushed reflection betrayed the truth. *Or . . . like someone in love.*

Elissa closed the closet door. Enough of that.

She checked the small dorm room to ensure everything was Starfleet precise, on her side and her dormmate's. Desks neat, padds and books aligned, bunks smooth and taut, with the folded-over sheets measured to exactly ten centimeters. Good. If there was a surprise inspection this morning, unlikely at this time of year, the room would pass. Since her first lab wasn't for another hour, she had a few minutes of personal time. She could place the call she'd been planning to make since she'd returned to her dorm room earlier this morning, the moment her evening liberty expired.

She took her personal communicator from her desk drawer, flipped it open. "Jim," she told it.

She needed answers. But most of all, she admitted to herself, she just needed to hear his voice again. *Idiot,* she scolded herself as she waited, impatient for the call request to go through.

It didn't.

For a moment, Elissa thought about leaving a message, but then had a sudden image of Kirk's communicator in the hands of the protectors. She snapped her own communicator shut, thought a moment, flipped it open again.

"Sam," she said.

This time, the call went through.

• • •

His apartment was a mess, and George Samuel Kirk didn't care. Unable—as usual—to sleep, he sat back on his decrepit green couch, bare feet resting on a rectangular utility table covered with encrusted Chinese food containers. The only sound came from the soft hum of the air pump in his salt-water aquarium. The only light came from the dawn slicing in through metal blinds, fragmenting the room's disorder even more with sharp swaths of light and shadow.

His communicator beeped.

The device lay beside his feet, beside the half-empty, open bottle of Stark whisky and the two currency wafers from Griffyn—the first an insult, the second blood money.

Sam hesitated, his stomach tight with fear. He knew from bitter experience that if he didn't speak with Griffyn *this minute*, there'd be someone at his door within the hour. That would be even worse.

Sam reached for the communicator, but hit the bottle instead and knocked it over. A quarter of its contents spilled out as he cursed and scrambled to catch it before it could roll off the table to the floor.

He caught it. Took a swig. Put it down carefully. Took a deep breath. Unfolded his communicator. Then relaxed.

Jimmy's girlfriend.

The ID on the small display was like a gift from the heavens, not because the call would be any easier, but because, although he couldn't lie to Griffyn, he could to Elissa.

"Hey, girl," he said.

"Can you talk?"

Sam heard the concern in her voice. He rubbed his face, to force alertness. "Yeah, I'm at the apartment." Because his brother hadn't come home yet, he'd assumed he was still with Elissa. But if she was calling, upset . . . "Is Jimmy with you?"

"I was hoping he was with you."

Sam swore. "When'd you see him last?"

"Last night. There was a . . . a bar on the waterfront."

"Which one?"

"Venus something."

"I know it. What happened?"

"We got in, but . . . Jim saw two protectors come in after us. He told me to leave and that . . . that he'd take care of it."

Sam's mind raced. That was Jimmy, all right. Taking care of everything. He looked over at his aquarium. The timer had switched on the light and he saw the orange-and-white dance of his clown fish, waiting for the morning's blessing of food from the sky.

Sam loved those fish. But with all his absences, there was only one reason they were . . .

"I haven't heard from him," Sam said, knowing why.

"You said you were going to—"

Sam interrupted before she could finish. He doubted the computers would already be listening to this call, but he couldn't take the chance. His little brother wasn't like him. Jimmy acted tough, tried to make himself out to be a maverick and outside the law. But Sam knew for certain that his little brother knew right from wrong. He might get a bit confused about where those boundaries were when it came to his family and friends, but if he was in the protectors' custody right now, it was only a matter of time before his inner compass kicked in and he did the right thing.

Sam envied him for that.

But he wasn't willing to get dragged down and shipped off to some rehabilitation center because of it. And he knew that as soon as Jimmy started explaining why he had built his override device, and who had helped him use it on that Starfleet staff car, the computers would go to work on all communications between the three of them, and that would be the end of it.

"I got rid of all that stuff that was cluttering up the place,"

Sam said, hoping Elissa would understand what he meant. She was an Academy midshipman, so it was more than likely she hadn't pushed the limits of proper behavior in her entire life.

"Oh . . . You don't think anyone else found it. I mean, all the stuff from the apartment?"

Sam gave her points for trying. "No."

"Then why didn't Jim come home?"

Home, Sam thought. *What a joke.* Home was a farmhouse in Iowa. There was nothing for either of the Kirk brothers there, except for a disappointed, bitter father and—

"Sam?"

"Look, he's going to be okay. He's a smart guy. He knows how to stay out of trouble."

"It's only . . . you know, in three days . . ."

Sam remembered what was going to happen in three days. "I'll have him call you as soon as I hear from him."

Elissa said nothing, but even over the silent circuit, Sam felt her worry.

"This is my brother we're talking about," he said. "You know he never lets anyone down, right?"

"Yes."

"Just go to classes or whatever it is you're doing now, and—"

This time, Elissa cut him off. *"Gotta go. Bye."* The circuit went dead.

Sam stared at his communicator, unsure what to do next.

After a moment, he decided the best thing would be to wait for his brother to call. Maybe Jimmy would know what to do about that thousand-cee card, because he certainly didn't.

Sam felt a wave of self-pity sweep over him. *Why can't I ever do anything without complications? It's not like I plan stuff to work out that way.* He looked over at the aquarium, envying his fish their lack of choices, temptations. Animals didn't cheat or betray their friends. He thought suddenly of Fizzbin, the big white Lab he and Jimmy had shared growing up on the farm. That dog was like Jimmy, never gave up on him, never stopped trusting him.

Sam swore again in the empty apartment, angrily brushed a tear from his cheek.

His clown fish flicked back and forth in their tank.

He'd feed them in a minute or two, after he had another drink.

And after that, Jimmy would know what to do. Jimmy always had a plan.

"Who was that?"

Elissa snapped shut her communicator and guiltily slid it into her desk drawer.

Zee Bayloff stood in the open doorway. She'd just come back from her morning run, short blond bangs plastered to her forehead, Academy-issue gray sweatshirt splotched with sweat.

"Let me guess," Zee said, still slightly out of breath. "Ji-m-m-m-m-m?" She drew the name out salaciously as she opened her closet and took out her pristine white dressing gown.

Elissa didn't turn around, wondering how much her dormmate had overheard. They'd been roommates during their plebe year, and Elissa knew they had no secrets left.

"Okay, something's wrong," Zee said. It wasn't a question.

"Three days until the honor board." Elissa stared out the room's north-facing window. The Academy's expansive green grounds and low-profile buildings stretched out before her, with the distant pylons of the Golden Gate Bridge just emerging from the low coastal fog fading in the dawn.

"Loosen up, Corso, it'll work out."

Fully indoctrinated in the ways of the Academy, Zee deftly

rolled her gray sweatshirt, shorts, and underwear and slipped them into the laundry bag at the bottom of her closet. She shrugged into her dressing gown and got her shower kit from the upper shelf.

"Yeah, well, whoever broke into the lab used my ID codes," Elissa said tightly.

"Did you do it?" Zee asked.

Elissa turned around with a flash of anger. "How can you ask me that?"

"That's my point, dummy. There's no way they can prove you did it because you *didn't* do it."

"That's not what the ID codes say."

"Codes can be stolen."

"By who?"

Zee gave Elissa a look of disbelief. "Who else?"

Elissa realized what Zee was suggesting, dismissed her sharply. "He wouldn't do that to me."

Zee didn't look at all convinced. "Even I've heard him go off about Starfleet and this place. He thinks any officer is a sanctimonious, self-important prig. And mids aren't much better."

"He's my friend."

"Was. Until you gave him what he wanted."

Elissa felt her face flush. "He's not like that."

"Look, face facts, huh? What's a guy who hates Starfleet as much as he does doing with a mid in the first place? I mean, as soon as he learned what you were, why didn't he put all thrusters on reverse?"

Elissa didn't mean to say what she said next, but it came out anyway. "Zee, I think I'm really in love with him."

"Great timing."

"You really think he's been using me to . . . to get my codes?"

Zee perched on the edge of the desk, put her hand on

Elissa's shoulder. "You know him a whole lot better than I do. What do you think?"

Elissa was honest enough with herself to know that part of Jim's attraction for her was that he seemed somehow lost and looking for direction—something she knew she could provide for him.

But now her mind swirled with terrible questions. What if that had all been an act designed to draw her in? What if Jim had always known exactly what he was after, and now that he had it, his antagonism toward Starfleet let him walk away from her?

Jim could destroy her dream of a career in Starfleet.

What if Zee was right?

10

"You're a long way from Iowa," Special Agent Gilfillan said. Her clear gray eyes were almost translucent in the brilliant overhead lights of the interrogation room.

Kirk gave her a smile across the interview table. "I guess. Where are you from?" He leaned back in his chair and stretched as if he didn't have a care in the world, as if he enjoyed being locked up in Starfleet Headquarters, slowly driving a Starfleet Criminal Investigative Service agent mad.

"Do you have any idea how much trouble you're in?" Gilfillan asked. Her tone was feather-light, as if, like Kirk, she had no concerns about being here for as long as it took, which meant, of course, she did.

Kirk continued his pretense of good-natured indignation. "I was in the bar, the Vulcan guy bumped into me, I overreacted. I'm sorry. I apologize. I'll buy him a new cloak. But we're talking about a bar fight, right? How is *that* a lot of trouble?"

"It isn't," Gilfillan agreed. "Stealing a Starfleet staff car is."

Kirk spread his arms wide as if to ask what more Starfleet could possibly want of him. "I've already told you—and everyone else here. It was the Vulcan guy and his . . . whatever that thing was, that let him steal it, okay?"

Gilfillan lifted a padd, turned it on. "You don't appear to have a record. At least, not much of one."

Kirk wanted to see whatever it was she was reading, but the special agent had angled her screen away from him. "Why would I?"

"Someone who can build an override like that, you'd think he'd be smart enough to go after civilian cars."

"Well, there you go. I'm not smart enough to build the override—that Vulcan obviously is. And since I haven't stolen any cars before, why would I be dumb enough to start now, with a *Starfleet* staff car?"

"Your brother, on the other hand—George Kirk."

"Sam," Kirk said. He kept his tone as unrevealing as he could.

Gilfillan looked up from the padd. "I'm sorry?"

"He prefers Sam."

Gilfillan looked back at the padd. "He *has* got a record."

"Not his fault. He was set up."

"Seven times?"

Kirk forced himself to speak without emotion.

"He made mistakes. He knows it. He doesn't make them anymore."

Gilfillan nodded as if she didn't care one way or the other. She touched the padd's screen. "Now you, as far as I can tell, you're a good kid. A bit of . . . oh, rowdiness, shall we call it, back in Riverside. 'Borrowing' a flyer. A few unsanctioned trips with school friends. Just a farm kid letting off some steam. Nothing noteworthy there. Plus, it's clear you care about your brother. Strong family connection. I'd say your parents raised you right. Good early experiences in responsibility."

Kirk looked down at his hands on the desk. *Bare feet slipping on frozen mud, thousands of corpses, charred, bloated, a cloying sweet odor so thick that—*

"Kirk?" Gilfillan's question brought him out of it. "You heard what I said?"

"So?"

"So you're a decent kid. A decent human being."

"And . . . ?" Kirk prompted the special agent to continue.

"And any decent person would realize the consequence of convincing the authorities that an innocent person committed a crime when he didn't: That innocent person would be unfairly punished."

Kirk met her piercing gaze. "How's that my problem?"

Gilfillan switched off the padd, laid it on the table. "You tell me."

She sat back, arms folded, waiting.

Kirk matched her, move for move, determined to beat the special agent at her game.

In silence, they both waited.

In the observation room, Eugene Mallory watched the feed from the interrogation room and tapped his finger on the table.

"He's pretty sharp."

The observation came from Special Agent in Charge Luis Hamer, the SCIS agent responsible for Starfleet North American operations. He was a tall man with a precisely trimmed beard and an ill-fitting suit, and clearly not pleased with being rousted from bed to liaise with Mallory on such a seemingly petty investigation.

"Not that sharp," Mallory said. "He's definitely hiding something."

"Yes. He stole the staff car."

"That's a foregone conclusion." Mallory picked up the small, cylindrical override device that SCIS had found on the Vulcan. "His DNA confirms it."

"Kirk doesn't deny touching it when the Vulcan tried to palm it off on him."

Mallory looked thoughtful. "There's something else, though."

Hamer took another swallow from his coffee mug, stared at the small display screen that showed Kirk and Special Agent Gilfillan in the interrogation room, staring at each other in silence. "The only reason I can think of to explain why the director told me to get over here is because you think one of these kids broke into the Academy lab, too, and stole that dilithium."

Mallory reexamined the override. "Forensics says a different transmitter was used. But both crimes used the same quantum code-breaking technique."

Hamer yawned, apparently still waking up. "So you're *not* convinced?"

Mallory waved the device at the small display screen. "On the one hand, your agent in there makes a good point. If Kirk's smart enough to make this kind of an override, why not use it to steal civilian cars? Much easier to get away with."

"And on the other hand?"

"If he's smart enough to make an override that lets him steal dilithium from a Starfleet facility undetected, then why risk everything two weeks later by stealing something as relatively valueless as a staff car?"

"If we're talking smarts, Mr. Mallory, I suggest we take a closer look at the Vulcan."

"His parents are on staff at the Vulcan Embassy."

"Good. That means he could smuggle the stolen dilithium off-planet in the diplomatic pouch."

Mallory gave the SCIS agent a skeptical look.

But Hamer had an answer for him. "Look, I deal with this kind of thing every day, and let me tell you, crimes committed by Earth residents aren't much more than background noise to the overall statistics. No one who lives here steals because of want or need anymore. In fact, when it comes to *real* crime, the kind we read about in the history books, more than eighty percent of what SCIS deals with—*and* the local protectors— can be traced to offworlders: human colonists, aliens, makes no difference."

The agent nodded to the screen. "Given a choice between

suspecting an Earth-born human or a Vulcan, if you want to play the odds, go with the alien every time."

Mallory hefted the override in his open palm. "Maybe some aliens. But have you ever heard of a *Vulcan* committing a crime?"

"You're forgetting something, Mr. Mallory. He's not just a Vulcan—he's a teenager." Hamer pointed at the override in Mallory's hand. "And his DNA is also all over that override, *and* on the six-thousand-credit currency wafer we found on him."

Mallory frowned, still trying to figure out what the connection could be between the dilithium and the staff car and the two teenagers in custody. He hated mysteries.

"Look at it this way, then," Hamer said wearily. "Technically, you're right—Vulcans don't break the law. But do you really think they *never* make mistakes? And isn't that pretty much what being a teenager is all about?"

Mallory put the override back on the table. "I agree, for now. We can't rule out anything." On the display, Kirk and Gilfillan hadn't moved. Mallory decided he at least had to give Kirk credit for being so self-assured. Unusual in a seventeen-year-old. "Let's see how Special Agent Rickard is doing."

Hamer leaned forward to tap a control, and the display switched to the second interrogation room.

"Interesting thing about human-Vulcan relations," Special Agent Rickard said conversationally to Spock. She pointed to the paragraph on her padd, not that the Vulcan could see it. "No extradition treaty."

Across the table from her, his hands folded in a contemplative pose in his lap, the tall Vulcan teenager said nothing.

"Apparently," Rickard continued, "it's never been a priority because there's never been a need. If you were Andorian, or Denobulan, we could find you guilty here and then off you'd go to serve your sentence on your own planet with your own people. But since you're Vulcan, nineteen, first offense, I'm going to guess you'll end up in rehabilitation in New Zealand. Starfleet's just opened a penal settlement there. Minimum security. Based on the Stockholm protocols. You'd be the only nonhuman in custody, so far."

Spock's mind filled with russet deserts, dry winds, the skies of home. The images and sensations calmed him.

"Actually," Rickard said, "it might be easier for you to serve your time here, rather than on Vulcan. I understand there's no crime on your planet, since crime's not logical. You'd be the first Vulcan to be convicted. Ever. Will there be repercussions for your family?"

Spock concentrated on the flow of air through his nostrils, into his lungs. He breathed deeply, pictured the intricate chemistry by which oxygen molecules transfused through his alveoli into his bloodstream to be captured by the copper molecules of his Vulcan metalloproteins, which then responded by turning green.

Rickard continued, undeterred by his silence. "I understand the Klingons were known to execute whole families if even one member committed a crime against the Empire. Maybe they still do. In a way, such action would be logical. After several generations, perhaps, one could eliminate criminal genes from the population. Did something like that happen on Vulcan?"

Spock recreated the taste of *plomeek* soup in his mind—specifically, the recipe his mother would make after the meditation festivals every fall. He began to analyze each aromatic component by class, ordering them by number of carbon rings.

"You know," Rickard said, "I'm beginning to think that's exactly what makes you people special." She lifted her right hand to rub the back of her neck. "I mean, how else to explain this unique emotional control you all have. This perfect focus. I have never heard of any humans that can—"

Mid-sentence she slammed her open hand down on the table, making a thunderclap in the small room, making her padd jump, and making Spock jerk up from his chair, wide-eyed and startled.

Rickard nodded. "I'm a lot better at this than you are, smart guy. So don't think you can play any of your alien games with me."

Spock felt angry at this human woman for abruptly shaking him from his meditative state. Then his anger doubled back on himself for even feeling anger. He forced his body to remain still, but failed to slow his pounding heartbeat and to stop a small muscle twitching in his jaw.

Even worse, he could see from the human's smug expression that she had detected the glaring evidence of his raw emotions.

"As I was saying . . . now that you're listening . . . I've never taken a Vulcan into custody. Matter of fact, there's no record of any Vulcan on Earth *ever* being taken into custody, let alone being charged with a crime."

Insultingly, Rickard was regarding him with curiosity, like a specimen. "There's a bit of history being made here, and I want to know why."

Before Spock could attempt reimmersion in meditation, he saw the agent shoot a glance at one of the optical imagers on the wall. Her expression changed to sharp annoyance.

An inner wave of elation swept over Spock. He knew that human expression. She had given up! He had successfully outlasted her primitive and emotionally manipulative interrogation techniques. The superiority of Vulcan mental discipline had triumphed. He felt the calm of the desert return to him, as if he himself walked in Surak's footsteps. It was wrong to do so, he knew, but he felt pride in his accomplishment.

Rickard's communicator chimed and she flipped it open. "Rickard."

A man's voice spoke. *"Hamer here. We're going to call it a day for now, Agent Rickard. Escort the young man to detention room B. We've called the Vulcan Embassy to let his parents know their son's been taken into custody, so they'll be coming by soon."*

Spock's face went slack with shock and once again the human noticed.

She deftly flipped her communicator shut, slipped it back inside her open jacket. "The Vulcan Embassy is right across the street. You won't have to wait long."

"On the contrary," Spock said stiffly, all emotional masking momentarily beyond his powers of self-control. "My parents might have been called, but I assure you they will not come for me."

Rickard stood, gestured for Spock to do the same. "Don't be so sure. Vulcans love their children, too."

"There is no reason to insult me further."

The agent's expression changed again and Spock recognized this one, also. Pity.

"No," the human woman said. "I suppose not."

Mallory watched as Rickard escorted the Vulcan youth from the interrogation room.

"You certainly called that one," Hamer said. "His reaction when I mentioned his parents was priceless." His eyebrows lifted. "I thought they didn't have emotions."

"They have them. They just don't express them the way we do. Maybe that kid missed a few lessons." Mallory stared at the display, even though all it showed now was the empty room.

Hamer cleared his throat. "You going to leave this to us, now, Mr. Mallory? I figure you've got to have more important things to deal with than a local theft."

Mallory did have other pressing matters. He knew the after-action report from Helstrom III would be coming in any moment, and that he'd have to process it for the meeting of his DGS steering committee. He closed his eyes, rubbed them, still seeing the captain's haggard face, the still bodies of the children. But still . . . there was something about this apparently minor case . . .

"The Vulcan didn't steal the staff car," Mallory said. "It's as you said, his reaction when he heard his parents had been notified . . . any teenager that concerned about what his parents think about him, he's not about to steal any kind of car."

"So the Vulcan wouldn't steal it, and the Kirk boy is too clever to steal it," Hamer said. "That leaves us with two teenagers with no motives to commit the crime, enough DNA evidence to find them both guilty, and a six-thousand-credit wafer that suggests *someone* sold *something* to a third party, further explaining why the staff car is still missing."

The SCIS agent regarded Mallory with annoyance, clearly losing interest in hiding his irritation at being ordered to let a Starfleet bureaucrat from a low-level planning office interfere in his case.

"Trust me, Mr. Mallory, those dots aren't hard to connect. So shouldn't you just leave this one to SCIS?"

"Not till I know what the connection is between those two kids and the Academy theft."

"You honestly think there is one?"

"We'll know when the parents get here."

11

"He's your son," Amanda said. "Our son. And we *will* go."

Sarek, son of Skon, Vulcan diplomatic attaché for scientific outreach and the development of unaligned worlds, kept his expression in serene and neutral repose.

His wife, however, narrowed her own eyes as her human anger grew. "Don't give me that look."

"What look, my wife?"

"The public look. The ambassadorial candidate look. The Vulcan look."

"Given that I am a Vulcan, logically I have no choice in the matter."

"And don't change the subject."

Sarek decided it was time to study anew the tapestry on the wall of their private quarters. It was an exquisite piece of early Sharielian impressionism, dating back fifteen hundred years on Vulcan, showing the dawn breaking over Mount Seleya.

Amanda could see that her husband was about to retreat into private meditation—his traditional method of dealing with their "discussions" concerning their son—but she wasn't about to allow that today.

She stepped in front of the tapestry. "Sarek . . . Spock's in trouble."

"He cannot be."

"Starfleet has him in custody. For *stealing*."

"Precisely. No Vulcan has cause to steal; therefore, the Earth authorities have made an error which they will in time realize and rectify. Spock will be released soon enough."

"They'll release him sooner if we go to Starfleet Headquarters and you explain that to them. Sarek, do you know how embarrassing this must be for Spock?"

"Embarrassment is a human emotion. Spock will feel no such thing."

"Ohhh . . ."Amanda stamped her foot on the hard red tiles of the central room. She had been married to Sarek for more than twenty years—half her life. She knew the Vulcan way of logic and emotional control was a better way than the hedonistic philosophies of Earth and so many other worlds. But still . . . when Sarek used Vulcan logic as a barrier to their emotional attachment instead of as an exquisitely precise enhancement of it . . .

She stormed to the hallway to get her cloak."All right, I'll go!"

She wrapped the rose-colored fabric around her slight shoulders, checked her auburn hair in the dressing mirror. Despite her love of all things Vulcan, she kept it long and swept up in a human style. Aesthetically, Sarek found it "exotic,"he said.

She saw him step behind her in the mirror. She lowered her eyes, not in submission but because, at the moment, she knew she could only glare at him.

"My wife,"Sarek said, so calmly and so reasonably,"please reconsider what you are about to do."

"Why should I?"

"Because of our agreement."

That prompted Amanda to look up and into the reflection of her husband's dark eyes.

"Regarding Spock,"Sarek added.

"We've gone past that."

"No, we have not."

Amanda sighed. She relaxed to let her mind fill with the simple Vulcan meditative rhythms she had mastered, dutifully concentrated on her breathing, turned to face Sarek.

"I am not unaware of our son's difficulties," he said. "I know what he faced on Vulcan. I know the taunts and torments he received from the other children when he was a child." Sarek raised his eyebrows in an expression of apology—a display of emotion that Amanda understood would have been shocking in any other circumstance than a private discussion between husband and wife. "I understand how that interrupted his concentration, slowed his studies."

But Amanda couldn't let anyone cast aspersions on her son, no matter how gently, not even Sarek. "Spock is an exceptional student. You know he's brilliant. Even by Vulcan standards."

"Of course," Sarek agreed quietly. "But the proper studies of a youth of his age involve more than a simple mastery of multiphysics and rote memorization of history. There is the matter of emotional control, and there, we must both admit, our son's abilities are not as certain as they should be."

"All the more reason we should go to him now."

"No. All the more reason we must abide by our agreement."

Amanda lost the threads of her meditation, forgot about her breathing. She was a mother who loved her son. She had to do something.

Sarek held up his hand, two fingers extended, a sweet gesture of consolation.

Amanda had never been able to resist Sarek's charm and his love. Nor did she now. She held her two fingers to his in the ancient ritual by which two separate beings formed the sign of long life and prosperity, showing how their lives were entwined.

"On Vulcan," Sarek said, gazing into his beloved wife's eyes, "our son faced unique circumstances because it was known that he was neither Vulcan nor human, but a blending of the two. But on this world, for his sake, we have kept that knowledge from the Earthmen, and his studies have proceeded as they should.

"For the two of us, or for you, to go to Starfleet and by that action reveal Spock's human heritage, what will happen to his studies then?"

After more than twenty years with this dear man and his people, Amanda was able to appreciate what her husband meant by those words and the way that he said them, and she lost herself to him all over again.

"You do love him, don't you," she said softly.

Sarek's expression betrayed an almost subliminal sense of his puzzlement. "Emotion has nothing to do with it. Spock will be a great scientist someday. For the sake of all those people and all those worlds that will benefit from his discoveries, it is logical that we do what we can to remove obstacles from his path."

Amanda smiled at Sarek, understanding. "Someone should go to him. To help straighten this out."

"I will make arrangements."

"I love you," Amanda said.

Sarek's face remained appropriately and lovingly neutral. "You are my wife," he agreed, "as I am your husband."

Amanda's smile grew as she savored the passion within that simple yet complex statement. Her husband and her son were her life, and nothing made her happier than knowing how close the three of them were, joined by such mutual love and understanding.

Everything would soon be made right.

12

Sam Kirk woke late that afternoon, head pounding, mouth dry. He pushed himself up from the faded green couch, blearily focused on the empty bottle of Stark's, cursed himself for not leaving at least a drop to help him wake up.

He hung his head, trying to remember what it was he was supposed to do. There was something, he knew. Something important . . .

He heard a sound behind him, twisted around.

George Joseph Kirk, his father, all six and a half feet and two hundred and fifty pounds of him, was delicately sprinkling fish food into the saltwater tank.

He looked back at his son, and Sam didn't have to focus to see the disapproval on his father's darkly tanned and deeply lined face. "I let myself in." His voice was deep, husky. Cold.

That much was obvious. Sam had a more important question on his mind. "What're you doing here?" He looked over by the door to the hallway, saw his father's old Starfleet duffel bag beside it.

"Jim's been arrested."

"What?"

"You heard me." Joe Kirk put down the cylinder of fish food and carefully closed the cover on the tank.

Sam stood, winced as he stretched out the kink in his neck. He looked over at a wall clock, an old one Jimmy had picked up in one of those shops he did odd jobs for in New Union Square. It showed Earth and Mars time, reconciling the two different day lengths and calendars. And all mechanical,

Jimmy had said, as if that was special somehow. Whatever, he had spent a week rebuilding it so it worked.

"It's after four," Joe said.

"Is Mom here?"

Joe went to the window, tugged open the slatted metal blinds. "Someone has to run the farm."

Sam couldn't take it. He'd been talking to his father for less than a minute and *this* had to come up again?

"Don't start." He walked unsteadily to the bathroom. He was pretty sure he had a block inhaler there. That'd calm down his head, make the old man a bit easier to deal with.

"When'd you see your brother last?"

Sam ignored the question, opened the medicine cabinet over the sink in the one-piece modular bathroom. He found the small cylinder of the inhaler, shook it. At least one dose left. He'd have to buy another.

He covered his nose with the soft plastic cup, turned the cylinder on, and inhaled as it buzzed.

When he opened his eyes again, his headache was already receding. He saw his father in the doorway and even felt revived enough to smile.

His father, true to form, scowled back. "Look at you." Pure disgust.

Sam waved his hand over the faucet to turn it on. "You let yourself in." He cupped the cold water, threw it on his face.

"When did you see your brother last?" Joe repeated.

Sam dried his face with a threadbare, dingy towel. "Last night. With his girlfriend."

"What did you get him into?"

"What's that supposed to mean?" He pushed past his father, went back to the main room, heading for the kitchen alcove.

His father stopped him with a huge, calloused hand on his shoulder, spun him around. "You listen to me, George."

"Sam." The name shot out of Sam like venom from a snake.

"I don't care what you want to call yourself." Joe Kirk looked around at the disaster that was his first child's apartment. "I don't care that you live like an animal. I don't care that you've thrown your life away."

"Good. You can leave any time." Sam tried to pull away, but his father wouldn't let go.

"Jim's another matter."

"Then why aren't you with him?"

Joe's temper flared and he grabbed a handful of his son's shirt, pulled him close. "If your mother could hear how—"

Sam pushed back with both hands against his father's barrel chest, solid muscle. "Lemme go!"

Joe didn't budge. "If Jim's in trouble, then I know why." He shook Sam. "You." Then he let go, and Sam stumbled backward. "Tell me what you've done this time."

"Nothing! It was all Jimmy's idea."

"What was?"

Sam realized he had already said too much, tried to backtrack. "Whatever he's in trouble for. I don't know. He had something planned with his girlfriend."

"Your brother doesn't get into trouble."

"Oh, you wish."

"He listened to me and your mother."

Sam waved his hands as if trying to erase this entire conversation. "For how long, Dad? And guess who's to blame for that? Not me. Not Mom." He turned to the small cooler, opened it, stared inside at open containers of engineered food, nothing natural, or appetizing.

"I gave you both everything you could—"

Sam slammed shut the cooler door so hard he could hear the containers inside fall over. He wheeled around to confront his father. "Stop it! You didn't even listen to what *we* wanted.

You gave us everything *you* wanted! Half the time, you weren't even there!"

"I had my job. I worked for Starfleet so my father's farm could be yours."

"But—I—never—wanted—it! Jimmy—doesn't—either!"

"It stays in the family."

"You think we're still family? After everything that's happened?"

Joe took a step toward his son, raised his hand, and just as abruptly dropped it.

"Look at you," Sam said accusingly. "You were getting ready to hit me, and you wonder why I left Riverside?"

Joe looked at him, eyes stabbing. *Jimmy's eyes.* "I've never hit you. I've never hit your brother."

"You didn't have to, Dad. You sent Jimmy to Tarsus IV."

Joe blinked. "That was a long time ago."

"Three years. He still has nightmares. I hear him. You don't."

Sam saw his father's body tremble, and braced himself just in case. "You're the eldest," Joe said thickly. "That was your trip."

"Right. Blame me."

"No one's to blame." Joe Kirk didn't meet Sam's eyes, but whether that was because of shame or sorrow, his first-born was not sure.

Sam's words spilled out of him in an angry rush. "Jimmy told me what happened there. Not all at once. It's not anything he likes to talk about. But you know what, Dad, if I had been there, I'd have done what they said. How's that make you feel? How do you think that makes *me* feel? *I would have done what they said.*"

Sam shook his head. The nerve block was wearing off. He was hungry. He needed a drink. And he didn't need or want to be having this conversation. He grabbed his jacket from the couch and headed for the door.

Joe stared at him, uncomprehending. "You're not leaving. We're going to see your brother."

Sam kicked his father's duffel to the side, viciously. "You see him. I can't. Someone's got to make things right!"

13

"Sit down, kid." Mallory indicated the chair across the table. "Is it James? Or Jim? Tiberius . . . ?"

Kirk sat down, leaned back, crossed his arms. "Does it matter?"

Mallory nodded at Agent Gilfillan, who looked weary after her long night questioning Kirk. Kirk took pride in having worn her down. At seventeen, he felt on top of his game, indestructible.

Gilfillan remained in the corridor, touched a control to seal the door of the interrogation room.

Mallory waited until the door closed before he spoke again.

"James, then. You don't look like a Tiberius."

Kirk shrugged. This man's assessments meant nothing to him.

"Old family name?" Mallory asked.

"My grandfather had a thing about him."

"The emperor?"

Kirk thought that was a strange question. "Yeah."

"Because there was another one. Not quite as well known. And not quite as bloodthirsty."

Kirk hadn't known that. "Another Emperor Tiberius?"

"No, a politician. Two centuries before the emperor. A strong spokesman for farmers' rights. I thought that might have been the connection. Was your grandfather a farmer, too?"

Kirk nodded, his interest somewhat sparked. "So no other emperors?"

"*Roman* emperors? No. But there was a Byzantine emperor with the same name about five hundred years later."

"You know a lot about history."

Mallory gave him a half-smile, the expression hard to read. "A little. Does it matter?"

Kirk grasped that he was being lightly mocked, but ignored that to push this curious exchange to whatever limits he'd be allowed to. "For my grandfather, it was definitely the Roman Emperor Tiberius."

"Any idea what the fascination was?"

Kirk shifted in his chair, engaged now despite himself, studying Mallory as intently as Mallory studied him. Kirk understood that they were each trying to get the other's measure.

"A life of contradictions, my grandfather said. Full of lessons."

Mallory appeared to be genuinely interested, which Kirk suspected was a ploy, just as his attempt to change the subject to Mallory's knowledge of history had been. "What kind of lessons?"

"A brilliant general who became a depraved and hated ruler. You know, find what you're good at and stick to it. That kind of thing."

"What are you good at?"

Here we go, Kirk thought. But he wasn't about to let this old guy win so easily. He pointed to Mallory's padd. "Special Agent Gilfillan had my life history on her padd. If you're her boss, you've got it, too."

"I'm not her boss."

This time, Kirk refused to ask the obvious question. Gilfillan had manipulated him that way, and he wasn't about to let it happen again.

Mallory didn't let the silence remain unfilled. Surprisingly, as if acknowledging Kirk's strategy, he turned on the padd.

Kirk's eyes raced across it. Even upside down, he recognized his own flyer's license ID image. But he didn't recognize the form it was displayed on, although he could see that the form had a Starfleet emblem at the top.

"I'm just someone who likes history," Mallory said, answering the unasked question anyway as he tapped his way through several other forms on the padd's display, as if reviewing them. Kirk had the feeling, though, that whatever was in his record, Mallory was like his father and had every word memorized already. "Can you guess why?"

Kirk tried another tactic. "You like to live in the past?"

But Mallory didn't even react to his attempt at an insult. "Patterns," he said. "You've heard that old saying: Those who don't remember the past are doomed to repeat it?"

"I guess." Kirk wondered what all this had to do with him.

"It's true," Mallory said with a curious frown. "For seven thousand years or so, humans appear to have lived in a permanent state of forgetfulness. Seven thousand years from the first agricultural communities to the great urban centers of the twenty-first century—not one generation free of war or famine or injustice. And then . . . we woke up. It took the worst war we'd ever experienced, but out of all that came Cochrane and a new generation that for the first time *wouldn't* forget. Because the pattern was broken. So no more wars. No more need. No more injustice. The world, *our* world, is the way it is today because *we* remember the patterns of history and we do not repeat them."

"You can skip the lecture," Kirk said. "I didn't steal the Starfleet staff car."

Mallory regarded him with cool amusement. "Did I ask you if you had?"

Kirk realized he had fallen for a more subtle interrogation technique. For the first time, he began to feel he was beyond his depth. He had no clue what Mallory was up to, only that his interrogator had some agenda as yet unknown to him.

"You were going to."

But Mallory shook his head. "You spent four hours denying it with Agent Gilfillan. Why would I waste time going down that road again?"

Kirk's eyes narrowed. What was this guy after? *What does he want from me?*

"Because I'm looking for patterns," Mallory said, answering his own question. He patted the edge of the padd. "I've got your whole life story to check. Most of it, at least."

Those words contained a threat, Kirk was sure of it. He tensed, waiting, wondering.

"Face the facts, kid. Whether you did it or not, the theft of that car *is* the reason why you're here."

Whether you did it or not. Kirk couldn't get his head around the meaning of that statement.

"For that reason alone, SCIS did what any investigatory body would do . . . checked your records to see if you've ever been involved in anything like this before."

Kirk sat up straighter. "Did they check the Vulcan's records?"

Mallory's response rebuked him. "I'm not here to talk about the Vulcan."

Kirk slouched in his hard-backed chair, sullen. "Whatever you say." He stared past Mallory at one of the imagers mounted high on the plain, dull, Starfleet-blue walls, letting whoever was watching know how totally uninvolved and bored he was.

"So here's my problem. Your records don't make sense."

"That's not my fault."

Mallory held the padd so Kirk couldn't see it, even upside down. "Didn't say it was. Have you ever been off-world?"

Kirk felt his stomach tighten. *Here it comes.* "Yeah, sure. Been to the Moon on class trips."

"Tranquility Park? The alien ruins?"

Kirk nodded.

"Anywhere else?"

"Uh . . . Pluto. The museums there."

"Jonathan Archer's ship?"

Kirk shook his head. He looked around, seeking another imager.

Mallory repeated his question.

"No."

"You don't like starships, I take it."

"No."

"Odd thing," Mallory said. He ran his finger across the padd's unseen display. "It says here you joined the Star Cadets when you were eight. Set a record for merit badges in your age group. Before that, you were in the Junior Explorers." He turned the padd around and Kirk was mortified to see an image of himself, age five, in a baggy blue jumpsuit with a ball cap pulled down so far it made his ears stick out like warp nacelles. His hand was engulfed by his father's. That was all of Joe Kirk that was in the image.

"Is that your father?"

Kirk's voice hardened. "Look, if you have something to say, say it. I'm not here to reminisce about all the goofy stuff I did when I was a kid, okay?"

Mallory tapped onto another page. "On 14 January 2246, you visited the Laurel Blair Salton Medical Clinic in Des Moines."

"So?"

"So you had a series of inoculations and protein inhibitors that in my day we used to call the Spaceman's Cocktail."

"What's that got to do with anything?"

"There's only one reason a thirteen-year-old gets that battery of injections. You were going to be exposed to an alien ecosystem."

Kirk took a chance to bring this unwanted intrusion to an end. He leaned forward to make his demand. "Is there anything in those records that says I *was* exposed to an alien eco-system?"

"Not a word," Mallory said, his attention still on the padd. "And that's what strikes my interest. It means your pattern's fractured somehow. Smart kid. Loves space travel. Junior Explorer. Star Cadet. Apparently obsessed with collecting merit badges. Plus top grades at school."

Mallory briefly glanced up at Kirk.

"Same patterns I see in the records of my bosses—Starfleet admirals, for the most part."

Kirk's face felt stiff. It was all he could do not to throttle Mallory, not to try to escape by any means.

Mallory went back to reading the padd. "So you get all the shots you'd need to go to an alien world . . . but you don't go anywhere. Far as the records are concerned, about a year later you went on a week-long school trip to Pluto, and that's all. Apparently, you haven't been off-world since."

"That's what I said." Kirk crossed his arms tightly, all too aware of the hammering in his chest.

"I'm more interested in what you didn't say. You got the shots. You didn't go anywhere. By the next school year, you were barely getting by. You 'borrowed' one of your teacher's flyers. I see the Riverside protectors have sealed a file on you, which means you got up to something. Maybe now you can see my problem."

Silence. Kirk stared down at the table. He wanted to run so badly he felt . . . *he felt the icy air burn his throat again as he screamed for Donny to keep going to the arena and heard the other kids with the red bandanas calling for him, hunting him, hunting them all because of—*

"So tell me, what happened three years ago?"

Kirk stared at the man, loathing him, loathing Starfleet, loathing everything and everyone who had brought him to this moment.

"Because something did happen," Mallory said.

At seventeen, Kirk's only weapon was defiance.

Mallory studied him for a moment, then turned off the padd, placed it on the table. Then he got up, went to the closed doors, and punched a code into the control panel there. The door remained closed.

Mallory took his seat again. "I turned off the imagers. Whatever we say now is just between us."

"Like I believe you."

"I'm not doing this for you, you know. I'm doing it for me. I work for Starfleet."

"Nice uniform," Kirk said.

Mallory looked down at his rumpled civilian suit. "Isn't it," he agreed, unruffled. Then he regarded Kirk calmly. "I have access to records SCIS doesn't even know exist. I've turned off the imagers because I need to keep those records secret."

"And you're going to tell them to me?"

"You already know them."

Don't say it, don't say it, Kirk thought wildly, but he said nothing, could say nothing.

Mallory placed his hands, palms down, on the table. "What do you know about a colony world called—"

"Nothing!" Kirk shouted. He leapt to his feet. "This is over, all right? You wanted to find out about a stupid stolen car, you asked your stupid questions. Now let me go!"

Mallory stayed motionless in his chair.

"Maybe I should tell you what I know about Tarsus IV and Governor Kodos. They called him the Executioner."

Kirk dropped back into his chair, his legs trembling so violently he could no longer stand.

There was nothing this man could tell him that he didn't already know.

He had been on Tarsus IV.

Three years later, he was still there.

14

Everything was wrong. Nothing was as it should be. Instead of sun, there was darkness. Instead of laughter, there was pain. Instead of life, there was death: four thousand bodies crisped by laser fire. A week after the colony's revolution, they lay blackened, bloated, unburied.

And in the midst of everything that was wrong, a boy.

His name was Jimmy Kirk and he was fourteen years old, plus a month more or less.

Fear overwhelmed him. His legs were rubber, his stomach a tensed fist twisting his insides, his arms ice cold, and not just from the gusting snow and ice that cut through his tattered shirt with each blast of wind.

He was being hunted, and he knew he was going to die at any moment.

His parents, his brother, his dog, his bed, they were light-years away. And his friends?

That's what chilled him more than the ever-present ice and snow.

His best friend, Matthew Caul, fourteen and two months, was the killer who pursued him.

He'd been running and hiding and foraging for days, and knew there was no hope he could run far enough, hide well enough. Foraging didn't matter because there was no food. He'd tried chewing dried grass dug up from the ice-covered ground, somehow managed to choke it down. But it had only made him gag and spit up harsh bile.

That had been three days ago, he thought. Maybe four.

That was something else that was wrong. There were no more days, no more nights, no sense of time at all. Only fear. Of his best friend. And death.

But still he ran. Tears frozen on his grime-streaked face. Yellow mucus crusted on his reddened nose. His lips cracked and flaked with dying skin. His bare feet beyond sensation. But still he ran.

The reason was simple. He was not alone.

The kids from his cabin. There were four left, out of twenty-four. Tay Hébert, nine. Edith Zaglada, eight. Billy Clute, seven. Donny Roy, four.

And since he was the oldest, he was the one in charge. That was the rule of the cabins, and the farms, and the colony.

Jimmy had always followed the rules. Always.

He heard shouted voices and looked up, frightened for his small charges.

The voices came from past the old supply depot, where the frozen-mud road turned toward the center of the colony.

He could still see tendrils of smoke oozing from charred wooden beams that once held up the depot's roof. Three of the building's gray brick walls were still standing, mostly, their windows blown out. Some of the adults had fought back on the night the governor had made his announcement.

But the governor's men had had the only guns.

The governor's men and the kids who'd helped them.

"Over there! I see 'em!" The words were faint against the wind, but clear enough.

Death was near. He had to save the children.

He looked around wildly, then pointed to the arena. "That way!" The domed structure had once held seats for twelve hundred people. The colonists had played soccer and lacrosse there, put on plays, rode their horses, held their general meetings. Now half the building seemed to have been flattened by a giant's fist. On the sagging roof that was left, strips of gray insulation waved in the wind like seaweed on a drowned shipwreck.

But he'd spied a small opening in one rubble-mounded wall. Small bodies could crawl through it. Adults couldn't.

He ran for the dark opening, half dragging little Donny while the others stumbled after him. No one cried anymore. That had stopped a day ago. They just did what he told them to do, trusting him because there was no one else to mind and nothing else to do.

He reached the wall first, set Donny down carefully, then launched himself through the opening. The broken blocks and mortar cut into his knees and hands, but what he'd hoped for was true. One quick glimpse confirmed that the opening was a tunnel. And it led into an undamaged part of the arena. He scrambled back to fetch the others.

"Hurry up!" he whispered to himself as he pulled them through. "Hurry up!" Then he gagged as the stink of rotting flesh swept over him. He whirled around and wished he hadn't.

Bodies. All over the floor of the arena. Contorted, pleading. Carbonized.

He covered little Donny's eyes with his hand and used his body to shield the others. "Keep goin'! Go! Get under the stands!" Weak sunlight from outside showed the way to a hiding place under the tiered seats.

They huddled there. Shivering. Trying not to think of the stench, and the terrors it brought back.

"Jimm-mee! Come out, come out, wherever you are!"

The challenge reverberated in the arena.

Jimmy knew that voice. It belonged to Matthew. His best friend.

He looked at each of the children in turn, shaking his head, and miming covering his mouth and then his ears. With wide eyes, they obeyed his call for silence but he saw their bodies shaking.

Approaching footsteps crunched heavily over frosted ground, over rubble, over bodies.

"We've got a sensor! We're gonna find you!"

Tay looked up at Jimmy with frightened eyes. "They know where we are," he whispered.

It was over.

Jimmy knew that he had failed.

"By anyone's reckoning, it was a disaster," Mallory said quietly. "And the worst of it was, everyone could have survived the famine. The Vulcan relief mission and a contingent of Starfleet Security forces got there less than a month after the massacre."

Mallory continued, "But with no records—the colony's processing center was destroyed—there was no way for anyone to know which of the eight thousand colonists Kodos had been before he took on that name and became governor. So all those responsible got away: Kodos and everyone who'd helped him seize power and carry out the slaughter . . . they all either burned to death . . . or escaped."

Kirk sat rigid, staring at nothing, no one.

"The news spread, of course. But so much was riding on tracking Kodos—if he was still alive—that the Bureau of Colonial Affairs kept a lot of the details under wraps."

Kirk didn't move.

"Specifically, that there had been nine survivors who could identify Kodos. I think the BCA wanted to make sure they were safe from retribution."

Kirk said nothing.

"Four of these eyewitnesses were small children, just kids. Three were saved by a fourteen-year-old boy."

Kirk made his decision. If he confessed to stealing the staff car, then Sam and Elissa would be protected. The Vulcan would be in the clear. And most important, he could get out of here.

But Mallory's next words caused him to hesitate.

"Interesting thing," Mallory said, "those witnesses' identities are so well-protected, even I can't get access to their names. Yet, if I could talk to that boy—and he'd be about your age today—I'd tell him he was a hero. And I'd tell him that the qualities he demonstrated on Tarsus IV are unique enough to make some people give him a second look, even grant him some extra latitude. If he ever needed help, that is."

Kirk started, surprised, when Mallory's communicator chimed sharply.

"Just a second." Mallory flipped the communicator open. "Mallory. Go ahead."

Kirk tried but couldn't hear a thing. That meant Mallory had a privacy earpiece so only he could listen to his caller.

After a few moments, Mallory said, "Agreed," then flipped the device shut and stood up. "Processing says you and the Vulcan have visitors."

Kirk pushed back his chair and got to his feet. His legs still felt unsteady, probably because of exhaustion. Though he had no idea what time it was, he knew it was well into the morning, which meant he hadn't slept for at least thirty hours. Maybe he wasn't completely indestructible.

"You looked like you were going to say something there," Mallory suggested. But when Kirk didn't reply, he didn't persist. He went to the door controls and entered his code. The door slid open.

"Maybe he wasn't a hero," Kirk said. "That boy on Tarsus IV."

Mallory turned around and regarded him quizzically. "Even with what little I know, it's pretty clear he risked his own life to save others. What would you call him?"

"He only saved three," Kirk said. "A lot of other kids died."

"Would you blame him for their deaths?"

"No. That's Starfleet's fault."

"Go see your visitors," Mallory said. "We'll talk again."

15

Spock sat cross-legged on the fold-down bench, hands steepled in the basic meditative form known as *shal-lo-fee*—the second foundation of inner breath. It was one of the first states of mindful balance he had achieved as a child, and he found it easy to enter even under the most disruptive of circumstances. And being locked in a holding cell in Starfleet Headquarters certainly was disruptive. He did not choose to repeat the wrenching sensation of attempting a deeper state of balance, and then being torn from it by an unexpected diversion. The one experience of that with Special Agent Rickard had been enough. Spock did not know what to think. He felt sure he had not betrayed his emotions.

As from a distance, he heard the holding-cell force field switch off and the security bars slide open. Spock held his position, satisfied that he had chosen the correct meditative strategy because the noise didn't disrupt the balance he had achieved: aware, yet restful.

And then, just as satisfaction began most improperly to turn to pride within him, he felt and heard the fold-down bench creak as a heavy mass impacted it and he was nearly pitched forward to the floor.

Spock caught himself, barely, all sense of calm gone because of—

Beside him. The human. Jim Kirk. Sprawled on the far end of the bench, back against the wall. He caught Spock looking at him.

"How's it going?" Kirk asked. From his tone, he did not expect or want an answer.

Which was just as well because Spock had no idea what

the human's words meant. "Could you clarify the question?"

Kirk glanced around the cell, apparently looking for something on the walls, then shifted sideways, closer. He spoke softly, as if trying to avoid illegal listening technology. "Look, I got this figured out."

"Indeed." Spock was no closer to comprehending him.

"But first I gotta know what you told them."

"Can you be specific? I told them many things."

"Great. Take me through the high, uh, points." He glanced at something on the side of Spock's head and gave a little snort of amusement. Spock reached up and pushed his long hair back over his ear.

"What did you tell them about the car?" Kirk asked.

"I know nothing about the car. Accordingly, I told them nothing."

"Okay, that's good. How about the override?"

"You put that in my pocket."

"Okay, and I said I stopped you from trying to put it in mine. So we balance out there."

"Except, my statement is truthful and your statement is a lie."

Kirk seemed to think that wasn't an important distinction. "Vulcans never lie?"

"Never," Spock lied.

"Okay, forget that stuff. It's not important anyway. Here's how it's going to work out." Kirk glanced at the door where the security bars were once again in place and the force-field emitters glowed around the frame. "These clowns can't—"

"I saw no clowns," Spock interrupted.

Kirk stared at him in silence for a moment, then began again, speaking slowly, as if he doubted Spock's command of human language.

"The SCIS agents can't figure out which one of us was involved with the missing staff car. And since they can't pin the crime on either one of us, they have to let us both go. Simple, right?"

Spock thought it over. The legal system on this planet was predicated on the principle that no innocent party should suffer, even if it meant some guilty parties might go free. Under those conditions, Jim Kirk had reached a valid conclusion. "Quite logical," Spock said. He was surprised the human was capable of such reasoning.

Kirk grinned, punched him on the shoulder. "That's what I said."

Spock drew back, startled. "You said no such thing. Why did you hit me?"

Kirk looked at his fist. "That wasn't a hit. That was . . . a playful tap. Congratulations . . . because our team's gonna win."

Spock began to feel uneasy, almost nervous. For whatever reason, after the human's initial display of logic, he was now reverting to spouting gibberish.

Even more surprising, the human indicated he had sensed Spock's true reactions, though Spock felt sure he had not betrayed emotions. Kirk shifted down the bench. "I apologize for the punch. It's a human thing. No offense."

"None taken."

"But we are going to get out of this."

"Good," Spock said.

"You said it."

Before Spock could correct that statement, Kirk closed his eyes and leaned back against the hard wall with both hands behind his head.

When Spock had decided the human had calmed down sufficiently, he said, "I do have one question."

Kirk opened his eyes. "Shoot."

"I have no weapon."

Kirk closed his eyes again and Spock wondered if he needed more rest. "Figure of speech, Stretch. What's the question?"

"I am curious about the clowns."

For some reason unfathomable to Spock, Kirk started laughing.

Spock concluded such a reaction must stem from something the aforementioned clowns had done earlier, and felt a strange mixture of curiosity and revulsion.

To a Vulcan, the idea that a specific class of performers existed whose sole purpose was to elicit from their audience an intensely personal emotional response *in public* was repugnant, but to Spock, it was also strangely fascinating. He often wondered what his response to a clown might be. One possibility was that such an encounter might confirm his mastery of self-control, and he would not laugh. But another, more troubling possibility was that he would lose all Vulcan reason and his human half would rise unbound to the surface of his mind and shame him.

Spock frequently had nightmares in which he arrived at school and suddenly broke into laughter or tears. Though he could never discuss such a thing with his parents or his peers, since accompanying his parents to Earth, clowns had become a constant source of concern to him.

"When we get out of here," Kirk said after he caught his breath, "I'm going to buy you a slang translator. Vulcans have slang, don't they?"

Spock knew what "slang" meant, and shook his head. "A word is what it is, or it is not. The Vulcan term is *kaiidth.*"

"A quantum language. How about that."

Spock stared at the human, struck by the insight that was both fascinating and true, and wondered if it was at all possible that what Kirk had just said was something that he had meant to say. Could this young human actually have knowledge of the quantum characteristics of energy and matter *and* the intellectual imagination to abstract that concept to the underlying cultural structure of Vulcan languages and dialects? It didn't seem possible.

"Indeed," Spock said, because once again, Kirk left him with no idea what to say in reply.

The force-field hum died, and both Kirk and Spock looked to the doorway as the security bars slid open again. Mallory entered with a younger man wearing the bright red shirt of a Starfleet Security officer. He was the first uniformed Starfleet member Spock had seen in Headquarters. The Starfleet officer was unsmiling, and carried a metal case with an indecipherable serial number stenciled on its side.

"James," Mallory said, then nodded at Spock. "And—" He glanced at his padd. "Mr. Spock, I have your first name here, but I will spare us both the embarrassment of listening to me try to pronounce it. Could you both stand, please."

Spock rose to his feet and stood as if at parade rest, hands behind his back.

Kirk got up slowly, dragging out the moment to show his disrespect for Mallory. Spock did not approve.

"We're in a bit of a bind, boys," Mallory continued. "Because of the override, we know that one or the other of you was involved in the staff car theft. What we don't know is which one of you it was."

Kirk gave Spock a sideways glance, and when Spock met it, Kirk winked.

Mallory gave no sign of having noticed the exchange. "Therefore, it seems the only plausible assumption is that you were working together, so Starfleet will be prosecuting you both for . . ." He checked his padd for the terminology, as if he had never had to say the words before. "Grand larceny. How archaic."

Spock kept his expression neutral, telling himself that

there was nothing humans could do that could surprise him.

Kirk's eyes flashed. "C'mon! I told you I never met this guy before last night!"

Mallory wasn't swayed. "It's not up to me anymore. You'll be talking to a judge. Hearing's set for next Thursday."

"Five days?" Kirk protested. "You can't keep us here five days."

"We can, but your records are more or less clean, so we won't." Mallory gestured to the security officer, and the man opened his case to reveal two gray metal bracelets.

"You're both free to leave," Mallory explained, "as long as you consent to wear these tracking modules. They'll transmit an alarm to Starfleet Security if you venture more than five kilometers outside the city limits. They're also linked together through a subspace transponder, and an alarm will be sent if you get within twenty meters of each other. Understand? One of the conditions of your release is that you have no contact with each other."

Spock dutifully held out his right hand.

Kirk grudgingly did the same. "Never saw you before," he said to Spock between clenched teeth. "Don't care if I ever do again."

Spock was curious about Mallory's evident self-control. He seemed to be unresponsive to Kirk's defiant attitude and statements.

The security officer snapped a tracking module around Spock's wrist, then Kirk's with a solid snap, the sound immediately followed by the sizzle of molecular bonding.

Spock studied the bracelet-shaped device with interest. "An efficient design," he said.

Kirk glared at him.

Mallory added another caveat to their instructions. "I'm sure I don't have to add that if either of you even attempt to remove the tracker, security officers will beam to your location and immediately return you to custody until the hearing. Any questions?"

Spock wanted to ask what powered the subspace transmitter and how the five-kilometer limit was determined: by following the city limits proper or by a radius measured from a central point to provide an average distance. It was an intriguing problem.

But Kirk said, "No. Can we go now?"

Mallory gestured to the open door. "Your father's waiting for you outside Processing."

Spock saw Kirk frown. "Great," the human said.

Mallory turned to Spock. "The embassy sent an attaché to escort you back to the compound."

"Of course," Spock said. "My parents have other business to attend to."

"Lucky you," Kirk said as he started toward the door.

Spock considered that puzzling statement during the short drive back to the Vulcan Embassy. He did not think of himself as lucky. Indeed, if he were not Vulcan, he decided he might envy Kirk for having the interest and attention of his father.

If he were not Vulcan.

16

Thirty-three years earlier, the shuttlecraft *Helen Hogg* had served with distinction on the *U.S.S. Endurance*. Among its most notable historic missions, the small, warp-three vehicle had carried delegates to the Babel Conference that had ratified the independence of Earth's oldest extrasolar colony world, New Montana, where Zefrem Cochrane himself had settled.

But, inevitably obsolete and outmoded, the venerable spacecraft had long since taken its last voyage. In the company of a dozen other fleet vehicles of various classes, it now spent its days in the vast hangar of the Tucker Systematics Center, being respectfully taken apart and reassembled by eager young Academy midshipmen.

The two mids who worked on the *H.H.* today were Elissa Corso and Zee Bayloff, gaining extra credits before the first semester of their second year began. Three days earlier, a fiendishly clever third-year lab instructor had set up a fault in the shuttle's impulse-power system that, bafflingly, also created an offset in the navigation system and made life support erratic. Now, even with most of the shuttle's hull plates removed and half the spacecraft's transmission network disassembled on the spotless gray plating of the hangar floor, the two young mids were no closer to resolving the issue than they were when they opened their first access panel.

So, for the moment, they did what any engineer would do: stood back and surveyed the chaos they had created from the once sleek vehicle, oblivious to the noisy tools and equipment of the other teams working on the other sacrificial shuttles and spacecraft scattered throughout the hangar, focusing only on the problem before them.

"This is what I'm thinking," Zee finally said. "What if there are three *separate* faults?"

Elissa wore her ball cap backward to keep the bill from hitting the circuits she'd been testing up close. She pushed it back even farther to scratch her hat-flattened hair. "Except Carmichael told us there was one underlying root cause."

Zee's blond hair was short enough that she didn't wear a cap, and somehow, on her, even the shapeless, pale-blue mechanic's overalls she wore seemed fashionable. "Maybe that's part of the test. The initial report was flawed, but since we didn't question it, we've just wasted three days on a false assumption."

Elissa tried to grapple with the part of that conclusion that troubled her the most. "You're saying Carmichael deliberately misled us?"

"Welcome to the real world," Zee laughed, and Elissa was surprised at her scornful tone. "If you were on the engineering staff of a starship and the chief told you to perform a specific repair, maybe the first step is to confirm the chief's diagnosis of the fault."

Put that way, Elissa saw the solution was obvious. "Carmichael's a hard case, isn't he."

"Yeah, but that's probably what makes him a good instructor." Zee gave Elissa a cynical smile. "People lie, fact of life."

Elissa sighed. "So . . . you deconstruct the nav components and I'll tackle life support?"

"Sounds like a plan."

The two slapped hands and went off in search of the new tools they'd need. That was when Elissa saw her company commander approach with an older civilian she didn't recognize.

"Ms. Corso," the CC barked. "Front and center."

Elissa instantly double-timed it to the two men. Her company commander was a fourth-class mid, rigid but fair, who kept his head as closely shaved as if he were still a plebe. The man with him was older, his hair white, his suit badly in need of a sonic wash to eliminate its wrinkles.

"Midshipman Corso reporting, sir." Elissa stood at attention.

Her CC referred to the visitor. "This is Mr. Mallory from Command. You're going to talk to him."

"Yes, sir." Elissa could guess what the topic of the conversation was going to be.

The company commander looked over at the disassembled shuttlecraft where Zee was already removing a square of inertial-damping mesh from the forward hull—part of the navigational positioning subsystem. "What's your status on that?"

"We've developed a new approach to solving the problem, sir."

"New approach. Good. I want a full written report by 0700 tomorrow."

"Yes, sir."

"Carry on."

Elissa and Mallory watched the fourth-year mid march off.

"Will that be a lot of work?" Mallory asked. "The report?"

Elissa remained at attention. "No, sir."

"At ease, Midshipman. This isn't an official visit."

That statement confused Elissa, but she relaxed. "Yes, sir."

"And I'm not an officer, so call me Mallory, and I'll call you Elissa, if that's all right."

"Yes, s—" She caught herself. "Mallory."

"So, I've just been reviewing your file, and I see you're facing an honor board hearing over the dilithium theft."

Elissa felt even more confused. This man worked at Starfleet Command, but dressed like someone who had never seen a proper uniform. And he was talking about her honor board as if it were something of passing interest, and not the reason for his visit. "That's correct." She managed to cut off the "sir" before she began to say it that time.

"For what it's worth, and I don't really know if I should be telling you this, but there's no evidence to suggest you actually took the dilithium yourself."

Elissa almost rocked back on her heels, so great was her relief. "Really?"

"You're not off the hook, though."

Elissa felt the weight of injustice descend on her again. "Permission to ask why."

"Your ID codes were definitely used by the actual thieves to gain access to the warp lab and to open the storage vault. So, at worst, you might be a knowing accomplice—which the investigators appear to doubt. But, at best, you were negligent in protecting your codes."

Elissa was back where she had started. "I can still be separated for that."

"You can."

Elissa still didn't know what Mallory wanted from her, unless it was to make her feel more miserable than she already did. She looked back at Zee, who was taking field readings off the damping mesh she had wired to a test bench. "May I ask if there is something else you wanted to talk to me about?"

When she turned back to Mallory, she saw that he did have another topic of conversation in mind. In his hand, he held Jim's override.

"Is this yours?" Mallory asked.

There were many ways Mallory might have asked that question, but he had fortunately chosen one that Elissa could answer honestly, without getting Jim in trouble.

"No, sir."

"I ask because it's programmed with your codes. This isn't the transmitter the dilithium thieves used, but it can do exactly the same thing." Elissa didn't risk opening her mouth, and Mallory stopped waiting for her to say something.

"Starfleet found this device in the possession of a young man: James Kirk."

Up to that point, Elissa had felt justified in not volunteering any new information that might hurt others, but she wasn't about to play games with someone from Command. If Mallory knew about her relationship with Jim, then there was no reason to remain silent.

"He's my boyfriend."

"Oh, I know. That's why I'm here. He was taken into custody last night on suspicion of stealing a Starfleet flyer."

"Jim would never do anything like that, sir—Mallory."

"Even so, it turns out that this device does have the capability of defeating the basic security lockouts on noncritical Starfleet equipment. It's very clever."

Mallory looked from the override to Elissa.

"Did you give him your codes so he could use them in this?"

Elissa could not lie to this man. Not just because she was a midshipman at Starfleet Academy, but because she was not the kind of person who would lie in any event. Which is *why* she was a midshipman.

So, even though she knew what she was about to say could lead to her immediate separation from the Academy, Elissa squared her shoulders and answered Mallory's question as befit a Starfleet officer candidate.

"I did give him my codes. But only *after* the dilithium went missing." Mallory didn't interrupt, so she continued. "Jim is convinced that the lab security isn't as foolproof as the investigators claim it is, and he basically built that override in a day to prove to me how easy it is to circumvent Starfleet security safeguards."

"And he demonstrated it by overriding the staff car's controls."

Elissa took another deep breath, knowing she was digging herself in deeper. "He did some research and figured out that the car and the lab had the same level of built-in security."

"Your boyfriend was right."

Elissa was surprised to catch a hint of what might have been admiration in Mallory's statement.

"Was there a Vulcan with you last night?"

"No, sir—Mallory." Elissa was surprised by the question. What did that have to do with anything? "I've never met a Vulcan on Earth, I mean, other than Ambassador T'Pol when she lectured here last year. But that was just a receiving line."

"Does your boyfriend know any Vulcans?"

"Jim's never mentioned knowing any." Elissa thought carefully. "I'd be surprised if he did. He's not the adventurous type. I mean, not when it comes to space and aliens and . . ."

"Starfleet?" Mallory suggested.

"He's not what you would call a supporter."

"But you are."

Elissa smiled. "I grew up on Risa. Half the population is alien."

Mallory slipped the override into his pocket. "Any idea what happened to the car?"

Elissa didn't know why this civilian hadn't mentioned Jim's brother yet, so she decided it would be all right if she didn't, either—unless specifically asked.

"Uh, when Jim tested the override, we were pretty much outflanked by the parking lot guards, so Jim decided we should get away in the car. Just far enough to give us a head start. We had no intention of stealing it. We parked it on a sidestreet by the waterfront, and that's the last I saw of it."

"You both left the car together?"

"Yes, sir." She caught herself again. "Mallory."

Mallory smiled. "I understand. It's a hard habit to break. I'm a graduate. Class of '22."

Elissa's attitude toward her questioner changed the instant she realized he'd experienced the same challenges she was in the midst of, and had succeeded. "Outstanding."

Mallory looked up, past the dazzling bright lights and structural braces of the arching hangar ceiling to what lay beyond. "When you get out there, serve on a Starfleet vessel, you'll find it's a bit less formal."

"*If* I get out there."

Mallory gave her a smile of commiseration. "Your honor board could break a lot of different ways. If you gave your codes to your boyfriend *after* the theft, the worst the board could rule is that you exercised poor judgment in not keeping your conduct adviser informed of what you were doing. That would mean demerits, maybe no liberty for a semester, but if Starfleet separated all the mids who committed minor infractions, I don't think there'd be much of an officer corps left. We tend to select for 'original' thinkers, and that does result in the rules being pushed to their limits on a regular basis."

"I would never knowingly violate the Academy's Honor Concept, and I would never break the rules, sir." Elissa didn't try to censor herself that time. If this man was an Academy graduate, then "sir" was what he deserved to be called.

Mallory paused, gave her a sharp look. "Again, when you get out there, on the frontier, sometimes you'll find that the people and conditions you encounter don't play by the same rules we do. That's when we need those original thinkers who understand our rules, but aren't afraid to make new ones."

Elissa sensed he was referring to something that had great personal significance to him, but it was not her place to ask for more details.

"Understood, sir." It was all she could say.

"By the way, I'd be happy to appear at your board as a character witness."

Elissa frowned, surprised. "Sir, you don't know me."

"Oh, I'm sure if we have further conversations—say if you happen to think of anything more that might help me understand the connection between you and your boyfriend and the override and the missing car—that would change. And I'd be able to appear on your behalf."

He's offering me a deal, Elissa thought indignantly. *Sell out Jim and Sam and get off with a few demerits and a slap on the wrist.* There was only one way she could respond.

"Thank you for your offer, sir. But this is my problem and I will deal with it."

"If you don't, you might lose your whole career."

But Elissa was an Academy mid, and she knew how a problem like hers could be solved every time. "All I have to do is tell the truth, sir. I have faith in the system."

Mallory nodded. "So do I." He held out his hand to shake hers. "A pleasure to meet you, Ms. Corso. But if I could offer a bit of advice?"

"Of course, sir."

"It's not enough to tell the truth. You have to tell the *whole* truth."

It was all Elissa could do to look him in the eyes, knowing how thoroughly he had seen through her.

"I understand, sir."

Mallory gave her a smile. "Well, if you don't now, you will soon enough. Good luck with the shuttle, Midshipman." Then he left.

Zee was beside her almost at once, using a towel to wipe an oily film of tetralubisol from her work gloves. "Who was he?"

"Some guy from Command."

"Trying to get you to confess?"

Elissa shook her head. "Thanks, but it's my problem."

"The more you tell me, Corso, the better chance there is I can help."

Elissa appreciated her dormmate's support but sometimes felt as if Zee were a bit too eager to learn bad news about anyone in their class.

"I'll be okay. The last thing you need is more trouble."

Zee gave up for the moment and they started back for the old *H.H.,* so many of its interior struts and spars revealed by missing hull plates that it resembled the half-decayed corpse of a mechanistic dinosaur.

"New semester, new Zee," Elissa's dormmate said. "I've learned my lessons."

Elissa was thinking, furiously. *Three days to go. Will I be able to say the same?*

17

"How can you and your brother live like this?"

"For one thing, Dad, it's cheap. For another, if you look around, we're not in Iowa anymore."

Kirk opened the cooler door, then wondered why. Of course, there was nothing edible in it. He'd been gone for a few days. And he was the shopper.

His father's tall figure blocked most of one window. Joe Kirk was staring out at the equally old and decrepit apartment building across the street. "That's not you, Jimmy. That's George talking."

Kirk took a deep breath to calm himself. "C'mon, Dad. His name is *Sam*."

"I know what your brother's name is. I gave it to him."

"And he doesn't want it. *You're* George Joseph Kirk. He wants to be his own man."

"Men don't run away from their obligations."

Almost of its own accord, Kirk's hand slammed shut the cooler door, nearly rocking the old appliance off its base. He turned to face Joe Kirk, angry with his father, but angrier with the heaviness of the tracking module fastened around his right wrist. "Let him go, Dad. He has no obligations—none that have anything to do with you."

"The farm!" Joe Kirk turned from the window, his bulk now silhouetted against the dirty panes. He was a big man, fifty-five, still strong, still powerful. He kept his hair in a crew cut, and two years out of Starfleet he still wore his service sideburns with laser-sharp points.

Kirk's eyes locked on his father's. "It's your farm," he said carefully, for what felt like the hundredth time. "Yours and Mom's. Not Sam's. Not mine."

"Ah, Jimmy . . ." Kirk's father spread his enormous hands as if they no longer had the strength to do anything. "Why are we like this?"

There were so many answers Kirk wanted to give his father, but he finally settled on the one that made the most sense to him, and Sam. Something he'd never had the courage to say before, so simply. "Because you keep trying to run our lives."

His father's shock looked genuine. "You're seventeen! You're not old enough to know how to run your life!"

"Who says? I'm doing fine!"

"*Jimmy!* You just got arrested by Starfleet for vehicle theft! Do you know how that reflects on me? On your mother?"

Kirk struggled to control himself. "Will you listen to yourself? Somehow, what Starfleet *thinks* I did—something they can't prove, by the way—reflects on *you*—and Mom! Dad, you've gotta stop this!"

The sudden silence made the cramped and dismal room seem even smaller.

Kirk could hear his father working hard to keep his voice down. "I know you didn't steal anything. You're not that kind of kid."

"Thank you," Kirk said flatly. "But I'm not a kid anymore."

Joe pressed his lips together, shook his head as if he were counting to ten. "Okay. Whatever you say. A young man. Whatever you want. *But*, I know that if a Starfleet car's been stolen, then somehow, your brother George—*Sam*—is behind it."

"You don't know that."

"Let me finish," Joe said sharply. "I know you don't agree, but give me some credit for understanding my boys. Your brother has always looked for the easy way, and it's always been in your nature to take care of him. Your mother says you'd take care of everybody, if you could."

"Sam doesn't need my help."

Joe regarded his younger son with pity. "Is there food in the cooler? I don't even have to look to confirm that. Because you've been in custody all night and Sam probably doesn't even know where to find the market. We both know he's got better things to do with whatever money he gets. However he gets it."

This argument was too old, too familiar, and wouldn't be settled soon. "Look, Dad, I'm tired. I'm going to bed." Kirk headed toward the door to the apartment's single bedroom.

His father reached out to catch his son's arm. "We need to talk."

"In the morning."

"At least call your mother, to explain."

Kirk pulled away from Joe. "Why don't you do that. You seem to know it all." He threw the door shut behind him.

The cramped bedroom was gloomy, and little bigger than the narrow cot that ran along one pockmarked wall. Kirk collapsed on it, his entire body trembling in the aftermath of all that had happened, his mind all the while searching to understand why he had behaved the way he had, afraid to find the answer.

What if that answer dragged him back to the killing ground of Tarsus IV? To the screams from those the hunters found? To the certainty of death, not just for him, but for the children who looked up to him, who trusted him to save them all?

Even as he closed his eyes, he sensed his father's solid presence outside his door. He knew his father's code would prevent him from entering. Not even to reassure his son.

A part of Kirk wished desperately that just this once his father would break his rule, do exactly that, and as if he was small again and lost in the fields of corn, his father would gather him up into his arms and tell him that everything was all right and that everything would always be all right.

Kirk opened his eyes and stared up at the ceiling, dry-eyed. He wasn't a child anymore. He was a man. And nothing would ever be all right, ever. Because no matter how much he did, it would never be enough.

For anyone.

Or for himself.

"The paragon of virtue was nicked?!" Griffyn's explosive laughter rattled the metal walls of his denlike office. It was a claustrophobic, mean room, with a low overhead, sited eight meters above the deck of the *Pacific Rome*'s main cargo hold. Through its narrow, outward-slanting windows, Griffyn could look down over his burgeoning enterprise and the underage workers who served it and him.

Sam stood nervously in front of the single, battered desk. He had tried to play an angle that he thought would free him from Griffyn's demand to meet his younger brother. But from Griffyn's delighted response, he had failed.

Griffyn caught his breath, directed his attention to the young woman gracefully arranged in a corner of an old sofa draped with what appeared to be dusty, antique tapestries. Her head was bent over a news padd, her legs tucked up under her. Sam knew her as Dala, Griffyn's sometime girl-friend.

"You've heard of this kid, right?" Griffyn asked her.

When she didn't respond, he snagged a thermal cup from his desk and threw it at the wall above her. It twanged off the metal and bounced onto the carpet-covered deck, finally roll-ing between two tall stacks of small shipping containers.

Dala looked up from her padd, unimpressed. She had painted iridescent blue butterfly wings around her eyes, and Sam thought the glistening indigo jumpsuit she wore fit her like a second skin. "I heard you."

"Who am I talking about?"

"Jimmy Kirk." Dala rolled her eyes. "It's always Jimmy Kirk with you."

Sam frowned, wondering what she meant, but he knew he didn't have the stomach to question Griffyn about it, or about anything. All he had to think about was how to keep Jimmy out of this.

Griffyn put his feet back up on his desk, roughly, and in the same movement grabbed a small clay object to avoid knocking it over.

The squat figurine looked old to Sam, but that was all he thought, because Griffyn's strange eyes were on him now.

"So, Georgie, what do you think we should do?"

Sam mustered all his courage. "Well, if Starfleet thinks Jimmy's involved in stealing cars, then he's probably going to be under surveillance, right? So . . . maybe it'd be better if you weren't seen with him?"

"You let me worry about that." Griffyn held up the clay figure and squinted at it with a frown. "But here's something you *can* worry about."

"Yeah?"

"Your little brother's a regular Star Cadet. You really think he's going to be able to keep his mouth shut when they start asking him questions?"

"What . . . what kind of questions?"

"Georgie . . . Georgie . . . he's going to give you up. He won't be able to help himself. They'll ask who stole the car, and he'll tell them."

Sam had never thought of that. "But, Griff, they think *he* stole it. So they won't ask him. And Jimmy won't do anything that'll hurt me. I mean, he wanted to fly the car last night because he knew if I got caught, my probation's over."

Griffyn swung his feet down, leaned forward, hands cupped around the figurine. "Exactly. They come for you, you're facing a few years of rehabilitation. Maybe send you off to one of those penal colonies where they rewire your brain. *Unless . . .*" Griffyn dragged out the moment. ". . . *you* cut a deal."

Sam suddenly grasped what Griffyn was implying and began speaking so quickly that his panicked words ran together. "Griff, no! No way. I'd never give you up. Never. No matter what they offered me."

Griffyn's grin was unnerving. "Guess what? I believe you. Because if you *ever* did anything that stupid, they'd find you gutted like a Tellarite on Andoria."

Dala snickered without looking up from the news.

"So, Georgie boy, if you don't think Jimmy's going to rat you out, and I know you won't rat me out, why do you think I said you have something to worry about?"

Sam nervously shook his head. He knew that half of whatever Griffyn said to him was just to keep him off-balance. But he couldn't conceive of any way to talk back. *Jimmy would know,* he thought. *He can handle creeps like Griffyn.*

"Who's missing from the equation?" Griffyn prompted.

Sam stared at him blankly.

Griffyn counted ostentatiously on the fingers of one hand. "Let's see . . . there was Kirk brother number one . . . Kirk brother number two . . . and . . ."

"Elissa?" The name shot out of Sam with geyser force.

Griffyn smiled approval. "Now you're firing on all thrusters. Consider this—she's a Starfleet midshipman, so she's committed to the truth. I could hold a knife to her throat to keep her quiet and she'd still tell me exactly what happened. Jimmy might not give you up, but his little playmate won't even think twice about it. Hell, she won't even think once. She'll just spill her guts. Which brings me back to you and your desire to not have your guts spilled."

Dala laughed softly to herself.

Sam could feel the sweat trickle down his forehead. "But,

Griff, she was just along for the ride. Jimmy'll never mention her. Starfleet will never know about her."

"So let's keep it that way. She's a sweet little Risan girl; we don't need to bring her into this at all. That means I let you keep your finder's fee."

The thousand-cee wafer was still in Sam's hand. He had just tried to return it to Griffyn, but his offer had been refused.

"That means," Griffyn added, "I still expect you to get your brother here—so I can fill him in on what's expected of him. Before he gets it into his head to do the right thing."

Somehow, from somewhere, without even weighing the risk of what he was about to do, Sam found the unexpected strength to stand up for his brother. "Jimmy's not involved in any of this. I don't want him hurt."

Griffyn rocked back in his chair, mouth open in mock surprise. "I'm impressed." His eyes went cold. "But I'm also disappointed."

Sam had trouble breathing as Griffyn got up, walked around from his desk until he was centimeters from Sam.

"Your little car theft stunt left a lot of dominoes out there that could start falling any second."

Griffyn leaned in closer to Sam's face, flicked his fingers to the left and right, as he described the consequences of those dominoes falling over.

"Oops, there's Jimmy blabbing, leading back to you, leading back to me. Oops, there's the girlfriend, trying to help Jimmy, leading back to you, leading back to me. You get it, Georgie? All those falling dominoes end up on *me*."

Griffyn's last gesture was to flick Sam's nose. Sam flinched, but made no protest.

"So I want you to ask yourself this question: Will I wait around for that to happen? Or will I destroy those other dominoes before they even fall?"

"I'll get him here," Sam croaked.

Griffyn patted him on the cheek like a dog. "Good boy."

When Sam left the *Pacific Rome* that night, he stopped on the pier only long enough to retch up everything in his stomach. He had never felt so frightened or so trapped, and he feared that this time not even Jimmy could make things right.

Spock stood in the center of the main room in his family quarters, calmly, because there was no other way for a Vulcan to stand.

His mother was near, her face taut with human worry.

His father's image gazed out at him from a wall-mounted viewscreen. Sarek was on a commercial flight to Titan to meet with a scientific delegation from Nren Prime—a Class-P world whose inhabitants felt more at home on that frozen moon than on Earth.

"Explain to me why you must return to Starfleet Headquarters," Spock's father said.

Spock looked down at the tracking module he wore. "I must appear for my hearing."

"But you told them that you did not steal the car."

"Correct," Spock said. "They did not believe me."

Sarek raised an eyebrow by an infinitesimal degree, signifying his great surprise. "But you are a Vulcan, Spock. You would not lie in a matter such as that."

"No," Spock agreed, "I would not."

Amanda touched her son's arm. "Spock, if the authorities need proof of your innocence, then surely you can provide them with an alibi. Since they know exactly when the car was stolen, all you have to do is tell them where you were when it happened."

"Her logic is flawless," Sarek said with Vulcan pride.

Spock agreed with a nod.

"Where were you?" Sarek asked.

Spock kept his attention fixed on his father's image because a perverse part of him—which he assumed was some last vestige of his human heritage he had successfully put aside—wanted to see Sarek's reaction to what his son was about to say.

"I was in the Garden of Venus—what humans refer to as a 'love bar.'"

Sarek nodded sagely. "An establishment for social gathering in which patrons celebrate and/or arrange various permutations of sexual assignations, typically to be explored at other, more private locations."

"Typically," Spock agreed, noting that his father's statement was word for word the definition from the embassy's briefing papers.

"What was the purpose of your presence there?"

Amanda interrupted. "Sarek, perhaps that's too personal a question."

Sarek looked puzzled, though only his closest family members would have known it. "Spock is not yet ready for his next *pon farr*. Therefore, he was not in the 'love bar' for the typical reason. Is that not correct, Spock?"

"Indeed, it is."

"Your purpose, then."

"At the time the car was stolen, I was engaged in selling a pre-Enlightenment *seleth* figurine to what is known as a 'fence'—that is, a dealer in stolen goods."

Amanda reacted with uncharacteristic shock. "Spock!"

Sarek, though, gave no reaction at all. "I see. The figurine was a forgery, of course."

"It was," Spock confirmed.

"What?" Amanda looked to the viewscreen. "How could you know that?"

"The only source of such figurines on Earth is the display of cultural artifacts in the Vulcan Embassy's reception hall. The value of such items is incalculable, and Spock would no more steal one than he would a Starfleet car."

Amanda shook her head in abject puzzlement. "Then why . . . ?"

"I am certain Father can explain the rest more succinctly than I," Spock said blandly. He had never spoken to Sarek so confrontationally.

"Sarek . . ." Amanda said, making no attempt to hide her confusion.

"Over the past forty-two days, Spock has come to me with what he believes is evidence that the most valuable items in the reception hall's display cases are being stolen and replaced with forgeries."

"And are they?" Amanda asked, still shocked.

Sarek said nothing.

Spock was not about to let his father continue with his denial of the problem. "Father . . . ?"

Finally, Sarek must have realized he had been outmaneuvered. "What I tell you now must remain in the strictest confidence."

Finally, Spock thought with an embarrassing sense of triumph over his father. He quickly suppressed it.

"The embassy staff is aware of the situation Spock deduced."

After a few moments of expectant silence, Amanda said, "That's all?"

Sarek reluctantly continued. "For reasons, quite logical, which I cannot discuss, the staff does not wish to stop the thefts at this time. That is all I will say on the matter."

Amanda's shoulders stiffened, and Spock realized he knew exactly how she felt.

"That is an unacceptable answer," Spock said, surprising himself as much as his parents with his rebellious attitude. "It is one thing to know that the embassy staff does not trust me, as if they think I am something other than Vulcan. But when you, my own father, treat me with a similar level of distrust . . ." He then delivered the harshest assessment any Vulcan son could make of his father. "I find your behavior toward me unsatisfactory."

Amanda was steeped enough in Vulcan ways to put her hand over her mouth in stunned silence.

The charged moment became worse as Sarek replied to the outburst, treating his son as harshly in turn. "I find your statement disrespectful."

"Stop it, you two!" Amanda said urgently. "I will not stand by and have you say such hurtful things to each other!"

"My father has the means to change the impasse he has created."

Sarek's eyes narrowed by a millimeter. "Your suggestion, Spock?"

"Tell me why you allow illegal activities to occur in this embassy."

"I cannot."

Spock realized he had balled his hands into fists behind his back, and was glad neither of his parents could see his outrageous loss of control. "I can only arrive at one logical explanation for your position."

"Explain."

"You do not trust me for the same reason the embassy staff do not—you believe me to be less than Vulcan."

Amanda stood before Spock and spoke as if in great pain. "Spock, that's not true. You know that's not true."

"Your mother is correct," Sarek said sternly.

"If my logic is flawed, then correct me," Spock challenged. "State another reason."

Sarek shook his head once, clearly in emotional distress. "I cannot."

"Vulcans do not accept me as Vulcan. The humans do not

accept me as human. What would you have me be, Father?"

Spock felt his mother put her arm through his. "Our son. Whom we love." She looked at the viewscreen. "And trust."

"Is that true?" Spock asked his father, and he was so upset that he no longer cared that his words caught in his throat.

"Your analysis of the situation is flawed," Sarek replied, as if he were speaking to a child. "We will discuss this further when I return." He leaned forward, and the viewscreen image switched from Sarek to a Vulcan desert scene.

"Spock," Amanda said, gently withdrawing her arm from his, "you know your father didn't mean any of that."

Spock relaxed his hands. "Unlike me, Sarek is Vulcan. He is incapable of saying anything except what he means." He gave his mother a small half bow. "If you will excuse me, Mother, I have my studies."

As Spock left Amanda speechless in the now silent room, he thought again of the human, Kirk, and envied him the closeness of his family.

When he was alone, he examined the gray metal bracelet of the tracking module, idly twisted it around his wrist. Something, at least, could be done about that.

18

Fourteen-year-old Jimmy Kirk shivered in the corner of his cabin with the other kids. He had draped them all with the thin blankets from their bunks, tried to make them think it was a dress-up game. But the heat and power had gone off yesterday when the governor's residence had been attacked, so Jimmy knew that whatever was happening out on the wide dirt streets of the colony, it was no game.

Near dusk of the second day, when most of the kids were in fitful sleep, the cabin public-address speaker had crackled to life, waking everyone. At first the younger kids were scared, but then the older ones figured out that if the colony's communications systems were back online, maybe that meant the power would be next, and then heat and running water—and food.

But the cabin stayed dark as an unfamiliar voice began to speak. "People of Tarsus IV, our colony faces difficult times. Governor Myron could not lead, and so, by the will of the people, I have taken that office in her place. The struggle we must now embark upon is dire, but measures can and will be taken to ensure this colony's survival. I ask all able-bodied adults to assemble at once at the storehouse complex. Ration cards are being prepared and will be allocated according to the group to which each individual is assigned. If you know of any elderly colonists, or others too ill or infirm to assemble, inform the guards at the storehouses so arrangements can be made for those people as well."

Whoever was speaking, the new governor Jimmy supposed, sounded so reasonable and authoritative that he began to believe that everything would work out. Maybe someone had found an-

other storehouse of grain that hadn't been spoiled by the fungus. And then a loud noise came over the speaker, like something heavy falling or a door slamming open. Another voice started shouting. "No! No! He's going to kill us! That's his—" There was another sound, then—a high-pitched hum that Jimmy knew well: laser rifle.

The second voice stopped in mid-sentence, followed by another sound of something heavy falling.

He heard a new voice call out, asking if the governor was all right. Someone else demanded to know who was responsible for guarding the door. Other voices, far away from the audio pickup, buzzed into incomprehensible growling.

Donny Roy and another four-year-old huddled closer to Jimmy. All the kids were afraid now. When adults fight, no child feels safe.

At last, the measured, reasonable voice of the new governor returned, as if nothing had happened to interrupt him.

"Make no mistake," the governor said, "this colony is in the midst of a revolution. And if this colony is to survive, the revolution must succeed. Assemble at the storehouses. Go into your groups. Obey the guards. That is how we will survive. By my order, Kodos, Governor of Tarsus IV."

The speaker clicked into silence.

The only sound in the dark, cold cabin came from a handful of whimpering children.

Then a fist pounded on the outside door. All the children gasped or cried out in surprise. And Jimmy heard the familiar voice of his best friend shout: "Jimmy! It's Matt! The governor wants to see you!"

The kids all looked at him through the gloom.

"He's got food! All we got to do is help him out! C'mon!"

Jimmy went to the wooden door. It creaked on cold hinges as he opened it.

Outside, lit by the hand torches they carried, exhaling clouds of frozen breath in the cold of growing night, Matthew Caul was waiting for him, grinning, accompanied by five other teenagers from nearby farms. They all wore red bandanas at their necks. "Tell the other kids to stay in the cabin for now. We'll come back for 'em after the governor's checked their records."

"Checked for what?" Jimmy asked.

"It'll be okay," Matt said again. "The governor's got food. All we got to do is help him."

Jimmy looked into his best friend's eyes and saw hunger there. Then he saw that Matt and the other teenagers carried laser rifles, just like the one he'd heard over the speaker.

"Why do you have guns?"

Matt's grin faded. "I told him you'd be okay. You want to eat, don't you?" He fell back on the same old argument. "All we gotta do is help him."

"Help him do what?"

"The right thing," Matt answered.

Then there was another loud explosion and—

—Kirk woke with a start, gasping, still feeling the deathly cold wind of Tarsus IV blow into the cabin through the open door.

He sat up, remembered he was in his brother's bedroom. Then he heard another loud noise, just like the one that had wakened him.

Joe Kirk was in the main room, snoring like artillery fire from the old holosimulations of the Romulan War.

Kirk slowly opened the bedroom door, saw his father on the couch, one arm folded across his eyes, deep asleep, apparently immune to the volume of his exhalations.

Kirk seized his opportunity. He walked quietly across the room, found his jacket where he had tossed it, checked the pocket for his communicator, then eased out the door into the hallway. He could hear his father all the way to the lift.

By the time he was outside and on the street, Kirk felt awake and a plan fell into place. The first order of business was the tracking module on his wrist. Something had to be done about it.

He pulled out his communicator, called the one person he knew he could always count on, despite what his father said.

"This is close enough," Kirk said. "Can you park?"

Sam peered through the grimy windshield of the rental landcar. The towering, flashing holosigns of New Union Square lit the street ahead in a rainbow explosion of shifting colors, as if a deep-space nebula had been blown apart by a supernova. In the confusion of light, the milling crowds of pedestrians made it hard to tell where the sidewalks ended and the road began. He could hear the rumble of their passing conversations warring with the come-ons from the holosigns and a dozen competing music broadcasts. There was no possible place to park. "Not a chance," he told his brother. "I could let you off."

Sam had taken Jimmy's call with reluctance. The only thing that was keeping him from doing what Griffyn wanted right away was the tracking module Starfleet had clamped on his brother. It was the perfect excuse for his not taking Jimmy to the docks. But with this new plan of his brother's to get rid of it, Sam didn't want to risk anyone from Griffyn's organization seeing them together. If Jimmy wasn't wearing the tracking module, then Sam had no excuse.

"How 'bout it?" Sam asked.

Kirk had a new plan. "Turn right up here. There's an alley by that surplus shop."

Sam turned right when the crowd let him, slowly made his way along a narrower, less crowded street. The holosigns here were fixed within their generator frames, and none of them projected their illusory images down to the street level. He checked the mix of businesses: mostly small restaurants, the inexpensive kind where all food was extruded from a machine in the back.

"There," Sam's brother said. He pointed to a small storefront where a crooked holosign showed the same loop of an antique starship stretching out as it went into warp drive, disappearing, then reappearing on the other side, nacelle lights growing brighter once again. As Kirk had said, there was a narrow opening between that shop and the next building on the street. "Turn in."

Sam stopped the car in the small blind alley. The headlights illuminated a lurid red sign that carried a warning in several languages and many different alien letter forms. The ones Sam could read stated that anyone who parked here would be eaten. "You're sure this is okay?" he asked.

"Yeah, c'mon," Kirk urged, and as quickly as that he was out of the car.

Sam followed his brother to the surplus shop with the infinite starship sign. "Wait here," Kirk said, then went in.

Sam remained on the sidewalk, looking through the front window to see what appeared to be the aftermath of an explosion in a wrecking yard. Every square centimeter of the shop was covered in rickety-looking shelves holding bins of all sizes and colors, crammed full of memory modules, isobinary chips, quantum isolators . . . Sam couldn't identify more than a tenth of what he saw.

Jimmy, though, looked right at home in the middle of the mess. He had one baffling piece of something in his hand already, and was laughing about it with the shopkeeper—a massive, dark-skinned alien with a startlingly white beard, two stubby antennae coming straight out of his forehead, and wearing what looked to be a scarred old 'plaser's apron. The shopkeeper laughed at whatever it was Jimmy said, then waved his three-fingered hand—or maybe, since the light was dim, Sam thought it might even be his tail—and nodded "of course" when Jimmy pointed at the wall behind him, obviously referring to the car.

Sam's brother came out of the shop a moment later. "No trouble. Joonie-Ben says we can leave the car there as long as we have to. Let's go."

Sam marveled again at how easy everything seemed to be for Jimmy. "Joonie-Ben? That alien?"

"Yeah," Kirk said as they walked quickly toward the main street. "It's his shop." Reaching the street, they pushed their way through a river of shoppers and gawkers until they came to the stream of people walking in the direction Sam realized that his brother planned to go.

"Get this, Sam: Joonie-Ben's mother was Arcadian and one of his fathers was a Xiicalli."

Sam wondered if he had heard correctly. "*One* of his fathers?"

His brother didn't seem troubled by the concept. "That's how Arcadians do it." He gave Sam's shoulder a punch. "You're the guy who's gonna be a biologist—you tell me."

Sam glanced back at the Arcadian's shop with a bemused half-smile as, for a moment, it all came back to him: his fascination with the processes by which chemistry became biology. He could remember reading something years ago about tri-sexual species, but . . .

Sam shook his head. Those details were lost in a mental fog, like so many other things from his childhood. "Haven't got a clue," he told his brother. For some reason, the loss bothered him.

Kirk nodded, accepting as always. "Anyway, the guy's an old boomer engineer. Got his start when his captain mothballed their freighter and let him sell it for parts. Been selling surplus ever since."

Sam looked at his brother, whose ingenuity never failed

to surprise him. "How'd you meet up with someone like that?"

"It's a good shop. I got some of the parts for the override from him. And if I listen to a few of his stories, he gives me a good price, too." Kirk pointed across the street to a small, arched gateway. "Down there."

Traffic was stopped dead, and Sam had no difficulty following his brother as they threaded through the stop-and-go landcars and flyers in wheel mode. The arched gateway led to another alley, though this one was lined on both sides with even smaller shops than Joonie-Ben's.

After a few more minutes, his brother pointed to a door between two fast-food extruder stands. Sam couldn't see any sign on it, and its dingy yellow paint was chipped and fading. But Jimmy walked up to it and knocked. Then he motioned for Sam to stand beside him. "They have to scan us."

Sam was familiar with a lot of places down by the docks that let in patrons only after they had been scanned. Such places mostly served offworlders, but that didn't mean there wasn't fun to be had for locals. "Jimmy . . . what kind of place is this?"

The door clicked open.

"My kind of place," his brother said, and led Sam in.

Sam took a quick look around, winced at the smell of some acrid mixture of old oil, citrus solvent, and burning insulation. The long, narrow room was even more of a mess than Joonie-Ben's shop. And this time, Sam didn't recognize *any* of the parts and pieces that were stuffed into every available space— even bins hanging from the ceiling.

"James T.!" an excited voice said loudly. It had to be loud to be heard over the unusual music that was playing. At least, Sam thought it was music. It might also have been a recording of cats yodeling, atonally and with no discernible rhythm.

Sam watched an oddly thin alien in Earth jeans and a fresh

white T-shirt step around a stack of what seemed to be empty computer cases. "Seemed to be," because some of them had fur growing from their sides, and were breathing.

"Torr!" Sam's brother said in recognition.

"It's not Saturday," the alien burbled. He sounded as if he was perpetually happy.

Sam had seen several of Torr's species in San Francisco before. Humanoid . . . segmented ridges framing his eyes and his high, lightly ridged forehead . . . Then the alien's smile turned into something worthy of the Cheshire cat by stretching remarkably as if to bisect his entire head, and Sam had it. Denobulan.

"Special project," Kirk announced. He held up his hand to show Torr his tracking module.

The Denobulan pursed his lips in admonishment. "A Starfleet 10-57 Mark B. Very sophisticated. James T., have you been naughty?"

"I'm trying to be," Sam heard his brother say. "That's why I need to get this off."

Then Sam saw Torr look curiously at him. "Is there anything else I should know?"

"It's okay, this is Sam."

The Denobulan relaxed. "Ah, Kirk the elder. A pleasure to meet you after all your brother has told me."

"Yeah, same here," Sam mumbled. He still couldn't get over this new side of his brother he was seeing. Sure, New Union Square was where Jimmy spent most of his weekends, sometimes worked, but who knew how or why or that he hung out with so many aliens. And aliens liked him.

Torr scratched at one of his extravagant peaked eyebrows, turned his attention back to Kirk. "I believe the law requires me to say that any attempt to block the signal of or to remove a certified law-enforcement tracking module is a violation of . . . I don't know how many regulations."

"That's pretty much what Starfleet told me."

"Right. I've done my civic duty," the Denobulan said happily. "What's the plan?"

"Earth's not exactly like Denobula."

Torr laughed. "Tell me about it!"

"Seriously, doing your civic duty isn't enough to keep you out of trouble if they figure out you helped me."

The Denobulan looked hurt. "But I've never opened up a 10-57 Mark B before."

"But you know how to take one off, right?"

"Taking it off is easy. Making Starfleet think that you haven't, that's hard."

"Not this time."

Sam watched as his brother held up the module again. "It has a subspace link to a second module—to let them know if the other guy and I try to meet."

The Denobulan brightened and gestured grandly to the back of the shop. "Use workshop number three. I'll bring you my best cutter."

"Thanks, Torr. An hour should do it."

As his brother offered the Denobulan a credit wafer, Sam wished he had his brother's easy confidence.

But Torr waved the money aside. "No, no, no. This is too exciting. Let me look at the pieces?"

"Just don't keep 'em around too long," Kirk warned. He motioned to Sam. "Let's go."

Workshop three was basically a closet at the end of a creaking hallway, but it had a brightly lit workbench with immaculate tools for just about any kind of delicate transtator work. Sam spent most of the first hour watching in awe as his brother deftly assembled what appeared to be a fat cylinder of silver mesh which he lined with the innards of four old communicators connected by glowing optical circuits. A fifth communicator, bulkier than the others and which Sam recognized as a Starfleet model, was connected to the cylinder by a conductive ribbon. His brother placed that communicator to the side, and turned it on.

When Kirk finally took a moment to lean back and stretch his arms, Sam had to ask: "Jimmy, I knew you were good at this kind of thing, but c'mon, you been going to night school or something?"

Kirk slowly rocked his head back and forth, making his neck crack. "All the manuals are in the public computers. Especially the old stuff. I don't know . . . once you figure out how the basic circuits work, everything else is just a combination of them. Put 'em all together the right way, and it makes sense, you know?"

Sam laughed. "No."

He watched Jimmy pick up a Pauli-exclusion probe, make an adjustment on its dial, then begin moving it near the circuit connections he had made, all the while monitoring the probe's tiny display of particle positions.

"Anyway, duotronics I can do. Transtators . . . it's all easy stuff. But quantum bypasses . . . that kind of thing . . . I leave that to the experts. I read the manuals, and it's like reading old Orion—can't figure it."

Sam quietly watched his younger brother's expert movements, deciding not to remind him that, as far as he knew, quantum technology was usually grown under the direct supervision of powerful artificial intelligence programs in factories floating in interstellar space. Nor did he say that he himself had trouble changing power nodes in his communicator.

"Okay, done," his brother said with pride. "Now I can get this off." He stood up from his stool and put his right hand into the open end of the mesh cylinder. "Sam, reach in from the other side, hold both sides of the module, and squeeze them together."

Sam did as instructed. The cylinder was just wide enough

for his hands to fit around Jimmy's wrist. "Now what?" he asked.

His brother flicked on the cutter Torr had brought him. It was a slender, wand-shaped device, with a small disk at the working end. As a high-pitched whine began to come from it, the disk suddenly glowed blue, then disappeared.

"Okay," Kirk said quietly, and Sam could tell he was concentrating. "Got it set for metal crystals, self-cooling, full rejection of soft matter . . ." He gave Sam a tight smile. "That would be my wrist and your fingers."

Then he carefully slipped the cutter into the cylinder and delicately moved the invisible disk toward the top of the module between Sam's hands.

Sam was fascinated and had no fear. If anyone knew what he was doing, it was his little brother.

He felt a mild vibration in the module, and then, almost anticlimactically, the noise stopped and the disk reappeared, no longer glowing.

"Pull it apart," his brother said, so Sam did.

The gray metal bracelet separated like soft candy.

"Leave the pieces in the cylinder, and that's that."

Sam carefully withdrew his hands from one end as his brother removed his hands and the cutter from the other.

Kirk rubbed his right wrist, even though the module had never been tight enough to cause discomfort.

Now Sam felt nervous. "I gotta tell you, Jimmy, I'm half expecting Starfleet Security to beam in any second."

Kirk grinned. "No way. The mesh and the four other communicators in there jam the alarm the module's sending out right now. And that communicator"—he pointed to the Starfleet model—"has a subspace mode, so I used it to retain the link between the identifier circuits in my module and the ones in the Vulcan's—just like Starfleet programmed them to do in the first place, thank you very much. Right now, the Vulcan tracker is doing the transmitting for both modules, and making it look as if the second signal is coming from about six kilometers away from the first."

Sam was pretty sure he understood the basics of what his brother had done—essentially using Starfleet's own technology against itself. But as much as he respected his brother's talents, Starfleet wasn't exactly stupid about this kind of thing.

"How long until Starfleet figures out what you've done?"

His brother was already carefully replacing every tool in its specific slot and holder, making the bench as neat and ordered as when they had entered the workshop. "They won't." He laughed. "Unless that Spock guy decides to disable his own tracker. But no way a Vulcan's going to do anything illegal, right?"

"Guess so," Sam said, not really sure. As far as he'd heard, Vulcans were notoriously dull and rule-bound. But you never knew.

His brother opened the workshop door and beckoned him. As usual, he was full of energy. "C'mon, driver, I'm late for a date."

Sam, as usual, followed in his brother's wake, trusting that Vulcans were indeed as predictable as Jimmy hoped.

They weren't.

19

In the mid-twenty-third century, on any aerial approach to San Francisco, the Vulcan compound was unmistakable.

The city itself was modern, with narrow soaring towers and wide-open green parks and colorful mixed-use plazas. A few older buildings of brick and concrete remained, survivors not of the third world war, which had left most of the city untouched, but of the three major earthquakes that cumulatively had done even more damage than the Great San Andreas Quake of '42. Geologists were still working hard at adapting Vulcan techniques used to bleed off the mechanical forces of tectonic activity, but for more than a century now, most earthquakes could be reliably predicted to within a ten-hour window with two to three weeks' warning. It had been decades since any earthquake had caused major destruction and disruption—additional evidence of the planet's becoming more and more of a paradise.

In the midst of the vast blooms and interlinked pathways of thriving vegetation, and the crisp white, silver, and muted tones of contemporary architecture, the Vulcan diplomatic compound was a distinctive patch of crimson and sand—the colors of home for the fifteen hundred aliens who lived and worked there. The blinding-white United Earth Embassy in Shi'Kahr City on Vulcan was no less distinctive in its alien setting.

One of the buildings in the compound, though, was noticeably different from the others. Instead of the gently upreaching, softly rounded lines of an ancient aesthetic shaped by the desert winds of Vulcan, it was low, hard-edged, and more reminiscent of an ammunition bunker. For this structure, called, with Vulcan efficiency, Utility Building 2, the logic of physics had overruled that of tradition.

Within the thick protective walls, the compound's independent power-generation equipment was housed, along with powerful subspace transmitters in direct contact with the homeworld, and—perhaps most importantly—the compound's own secure transporter hub, which guaranteed that all personnel would be beamed through quintuply-redundant Vulcan technology, rather than the comparatively reckless triply-redundant systems tolerated by Earthmen.

In fact, the Vulcan compound's transporter system was so safe and secure that in more than a century of operation, not one warning alarm had sounded except during training and maintenance drills.

Until tonight.

When the radiation alarm sounded in the main control room, two transporter technicians were on duty. Within half a second, they had ended their discussion of non-Surakian modes of logic and begun the test procedures required to determine if the alarm had activated because of a fault in the warning subsystem or because of an actual—and unprecedented—radiation leak.

All five independent radiation monitor screens displayed on the main console indicated identical levels of high-energy particles leaking from the annular-confinement-beam generator, indicating, in turn, a serious shielding failure that had cascaded through five different protective systems.

Neither technician understood how that could be possible. But, since they were now being bombarded with enough radiation to have killed a human and to cause themselves troublesome health problems, they swiftly set all controls to a "safe" mode and walked quickly to the main doors. As trained, they would report to the infirmary for radiation treatment while the technicians for the next scheduled shift would don radiation suits and commence repairs.

Within thirty seconds of the alarm, the main transporter control room was empty and unguarded.

Thirty seconds after that, Spock walked in. He headed to the main console and inserted a black data card. Three new programs began running in the transporter computers. The first replayed and then altered the security imaging file to show that after the technicians left the chamber, no one else had entered. The second erased the fractal program that had reproduced the effects of a radiation leak in the five different monitoring systems. The third program entered two sets of transport coordinates into the controls and began a fifteen-second countdown.

Spock crossed unhurriedly to the transporter platform and stepped onto the right-most lens. Then he waited, hands behind his back.

A few seconds later, he dissolved into a glittering matter stream and faded from sight.

Except for his tracking module.

It landed on the platform when the elementary particles comprising Spock's right wrist lost cohesion.

A moment later, the matter stream reformed on the left-most lens, and Spock reappeared. When movement was possible again, he walked over to retrieve the fallen module and put it into the pocket of his cloak.

He returned to the console, removed the black data card, and inserted a blue one. The program it contained erased the transporter log.

Spock pocketed both cards, then left. It had taken him all of ninety seconds to defeat the Starfleet module, and though he knew it was wrong, he felt proud of himself.

How anyone could mistake him for a human, he just didn't know.

• • •

On Spacedock, the nine representatives seated around the table in the narrow, windowless conference room were silent. The images on the viewscreen and the charts showing the spread of the atrocities were that disturbing, that alarming.

The sole reason Mallory's misleadingly named Department of General Services existed was to deal with those things the regular Starfleet did not have to contend with in its mission of exploration. The fact that his department was not included on most organizational charts, its presence and actions nothing more than a line or two in the yearly allocation reports, did not concern him. Because the universe was not yet as perfect as the leaders of the Federation and of Starfleet wished to see it and tried to make it, it was his responsibility to confront those imperfections.

So, at this meeting, it was his responsibility to ask the one obvious, and unanswered, question.

"Could it be Kodos?"

In the subdued light of the hushed room, eight grave-faced individuals turned from the viewscreen and its dreadful images of children mutilated by Starfleet weapons.

Facing Mallory were two Starfleet admirals, four civilian analysts, and two elected representatives of the Federation Council, here to provide oversight. Both admirals were regional commanders of the specialized security forces in charge of colonial defense, whose usual most pressing concern was tracking Orion pirates. The civilian analysts were from Starfleet Command, representing expertise in colonial affairs, the history of the Helstrom Nebula Development Region, interstellar treaty law, and deviant psychology. The final two members of the committee were elected representatives from the Federation Council: a human from New Montana, and T'Rev of Vulcan.

The senior admiral, Elias Mathur, was the first to respond

to the possibility Mallory had raised. "You mean, is this war-lord they call 'the general' and Kodos the Executioner one and the same?"

"It's something we must consider," Mallory said. "Both men are brutal. Both appear to be driven by some strange concept of eugenics. And both use children as their fighting forces."

"Governor Kodos used children?" The representative from New Montana was Mer Proctor, a novice, newly appointed to the innocuously named DGS Steering Committee.

"The reports of the time are unequivocal," T'Rev explained. He had been a member of this committee for more than ten years, and Vulcans had led the first relief mission to Tarsus IV.

"In some cases," he continued, "entire families were de-stroyed. That is what one would expect if Kodos followed a strict interpretation of eugenics. By killing every member of a family, he would have successfully eliminated undesirable ge-netic traits from the population pool.

"However," T'Rev added without emotion, "the eyewit-nesses also report that some of the young were not termi-nated, even though their parents were. That is not the action of someone following a program of eugenics. That could be construed as an act of recruitment."

"But why children?" This time, the question was asked by the civilian specialist from Starfleet's legal division, Chinatsu Rin, severe in appearance, with stark black hair framing the pale features of one who had grown up in the armored pres-sure domes of Venus.

"Several explanations are possible," T'Rev said. His neutral tone and bland expression gave no indication that he was dis-cussing the brutalization of children. "In terms of the specific conditions on Tarsus IV, Governor Kodos clearly viewed him-self as a savior. While his actions were unconscionable, his goal was logical: He wished to save as many colonists as possible. Children require less sustenance than adults. Therefore, for every adult he executed, two children could receive enough food to survive. It was an equation born in madness, but an equation nonetheless."

Unlike many at the table, Admiral Mathur was well-versed in the darker realities of interstellar exploration. He folded his hands before him. "What are the other explanations?"

T'Rev's explanation was chillingly pragmatic. "For a leader seeking an army willing to do his bidding without question, children's minds are more malleable. Their thoughts are not complex. They have little sense of their own mortality. They can be coerced by rudimentary expressions of punishment and reward. Perhaps, most importantly, their moral and ethical notions of life are not fully formed, and thus can be shaped by a charismatic leader."

The civilian psychologist, Tyler Light, nodded in agreement, one hand absently stroking his gray beard. "All eyewitness accounts confirm that Governor Kodos was extremely compelling. It seems some of those chosen for execution submitted willingly after listening to his rationale."

"Though I would argue that this new warlord is insane," Rin added, "his actions do seem deliberate, his strategy"—the legal specialist gestured to T'Rev—"well thought out, it appears."

"But he's using *children* to fight his battles." Darskin Sauder was the second admiral, and he had just been promoted to command rank because of his heroic actions in defusing the Trimega Insurrection without firing a shot—precisely the cool-headed, nonviolent approach Starfleet sought out and rewarded in its officers. Yet Mallory had seen the young man's face blanch as the images of the recent casualties had appeared on the screen.

"How is that 'well thought out'?" Admiral Sauder looked stricken, as if he, personally, were responsible for what had happened. "We all saw the report from Helstrom III. Our security forces slaughtered those . . . those innocents."

Mathur regarded his young fellow officer with compassion.

"A case of brilliant albeit regrettable tactics. As soon as our senior officer on the ground believed his forces had mistakenly engaged noncombatants, he quite correctly broke off the attack and withdrew so he could ask for new orders. During that withdrawal, the warlord's second team was able to reach Helstrom III's undefended power generator and set the charges."

Sauder's voice rose with anger. "So this criminal just . . . sacrificed those children, knowing what would happen to them?"

"And nearly succeeded in erasing Helstrom III's colony, which appears to have been his objective. Keep in mind that at least four other colonies have been destroyed or suffered forced evacuation over the past two years."

Ahmed Najoori, a small, quiet scholar unheard until now, held up a hand to draw the others' attention. "Governor Kodos tried to *save* Tarsus IV. Do we have any evidence that these new attacks are due to him as well?"

"I've simply raised the possibility, Mr. Najoori," Mallory said. "We'd be in a better position if we knew this so-called general's long-term objective. *Is* there anything of any strategic value among the worlds of the Helstrom Nebula?"

The civilian historian shook his head. "Twenty-three primary star systems. No indigenous intelligent species. Nine Class-M worlds and two Class-M moons suitable for colonization. Six other worlds suitable for terraforming. Thirty gas giants for raw material . . . those can be found in almost any system." He paused, then summed up: "There're just planets. Nothing special."

Mallory turned to the legal specialist. "Ms. Rin, are any of the Helstrom worlds part of a territorial dispute?"

She shook her head as well. "With no spacefaring species within fifty light-years, they're covered by the Babel Expansion Treaty of 2312. Jointly administered by the six Federation worlds closest to the nebula. No disputes. Settled law."

Mallory looked around the table at the other eight attendees. "So if it is Kodos who's behind these attacks, there's *nothing* we can point to and say *this* is what he believes he's protecting?"

Mallory's communicator beeped. He checked the display code—it was his assistant, overriding his privacy lockout. He looked up, disregarding Sally's summons. This meeting was too important to interrupt and reconvene.

But no one chose to respond to his question, so Mallory took the lead again. "The Federation will not abandon the remaining colonies in the nebula to a warlord," he said firmly. "Clearly, we need a next step."

"Several steps," Admiral Mathur said.

Mallory ignored a second beep from his communicator. "What do you need from us, Admiral?"

Mathur thought a moment. "The highest priority is to work out some way to predict what the general's next target will be. We have a lot of firepower in the sector. I can assign more ships over the short term. But first we do have to find out what it is he wants. Then, maybe, we can anticipate his moves."

"All right," Mallory said. "My department will set up a study group at once. What else?"

"New rules of engagement. What do I tell my people when they're attacked by children?"

Mallory had anticipated this question and had made his decision: This was the time to take the wraps off a secret project.

"This is strictly 'need to know,' not to be repeated outside this committee."

All eyes were on him now.

"Starfleet Technical is actively redeveloping personal phase-weapon technology."

Tyler Light snorted. "And will we be bringing back blunderbusses and flintlocks, too?"

Mallory understood the psychologist's skepticism. Personal phase weapons dated back to before the founding of the Federation, and had been on their way to becoming standard-issue sidearms throughout Starfleet, praised for their ability to safely stun combatants. Then had come the Romulan War, and though no Romulans had ever been engaged in face-to-face combat, too many humans had fallen before the onslaught of the Romulans' laser-armed robotic forces.

By the end of humanity's first and, it was hoped, last full-scale interstellar war, phase weapons had been replaced by much more powerful class-eight laser weapons, which added stimulated subspace energy frequencies to those of traditional laser light. The result had been a powerful new type of combat weapon with a far more efficient use of energy, and capable of blast and penetrative effects that the designers of the antique class-one lasers could never have envisioned.

The one drawback, though, was that it was notoriously difficult to employ a class-eight laser as a nonlethal weapon. Too far away from the enemy, and the laser would only prove annoying. Too close, and the laser could stun the target permanently, eliminating even the possibility of regaining consciousness. Thus Starfleet had gone back to basics and for years had been attempting to marry the blast effects of the standard-issue class-eight laser with the humane stun settings of the old phase-weapon technology.

According to the latest evaluation reports Mallory had read, it appeared Starfleet had finally come close to solving the technical issues and was ready to deploy, on a test basis only, a new weapon dubbed the "phaser," which combined the best of both earlier systems.

Mallory now declassified this for the committee, and promised Admiral Mathur that his forces in the Helstrom Nebula would be the first to receive the new phasers. Any engagement with the general's child army would be conducted with stun weapons and not deadly force.

"Do you know when these weapons will be available?" Admiral Mathur asked.

"No."

"What do I tell my people in the meantime?"

Mallory had no prepared response ready. "They will have to use their best judgment."

"And fire on children?" the senior admiral challenged.

But Mallory had seen even more of the universe's darkest corners than Mathur.

"Admiral, it is Starfleet's duty to protect the lives and well-being of all Federation colonists. If the general's forces attack another colony and Starfleet Security forces are called upon to defend that colony, your people will be firing on the *enemy*. I'm sorry, but I can't put it any plainer than that."

The admiral stood, his posture rigid.

Mallory chose to go along with the moment and end the meeting. He got to his feet as well.

"Just be damn quick with that study group," Mathur growled as he exited the room. "We need to know what this fanatic's thinking."

As the rest of the committee members left, Mallory finally flipped open his communicator.

"This'd better be good," Mallory warned his assistant.

"Special Agent in Charge Luis Hamer needs to talk with you."

Mallory automatically assessed his assistant's tone, found no evidence of worry, and switched his attention from the tragedy on Helstrom III to yesterday's excitement at Headquarters. He checked the time display on the viewscreen. "That took the boys longer than I thought."

"Say again?"

"Never mind, Sally," Mallory said. "I'll take the call in my office."

20

Two minutes later, the image of the angry SCIS agent appeared on the deskscreen in Mallory's office.

"I told you you were making a mistake, *Mr.* Mallory." Hamer was thoroughly annoyed and not bothering to hide it.

Mallory suppressed a smile, understanding that the agent's emphasis was to underscore his displeasure at being forced to take orders from a civilian bureaucrat who headed one of Starfleet's lesser known, and least useful, departments.

"One of the boys removed his tracking module, did he?"

"You expected this?"

"Whoever built that override wouldn't have any trouble defeating a standard tracker. As a matter of fact, I was expecting you to call a few hours earlier than this."

Mallory made a mental note to write a glowing letter of commendation to soften any lingering resentment the agent might develop for having been kept in the dark.

"So which one was it?"

"Which one?" Hamer repeated as if confused.

"We needed to know which one of the two kids built that device. So, putting them in the modules was the test. Whoever got out of his is our resident genius."

What Mallory didn't understand was why the SCIS agent suddenly looked pleased. "So?"

"They *both* removed the modules. At exactly the same time. About twenty-five minutes ago."

There weren't many times Mallory was surprised in his line of work, but this was one of them.

"They're better than I thought," he said softly, not caring if the agent heard him. "They really are working together."

Hamer had the decency not to gloat excessively, but Mallory didn't begrudge him the moment. "Shall I send out a fugitive alert to the protectors and travel hubs?" the agent asked.

"Not at this time, thank you. With any luck, now that the boys are out of the trackers, they'll lead us to whoever it is they're working with."

Hamer's mood darkened. "Except, without the trackers, how can they lead you anywhere?"

"Oh, we have our resources," Mallory said, and unlike Hamer, he didn't gloat.

At 0200 local time, another of Spock's fractal programs became active.

Operating in a highly distributed pattern that was too diffuse to trigger a security alert in the Vulcan compound's computer network, the program diverted the feed from the imagers in the main reception hall and then processed it to remove Spock and his activities before resending it to the databanks.

Free from surveillance, Spock approached a display cabinet along the back wall. It was from a pre-enlightenment museum on Vulcan, long buried under once-radioactive rubble, now meticulously restored and decontaminated. Because it predated Surak's teachings, the cabinet was intricately carved, with complex ornamentation of intertwined beasts and leaves brought into high relief by careful shading with a blue vegetable dye, unique to the era in which the piece was built.

Earthmen invariably declared that the ancient relic was breathtakingly beautiful. The Vulcans who were posted here were pleased to provide an aesthetic experience to their hosts. Those same Vulcans, though, preferred the simpler lines of the cases that flanked the cabinet. Those pieces were constructed much later in Vulcan's history, and the subtle abstract designs carved into their woodwork tactilely expressed an equation for deriving prime numbers. That meant they were pleasing to look at, *and* educational. A far more logical style of design.

Spock, however, found the older cabinet more interesting, not that he'd ever admitted his preference.

But this night, his interest in it was not because of its beauty. Inside, protected behind doors of rose-tinted glass made from the sands of the sil'Rahn Desert in Vulcan's southern hemisphere, there rested the embassy's collection of primitive clay figurines produced by the planet's earliest known culture. One of the figurines in the display was the original from which Spock had fabricated the forgery he had sold to Dala. Twelve others completed the collection.

From his other late-night visits to the reception hall, Spock had determined that five of the thirteen were, in fact, forgeries, replacing originals that had been stolen and sold by the real theft ring operating from the Vulcan compound—a criminal enterprise that Sarek had now admitted the staff knew about, yet would not interfere with.

Spock had deconstructed the logic of his father's position over and over, and had been able to come to one conclusion: Whoever was responsible for the thefts was known to the staff, and the staff had deliberately chosen to ignore the crime. Only two possibilities existed to justify that decision.

The first was that the person responsible was a high-ranking Vulcan official, and disclosure would disrupt that official's dealings with the United Earth government, the Federation Council, or some other equally important body.

The second was that the person responsible was a prominent member of the embassy's local staff—a human. In that case, disclosure of the crime would prompt a disruption in Vulcan-Earth relations.

With the fervor of youth, Spock viewed both ethically flawed positions as typical of so-called pragmatic adults, and an affront to all that the Vulcan culture stood for.

Some of the staff who worked in the compound had been on Earth for more than twenty years, so Spock understood how their ethical standards might have been eroded in that time. After all, in the more than twenty years his mother had spent among Vulcans, she readily described how she had changed, willingly embracing the benefits of the Vulcan way. No doubt the Vulcans posted to duty on this world had reacted in a similar though less positive fashion, and embraced the slippery ethics of the nonlogical.

Spock had done the right thing, he knew, first by noticing that figurines were being stolen and replaced, and then by reporting what he had learned to Sarek.

That his father's logic had also been made uncertain by his exposure to humans was regrettable, but not surprising. Sometimes Spock wondered how Vulcan culture could survive in the hands of the older generation, who often seemed to have lost touch with the pure message of Surak.

In any event, whatever the future might hold for his world, Spock did not consider himself obliged to follow it into ethical decline. He had tried to work within the rules, but if those in authority here refused to abide by the same conditions, then he had no logical choice but to proceed on his own to gather insurmountable evidence that he could present to authorities on Vulcan.

If that meant prominent Vulcans or human staff would be called upon to account for their transgressions, then so be it. The teachings of Surak were clear to every Vulcan who cared to study them, and Spock was Vulcan—he would permit no equivocation, human or Vulcan, to deter him. Logically, he could do no less than what he did now.

He used a small scanner he had borrowed from the scholars' library that the compound maintained for Earthmen. The palm-sized device was specially calibrated for archaeological use.

He aimed it at the figurines behind glass. Each one registered with an authentic spectrographic and isotope-dating profile.

Then he inserted a polykey into the antique cabinet's security latch—a feature not found on the cabinet as originally built, but considered necessary on a planet that still had occasional crime. No offense intended to the Vulcans' human hosts.

The key vibrated, its nano-scale filaments filling the mechanical space reserved for a standard key, then transmitted an encoded magnetic pulse that he had already decrypted from the databanks.

The cabinet doors clicked open. Without the barrier of the rose-tinted glass between him and the figurines, Spock scanned them again.

Six registered as forgeries now.

The scheme was clever, Spock admitted. Somewhere in the frame of the door there was a series of sophisticated transmitters that responded to the pulses from any type of scanner or sensor. That triggered each device to return a fabricated sensor signature for the figurine it was paired with, containing all the details necessary to confirm the figurine as an original.

Spock had deconstructed the transmitters and had built one of his own, which he had placed in the forgery he sold to Dala. The human female's sensor had been tricked by the false signal, and she had accepted it without realizing the deception, and without suspecting that she had taken into her possession an inert lump of fired clay, not much more than ten days old.

But that detail was for the next stage of his operation. For now, Spock was eager to try his newest discovery—an algorithm that would allow him to read the security log on the cabinet, and see who had last opened it.

Whoever was stealing the figurines clearly was able to manipulate the security imagers in the compound as easily as he could. He had watched the recordings after each theft, and there was never the slightest indication that anyone had entered the reception hall, opened the cabinet, and replaced a figurine.

But the security register installed in the cabinet was separate from the main network. Every time a key was inserted into the lock, the register noted the biosignature of the person holding that key.

Spock now used a small, personal bicorder to transmit his algorithm to the security device that monitored the lock.

Vulcan codings scrolled rapidly across the bicorder's screen as the register was decrypted.

With inner calm befitting a Vulcan, he waited patiently for his mathematical innovation to complete its work. In just a few seconds, he would have the name of the person responsible for the thefts, and he faced that moment properly this time, without the emotion of pride.

The screen flashed. The algorithm completed its work.

Spock read the name of the thief, numb not from self-control but from shock.

The thief was his father.

21

At 0600, slowly in the dawn, the Academy came to life.

Small groups of newly returned upperclassmen, male and female, jogged along park trails, anxious to get back into peak shape after either a short liberty or a specialty summer posting to a low-gravity environment.

Instructors poured out from the monorail station or beamed into the Erickson Hub or simply cruised through the main gates in their personal vehicles.

In just over a week, the new plebe class of almost a thousand young men and women would assemble for a two-week indoctrination session prior to the start of the first semester. A whirlwind of activity would immediately commence as the Academy's full complement of almost four thousand midshipmen—from first-year plebes in basic grays to upperclassmen in metallic shirts—dug in and applied themselves to their studies.

But that whirlwind was still in the future. For now, the leafy grounds were a peaceful contrast to the inner turmoil Elissa Corso suffered as she thought about the honor board hearing she faced in two days.

Zee Bayloff strolled beside her on the path that linked Archer Hall and what the mids called Regurgitation Row—the Academy's food distribution complex. The two dormmates were wearing their standard gray midshipman's uniforms—after breakfast, they planned to do research on propulsion faults before returning to Tucker Center and their disassembled shuttlecraft.

Elissa walked, head down, in self-absorbed silence.

"Hey, Corso," Zee said, sounding far more upbeat than anyone should without her morning coffee, "do you remember that first orientation meeting after you got your acceptance?"

Elissa didn't reply, but she remembered.

"I was in a group of about fifteen," Zee prompted, encouragingly.

Elissa brought up the memory of her first orientation meeting. "Yeah, I was the only one on Risa who got in that year. I had my meeting with a lieutenant on the *Lexington.* It was the first one he'd given."

"That had to be exciting, being on a starship."

Elissa shrugged. "Yeah, I guess it was." Back then, in the full flush of her astonishment at actually being accepted into the Academy, the unsullied promise of a Starfleet career still lay before her. She'd been only seventeen, yet the crew of the *Lexington,* at Risa for shore leave, had welcomed her as a sister-in-arms. They'd even let her stay aboard in visitor's quarters for three days. The officers had regaled her with tales of their own Academy experiences, heaping welcome advice upon her. Specialists from every department had made a pitch for their particular area of expertise, saying how much they'd enjoy having her back. Captain Korolev had even let her take the center chair on the bridge.

When she'd finally beamed back home, she could have floated on air without antigravs. To be part of Starfleet had always been her lifelong dream.

Now, she could lose it.

"Did they give you the standard lecture? You know, about what you could expect here?"

"Zee, I got three days of lectures."

"The official ones, Corso. Me, I remember this one part, where the recruiter told us that, in any other educational institute, we'd be given a standard speech on our first day. The instructor, or whoever, would tell us to look at the person on the right, then look at the person on the left, and then keep in mind that in four years, only one of those three people would be graduating."

Elissa nodded glumly."Yeah, I got that, too. It was on a recording in the ship's library."

"So you remember what the rest of it was? How for centuries, the most elite academies have been completely different from universities and colleges? That going back to the old Naval Academy at Annapolis, or the Space Force Academy at Colorado Springs, those institutions didn't exist to drive students out. That after all the time and effort they had expended to seek out and select the best of the best, they were committed to retaining each member of the first-year class."

Zee gave Elissa a friendly bunt with her hip, obviously trying to cheer her friend up any way she could. "When we looked to the left and right on our first day, remember what old Superintendent Lee said: It was each mid's duty to do all we could to make sure those same people were at our side on Commissioning Day."

Elissa's dormmate tucked her chin into her neck and intoned in a mock impersonation: " 'Not one member of Starfleet will ever be left behind, in space, or at the Academy.' " She laughed."And he was sort of right. I mean, the attrition rate here is something like fifteen percent, compared to around forty at most civilian institutes. And most of the attrition is due to accident or—"

"Honor violations," Elissa interrupted as they passed by a freeform flowerbed planted with martian zinnias that changed color according to the angle of the sunlight. She gave Zee a reluctant smile to show she appreciated her efforts.

"That speech we got, that was for any mid who gets into academic trouble. No one fails out of the Academy. I'm not worried about that."

Zee nodded vigorously. "Good, because the point I'm trying to make is that Starfleet wants to hold on to as many mids as it can. You've got the benefit of the doubt working for you, so it only makes sense that the board's going to bend over backwards to find some kind of reason to keep you here."

"Sure," Elissa said. "On probation, no liberty, loss of privileges."

"Will you stop being such a drudge? Who cares about any of that? The point is, you'll still be here and, don't forget, at graduation, if you haven't totally screwed up, those records'll be sealed."

"Thanks, Zee," Elissa said quietly. "But I'd know. And honor violations . . . that kind of record has a way of spreading outside the system."

"Good morning, ladies, you're both looking great today."

Elissa and Zee both whirled at the same time to flatten the boorish second-year mid who had suddenly run up behind them, only to realize it was Jim Kirk.

"Very smooth, sport," Zee said sarcastically.

"Jim!" Elissa looked around nervously to see if any instructors were near. "Do you know how much trouble you can get into wearing that uniform?"

Kirk threw his arms around the shoulders of both mids and kept walking. "A lot less trouble than I'm in right now."

Elissa was not through scolding him. "Where'd you get it anyway?"

"Let's just say it was hanging around. I'll get it back before it's missed."

"You're impossible."

"That's what they told Zefram Cochrane," Kirk said.

"Jim, I'm serious, you can't be here."

Kirk stopped and Elissa and Zee stopped with him.

"Elissa, *I'm* serious. I need to talk to you about the board." Before she could argue, Kirk gave Zee an apologetic smile.

"And it's probably better that you don't know about the conversation. Just in case anyone asks."

Zee shrugged, but she didn't look happy to leave Elissa with Kirk. "Thanks, I certainly wouldn't want to tell a lie. You two have fun." She looked meaningfully at Elissa. "Corso, if this starts getting too much for you, just call me and I'll do anything I can to help, okay?"

Elissa gave her a hug of thanks. "It'll be okay. Enjoy breakfast for me."

"Mmm," Zee said. "Retextured protein blobs with syrup. Who'd miss that?" She gave Kirk a look that swept him from head to toe. "You almost look good in that uniform, hotshot." She winked at Elissa. "Almost."

Then Zee turned and left, glancing back only once.

"Wild guess," Elissa said when they could talk alone, "you've got a new plan."

Kirk took her arm and propelled her along the path. "Let's keep walking, just two mids heading for the monorail station."

Elissa tensed and slowed her pace. "Why there?"

Kirk pushed her to quicken her step, kept his voice cheerful. "I had a run-in with Starfleet Security yesterday."

Elissa groaned. "Right. Sam said you didn't come home. And I got visited by some tough guy from HQ."

"White hair? Name Mallory?"

Elissa felt like melting away into nothing. Her shoulders sagged. "They know about the staff car, Jim. They know about us. It's all over, isn't it?"

Kirk's stride didn't falter. "No! In fact, it's what happened at Starfleet that made me realize there's another way to prove you're innocent."

"You mean, like the override was going to prove it?" Elissa pulled away from him. The path they were on now wound through a grove of genetically reconstructed elms.

Kirk took her arm again, insistent. "Mallory's got the override now. You can definitely tell the honor board about it. He'll have to produce it."

Elissa shook him off again and started walking away. "Don't worry. I will. I have to."

Kirk hurried after her. "I know—will you stop for a second? This is important!"

Elissa wheeled around, furious. "I know it's important! It's my life!"

"And I want to help make it right!"

"All you've done is make it worse! You don't even like Starfleet!"

"But I like you. I want to help. And I know how to do it now."

Elissa stood facing him. "Okay, then. Convince me."

Kirk took a breath, then launched into what Elissa realized was something he'd been practicing. "I didn't think of this until last night, but it suddenly came to me that security systems have two separate functions."

"Keep going."

"First, they're designed to stop people from breaking into something—a car, a safe, a databank, whatever." Kirk held up a finger to make a point. "But then, because no security system can ever be one-hundred-percent foolproof, they have a second function." Kirk looked at her expectantly, waiting for her to realize what he had realized.

"Not foolproof . . ." Elissa said, working it out. "I know—their second function is to alert someone that they've failed."

Kirk beamed. "That's it! That's how the guards came after us so quickly in the parking lot the other night. My override broke through the security lockouts on the car—"

Elissa continued, spurred on as Kirk's enthusiasm became hers and her spirits lifted. "—so the system sent out an alarm saying it had been defeated."

She stiffened as Kirk made a move as if to hug her, then didn't. Elissa bit her lip, relieved. There were other mids on the path and the Academy's fraternization rules were strictly enforced.

Kirk rushed on, not seeming even to have noticed how close they had come to breaking yet another rule. "Which raises a really interesting question about what happened in the warp lab."

Elissa caught what he meant at once. "The security lockout on the dilithium vault didn't send out an alarm."

"Exactly! And listen to this: Mallory confirmed that my override worked just like the one that was used to break into the dilithium vault—by transmitting signals to the security system. But, to stop an alarm from going out, I would've needed a *second* piece of equipment to either jam or block the signal. And that second piece of equipment—"

Elissa gasped as she understood what Kirk was about to say, and then they said it together: "—had to stay in the lab!"

Kirk pointed in the direction of the monorail station. "Let's go get it."

But Elissa wasn't yet convinced. "Hold on. What makes you think it'll still be there?"

"Because nobody's found it."

"Yeah, well, I hate to be the one to give you the bad news, but you're not the smartest person on the planet. If you figured this out, Security did, too."

Kirk grinned. "They're smart, but they don't have you for a girlfriend."

Elissa hated it when Jim turned on the charm as she was trying to be serious. "And that's important, why?"

"Simple. The first investigators checked to see whose codes had been used to open the vault—your codes. As far as they were concerned, that was the end of the investigation.

But I—your boyfriend—*know* you're innocent, so I kept digging. Which Security didn't do."

"One problem," Elissa said. "Even if you're right, and whoever did it used an override *and* some kind of jammer, why'd they leave the jammer behind? Why not take it with them?"

"They needed it to keep working so they could leave the lab."

Elissa thought it through, found one loose end. "So why didn't they go back and get it during normal hours?"

Kirk shrugged. "Maybe they did. Then again, maybe they haven't had a chance yet because of all the extra security measures that've been put in place. The point is, we won't know until we go look for ourselves."

"Even if I accept everything you're saying, what I have to do is tell my conduct adviser and then have Academy Security check the lab."

Elissa was surprised to see Kirk's boundless enthusiasm suddenly vanish as he became graver than she had ever seen him. "Elissa, I know you don't want to hear this, but Starfleet isn't the perfect organization you want it to be."

Elissa glared at him. This was the one topic of conversation the two of them had promised each other they'd never discuss. They'd had too many arguments because of it. "Don't even start," she warned him.

"I don't want to fight," Kirk said, trying to sound reassuring, "but come on, you have no motive, there's no DNA evidence putting you in the lab, and how the hell do they think you got the dilithium off campus? The fact is, you didn't do it and someone in Starfleet Security is making a *huge* mistake thinking that you did. So do you really want to risk your career by trusting someone like your adviser who's capable of that kind of mistake? That's all I'm saying. That's it."

"Mallory already told me there was no evidence that *I* personally stole the dilithium."

"But they're still making you go before the board."

"He thinks they'll settle for finding that I didn't protect my codes."

"That's great. That means they don't think you're a thief. But has anyone from Security come and told you that? Has your adviser passed on the good news, told you not to worry so much?"

Elissa shook her head.

"It's a bureaucracy, Elissa. The cogs start turning and no one cares about the little people that get ground up in them. The truth is, if you want to do something—anything—to change Starfleet's way of doing business, you're going to have to do it on your own. The system's already made up its mind about you, and that system is not about to help."

Elissa stared at him, confused. She didn't want to believe what Kirk said about Starfleet—she *couldn't* believe it. But she also couldn't argue with his analysis of what the Academy's security investigators had and hadn't done. Maybe every big organization, no matter how well-intentioned, always had a few people who didn't measure up. And maybe her conduct adviser was one of those, someone who just wasn't watching out for her best interests in the way that Starfleet, at its best, would demand.

"Elissa . . . trust me. This won't be like overriding a staff car. We're only going to look for something that someone else put there, and when we find it—*if* we find it—then we'll tell someone who can help us. Maybe that Mallory guy."

Elissa took a deep breath. "Ground rules: We don't break into anything. We don't take anything."

Kirk didn't argue. "All we need this time is information."

"And if we don't find it?"

Kirk gave her his most winning smile. "Then you can dump me, and Zee can have me."

"You're such a liar."

"That's why you love me."

"No, I love you because you're arrogant and insufferable."

"Two of my best qualities." Kirk pointed down the path. "Monorail station?"

Elissa made her decision.

22

After his morning meditation, Spock remained in his private room, continuing his study of classic Earth literature. As always, he was fascinated by the conundrum that study presented. How any culture could give rise to masterworks with the brilliance and sensitivity of J. Susann's *Valley of the Dolls* and *Once Is Not Enough,* yet, within decades of their publication, engage in a devastating global war, was an enigma whose solution still challenged finer Vulcan minds than his. Not that that stopped Spock from trying, which was why, for the third time since coming to this world, he once again began to read H. Miller's *Tropic of Cancer*, in a diligent search for answers.

In less than an hour, he had finished the novel, his usual speed reduced by the number of times he had had to backtrack and reread particularly descriptive passages, not trusting them to memory, and scarcely able to believe them.

Then, having heard Sarek exit their family's quarters to go to his office in the main embassy building, Spock put on his cloak, felt for the weight of the tracking module in its pocket, and left his room.

His father's study was, of course, unlocked. This part of the compound rarely had human visitors, so security precautions were more typically Vulcan—which is to say, there were none.

Spock stood in the hallway by the study's closed door and listened carefully. He could hear in the main room the "Flower Duet" from the Earth opera *Lakme,* the twenty-second-century recording of the Sydney Opera Company, considered definitive by Vulcans. It was one of his mother's favorites, and true to her schedule, she would now be tending the plants on the courtyard balcony. She was not due to teach at the compound school until this afternoon.

Knowing he would not be disturbed, Spock pushed the door that opened into his father's private sanctum. The room was dark, the "Flower Duet" becoming softer and more distant, all sound muffled by the thick carpets and wall hangings.

Spock moved toward his father's desk, an heirloom carved from a single block of Vulcan *wehk* wood. Its polished surfaces revealed the striations of the hundreds of vines that had grown cooperatively, then fused into one organism. The distinctive markings most resembled ripples frozen on a rich sea of mahogany and oak.

Sarek's personal computer terminal, which sat on the top of the desk, was installed in a frame made of the same wood, pleasing to the eye.

Spock sat in his father's chair and accessed the terminal—he had long ago deduced Sarek's personal codes, more as a mathematical exercise than for any other reason. Even on Vulcan, sons and fathers inevitably fell into competition.

Then he called up his father's daily schedule. Spock raised an eyebrow at its extent. It went back seventy-five Earth years, to the first entry Sarek had made when he was the equivalent of seven Earth years old. But for Spock's purposes, he only needed the details of his father's activities since being posted to Earth, so he isolated just that dataset and captured it on a red data wafer.

He switched the terminal back into standby mode, pocketed the wafer, and stood, ready to—

Amanda was standing in the doorway, wearing a gardening apron, holding soil-stained cloth gloves. She made no attempt to hide her human indignation. "What are you doing?" she demanded.

Spock had no trouble maintaining his equanimity. "I am

preparing to meet with one of my father's 'business associates.'"

"Does Sarek know?"

"I would prefer he did not."

Amanda suddenly looked to her son's wrist. "Spock, where's the tracking module?"

"I have removed it."

"They could take you back into custody!"

"Since they have not, it is obvious I was able to remove it in such a way that it did not send out an alarm."

His mother stepped into the room, her concern turning to fear. "I don't care that you know *how* to take off the module. The point is, it's against the law. You know better."

What Spock knew was that he had only a few hours to complete the task he had set for himself before his father returned and realized his terminal had been accessed. This was no time to debate his mother.

"Will you report me, Mother?"

Spock could see Amanda wring the gloves she carried. "Logically, I should. Ethically, I must."

Spock accepted her decision calmly. His plan had failed. He could not blame his mother for doing what she must. She was only human.

"But I'm your mother," Amanda sighed. "And one thing mothers have to do is to know when to let go. You keep telling your father and me you want to be treated as a Vulcan, and we do treat you that way, though you somehow don't seem to realize it. You keep telling us you want to be treated as an adult, and that's something your father and I have always worked toward, giving you more and more responsibility as you've proven to us that you can exercise it. But you're so young. You're just nineteen."

Spock wondered if he would ever understand human logic, even that of his own mother.

"You don't know how much your father and I discuss you, ask ourselves if we've done the right thing, not done enough . . . You are in our minds—*and in our hearts*—every day. Every day. And still, somehow, you don't seem to know it."

Spock had no time to waste. If Amanda was not going to report him, then he needed to go at once.

"Mother, I know you care for me. If I have not shown you proper respect for that care, then I regret it, and I will strive to do better in the future."

Amanda shook her head as if she couldn't understand him. "Spock, the embassy staff *cares* for you. Your father and I *love* you." She waved her hand before he could protest further. "Oh, I know 'love' isn't the word you'd prefer to hear said aloud, but it's true. And not even Sarek would deny it. He is so proud of you, has such hopes for you."

"I regret that I cannot reciprocate."

"How can you say that?" Amanda spoke as if he'd struck her.

Spock repeated what he had said earlier. "Mother, I have work to do. If you are not going to report me, then I must go."

"There will be consequences to what you're doing," Amanda said, now sounding more Vulcan than human. "If you choose to act on your own, you must take responsibility for your own mistakes. Neither Sarek nor I will permit less."

"I am aware of that." He fixed his dark eyes on her, the teenager's challenge to his parents. "Just as my father must take responsibility for what he has done."

He left then, before his bewildered mother could reply.

There was so much that needed to be corrected in his family and in the embassy. But at last he was free to do something about both conditions, and act not just as a privileged son, but as an adult.

He was going to change his world for the better.

Even at the age of nineteen, he knew with certainty that he was the only one who could.

The Lily Sloane Complex—the Academy's warp physics teaching lab—was, for safety reasons, located on an artificial island in San Francisco Bay that was linked to the main Academy grounds by a pair of monorail tracks with automated cars. The cars were in continuous operation, ferrying maintenance personnel, instructors, and mids back and forth to the lab.

The four-minute ride was something most passengers looked forward to because of the startling moment when each car passed through the complex's hemispherical force field that protected not the island, but San Francisco, from a potentially disastrous warp-core breach. There was always an exciting interval in which the monorail car seemed to suddenly slow, then dip into a steep dive, then right itself, as the field softened to permit the passage of the slow-moving object and the local gravitational field was distorted. No such softening would occur, though, should the Sloane Complex suddenly blow apart and the rubble spray out at supersonic velocities. In that case, all riders on the cars knew the force field would remain at full strength and, to an outside observer, appear to instantly fill with fire and black smoke.

Such a catastrophe, of course, was a worst-case scenario. The complex's containment and safety systems were maintained at the same readiness level as those on board a starship. Its static warp core—used in advanced instruction for mids and engineering specialist recruits from the Starfleet Training Center across the bay—was seldom operated at full power. Starfleet was not an organization known for taking unnecessary chances.

The complex itself was a set of twelve buildings, only three of which were generally open to mids: the main lab, called Lily One; the subsystems lecture facility, called Z. Hall; and the warp-core facility, affectionately known to the mids and instructors as Ground Zero. The other buildings ranged from monorail maintenance facilities to two power plants, and a combined operations center that oversaw communications and transporter services, and flight-traffic control for the island's small landing port.

The ops center was Jim Kirk's first target.

"Now that's more your style," Elissa said as Kirk modeled his newest "borrowed" uniform—maintenance overalls. "But most of those guys, they're in their twenties, at least."

Kirk pulled his cap visor down, spoke in a deep voice. "Sorry to disturb you, ma'am."

"You do realize this isn't a joke?" Elissa was already uncomfortable being in one of the ops center's supply rooms, sorting through the uniforms of off-duty personnel. Kirk's levity was not reassuring.

"Sure do, ma'am." Kirk spoke in the same deep voice.

"Stop that right now," Elissa warned him. "Just tell me what we do next."

A smile tugged at the corners of Kirk's mouth, but he obeyed, sensibly. "We need to get to a maintenance terminal so I can check work orders."

"What kind of work?"

"Whatever kind of work had to be done in the warp lab three weeks ago, before the theft." Kirk made a sweeping gesture in the direction of the door, indicating she should precede him. "As soon as we find those records, we find the name of the real thief."

There was a bank of maintenance terminals outside the staff cafeteria, and Elissa followed Kirk as he walked up to it as if he had worked at the Sloane Complex for years. Inwardly she cringed as he even drew attention to himself by nodding and smiling at the other maintenance workers. He had no fear.

Then he reached into a pocket of his overalls and drew out an ID card.

"Where'd you get that?" she whispered, eyes wide with disapproval.

"It was in the pocket. That's why I picked this one."

Elissa mentally castigated herself again for going along with this.

"C'mon, Elissa. It's not like it's valuable or has a security clearance or anything."

Elissa grimaced. She had no one to blame but herself. Naively, she had believed that all Jim wanted to do was to check the lab in person—and the only thing remotely wrong with that was that he would have been wearing a midshipman's uniform. There most likely was some kind of regulation prohibiting a civilian from impersonating a mid, but she was sure it had to be a much lesser offense than stealing a Starfleet car.

Now, though, Jim wasn't just dressing like an Academy maintenance worker—by using the stolen ID to access the terminal, he was *impersonating* a worker. That wasn't against regulations—that was against the law.

"Please," she urged him now, "don't do it."

But he'd already waved the card past the terminal's sensor and a welcome screen appeared. "See?" he said blithely. "I don't have to do anything else—no lies, no misrepresentation."

Elissa felt the hand of doom settle on her and her lost career. Jim was wrong. Just waving the card was misrepresentation. But as he'd instructed her, she kept her eyes fixed on the terminal as other complex workers and staff walked into and out of the cafeteria. Jim's plan called for her to be a student instructor being given an orientation tour.

A work schedule screen appeared on the terminal. Whoever Jim was impersonating wasn't due to come on shift for another three hours, so it wasn't complete.

"See," Kirk said to her. "The computer thinks I'm early so it's not even asking me to input a start code."

"That doesn't make it right," Elissa muttered through clenched teeth.

Kirk confidently entered a search command. "Starfleet punishing you for something you didn't do isn't right either. And I don't have any trouble figuring out which situation is worse."

In response to his request, the screen changed. Now it displayed a maintenance schedule for the main warp lab. Kirk immediately adjusted it to show only the past three weeks.

"Here we go," he said. "Equipment upgrades."

Elissa looked left and right, surreptitiously, to see if anyone was watching them, but no one was.

Kirk was scanning the screen, moving his finger over it quickly. "Looks like they've already replaced the stolen dilithium with a new shipment . . . There it is!"

Elissa turned her attention back to the screen. "What?"

"Read."

The paragraph Jim was pointing to was part of the warp lab's maintenance log.

Elissa dutifully read the paragraph. On July 15, the vault had been emptied of 3.2 kilograms of fully expended dilithium. On the nineteenth, the vault was degaussed and the holding frames were removed so the interior vault walls—about a cubic meter in volume—could be polished down and resealed. Five days later, new holding frames had been installed, the security system upgraded, and a new code combination set by the lab's director. Then, on the twenty-sixth, three kilograms of partially expended dilithium crystals had been delivered under guard from Spacedock to be locked in the vault for demonstration use in the coming semester.

"Okay, I read it," she hissed at Kirk. "What am I supposed to see that I don't?"

"July twenty-fourth," Kirk told her, "that's when the security system was upgraded. So any device that could circumvent the new system had to be installed either at the same time or between that date and the twenty-sixth when the new dilithium arrived. A three-day window of opportunity. Simple as that."

"Try again."

"We only have to find out who entered the lab during that three-day period. Since there were no classes being taught, and no other maintenance work scheduled, it can't be very many. And one of them will be our thief."

Elissa studied him, thinking hard. A little of Jim's explanation made sense to her, but it still didn't solve their biggest problem.

"Even if we do find a list of people who entered the lab, *then* what do we do? We're not protectors. We're not Academy Security. I'm just a mid and you're . . . . you're a . . ." Elissa couldn't think how to characterize her boyfriend.

"A genius?" Kirk said with a grin.

"A teenager, like me," Elissa said bluntly. "The two of us have no power. We can get as much information as we want. But we can't *do* anything with it."

Kirk flushed, his mood darkening in a flash. "*I'll* do something."

At once Elissa took his hand. "Jim . . . I know you want to help me. But this—" She nodded at the maintenance records on the screen. "—this is as far as we can go on our own. We need help."

She could see Kirk struggle and fail to subdue his frustration. "I would never—" He suddenly stopped, pulled his hand away from hers.

They both realized handholding had been a mistake. They both looked around the hallway.

They were alone.

"Something isn't right," Kirk said. "Let's go."

They walked as fast as they could without running down the corridor, heading toward the ops center's main doors.

The moment they turned the corner, Elissa's heart sank.

Mallory was waiting.

23

Kirk's first instinct was to run. But then his brain took over and he remembered he was on an island and the only way off, short of hijacking a flyer, was to take a monorail car deeper into the heart of enemy territory. There was nowhere he *could* run.

"Ms. Corso," Mallory said pleasantly. "James." He held up the sensor unit of a Starfleet tricorder. The second part of the device hung from a shoulder strap at Mallory's side.

"I've been following what you pulled up in the maintenance records," Mallory continued. "For what it's worth, I think you're onto something."

Kirk was incapable of giving in to Mallory, or to any authority figure. And the fact that he felt trapped only drove him to counterattack. "Then stop going after Elissa!"

"Jim, don't!" Elissa broke away from him, attempting what he couldn't—diplomacy. "Mr. Mallory, he was only trying to help me. We were just on our way to see my adviser and—"

Kirk cut her off. "No, we weren't."

Mallory looked from Elissa to Kirk. "I see. A difference of opinion."

"Yeah? A year at the Academy and she's too afraid to ask any questions, rock any boats," Kirk said hotly. "But I'm not!"

Elissa grabbed his arm to stop him, but Kirk pulled away, walked right up to Mallory. "You should know that there's nothing more important to her than a Starfleet career."

"I have no reason to doubt that. I'm familiar with her file."

"Then how can you think Elissa had *anything* to do with stolen ID codes, much less kick her out?"

"As I told Ms. Corso, the most likely outcome is that the Academy will find her negligent for not safeguarding her ID codes. Separation is unlikely."

"Can you guarantee that?" Kirk challenged Mallory.

"Jim—please don't make it worse!"

"Elissa, you can't give in to this rotten system. You're not negligent. You can't stop fighting just because you think it's the easy way out. What do you think'll happen the next time they need a scapegoat to cover up something else *they've* done wrong?"

Kirk turned to Mallory again. "Can you stop what they're doing to her?"

Mallory didn't move back, just looked curious. "Why is that so important to you?"

Kirk regarded him with scorn. "Why isn't it to *you*? Isn't Starfleet the almighty guardian of truth and justice throughout the galaxy?"

For a moment, Mallory's stern face cracked into a smile. "You haven't answered my question."

Kirk blinked, rapidly rethinking Mallory's presence here. *Is he offering* me *some kind of deal? But why?* Just as quickly, he realized it didn't matter. Just the fact that an offer might be in play implied there was something he knew that Mallory didn't, and that Mallory would trade.

He tested his supposition, named his price. "Drop the charges against Elissa."

"I don't have the authority to interfere in an independent investigation."

Kirk didn't believe him. "I think you do."

"And I don't think you know how Starfleet really operates."

"You asked what's important, I answered. Take it or leave it."

Mallory looked amused. "You think this is a negotiation?"

"I think it's a trade."

Mallory nodded, thoughtful. "All right, try this." He turned to Elissa, who had gone pale, her posture rigid as if she were willing herself not to collapse. "Ms. Corso, I can't tell the Academy to stop the proceedings against you. But I can ask them to postpone your honor board hearing on the grounds that you're helping Starfleet Security in an ongoing investigation that might be connected to the dilithium theft. I can also make it clear that Security is convinced you had nothing to do with that theft." Mallory looked back at Kirk. "Is that acceptable?"

Kirk shook his head. "A postponement doesn't do anything."

Mallory disagreed. "It lets me go forward with an investigation that can clear this young midshipman of all wrongdoing. If we find the real thief, and if we find out how that thief obtained her codes without her knowledge, then I can give that evidence to the board and *they* can stop the proceedings."

Kirk saw Elissa's tense face lighten with relief. "Jim, that's our way out of this. Starfleet Security will investigate. They've got better resources than the Academy investigators. They'll find the truth."

But Kirk wasn't ready to declare victory yet. He looked at Mallory, his gaze wary, measuring. "Give me one reason why I should trust you."

Mallory pulled out his communicator, kept it closed. "How about I remind you that you're in a restricted area of a Starfleet facility. You're wearing stolen clothes. You've illegally used a stolen ID card to access restricted Starfleet data on a Starfleet computer system. And every illegal act you've committed since arriving at Sloane is recorded on security imagers."

Mallory held up his communicator. "I just have to flip this open and make one call, and you'll be beamed up to a maximum-security holding cell on Spacedock. I doubt your trial will take more than half a day. And then, *if* the judge is in a good mood, and *if* he considers that you're a minor, you'll be lucky to only get two years of rehabilitation at the Starfleet penal colony on Mars. Terraforming. I believe the historical term is 'hard labor.' "

He paused as Elissa again tugged at Kirk, who again pulled away. The outcome of this confrontation still wasn't clear to Kirk.

"But," Mallory added, "I haven't flipped this open, and I won't for now, because you're right. The truth *is* important to me. So, to find the truth, I'm willing to give you the benefit of the doubt and consider your illegal acts as the well-intentioned mistakes of a misguided youth. Something I will only do *once*. Do you understand?"

If there was anything Kirk hated more than being forced to do something, it was admitting the enemy had outmaneuvered him. And Mallory had. "Yeah," he said.

Mallory's eyes bored into him. "I suggest you make that, 'Yes, Mr. Mallory.' "

"You . . ." Kirk was about to say something completely different, involving words he wouldn't normally think of saying in front of Elissa, but Mallory snapped open the communicator in his face.

"Sorry, didn't hear that," Mallory said evenly.

Kirk took a breath and, for Elissa's sake, forced out the hated words. He heard her gasp behind him. "Yes . . . Mr. Mallory."

Mallory put his communicator away, spoke crisply. "Ms. Corso, you have lab time booked at the Tucker Center. I suggest you use it. Your adviser will get in touch with you about the postponement of the hearing. And we will talk again."

Elissa snapped to attention, still ghostly pale. "Yes, sir, Mr. Mallory. Thank you, sir." Then she looked at Kirk, hesitating just a fraction, so much between them still unsaid.

Kirk frowned. "Just go. I'll call you."

Elissa marched off, and Kirk folded his arms and leaned against the wall. No one was going to make him stand at attention. He was a civilian. "What now?"

"Time for your half of the bargain."

Mallory wasn't wasting any of his attention on Kirk's posture or attitude, and Kirk knew why. The man had already made it clear who was in command.

"Shoot," he said.

"Where's Spock?"

"The Vulcan?"

"Your partner."

"What?"

Mallory's stern expression let Kirk know he wasn't in the mood for games. "I'm serious about sending you to rehabilitation, kid. Yesterday, Starfleet put a tracking module on each of you. Last night, they both came off at the exact same time. How stupid do you think we are?"

"You're joking, right?" Kirk laughed. "Stretch took off his module, too?"

"Stretch?"

"Spock."

"I'm losing patience here."

Kirk decided Mallory had zero sense of irony. He shrugged. "It's like this. You had the two modules talking to each other over a subspace link, so you'd know if Spock and I tried to meet. So what I did was set up a subspace echo of that signal. When I took apart my module and it stopped working, I knew you guys would pick up the echo through Spock's module."

"Why didn't your module send out an alarm when you took it apart?"

"I jammed the signal."

Mallory's surprised face was a sweet reward to Kirk. "You

had Spock's module sending out a location signal for both modules, so when Spock removed his, it registered as if both had been switched off at the same time."

Kirk bowed for the crowd. "Thank you, thank you."

Mallory reached out and forced Kirk's head back up. "I'll say this one more time—you're in real trouble, kid. So cut the smartass routine."

But challenging Kirk was like turning on a switch. He pushed Mallory's hand away. "Yeah, well, I can handle trouble."

Mallory smiled unpleasantly. "And I like a challenge." He grabbed a fistful of Kirk's overalls at the shoulder, yanked Kirk off-balance, and flipped open his communicator. "Mallory to Sloane Complex control. Two to beam to HQ holding. DGS priority alpha five one five. Acknowledge."

Kirk was left to struggle uselessly, unable to loosen the man's solid grip, furious with his helplessness. "You can't beam me anywhere! I have rights!"

"Sloane Complex control to Mallory, acknowledging your DGS priority alpha five one five. Stand by for force-field attenuation . . ."

"I said let go!" Kirk shouted. "Help! Help! I'm being kidnapped!" But the halls remained deserted.

Kirk winced in disbelief as much as in pain as Mallory shoved him against the wall.

"You're not being kidnapped, kid—you're being arrested."

"Energizing . . ."

Then Kirk felt the known world disappear as the ops center corridor, the bank of maintenance terminals, and everything around him except his captor dissolved into light.

A moment later, or perhaps days later, Kirk felt solid feet under his ground again . . . or was that solid ground under his feet?

He shook his head, disoriented. He looked around. Mallory still stood beside him, his grip still on his shoulder, but everything else was *different.*

For just a moment, he glimpsed the interior of a transporter room. Two technicians were at a console.

Kirk looked down. He was standing on a glowing disk. He looked up. Another glowing disk was above him.

Mallory gave him an unsympathetic look. "First time?"

Then one of the technicians said, "Energize," and it all happened again.

This time when solidity returned, Mallory let go and Kirk dropped to his knees and retched.

"Oh, come on. It's not that bad."

Kirk raised his head, wished he hadn't, wiped bitter liquid from his face. "You . . . *disintegrated* me. Twice."

Mallory hauled Kirk back to his feet. "Well, since I put you back together again both times, we're even."

Kirk felt dizzy, but he pretended to be even dizzier, rocking back and forth as he looked around at this new location.

He and Mallory had been transported to an open plaza outside Starfleet Headquarters. *Outside.* Kirk hid a smile. Mallory was an idiot. "I think . . . I think I'm going to pass out," Kirk said weakly. He started to wobble.

Mallory guided him to the edge of a planter. "Some people are sensitive the first few times, but disorientation should only last a few seconds."

Kirk hung his head between his knees, groaned. "Got this inner ear thing . . . gonna be sick again . . ."

Mallory sighed. "Let me get some help."

"Some water . . ." Kirk moaned.

"And some water. Just stay put."

Kirk grabbed his stomach and rolled onto his side on the

edge of the planter. "I can't move. Why won't it stop spinning?"

Mallory went up the stairs, two at a time.

Mallory's assistant was waiting for him by the main entrance. "Got your priority code." She pointed out toward the main plaza. "Is that the Kirk kid?"

Mallory looked back to see someone in a maintenance uniform racing at top speed toward a subway entrance, expertly weaving in and out between other pedestrians, fully recovered.

"That's him."

"Where's he going in such a hurry?"

"He thinks he's escaping from Starfleet."

"Ha," Sally said. "He's got a lot to learn."

Mallory looked thoughtful. "So do we—from him."

24

For Abel Griffyn, the best part of being assigned to Earth was that he did not have to fear being killed in his sleep every night—always a possibility in the camps on the frontier.

And then there were the women here. In the camps, the sexes had separate quarters. Fraternization was a reward for both sides, rarely given. But on Earth . . .

When Zee Bayloff appeared in the doorway to his office on the *Pacific Rome,* Griffyn casually reached out and crushed Dala to his chest.

"Interrupting something?" Zee asked.

Griffyn took a moment to enjoy the annoyance and jealousy in her voice.

Dala also knew how to play the scene. Slowly, she stood back from him, letting her hands trail across his chest as she smiled at their visitor, and only then appeared to remember to adjust the seal on her shimmering red skinsuit. "Zee."

"Dala." Zee moved to the side so she wouldn't block the door. "Why don't you find another playmate down on deck? Unless they're as sick of you as I am?"

Dala looked at Griffyn. "I'm not going anywhere, am I?"

Griffyn waved Dala over to the battered couch, where she curled up gracefully and blew him a kiss.

He came out from behind his desk and sat down on it. He spread his arms wide to welcome Zee, knowing how much it would bother Dala. He hadn't been able to make up his mind between the two, so he hadn't. He loved Earth.

"How's my little admiral?" he teased. "I miss your uniform."

Zee was wearing baggy green pants and a loose jacket that made her shapeless, unremarkable.

But Zee stayed by the open doorway. "Drop dead."

Griffyn laughed and let his arms drop to his sides. "You first. Dala's always telling me no one needs to see a mid hanging around my ship."

There was a soft hissing noise from the couch, and Griffyn glanced over to see Dala expertly using a cosmetics wand to touch up the iridescent red butterfly wings painted over her eyes. He smiled.

But Zee kept her eyes on Griffyn. "Kirk's got some new plan for helping Elissa."

Griffyn stopped playing. This was business. "So what is it?"

"They wouldn't tell me. But I watched them take the monorail to the Sloane Complex."

"They won't find anything. The investigators didn't."

"I don't know about that, but when Elissa came back— without Kirk—she was in a lot better mood. She said she expected the honor board to be postponed and then dropped. I think they did find something. And we both know what it was."

"Did you take the jammer out of the lab?"

"Me? I can't get in there again. You were going to arrange that."

Griffyn heaved himself off his desk and moved toward Zee. He could feel Dala's eyes follow every step.

"But you're my best insider at the Academy." For Dala's benefit, he traced Zee's cheek with a long-nailed finger. "My little admiral."

Zee slapped his hand away. "Until this thing gets wrapped up and Elissa takes the fall for the missing dilithium, I'm not doing anything to draw attention. If you have anyone else at the Academy, use them, not me."

Griffyn stepped back, hooked his hands into his gunbelt. "We have an arrangement."

"I've done *everything* you've asked. But if they catch me taking out the jammer and figure out why . . . they won't just kick me out of the Academy, they'll put me in rehab. Then I'm no good to anyone. And what's the general going to do when he finds out he's lost his best chance for getting a spy in Starfleet because *you* fouled up?"

From the couch, Dala gave a theatrical sigh. "Just kill them, Griffy."

Griffyn didn't appreciate the interruption. "Kill who?"

"All of them. Kirk. His brother. No more interference."

"They're already on the list," Griffyn said. "But first—" He ruffled Zee's hair. "—Zee's right, I need to protect the general's property here. Elissa has to be tagged for the dilithium. Officially. After that, well . . . accidents will happen."

Just as Zee knocked his hand away again, Griffyn heard the sound of multiple laser shots hum from the cargo deck and voices shout for someone to stay where he was.

Griffyn whipped over to the slanting windows, hand going to the laser pistol holstered on his belt. He froze as he saw the kids on the deck swarm a tall, dark-haired teenager in a black cloak. As the kids dragged him away from the holographic wall, the teenager's long hair flew up and—

"Dala!" Griffyn said. "Get over here!" He pointed at Zee. "You . . . stay away from the window."

Dala was beside him at once.

"Is that your Vulcan?"

"Spock," Dala exclaimed. "That little creep."

"If I find out he followed you here—"

Griffyn pounded his fist on the window and the kids on the deck looked up. "Hold 'im there! I'm coming down!"

• • •

All the machinery on the cargo deck was correctly powered off when Griffyn stormed down the metal staircase with Dala in tow.

His five guards—the general's best, aged twelve to fifteen—had their laser rifles trained on the captured Vulcan. Two of his mechanics, both sixteen and muscular, secured him with arm holds. Even one of his eight-year-olds was brandishing a flashdriver in hopes of using it as a weapon if the Vulcan teenager tried anything.

The rest of his gang of kids had formed a wall between their prey and any escape route.

Griffyn looked to the back of the cargo deck to make certain his other visitors of the day had the presence of mind to stay out of sight, then told his mechanics to let their prize go.

The instant they released their arm holds, Spock straightened, apparently unhurt and unperturbed by the sudden violence of his capture.

"He just walked through the screen and started yammering," one of Griffyn's guards reported.

"I merely asked to meet with you, Abel Griffyn," Spock corrected.

Griffyn hated Vulcans. Their lack of fear was disconcerting. He yanked Dala closer. "You mean me or your girlfriend here?"

"She is not my girlfriend," Spock said. "I did not expect her to be here. I came to speak to you."

"How'd you know where to find me?"

"You have dealings with my father."

Griffyn didn't know what Spock meant by that. "Do I?"

"His name is Sarek. He works at the Vulcan Embassy. Five times in the past sixty-eight days, my father has come here to sell you a valuable artifact which he has stolen from the collection in the—"

Griffyn suddenly realized what was going on, needed to cut this short. "I thought you were the one selling them."

The Vulcan teenager's steady gaze flickered for an instant. "I sold one to this woman," he said.

"You working for your father?"

Now Griffyn saw Spock's impassive expression change again. This time to confusion. *What kind of Vulcan is this kid?*

"At the time I sold the artifact, I did not know Sarek had sold others."

"Quite a coincidence," Griffyn said, intrigued. "Two thieves in one family. And a Vulcan one at that."

Now Spock plainly looked indignant.

"I am not a thief." But as soon as he'd said those words, he appeared to regret them.

Griffyn was amazed. He had never seen any Vulcan react this way. He tightened his grip on Dala, who glared at him and hissed, "I told you he was different."

"So, Spock, how'd you know how to find me?" Griffyn felt Dala's body become rigid beside him.

Spock hesitated, as if making certain what he said next was appropriate. His face returned to typical Vulcan blankness. "This location was encrypted in my father's computer."

"Very good."

"I do not understand why you would think it was 'good' that evidence of your illegal dealings exists in a computer in the Vulcan compound."

"Someday I'm sure you'll figure it out." Griffyn held out a hand to one of his guards holding a laser rifle, snapped his fingers. "Disruptor."

"What did you give my father in return for the stolen artifacts?"

The guard tossed Griffyn a Klingon hand weapon. It was an ugly thing, with dangerously sharp, diamond-shaped blades on the side, to be used as a slashing weapon when the power cell was exhausted.

Griffyn checked the weapon's settings. "Your father has . . .

let's call them 'needs' that Vulcans aren't supposed to have."
He showed the disruptor setting to his guard. "Is this for
heavy stun?"

"One more notch," the teenager said.

"Oh, right—I keep getting those little number things
mixed up." Griffyn nodded his thanks. "Glad I checked. I
would've set his ears on fire with that one."

"What needs?" Spock asked hesitantly.

With his free hand, Griffyn shoved Dala away from him.
She quickly moved to take cover behind the guards. "Dala
could give you all the sordid details of the recordings she
made of all the special ways she paid your father, but you
might be too young to know."

Spock regarded him in stunned silence.

"I . . . I do not believe you."

"Ask me if I care," Griffyn said. He aimed the disruptor at
Spock and fired.

Spock dropped to the stained metal decking with a clang.

Griffyn tossed the disruptor back to his teenage guard.
"Tell Kest and Strad to get out here."

The young guard ran aft, skirting around the remains of
several unidentifiable machines that had been scavenged for
parts. He returned in under a minute with two consular
agents from the Vulcan Embassy who'd concealed themselves
when Spock arrived.

Griffyn studied the two agents. He'd been dealing with
them for the year he'd been on Earth. And they behaved like
Vulcans were supposed to. They betrayed no sign of what they
thought or felt at seeing one of their own collapsed on the
deck, unconscious.

"Either of you know this guy?"

"Spock, son of Sarek," Kest said.

"He said his father works at the embassy."

"That is correct," Strad confirmed. "Sarek is the diplomatic attaché for scientific outreach and the development of un-aligned worlds."

"And he's the mark you set up."

"Correct. We knew discovery of our thefts would be inevitable. Therefore, we placed incriminating evidence in Sarek's computer so that when an investigation began, he would be suspected."

Griffyn walked over to look down at Spock. "But Sarek's kid found the evidence first."

"Apparently so."

"I told him that if he went public with what he found, I'd release some recordings that would ruin his father's reputation."

The two Vulcans stared at him blankly.

"The nature of the recordings?" Kest asked.

Griffyn pointed his thumb at Dala. "Sarek and Dala, you know."

"Know what?" Strad asked.

Sometimes Griffyn couldn't get over how dense Vulcans were. "Sex. Vulcans do have sex, don't they?"

Strad looked at Kest, who nodded. "Yes," Strad said.

Griffyn could feel his neck getting red. He spelled it out for them. "So are sex recordings enough of a threat to keep the kid quiet about coming here?"

The two agents looked at each other again as if in telepathic conversation. Kest was the first to speak. "It is unlikely Spock would believe you."

Griffyn rubbed his hands over his face. "That means I have to kill him."

"But," Kest went on, "if you could manufacture an image that appeared to be from such a recording, it could take several days for Spock to confirm it is false."

"Even then," Strad said, "the possibility that fraudulent recordings of his father could be distributed on Earth would be enough to keep him from reporting what he has found to the authorities."

Griffyn stared at the two consular agents for a moment, trying to decide if their solution came out of logic or some buried emotional need to say anything that would stop him from killing Spock. But in the end, he decided, it didn't matter.

"Five more days and we'll be finished here. If he talks after that, who cares. Can you get me some images of Sarek?"

They both answered. "Yes."

"Will you make sure the kid sees them?"

"Yes." Both again.

Griffyn gave Spock's inert form a vicious kick, and felt no response. "Then get him outta here. Take his communicator and leave him on a corner somewhere. It'll give him time to think on the long walk home."

As the two Vulcans lifted Spock to his feet, Griffyn's own communicator chirped. He checked the identifier code on its small display.

"This day just keeps getting better," he said.

Sam Kirk was calling.

25

"You're sure you want to do this?" Sam asked.

Kirk tapped his fingers on the passenger console of the rental car, and Sam knew his brother was thinking through the problem. That was another thing about him—you could actually see Jimmy stop and think things through. Most of the time, at least.

"It's not like I have a choice," Kirk finally said. "There's no way I can get anywhere near the Academy again. And I really need to get access to the maintenance computer logs at the Sloane Complex." He gave a tired smile. "If this guy you know is as good as you say he is, then, okay, I want to do this."

Sam peered through the rental car's windshield at the night rain, then checked the time. It was the 10:15 shower, scheduled to end at 10:30. The windshield's repulser field wasn't properly aligned, and a few raindrops hit the transparent aluminum, smearing the streetlights into streaks of hazy rainbow colors.

"Okay," Sam said. "But just so you know. This guy, he's not just into computers."

"I don't need to know that, Sam."

"Yeah, you do."

Kirk gave him a glance. "Is he some kind of crook?"

"He's not from Earth." Sam knew that was all he had to say by way of explanation. It was widely accepted that Earth didn't produce hard-core criminals these days. But there were a lot of other planets in this galaxy, and not all of them were as perfect as the homeworld of humanity.

"Then he's going to want something."

"He'd go for your override in a minute."

Kirk sighed. "That guy from Starfleet said they hadn't found the staff car. You didn't ditch it, did you." The last was a statement, not a question.

Sam couldn't meet his brother's eyes, looked out at the rain. "I needed the money."

"Sam, I told you I can get a full-time job in one of those shops in New Union Square."

"Not that kind of money."

Kirk put his hand on his brother's arm. "What kind of trouble are you in?"

"Old trouble, Jimmy. Nothing new. Just some old debts to pay back."

"And you're in debt to this guy . . . this criminal."

Sam nodded unhappily.

"Say I give him an override, would that cover what you owe him?"

Sam had never felt so conflicted. He'd made so many bad choices that he couldn't see a way out this time. The last decent option left to him was to keep his kid brother from following in his footsteps.

"Jimmy, you can't do that."

"Sure I can. Look, Starfleet already has my override. For sure, they'll take it apart, see how I did it, add a new layer of security to their low-level stuff, and then it'll be useless. So, if I give the specs to your friend, there's no harm done. He gets something he *thinks* is valuable, and I get to find out the name of the person who's causing all this trouble for Elissa. I don't have a problem with that."

The rain stopped. Sam checked the readout on the controls. Ten-thirty, sharp. "Okay," he said, hands tight on the controls. "Just as long as you know what you're getting into."

Kirk's forehead creased. "Is there something else I should know?"

"Naw." Sam switched the car into ground mode. "It'll just be a simple trade."

Kirk settled back in his seat, and Sam loved his brother for being the one person in the world who trusted him, and hated himself for not telling him that was exactly what he shouldn't do.

Sam drove toward the docks.

Kirk whistled in appreciation as his brother drove the car through the holographic screen and into the cargo deck of the *Pacific Rome.* "Very nice . . ."

"Try not to look around too much," Sam cautioned him. "They're a pretty jumpy lot."

Kirk saw five guards approach the car with laser rifles leveled. "Got you." Then Kirk sat forward. "Sam, they're . . . kids."

There were a few hundred colonists at the storehouse by the time fourteen-year-old Jimmy Kirk reached it. Dusk had given way to night and the unfamiliar stars of Tarsus IV shone through the cold air, forming constellations he didn't know.

"Is this where Governor Kodos is?" Jimmy shivered violently. All he had was his light jacket. Matthew and the boys with him had heavier parkas, and gloves to keep their hands from freezing as they gripped their laser rifles.

"Somewhere," Matthew said. He was looking around, past the clusters and knots of colonists: men, women, families with children. A line of sorts was forming by a refueling station. Jimmy saw floodlights there, tables set up with computer terminals. The adults who seemed to be in charge wore red bandanas, like Matthew's and the other boys'. They were scanning colonists' hands and eyes, handing out colored cards. For rationing, Jimmy thought. Though he didn't see any food.

"We need to go over there," Matthew said.

Jimmy looked where his friend pointed, toward a smaller table set up under a single floodlight by the loading dock of one of the storehouses. There were two older boys and a girl working at it. Jimmy recognized one of the boys: Griffyn. He was nineteen, so he was allowed to operate flyers and usually drove the visiting kids around on leisure days. His parents had one of the big farms in the valley. They even had horses. Jimmy had ridden one of them.

"Here he is," Matthew said as they approached the table.

Griffyn looked at Jimmy as if he were one of the horses, as if he were being inspected.

"Jimmy Kirk, right?" he asked Matthew.

"Yes, sir."

Matthew and the other boys hung their rifles on their shoulders and stood in a line like soldiers at attention.

Griffyn tapped the computer terminal on the table. "You've got a good file, Kirk. Prime qualities. It's what the gov likes to see. You're on the list."

"What does that mean?" Jimmy asked, puzzled.

"It means you're going to be okay," Matthew said quickly. "Food. Parka. Everything you need."

"That's great." Jimmy's teeth chattered as he spoke. He didn't want to appear ungrateful, but why wouldn't he be getting everything he needed? Everyone knew food was going to be tight for the next few weeks, but the fungus hadn't ruined any parkas as far as he knew.

Griffyn held out a red bandana. "Are you on board?"

Jimmy stared at him without understanding.

Griffyn scowled at him, impatient. "Matt, explain it to the kid."

"You just got to help out, okay?" Matthew dropped his voice almost to a whisper. "There's not as much food as everyone thought. The fungus got into even the processed stuff. So things are going to get tense, you know. The governor needs help to keep everyone under control."

Kirk looked around at the other kids with their rifles. "How do we do that?"

"We protect the food we do have. Do what the governor says. Round up any troublemakers. That sort of thing. Sort of like protectors."

Jimmy nodded to Matthew. That all made sense. "Okay, sure. I'm on board."

Griffyn threw the bandana at him, and Matthew caught it. "He's going to need a coat, too."

Griffyn said something to the girl, and she hopped up onto the loading dock and went into the storehouse.

Matthew helped Kirk put the bandana around his neck like the other boys. Kirk's fingers were shaking too much to tie the knot.

Kirk thanked his friend, then asked the most important question he could think of. "How about coats and stuff for the kids in my cabin?"

Matthew shook his head. "The governor checked their files. Nobody's prime. You're the only one."

"Who'll take care of them if I don't?"

"Don't worry. Someone will. Maybe us. Maybe one of the other teams. The way the governor's working it, everyone's going to be taken care of. You just have to do what you're told now." Matthew leaned closer. "And don't ask so many questions, okay? If Griffyn doesn't like you, he can take you off the list."

Just then the girl came out of the storehouse with a parka and gloves and even boots for him to put on. Almost immediately, Jimmy felt warmer. And guilty. He hoped the kids from his cabin would get theirs soon.

Then Griffyn came to him with a laser rifle. "You know how to use this?"

"Of course," Jimmy said. All the kids visiting Tarsus IV had been given lessons in essential farm skills to protect livestock from predators. Not that there was any livestock left in the colony. When the fungus had struck the animal feed stores, the ostriches and transcattle had all been slaughtered. But it was already too late.

The fungus had already entered the livestock's systems and made the meat toxic.

Griffyn shoved the rifle into his hands. "Good. Then here's your first ration." He gave Jimmy a concentrate bar, too, and laughed when Jimmy shoved nearly the entire bar into his mouth at once. "There'll be more when your team's finished their next assignment."

Jimmy chewed vigorously and swallowed hard as Matthew stood to attention like a soldier again. "What are your orders, sir?"

Griffyn grinned—he obviously liked the way Matthew behaved toward him. "Get back to the kid's cabin, take care of the others there. Should be twenty-three left."

Jimmy felt proud. His team was going to take care of the kids in his cabin. Right away.

"All of them?" Matthew asked, frowning.

Griffyn's grin vanished. "Do you have a problem with that?"

"No, sir."

Griffyn touched Matthew on his shoulder. "That's what I like to hear." He looked over at Jimmy. "Just be sure your friend here does his part. Understand?"

"Yes, sir."

Jimmy felt certain there was something else going on that Matthew and Griffyn hadn't told him about. Why would anyone think he wouldn't want to help the other kids in his cabin?

"Ready to go back?" Matthew asked.

"Yeah, but—"

All heads turned toward the main tables as a shriek interrupted Kirk's question about picking up supplies first.

A young mother with a toddler in her arms was screaming something at two teenagers in red bandanas.

The teenagers were trying to pull the child from her and she was fighting back.

Jimmy's eyes widened. Why weren't the other adults there stopping them?

Then he saw the reason.

Other teenagers in red bandanas had rifles aimed at them, preventing anyone from coming forward.

Suddenly, the young mother broke away and began running madly across the lot between the storehouses. Jimmy could see that her path would take her right past Griffyn's table.

"Take her down, Matthew."

The coolly delivered instruction didn't register for Jimmy, not even when he saw his friend toggle his rifle off safety mode, heard the power cell ramp up.

The woman was fleeing for her life, her child's legs kicking out. Soon she came close enough for Jimmy to see the tears glistening on her face. Each breath escaped her in a cloud of vapor.

All she cried out was, "No . . . no . . . no . . ."

Then a red beam of energy stitched the darkness between the muzzle of Matthew's rifle and her head.

She hit the ground with all her forward momentum, crumpling into a ball and rolling once as the child flew from her arms, wailing.

Another teenager raced up to the woman's body, fired another beam into her, then almost casually shot the toddler, too.

Jimmy was too shocked to cry out. He could barely catch his breath.

His friend, Matthew, was expressionless as he lowered his rifle. But he smiled when Griffyn tapped his shoulder with a bar of food.

"Good shot," Griffyn said. He passed out bars to the rest of Matthew's team, held out a last one for Jimmy. "Any questions?" he asked.

Jimmy was fourteen, scared to death, and surrounded by lasers.

He took the food.

He asked no questions.

26

"Come out, come out, wherever you are!"

Kirk knew that voice. He gulped down a deep breath to steady himself. "Sam, who are these people?"

But even before the doors to their rental car were jerked open, Kirk knew the speaker's identity. His throat tightened.

Sam got out of the car, silent.

The moment Kirk stepped out his side, he was shoved against the vehicle with a rifle muzzle under his chin.

"Jimmeee." The word came out in a burst of laughter, and Kirk twisted his head to see the person who could *not* be here, but was.

Three years older but easily recognizable. Matthew Caul. From Tarsus IV.

"I heard you got away, but there were so many stories going around . . . so many lies about Kodos and the teams. . . . How're you doing, pal?"

Matthew pushed aside the rifle that pinned Kirk to the car, but three other rifles still kept Kirk in their sights.

"Not going to say hello to your best friend? The guy who kept you alive on T-IV?"

Kirk fought down the desire to tell Matthew what he really felt. "You also tried to kill me."

"Only after you blew your chance. Your choice. Your fault. Wanna do something about it now?"

Kirk knew if he took a step forward, he'd be cut down. He focused on his mission. He had promised to help Elissa, and that's why he was here. So he only had one option.

"Yeah," he said with a rueful smile. "I really did blow it, didn't I?"

His former friend stared at him, awaiting more.

Kirk obliged him. "You guys were right, and I couldn't see it. I mean, there's no way the governor could've known the Vulcan ships were already on their way. Communications were down."

Matthew nodded, still judging his former friend's sincerity.

So Kirk went all the way. "With what he knew at the time, I figure Kodos did the right thing. It was a tough situation. It needed a tough solution."

Matthew chewed the inside of his cheek. "So you're okay with everything?"

Kirk forced himself to look apologetic. "Are you okay with me? I almost got you shot up by those Starfleet goons."

Matthew shot a glance at Sam. "He's your brother. You buying any of this?"

Kirk kept his face from betraying his concern. Could he count on Sam? Would his brother know enough to play along?

Sam shrugged. "He doesn't talk about Tarsus IV all that much. But when he does, yeah, he knows he screwed up. He keeps saying he wishes he'd gone off with his friends there instead of being shipped back home."

"You finally came to your senses, huh?" Matthew asked.

Kirk chose his strategy. "I've got my own thing going now," he said with mock bravado.

"Big deal. You're stealing Starfleet cars." Matthew stopped and put a hand to his ear, then turned away, as if listening to something he didn't want to share. Kirk guessed he had a privacy earpiece, like the one Mallory had worn.

Mindful of the three rifles trained on him, Kirk risked letting his gaze wander. He noted a wall of angled windows that overlooked the main cargo deck. A metal staircase led up to a door beyond them.

The lights behind the windows were out, so Kirk could only see distorted reflections of the deck in their dark surfaces. But there was someone up there watching. He knew it.

Matthew turned back to him, no longer listening to unheard voices. "I hear you need to break into a Starfleet computer system."

Kirk relaxed. Someone above Matthew had accepted his cover story. He could move to the next stage of his plan. "Sam says you have an in."

Matthew gave him a skeptical once-over. "It's going to cost."

"Sam also says you could use more Starfleet cars," Kirk offered. "I can give you the plans for my override."

"Just give us the override."

Kirk knew Mallory would be holding on to the only one he had, so he continued his bluff. "My first one had a few problems. I'll make you a new one. It'll work better."

Matthew put a hand to his earpiece again. "How long?"

"A day to get the parts, a day to build it."

Matthew listened, then nodded. "We don't have the time for that."

Kirk hadn't expected his offer to be refused, suppressed a flash of panic. "Come on, two days? Then you can lift all the Starfleet cars you want."

"There's something else you can do for us."

"Like what?"

"There's a guy at Starfleet we think you know. Eugene Mallory."

Kirk kept his face blank. "So?"

"We're interested in one of his investigations."

"Which one?"

Matthew ignored his question. "We need an inside guy we can trust."

Kirk glanced at Sam, seeking insight, but his brother looked just as confused as Kirk felt.

"If I go anywhere near Starfleet," Kirk said slowly, "they'll put me in custody."

"That's perfect," Matthew said. "We know all about Elissa and her honor board hearing. We know why you want access to the Academy's computers."

Kirk looked back at Sam in surprise. How much had he revealed? And why?

Matthew sneered at Sam. "Forget him. It's not as if we need your brother to tell us what's going on at the Academy." He studied Kirk as he made his proposition. "What we want from you are the details of the dilithium theft investigation."

That's when Kirk understood *exactly* what was going on here.

Matthew's gang had stolen the dilithium.

"If I show up on Mallory's doorstep," Kirk said, wishing he could punch Matthew's teeth down his throat, "they'll put me in detention. What could I do in there?"

"You'll still see Mallory and he'll talk to you. Then in three days you'll have your hearing, they'll probably find you guilty of something. You'll appeal, get released, and you'll come back here and tell us everything he said."

Matthew stopped again, hand to his earpiece. "In exchange, we'll arrange unlimited access to the Academy's computers for, say, an hour."

"What if they lock me up and send me to a penal colony?"

Matthew seemed amused by the possibility. "That's one way to get your brother off the hook. But that's not the way Starfleet works."

Kirk was backed into a corner. The only thing to do was to turn himself in, tell Mallory everything, and lead Starfleet back here for the dilithium. Elissa would be cleared and he'd have the satisfaction of seeing at least one of Kodos's enforcers face justice.

He nodded. "Okay. An hour will do it. Sam can drive me over to Starfleet Headquarters and I'll turn myself in right now."

"Oh, that reminds me," Matthew said casually. "I forgot to mention the details." He swung some kind of alien hand weapon up from a holster and shot Sam with an energy beam.

"Sam!" Kirk was thrown back against the car with a rifle butt rammed in his stomach.

He doubled over, dropped to his knees, gasping for air as Matthew grabbed his hair, forced his head back, stared down at him.

"Your brother's only stunned this time. But we don't want you to have any smart ideas, so we're tucking him away in a safe place . . . until you come back with what we need to know. And if you don't deliver"—Matthew held up the disruptor—"this has five settings past stun, and the top one won't even leave ashes behind. Your choice, Jimmy."

He held the weapon's emitter to Kirk's forehead.

"You going to do the right thing?"

27

Spock had finally achieved the second foundation of inner breath when he heard the holding cell's force field power down and the security bars slide open.

He opened one eye in time to see a red-shirted security guard in the doorway remove a pair of inductance cuffs from Jim Kirk.

Spock didn't even pretend to try to resume his meditative state. With Kirk about to become his cellmate again, what was the point? He doubted even a *Kolinahr* master could—

"Hey, Stretch—what's new?"

Thud. Kirk was sprawled on the fold-down bench and once again Spock was almost pitched onto the floor.

Spock sat up, feet flat on the floor, shoulders square, stared straight ahead. "I have been taken back into custody because of your manipulation of the tracking modules."

Kirk leaned forward, waved his hand in front of Spock's eyes to get his attention. "Excuse me? You're saying it's my fault?"

"I did not deactivate mine."

"Yeah, but you got out of it, right? That's what Mallory told me."

Spock ignored Kirk with practiced Vulcan indifference.

Kirk snickered. "I bet you thought those things only sent off alarms when they were broken. You didn't know just taking them off your wrist would register."

The human's smirk was insufferable. But that was precisely what Spock had assumed, incorrectly as it turned out.

He composed his riposte calmly. "If there was no way to

remove the module without forcing it apart, then for what logical reason would it have an alarm to register that it had been removed *without* being forced apart?"

"Maybe they were worried you might gnaw off your own hand, get out of it that way." Kirk shrugged. "But you can always grow a new one, right?"

It was difficult to disregard the human's deeply flawed reasoning, and ignorance, but Spock did his best. "I used a transporter."

"Ah, very nice," Kirk said, with what seemed to be real admiration. *Why?* Spock thought. The human's next words were just as puzzling.

"I just got beamed for the first time," Kirk said as he leaned nonchalantly back against the wall. "Thought I was going to heave."

Spock looked at him blankly.

"Regurgitate . . . throw up . . . vomit—"

Spock cut him off abruptly. "I am familiar with most of those terms." He was beginning to feel as if he might be sick himself.

"What do Vulcans call it?"

Spock found it hard to believe he was engaged in such dialogue. "Are you not concerned about the situation we are facing?"

"Of course I am. Why do you think I turned myself in?"

Spock raised both eyebrows, and just as quickly lowered them. For some reason, he had made the human smile.

But Kirk took his unspoken question seriously. "It was the logical thing to do—what were the odds of someone like me evading Starfleet? How'd you get here?"

Spock considered the doorway again, the bars once more in place, the force-field emitters glowing. "I was taken into custody by the protectors. While walking. They brought me here."

Kirk straightened up with apparent interest. "You were just walking. . . . Why'd you take your module off?"

Spock countered with a question of his own. It was an old tactic: childish, perhaps, but effective. "Why did you remove yours?"

"So they wouldn't know where I was."

"My reason was the same."

"Okay, but you're a Vulcan. You people don't lie, cheat, steal, break the law. Where would you be walking that you wouldn't want anyone to know about it?"

"Why did you not want Starfleet to know where you were?"

"I'm trying to do a favor for a friend, and she'd probably get into a lot of trouble if Starfleet knew I was meeting her."

"You removed the module not to help yourself, but to help your friend."

"You got it," Kirk said, flopping back against the wall. "Plus, I have to say, it was fun. Outsmarting Starfleet technology. They're a bunch of losers, and I like reminding them of that."

Spock was both fascinated and appalled. Did this young human know nothing about the history of the Starfleet? How it served the Federation's noblest goals, was a pillar of scientific advancement, interplanetary cultural understanding, and a responsible force for providing security to the Federation's borders?

"It would seem you are unaware of what is one of your species' greatest contributions to interstellar civilization," Spock said politely.

"Maybe Starfleet started out that way," Kirk replied. "But I can tell you, I've seen it up close and personal. Oh, they talk a good game, but when it comes to helping people who really need their help, they're just like everyone else—looking out for themselves, not others."

Spock was not sure, but he thought he detected the human emotion of melancholia, one his own mother sometimes exhibited, and which, in his experience, could be corrected with reason. "Your statement is not valid. In fact, you have contradicted it yourself."

"Really."

Spock felt encouraged and pressed on. "Not everyone looks out for themselves to the detriment of others. You, yourself, told me you knowingly risked punishment by removing your tracking module to help your friend."

Kirk's lack of response suggested he had no counterargument, so Spock continued with his line of reasoning.

"If you are capable of such altruism, why can you not accept that an organization of like-minded individuals can do the same?"

"Because they don't," Kirk said flatly. "Not Starfleet."

"You are mistaken."

"You can talk all you want, Stretch, but all the logical arguments in the galaxy can't beat what I've seen with my own eyes."

With that, Kirk closed his eyes.

Whatever emotions were at work in the young human now, Spock was unable to sort them out. What was obvious was that Kirk was attempting to conceal what he truly felt. *Like a Vulcan,* Spock suddenly thought, surprised. That Amanda, his mother, did so was not remarkable, because she was a student of Vulcan ways. But that other humans might do so for . . . for other, alien reasons of their own—

"Well?" Kirk asked, eyes open again. "Do you have something to say, or are you just going to keep staring at me?"

Somewhat tardily, Spock remembered his cultural briefings. Humans regarded staring as a challenge. "I apologize." He leaned back against the wall, adopting Kirk's posture to put him at ease—another lesson from his xenophobia-avoidance studies at the embassy. "But you are still mistaken about Starfleet."

"You never give up, do you?"

"Not when I am right."

A broad grin brightened Kirk's face. It was as if the sun had dispelled dark clouds. Spock felt dizzy just being near such a mercurial being.

"How 'bout that, Stretch. You're just like me."

Spock closed his eyes, horrified.

"Prisoners?" Kirk repeated. "I thought we were being held in detention as people of interest."

Commander Bearden, a bored-looking Starfleet officer in a gold command shirt, checked a screen on his padd. He and a younger officer, Lieutenant Commander Norse, a plain-looking woman also in command gold, had just entered Kirk's and Spock's holding cell. They'd introduced themselves as the legal officers assigned to be the prisoners' Starfleet-appointed advocates.

"That's how you were originally detained," Bearden confirmed, sounding as disinterested as he looked. "But when you reneged on your release agreement and removed the tracking modules, the charges went from nonjudicial offenses to court-martial."

Spock cleared his throat and spoke with utmost respect. "May I ask how it is we are to be tried at court-martial without being members of Starfleet?"

"To begin with," Lieutenant Commander Norse said, looking at each of them in turn, "by stealing the staff car from a Starfleet facility—that is, the overflow parking lot outside the Academy—you committed an act of property violation that falls under Starfleet jurisdiction. You may well have been able to challenge Starfleet's authority in that matter with a civil hearing, but then, when you signed the release forms presented when you received your tracking modules, you agreed to vacate your right to a civil hearing and submit to Starfleet's jurisdiction."

"We're minors!"

Norse, unsmiling, showed Kirk the forms on her padd. "Your father co-signed your form—" She tapped a control, and a form written in Vulcan notational script appeared, which she showed to Spock. "—and your duly appointed guardian co-signed your form."

Bearden summarized their situation. "You committed a crime against Starfleet property, you broke an agreement you made with Starfleet, and the result is that you are now subject to Starfleet rules and regulations."

"Quite logical," Spock said.

Kirk glared at him. "Are you nuts?!" He glared at the officers. "I want a real lawyer!"

Norse referred to her padd. "The next opportunity you'll have to argue civil jurisdiction will be if you're found guilty and appeal."

"If?" Kirk repeated angrily.

Spock followed up for both of them, more diplomatically. "Is there a chance we will not be found guilty of the charges against us?"

"Very unlikely," the lieutenant commander said. "Actually, there's little hope at all that you won't be found guilty of something."

"The whole system's rigged," Kirk complained. "Someone's probably already denied our appeal—before we've even made it!"

"There is another option," Norse suggested. "You *are* minors. Spock has no record of any kind, on Earth, Vulcan, or any of the worlds he's lived on. You . . . well . . . so far there's nothing in your record that goes to a pattern of intentional criminal behavior."

Spock looked at Kirk.

"Moving on," Kirk said.

"Upon review of the charges and your records," Bearden said, "we strongly suggest you plead guilty to all offenses. As minors, first-time offenders, with no indication of criminal intent underlying your actions, the Starfleet judge will give you both suspended sentences, most likely a year in which you'll have to be on your best behavior, and then, when you each turn twenty, the records will be sealed."

"Huh," Kirk said, considering. He turned to Spock. "Works for me. What about you?"

"There is only one problem with that solution," Spock said. "I did not steal the staff car."

Kirk stared at him in disgust.

Norse looked almost apologetic. "Mr. Spock, I understand your concern. I am bound to do what you direct me to do, and if it is your wish to have me defend you, I will do so to the best of my ability. But if you are then found guilty of the car theft, the judge will not contemplate suspending your sentence. You *will* serve time in a Starfleet penal colony." She paused for emphasis. "And keep in mind that even if I present a successful defense of your role in the car theft, it's unlikely any defense will work to find you not guilty of destroying the tracking module and reneging on your signed agreement with Starfleet. Even if you avoid being convicted of the car theft, the judge will still insist on your serving time for the secondary offenses."

"What did I tell you?" Kirk muttered to Spock. "Starfleet's true colors."

Bearden looked as if he were in a hurry to conclude the visit. "It's up to you now," he said crisply. "Plead guilty, and you're both on your way home tomorrow afternoon. Plead not guilty, you'll be held for trial, say another month in here, and then end up in a penal colony."

"Come on, Stretch," Kirk urged. "You know what the logical choice is."

"Yes," Spock agreed, "but in this case, the logical choice is also the wrong choice."

"Let me put it this way," Kirk said. "You really want to have me for a cellmate for a year?"

And with that, for Spock, the correct and only solution became clear.

28

"Guilty, Judge. All counts."

Starfleet Judge Mahina Otago was a small, stern woman with admiral's stripes on her dress shirt. She didn't seem surprised by the plea. "Both defendants?"

Commander Bearden nodded at Kirk and Spock. Both teenagers stood with him at their table, flanked by Lieutenant Commander Norse. A yeoman in red operated a court recorder by the judge's bench of polished golden oak. The whole courtroom was paneled in golden oak. Kirk felt he was in a museum. Starfleet was that old and out of touch.

But he tried hard not to look as uncooperative as he felt, even though the Starfleet flag behind the judge's bench was enough to knot his stomach. Instead, he ignored it long enough to say what he'd been told to say, "Yes, Judge."

Spock repeated the same words beside him. Kirk couldn't believe how calm the Vulcan seemed to be.

The judge entered some notes on her padd. "Very well." She looked up. "Anyone have anything to add before the court pronounces sentence?"

Kirk balled his hands into fists, using all the self-control he possessed not to blurt out something that would only get him into more trouble. Beside him, Spock didn't move or change expression, which only annoyed Kirk more. He glanced back into the gallery and saw his father, jaw tight, face implacable. He also glimpsed the two Vulcan consular agents he'd seen outside the Garden of Venus the night he and Spock had been taken into custody.

No one disturbed the oppressive silence in the court.

Kirk felt Bearden nudge him and he turned back to face the bench.

"Judge," the commander said, "my colleague and I wish to remind you of our clients' youth, their exemplary records, and their sincere regret for their immature prank."

The judge looked at her padd. "It says here a Starfleet vehicle is still missing. That's more than a prank."

"With respect, Judge, if you will note the custodial officers' report, my clients were charged with taking the car from Starfleet property, but not with its actual loss, which occurred after my clients had abandoned it."

"Hair-splitting, but duly noted." The judge wrote again on her padd.

Kirk felt his chest tighten as if her deliberate slowness was actually suffocating him. Yet he knew he was powerless to bring this ordeal to a faster end.

"Anyone else?" the judge asked perfunctorily. After a few moments, she continued. "This isn't the kind of case I usually see. I think one of the reasons for that is because of the high regard people have for Starfleet."

Kirk dug his fingernails into his palms. She was going to give them a lecture before she passed sentence. He wasn't sure he could last through it.

"And so I have to ask myself," the judge continued, "why it is that you two boys don't share that same regard. Why you thought that taking a *Starfleet* vehicle was a good idea. And why you thought that you could enter into a legal agreement with Starfleet, and then ignore it."

Kirk gave Bearden a quick look. Was the judge expecting him to say something? Bearden shook his head once, then nodded to get Kirk to pay respectful attention to the judge again.

"Because," the judge said, "those actions aren't youthful indiscretions. And at your ages, I'm not convinced that writing these incidents off as such will be what's best for you. If you have such disdain and indifference for authority today, who knows what you'll be capable of a few years from now?"

As the judge droned on, Kirk began to feel his anxiety diminish. He knew exactly what she was doing now. He'd had his share of lectures from self-righteous authority figures. The judge was amplifying her threats, so he and Spock would be pathetically grateful when she announced that their punishment would be less severe than it could have been. *The old hammer and feather,* Kirk thought scornfully.

"But it would be wrong of me to simply send you to a penal colony."

Kirk was impressed. This judge was *really* laying it on.

"I don't think simple punishment as such is in your best interests—or in Starfleet's. What I believe *is* in your best interests, *and* Starfleet's, is for the two of you to learn the value of respecting authority—"

Kirk adopted an expression of deep contrition, letting the judge know how seriously he took this, and how right she was. He waited, impatient, for whatever petty atonement she required of him.

"—and the value of Starfleet itself." The judge lifted her wooden gavel. "Therefore, I am willing to let you both take the first step in what I hope will be your new path toward adult responsibility, by offering you each a choice of sentence."

Kirk blinked. *Sentence?*

"James Kirk," the judge said formally, "and . . ." She appeared to check Spock's first name on the padd, thought better of trying to say it. ". . . Mr. Spock, it is the order of this court-martial that you serve a sentence of two years in service to Starfleet, either as prisoners at the Starfleet penal colony in New Zealand, or as enlisted personnel in Starfleet itself."

"What the—" Kirk couldn't complete what he was about to say because Commander Bearden clamped a hand over his mouth.

"I'll give you a day to reflect on your decisions. We'll reconvene here at eleven hundred hours tomorrow morning."

The judge lightly tapped the gavel on its stand.

"This court-martial stands adjourned."

Admiral Otago entered her office, closed the heavy wooden door behind her, and shook her head in disgust. "That was a travesty."

Her visitor didn't contradict her assessment. How could he? "I agree," Mallory said.

Otago dropped her padd on her desk, letting the sharp smack it made reflect the frustration she felt. "Then why force me to do that, Eugene? They *are* just kids. So one of them's a bit of a hellraiser. Show me any Starfleet brat who isn't. But a *Vulcan*? Found *guilty*? I'm going to be up before a review panel so fast I'll be my own warp engine."

Mallory laughed. "I'll handle the review panel."

Otago regarded him sourly. "Six admirals and you'll 'handle' them."

"I told you this was big."

"And this . . . well, let's call it what it is: an illegal manipulation of Starfleet's Uniform Code of Justice, has been signed off on by your oversight committee?"

Mallory got up from the official visitor's chair, an antique wingback Otago had had recovered in an exuberant tropical print—not the usual sedate choice for a Starfleet judge's office.

"It's not illegal, Mahina. There's nothing in the UCJ that prevents us from using deception to penetrate a criminal conspiracy."

"Except that those two civilians aren't part of the conspiracy, and they aren't even part of Starfleet. They're innocent bystanders."

"That's what makes them perfect for this."

"Perfect spies, you mean." Otago smoothed her shimmering jacket to compose herself. "Because, of course, they don't *know* they're spies, right?"

Mallory had worked with the judge long enough to understand the dilemma she faced. "I told you this morning, they're in no danger. My department would not put innocent civilians in harm's way. My oversight committee wouldn't allow it, and neither would I."

Otago sat behind her desk. She reached down and pulled off her regulation black boots, inspecting her swollen ankles with a sigh. "So how does this end?"

"It ends well."

"Details, please."

"Tomorrow morning, those two will be back in your courtroom, and they will choose to enlist in Starfleet."

"Right!" Otago exclaimed in disbelief. "No Vulcan has ever joined Starfleet as an enlisted recruit, and I guarantee you their ambassador will raise hell in the Federation Council before one of theirs is forced into a decision like that. The comm lines will already be burning up. Spock is most certainly not going to be here tomorrow morning."

"If that happens, it happens. I'm prepared to lose one."

"Which leaves you with Kirk?"

"He's already involved with what's going on. He's the one I really want."

"Yet from his record it appears this Kirk kid has such animosity toward Starfleet that if I gave him the choice, he'd rather serve ten years in an Andorian ice prison than one year in the service."

"Look into his earlier records. If anyone was born to be in Starfleet, this one was. He's just forgotten, that's all."

"How do you 'forget' something like that?"

Mallory said nothing.

Otago wasn't happy, but she understood. "The silent treatment. That means we're talking something classified."

Mallory remained mute.

Otago rolled her eyes. "Something so classified, you can't even tell me it's classified." She massaged her tired feet. "If it's that critical, how do you know they're not in danger?"

Mallory found his voice again. "We've had their biosignatures under constant satellite surveillance from the moment they were released from custody."

"That doesn't strike you as a violation of their civil rights?"

"As civilians, perhaps. But as witnesses under protective custody, completely legal."

"Did your 'witnesses' consent to be followed by an all-seeing eye in the sky?"

Mallory pointed to her padd. "It's in the case file. They and their guardians signed off on Starfleet surveillance as a condition of release."

"That was for the tracking modules."

"We, uh, we might have neglected to be that specific in the forms. They just include boilerplate descriptions of generic surveillance methods."

Otago paged through the case file on her padd, found the forms, scanned them. "You really know how to cover your backside, don't you?"

"Everything's been done by the book."

Otago tapped her padd off as if she were wielding her gavel. "Well, all I can say is good luck to you and your Machiavellian schemes. Because I don't think those two boys have read that particular book, and I guarantee you this isn't going to work out the way you planned."

Mallory held out his hand with a challenging smile. "Dinner on the shores of Lake Armstrong?"

"You know I hate the Moon." But she shook his hand, taking the bet. Then her deskscreen chimed. It was her yeoman. The legal attaché from the Vulcan Embassy was calling.

"So it begins," Otago said. "Do you take this, or do I?"

But Mallory was already on his way out the door.

29

"Do you understand what I just told you?" Commander Bearden asked.

Spock was sitting across from the legal officer in the familiar interrogation room. It was now being used as a private conference area for prisoner and advocate. "Yes, I do," Spock said.

Bearden frowned. "Then what's the problem? You can be out of here in an hour." He pushed a thin folder across the table to his client. The notational staff of the Vulcan Embassy was embossed on the cover. "Just sign."

Spock stared at the folder, didn't touch it.

"What am I missing, Mr. Spock?"

Spock thought about that. "Nothing of which I am aware, Commander."

Bearden took out a small white cloth and mopped his brow. "There are two consular agents in the reception area waiting to escort you back to your embassy, where you will transport up to the starship *T'Klass*. Three days later, you'll be home and enrolled in the Vulcan Science Academy. Starfleet's Judge Advocate General has already signed the agreement that accepts your enrollment there as meeting the terms of Judge Otago's sentence to enlist in Starfleet."

"All of this arranged in less than two hours," Spock observed.

"I gather your father's an important man in diplomatic circles."

"Indeed."

Bearden's eyes narrowed. "Mr. Spock, excuse me if this is

too personal a question, but do you and your father get along?"

Spock knew the answer, but it was not something to be discussed with anyone outside the family, let alone an alien.

He did not get along with his father, and the fault was entirely Sarek's. His refusal to explain to his own son why Vulcan artifacts were allowed to be stolen from the embassy's collection was evidence enough.

Spock knew his father was somehow connected to the thefts, just as he knew the human Abel Griffyn was lying when he implied that Sarek was seeking sexual favors as recompense. There was, however, no logical path he could find that would unite those two facts. Yet, it was obvious that Sarek, by brokering this deal with Starfleet, was only doing so to prevent his son from continuing his own investigation of the thefts.

Spock could not allow his father to control his life so blatantly.

He was nineteen now, an adult. He was fully capable of accepting responsibility for his actions. Especially, Spock thought, when his actions were logical and correct.

He'd decided to accept the judge's offer of enlisting in Starfleet. That was the best way to continue his investigation, because the Starfleet Training Center was just across the bay. Even after one week of basic training, he'd learned he'd be given weekend liberty, and for that week he'd have access to library computers during his personal time.

His mother had correctly said there would be consequences, and he welcomed them now, affirming his new maturity.

"My father and I enjoy a close relationship," Spock lied, "as fathers and sons do." He moved the embassy folder back across the table to Bearden.

"You're enlisting in Starfleet, then."

"It is the most logical decision," Spock said.

There was another truth that Spock was not sharing with the commander or anyone else: As he contemplated the prospect of living his own life without parental guidance, of never again being shuttled from one diplomatic compound to the next, under constant surveillance from his mother, his father, the embassy's staff and their agents—the small, hidden, human part of Spock found that prospect . . . thrilling.

"I know it's unfair," Lieutenant Commander Norse said to her client. "But my request for an appeal was denied until you've chosen a sentence. *Then* I can protest it."

Kirk paced the length of the interrogation room, back and forth. He was furious that he'd been trapped so easily. The consequences of his stupidity were enormous. If he didn't return to the docks with details of Mallory's dilithium-theft investigation, his brother would be killed. And without proof of the real thieves, Elissa would be drummed out of Starfleet at her honor board hearing.

"*I'll* protest it," Kirk raged. "I'm going to tell that judge—"

"Sit down!" Norse ordered. "You will not tell the judge *anything.* Do you understand, mister?"

Kirk stopped pacing but refused to sit. No one was going to tell him what to do. Never again. "What I understand is that you and the commander lied to me."

Norse was incensed. "We did not. We presented the best option available."

"And it turned out to be the wrong one, didn't it?" Kirk felt like throwing his chair at his advocate. "What a surprise—Starfleet geniuses make a mistake and I'm the one who pays for it!"

"We did not make a mistake!" Norse said. "The judge is completely out of line—the appeal *will* succeed."

Kirk finally sat down at the conference table. "How long will it take?"

"A week . . . maybe two."

"And meanwhile?"

"You'll be over at the STC. You'll live."

"Forgive me for not having much faith in your legal judgment."

The lieutenant commander was clearly nearing her limit of tolerance. "You are not making this easy."

"Me?!" Kirk said bitterly. "I'm the one who did what you said and lost two years of my life! And now . . . now you're telling me what to do again and how do I know the appeal judge won't say, Oh, the first judge went too easy—let's add another two years to the sentence?"

Norse gripped the back of her chair, and Kirk could tell *she* was close to throwing it at him now.

"There is no legal basis for extending your sentence," the officer insisted. "There is no legal basis for the sentence the judge gave you today. Do you understand what I'm telling you? The appeal will succeed because the law is on our side—your side."

"Starfleet law. I don't think so."

Norse suddenly came to some decision. She sat back down at the table, all tension gone. "Then I take it you'd like another advocate to represent you."

"Yes," Kirk said. "Like someone who knows what he's doing. A real lawyer, not someone in uniform."

"I will put in that request," Norse said evenly. "But you will still need me to be with you tomorrow when you give the judge your decision."

"I'm not going to give her one."

Norse shook her head. "You have to. You can't appeal the sentence until it's been pronounced. Give her a decision, then your new lawyer can start to work on the appeal right away."

"New Zealand."

"That's halfway around the world."

"So?"

"The Starfleet Training Center is ten minutes from here."

Kirk put his hands on the table and leaned forward. "My point exactly."

Norse made a note on her padd, then got up, padd tucked under her arm. "I hope you don't regret your decision."

The moment the door closed behind her, Kirk regretted everything.

The 511 Lounge was one of the pleasanter public areas on Spacedock, and Mallory always enjoyed an excuse to sit at one of its tables. Out the main viewports that stretched up three decks, the vast interior of the facility's main drydock could be seen. Right now, two starships were in port for replenishment—the *Exeter* and the battered science vessel *Endurance*. Several other, smaller vessels filled the lesser berths, but the center of attention, closest to the lounge windows, was the starship berthed for major upgrading—the magnificent *Enterprise*. The *Constitution*-class beauty had been in Spacedock for five months now, and her refit was almost complete.

Mallory studied her, as an artist might gaze at an old master. He could see shipwrights working on her port engineering hull, sputter-sealing plates so that it was no longer possible to tell which were originals and which were replacements for those damaged during the failed boarding attempt by Orion pirates.

Mallory guessed that one of the small, environmental-suited figures was probably Chris Pike himself. The ship's new captain had been a familiar figure on Spacedock these past five months, taking a literally hands-on approach to the refit. Rumor was that Pike had spent four days actually doing welding on the new bridge, and had even been seen with his shirt off, unloading supplies from the cargo transporters. True or not, the refit of the *Big E* was running three weeks ahead of schedule, a tribute to the expertise and enthusiasm of her crew and her captain.

"Mr. Mallory."

The crisp enunciation of his name summoned Mallory from his reverie. He stood to greet his guest. "Representative T'Rev, thank you for meeting with me, off the record, as it were."

The distinguished Vulcan gave a small nod of acknowledgment. But what he was thinking, as usual, Mallory couldn't judge.

As they took their chairs at the small table, a server arrived with a service of ginger tea. T'Rev had been on the DGS Steering Committee long enough for Mallory to know the official's preferences, if not his thought processes.

Mallory politely poured for his guest. "This extract is from the new greenhouses in Utopia Planitia. They can be opened to the martian atmosphere during summer days, now. Apparently, the taste is quite distinctive."

T'Rev savored the scent of the tea. "I have heard that. I appreciate the chance to experience it for myself."

With his token bribe offered and accepted graciously, Mallory went straight to the reason for the meeting. Vulcans weren't known for small talk. "I need a favor."

T'Rev raised no objections, merely sipped his tea and drew in a breath of air with a delicate slurp.

"The son of a member of the Vulcan Embassy staff has been charged in a petty offense against Starfleet property."

T'Rev gazed at the small pottery cup in his hands. "Spock, son of Sarek."

Mallory nodded, unsurprised that the Vulcan representative already knew what this meeting was about. His own office had been flooded with calls.

"Apparently, an agreement has been reached between your authorities and Starfleet to have Spock's sentence served on Vulcan, as a student at the Science Academy."

"If I may interrupt to bring your preamble to its logical conclusion . . . ?"

"Of course," Mallory said.

"There is no need for you to ask me to intercede, as inappropriate an action as that would be. Spock has rejected the agreement."

Mallory was honestly taken aback. "Really?" Then he remembered that that wasn't the sort of question to ask a Vulcan—why would they say anything that wasn't accurate? "I mean, I find that an unusual decision. For a Vulcan."

"Spock is an unusual young man."

Mallory contemplated the delicacy of T'Rev's statement. "May I ask in what way?"

T'Rev put down his tea cup, positioning it just so in relation to the serving pot, the serving dish of honey, the spoon, and the crisply folded linen napkin. "He has a unique family background which I am not at liberty to discuss."

"Ah," Mallory said. He had a good idea what "unique" might mean in this circumstance. Somewhere in Spock's family background, alien DNA had joined his bloodline. Having seen the young man up close, he'd have to guess the alien ancestor, in Spock's case, was a human.

As a rule, Mallory knew, alien hybridization was a difficult undertaking. However, to the ongoing bafflement of researchers, most humanoid species in the quadrant shared intriguing genetic similarities. And there was much ongoing debate about the implications of those similarities. One school argued that there was some thus-far undiscovered principle of nature that meant that independently arisen carbon-based life-forms could evolve only along certain specific paths. A more radical outlook maintained that the humanoid species in this region of space shared an ancient and mysterious ancestor. Nothing had as yet been determined.

But, whatever the reason, human-Vulcan hybridization was not impossible. Yet given the historic Vulcan sensitivity to human emotions, Mallory appreciated why a Vulcan family would not be eager to share the news of a human ancestor.

"I understand," Mallory said, letting T'Rev know he would not pry.

"Of course," the Vulcan said, "Spock's unique background in no way impairs his judgment."

Mallory suppressed a smile. To a Vulcan, that comment was no doubt a necessary clarification. To a human, though, it could be seen as an insult.

"In fact," T'Rev continued, "the reason the agreement between the authorities and Starfleet was so quickly arranged is because the Science Academy had been expecting to receive Spock as a student."

"He was already accepted there?"

"Not formally," T'Rev explained. "However, Spock is well known to the governors. Even at his young age, he has authored several significant scientific papers in a variety of subjects, from archaeology to Klingon literature."

"Eclectic interests," Mallory said amiably.

T'Rev nodded gravely. "Which is why Spock's father arranged Spock's acceptance at the Science Academy, to help channel his son's as yet unfocused intellect into a single field. Astrophysics. The science specialty of his father and his grandfather."

"A family tradition."

"An Earth term, but in this instance correct."

Mallory realized he now knew why Spock had rejected the sentence arrangement. However many generations removed, there was a human side to him, and it was rebelling against authority. It was clearly time to move off this particular topic.

"Would you happen to know which of the judge's two options Sarek's son will choose at his sentencing?"

"I regret that Spock is not acting in a logical fashion, and so I find myself unable to predict his decision."

"I understand," Mallory agreed, knowing full well there was only one decision that would be suitably rebellious.

A Vulcan enlisting in Starfleet, he thought. What an opportunity.

"And now," T'Rev said, "may I request of you some information that could also be considered off the record?"

Mallory liked nothing better than to have a member of his oversight committee owe him a favor. "Of course."

"It also concerns Spock."

Mallory waited, intrigued.

"Sarek reports that his son has deduced that a theft ring is in operation at the embassy."

For a moment, Mallory was unsure how to respond. "I've met with Spock. He said nothing about it."

"It is likely he considers it a Vulcan matter."

"That would make sense."

"Thank you," T'Rev said politely. "Would Spock's arrest on what are obviously false charges be connected to that operation?"

Mallory waved away the server who approached the table to refill their tea. "We were originally interested in someone else. A human teenager we arrested with Spock. The technique he used to steal the staff car was identical to the one used to steal dilithium from the Academy."

T'Rev gave Mallory a searching look, as if trying to decide if he were telling the whole truth. "According to the latest briefing I have read, Starfleet believes the dilithium was stolen by the same criminal organization to whom our agents are selling the stolen artifacts."

Mallory nodded. "Because of your embassy's ongoing assistance, we're close to identifying all members of the group. We even know where they're based. But we still don't know for whom they're working or why they're stealing the strange assortment of items they've been stealing. What *is* clear is that they have a source of information inside Starfleet. Right now, we don't know who or what that source is."

"Is there a possibility that this other teenager is connected to the criminal organization?"

"Definitely," Mallory said. "But not by way of criminal activity."

"How else could he be involved?"

"I think it's through a midshipman, Elissa Corso—the other teenager's girlfriend. She's the one all the evidence points to in the dilithium theft. I think what happened is that she was set up by the real thieves. What they didn't count on is that her boyfriend—his name's James Kirk—took it upon himself to prove her innocence. Somehow, he figured out how the dilithium was stolen, built a clever little device to demonstrate the technique, and then . . . things just got out of hand."

"In the final analysis, then, neither Spock nor this James Kirk deserved to be arrested."

Mallory smiled. "Spock? No. Kirk? He needs a good slap on the wrist. But he's no criminal. Just confused. Just as Spock seems to be."

T'Rev took in a sharp breath as if he'd been insulted.

"No disrespect, Representative. But perhaps the teenagers of our two species aren't all that different when it comes to navigating the shores of adult responsibility."

"Perhaps," T'Rev said, letting Mallory know this wasn't a topic to be explored. "May I ask, then, why the two teenagers have been subjected to this treatment, when it is clear they do not deserve it?"

"In confidence," Mallory replied, letting T'Rev know this

also was not a topic to be explored, "observation from a distance isn't enough. We need a way into that organization—one that can't be traced back to Starfleet."

T'Rev understood. "Because any Starfleet operation could be exposed by the organization's unknown source."

Mallory nodded.

"One last request." T'Rev proceeded without waiting for Mallory to grant permission. "Leave Spock out of this."

"That I can't do."

T'Rev did not accept defeat easily. "That is illogical. You recruited him for the operation, you can exclude him."

"Truth is," Mallory said, "Spock recruited himself. If he had chosen to return to Vulcan, I wouldn't have tried to stop him. But he's elected to stay, and so, when it comes to his dealings with the criminals, Starfleet can't be seen to be involved with him."

"Mr. Mallory, if young Spock comes to harm because of this operation, the relations between your world and mine could be severely harmed."

Mallory took the warning seriously. "I trust in your logic too much to think you would allow that to happen. You and I both know the threat the Federation is facing on the frontier. A threat that Vulcan analysts cannot predict. A threat that we cannot combat without committing atrocities. This is not a time for dissension in our ranks. If there is the slightest chance there's a connection between these criminals we're chasing on Earth and the warlord who's attacking our colonies, then finding out who he is and what he wants is more important than interrupting the social life of two teenagers for a few weeks."

T'Rev gave Mallory a withering look. "Spock is Vulcan. He does not have a 'social life' to interrupt."

"That's probably why he chose to stay on Earth."

T'Rev rose to his feet. The meeting was over. "Thank you for the tea, Mr. Mallory."

Mallory stood as well. "Thank you for your time," he said formally.

As the Vulcan walked away with regal bearing, Mallory sat down again and stared out at the *Enterprise*. In the days when he'd served on the *Constitution*, the first of this great ship's class, life had seemed simpler. He'd never had to choose the lesser of two evils.

Now he did. And he wondered what kind of a man—or a monster—that made him.

30

"I met your father out front."

Kirk turned his back on Elissa and the force field that confined him to the small, one-person holding cell. He'd been separated from Spock as soon as they were led from the courtroom. He half suspected the Vulcan had cut some kind of deal, leaving him the only one to get punished. And for what? *Nothing.*

"He wants to see you, Jim."

"Well, I don't want to see him, okay?"

"They've canceled my honor board hearing."

Kirk turned around to face her. "You said they postponed it."

Elissa's smile was brilliant. "They did, but my adviser just called me. He said someone from Starfleet Security showed up, presented the results of their own investigation, and the Academy dropped the charges against me.

"Jim, they're not even coming after me for not protecting my codes."

"That's great."

"You could sound happier."

"C'mon, Elissa . . . The only reason I built the override and used it on the staff car was to prove you were innocent." Kirk shook his head in frustration at how everything had gone wrong for him. "And then Starfleet Security waltzes in and makes it all go away *today*, instead of a week ago!" He slammed his hand against the wall beside the cell door.

Elissa had the decency to look sorry. "I guess . . . I guess we both should've had more faith in the system."

Kirk didn't trust himself to say anything in response to that garbage. "At least . . . it's over. I'm happy for you."

Elissa went to reach for Kirk, remembered the force field. "Me, too, because Starfleet Training Center's a lot closer than Sam's place. We can take the monorail to visit each other . . . What?"

Kirk just looked at her, and that told Elissa all she needed to know.

"New Zealand?" Elissa's eyes flashed.

"I know exactly what I'm doing."

"So do I. You're running away again."

"What 'again'?"

"What about your father's farm? You ran away from that, and him. And now you're running away from me."

"I'm not," Kirk protested.

"Then why New Zealand?"

"It's the right decision for me." Kirk couldn't tell Elissa it was the only way out of his impossible situation. That it was the only way he could save his brother. Matthew had said it himself: If Kirk was locked up and sent to a penal colony, Sam would be off the hook.

"But not for me . . . us . . ." Elissa's eyes were bright with unshed tears. "I thought . . . I thought this was actually going to work out for us, you know? You'd do great at STC. You could be an engineer . . . a pilot . . . anything you wanted to be."

"Not in Starfleet."

"Why not? Your life's a mess! And here you are throwing away another chance to fix it!" Elissa moved as close as she could to the security bars. "Don't you get it? That's why you're always so eager to help me, and Sam, and stray dogs, and any stranger that walks by. So you don't have to help yourself."

Kirk reacted swiftly, overcome by frustration, by what he couldn't tell her. "If my life's a mess it's because I tried to help you!"

"Jim, your life's a mess because you're not in school. You're doing odd jobs in the back of technology stores. You're living on your brother's old couch. No wonder your father's worried about you. So am I. And you're not letting any of *us* help *you*."

Kirk could see it in her eyes. Elissa was working herself up to leave. Not just this detention facility in the lower levels of Starfleet Headquarters—she was getting ready to leave him.

"You know what's really sad?" Elissa said. "You say you hate Starfleet, but that's always going to be a part of me, and you knew that when you met me. The real story is you won't admit how much you want what I have. It's like I was your surrogate Starfleet."

Kirk knew there was nothing he could do now but end this conversation, and this was the perfect opening. " 'Was'? You're telling me we're over?"

"You're the one going away for two years. You told me." Then she was gone, without a single look back.

Kirk stood at the sealed door, thrumming with unrelieved frustration, until the one mindless thing he could do occurred to him. He punched his fist into the force field. Savagely.

A minute later when he came back to consciousness, lying flat on the floor, he had a different kind of pain to deal with.

"You hear what I'm saying, Georgie?"

Sam flinched as he saw spittle fly from Griffyn's mouth. He'd thought last night had been the worst experience of his life, but he was wrong. What was happening now was much worse.

Last night he'd been forced at disruptor point into a storage locker on the lowest deck of the *Pacific Rome*. The cold of San Francisco Bay had seeped through the hull, and he'd felt as if he was going to freeze to death. There was no light, no food or water, and nothing but hard deck plating to sit on. But it was too cold to sit for long, and he had had no choice but to walk back and forth all night, three steps in each direction, trying to stay warm.

Now he was in Griffyn's office, his hands bound behind his back by power cable. Beside him were his guards—two Vulcans! Sam had no idea where they'd come from or why they were working with Griffyn. Dala was also in the small, cramped room. Her blood-red skinsuit was the same vivid color as her glistening, tied-back hair. And instead of a new genus of butterfly painted across her eyes, this time she'd colored her entire face Andorian blue. Somewhere behind him were Matthew and two other kids Sam didn't know by name. The kids held lasers aimed at him.

Griffyn stalked back and forth before them all, in a rage. Sam knew he was only moments away from being shot. But terrified as he was, he was also freezing, exhausted, and he knew he couldn't think straight. He began to moan in fear.

"Less than a day after your brother goes crawling back to Starfleet, his girlfriend's cleared! No questions. No more investigation. You tell me why and you tell me now!" Griffyn slapped Sam's face.

The blow shocked Sam into a semblance of coherence. "Griff, please . . . I told you. Jimmy would never give you up. He never would."

Griffyn stared into Sam's eyes like a jungle cat. "Face it, dead man—your brother had a choice to make: you or his girlfriend. Guess who he chose."

Sam trembled. "Jimmy wouldn't do anything to hurt me. He wouldn't. I swear."

"Then give me one reason why they'd clear Elissa Corso."

Sam gathered all his remaining strength. "Because . . . because she didn't do anything. Starfleet can figure that stuff out."

Griffyn grabbed Sam by the throat with one huge hand. "I

planted too much evidence against her for Starfleet to clear her just like *that*."

Sam began to gag, his vision blurred.

Griffyn released him abruptly, and the Vulcan guards caught him, one to each side, kept him on his feet.

"I'll give you a reason, Georgie," Griffyn growled. He strode over to the kids with lasers, stood between them. "Someone sold me out. And if it wasn't little Jimmy . . . then it was someone else who's standing here. *Right here!* A traitor with the guts to look me in the eyes and say he didn't do it." Griffyn suddenly pointed at Dala. "Or *she* didn't do it."

Dala laughed dismissively. "Like I'm going to turn in the only guy who can get me off the dullest planet in the galaxy."

Griffyn mimicked her laugh. "Oh right, you only care about yourself." He held out his hand to Matthew. "Disruptor," he said.

Sam felt his legs begin to shake, his knees lose their strength. The only reason he was still standing was because the Vulcans were bracing him.

Matthew slapped the Klingon weapon into Griffyn's hand. He set the dial without looking.

"Now, Georgie, here, he cares about all sorts of things. Like his brother. Like doing the 'right' thing. As if he could . . ." Griffyn raised the disruptor. "I can't have traitors in my organization." He motioned with the weapon, back and forth. "You two, let him go."

Sam closed his eyes, all hope gone.

But the Vulcans kept their grip on him.

"I believe this one could still be a valuable source of information," one said.

"Yeah? Well, that's why I'm the boss and you two are lackeys. Let him go so the chain reaction from this thing doesn't spread."

The Vulcans stepped back and Sam fell to the floor on his knees, waiting.

"Look up, Georgie," Griffyn said. "You don't want to miss this."

He fired.

The Vulcan on Sam's left blazed with incandescence, and as his form began to fall, he simply faded from existence. A moment later, the second Vulcan disrupted into nothingness.

Dala waved her hand in front of her nose, making a face at the acrid smell of electricity and burned flesh. "Griffy, you really think those guys had the *butlh* to sell you out?"

Griffyn rubbed the side of his face with the disruptor muzzle. "Who knows? I'm almost done here and it never hurts to tie up loose ends."

Griffyn bent down to Sam. "Does it, Georgie?"

Sam nodded, still in shock.

Griffyn casually gestured with the weapon as he continued. "Because I still need to talk to your little brother. Find out what Mallory said to him about Elissa. And I'm not going to be able to do that if he gets shipped off to New Zealand, am I?"

Sam found his voice. "But Matthew said you'd let me go if Jimmy got sent away."

Griffyn jammed the disruptor against Sam's cheek. "Matthew works for me and so do you, Georgie. Understood?"

Sam nodded, breathing again only when the disruptor moved away from him.

"So go talk some sense into Jimmy. He's going to take the Starfleet option, so he can stay in town and I can talk with him."

"Okay, Griff. I'll do that." Sam hated the way his voice quavered, but he couldn't steady it.

"I know you will." Griffyn nodded back at the kids with rifles. "Because you're not your brother and there's no place you can hide from me or them. And if you don't do what I want, I'm not going to disintegrate you. I'm going to burn you. Slowly. That's a promise."

Griffyn stood up, snapped his fingers at the kids with rifles. "Get him out of here."

Sam forced himself to his feet, allowed the two kids to untie his hands, escort him out of the office. Gradually, his breath came back to him, then his strength. He knew he was going to need both if he and Jimmy were to get away.

He wasn't stupid enough to lead his brother back here.

He and Jimmy were loose ends. And before Griffyn left Earth, he'd kill them both.

31

"Morning, Stretch."

Spock had anticipated Kirk's arrival in the joint holding cell, and so had decided not to meditate. With Kirk around, there seemed little point.

"Good morning," Spock said as the guards who had escorted Kirk to the cell resealed the door with force field and bars.

Kirk tugged on the shoulder of his bright orange jumpsuit with the word prisoner printed across the front, up the arms and legs, and across the back. "Snappy uniforms, huh?"

"A sensible precaution for most prisoners." Spock wore the same type of clothing. Of his personal belongings, he'd been allowed to keep only his IDIC medallion, which he wore beneath the jumpsuit. He was gratified, but surprised that the guards had not bothered to scan it, so its secret was undetected.

Kirk sat down on the bench beside Spock. "Y'know, I didn't expect to see you here today."

"Indeed."

"I figured they would've packed you up back to Vulcan by now."

Spock was impressed that Kirk had that much insight into interplanetary politics. "The opportunity was offered," Spock said.

"Why didn't you take it?"

Spock declined to get into family business with this troublesome human. "All things considered, I concluded remaining on Earth is a better choice for me at this time."

Kirk leaned forward, resting his arms on his legs. "Let me guess, you're signing up for the STC."

"Correct."

Kirk laughed. "Sucker."

Spock wondered what a confection had to do with anything they'd been discussing, but had learned his lesson—asking this human to explain himself generally resulted in further confusion. Thus, he used his standard reply: "Indeed."

For some reason, that prompted further laughter from Kirk. It ended when a red-shirted guard appeared at the doorway.

"Kirk—visitor."

Spock was fascinated to see how quickly Kirk went from expressing humor to concern.

"Tell my father I'll see him in the courtroom."

Spock was puzzled by the negativity he detected in the young human's manner. He'd supposed Kirk's relationship with his father would be more positive—not like his relationship with Sarek. Then again, having witnessed the speed of the human teenager's changing emotions, perhaps the nature of their child-parent relationship also changed throughout the day.

Spock did recall hearing that humans were prone to that—his own mother, of course, being a welcome exception to the general pattern.

"It's not your father," the guard said with disinterest. He gestured to the side, and a human Spock had never seen stepped nervously into view.

Again Kirk underwent a change in his emotional state. He jumped to his feet with joy, crying, "Sam!"

Spock marveled that such beings had ever achieved a technological civilization.

Kirk stood as close to the force field as he could, making sure he blocked Sam's line of sight to Spock, and spoke in a barely audible whisper.

"Keep your voice down—you wouldn't believe how good this guy's hearing is."

Sam didn't look as if he cared. "Nice to see you, too."

Kirk knew time was limited. He and Spock were due in court in the next ten minutes. "Yeah, yeah, I know. How'd you get away?" Then, just before Sam began to answer, Kirk held a finger to his lips, mouthed, "No names!"

Sam seemed distracted or nervous or tired, Kirk couldn't be certain which.

"Okay," Sam said, "the *guy* let me go."

Kirk guessed the "guy" in question was either Matthew or whoever Matthew had been listening to on his privacy earpiece. "Did the guy say why?"

From the way Sam nodded, Kirk knew—his brother was nervous.

"You can tell me," Kirk prompted.

"I'm supposed to convince you to stay in San Francisco."

"You mean, enlist."

Sam's face tightened. "I know what that means to you, but . . ."

Kirk hated the force field. He needed to touch his brother, to tell him it was going to be okay—that he would make everything okay for him, that he always would.

"Talk to me, Sam. Why does he need me here? He's got to know they dropped the case against Elissa. There's nothing more I can tell him."

"Uh, the guy told me he still needed to know what Mallory said to you. About *why* the case was dropped."

"But I haven't seen Mallory since I got back here." Kirk tugged at his prisoner jumpsuit to illustrate his next point. "This didn't exactly go as you-know-who planned."

"I don't think it matters, Jimmy. The . . . the guy . . . says he's almost finished here, and Dala—" Sam caught himself.

"—his girlfriend said something about going away, so . . . so I think he's getting ready to leave—you know, like Earth."

Kirk wasn't getting it.

"He wants to tie up loose ends." Sam said in such a low voice Kirk had to strain to hear what he was saying over the hum of the force-field emitters. "That's you and me, Jimmy. He's going to kill us both."

Kirk blinked. Having seen Matthew in action on Tarsus IV, he knew that was possible, but—

"Sam, listen . . . if he's going off-planet, then he doesn't have to do anything to us. If he's a thief, no one'll bother going after him. But if he's a murderer . . . they'll track one of those anywhere. This guy's too smart to risk drawing that much heat."

Now Sam's voice was so soft, Kirk had to read his lips. "He's already killed some people." He looked both ways along the corridor outside the hull, then mouthed the words, "Two *Vulcans*."

That made absolutely no sense to Kirk. He mouthed back, "What were Vulcans doing there?"

Sam gestured palms up, indicating he didn't know. "I saw him do it."

Kirk thought a minute, then he had it. "He faked it. He was just trying to shake you up."

Sam shook his head. "They *disintegrated*, Jimmy. He used that alien gun—you know the one."

That stopped Kirk. It was time to accept that events had moved far beyond anything he could handle on his own. "We gotta tell someone, Sam."

Sam's reaction was instant panic. "No! We can't! We've got to run! Go into hiding!"

"Shhhh!" Kirk hissed.

Sam dropped his voice to a desperate whisper. "I mean it, if we go to him, he's going to kill us. And he'll kill me if you go to New Zealand. But if you stay here, we can run away together. You know how to do that, Jimmy. I don't!"

"Get real, Sam," Kirk said quietly. "If I run off with you, Ma—the *guy*—is the least of our worries. Starfleet will come after me. That's who we have to tell! Wait till they hear the guy killed—" He mouthed the word *Vulcans!*

Sam clasped his hands together, pleading. "Please, please listen to me. Enlist. Stay close. Then all we have to do is stay hidden long enough for the guy to leave. Then . . . then you can tell Starfleet anything you want. Just let him leave and we'll be safe and Starfleet can go find him! You said that yourself!"

Kirk hated it when someone—even Sam—used his own reasoning against him.

But it was too late to say more. The guards were coming down the hallway with Commander Bearden and Lieutenant Commander Norse.

"Please," Sam said one last time, and then he was gone.

As soon as the door deactivated and opened once again, Spock stepped up beside Kirk and looked at him with dead-calm intensity.

It was as if the Vulcan had heard every word.

No one in the world outside the holding cell seemed too interested in the fate of two teenagers in trouble. That was the first thing Kirk thought as he was led through the side door and into the antique courtroom.

In the gallery, Kirk saw his father, regarding him today with sorrow instead of anger. Beside his father: Sam, his face drawn with worry. On another gallery bench, Kirk saw a single Vulcan, tall, distinguished, in a simple civilian suit.

"Is that your father?" Kirk asked Spock as the two of them sat down at the defendant's table.

"No. He is Representative T'Rev, of the Federation Council."

"Is he here to talk some sense into you?"

"I do not know. I have never met him."

Kirk scanned the other faces in the gallery. There weren't many, and all belonged to humans, some of whom were in uniforms. He noted two civilians, but didn't recognize them, so he decided they were here for some other case.

As he wondered why neither of Spock's parents had bothered to show up, Kirk realized the two Vulcan agents from the Garden of Venus weren't present, either. But they had been present for the sentencing hearing.

Two Vulcans, he thought. He leaned close to Spock, shoulder to shoulder, felt Spock ease away. "What happened to the two agents from your embassy? The guys who were here yesterday?"

Spock turned to Kirk with laser-focused eyes.

That was when Kirk knew. "You heard what my brother and I talked about."

Spock didn't give Kirk the satisfaction of an emotional response. All he said was, "Every word."

Kirk grimaced. There was no way this Vulcan was going to keep anything secret. "We need to talk."

"Agreed."

Then the door by the judge's bench opened and the yeoman in red stepped out to announce, "All rise."

Kirk, Spock, their legal officers, and the observers in the gallery stood as Judge Mahina Otago entered and took her place behind the bench. She spent a few moments making sure her padd was turned on, checked a set of documents with the yeoman, then tapped her gavel lightly.

"Good morning, everyone. This court-martial is in session. Are we ready to proceed?"

Bearden replied that he, his colleague, and the prisoners were ready.

"Very good, Commander. Mr. Spock . . . have you had time to reflect on the options I presented to you yesterday?"

"I have, Judge."

"What's your choice?"

"I choose to enlist in Starfleet."

"So ordered." The judge tapped her gavel. "Anticipating your decision, I have spoken to the commandant of the STC, and he has agreed to assign you to a new squad of recruits who will begin indoctrination and basic training tomorrow. May I add that if you fail to live up to the duties and effort expected of you as an enlisted recruit, you will not be separated from the service, you will be sent immediately to New Zealand. Is that understood?"

"Yes, Judge."

The judge looked relieved. "May I also say that I believe you have made a wise decision, and that, *if* you behave yourself, Starfleet is fortunate to have you."

"Indeed," Spock said.

Kirk suppressed a snort of disgust. As far as he could tell, anytime Spock didn't know what to say, he said, "Indeed."

"And now, Mr. Kirk," the judge said. "I understand you have an affinity for the South Pacific, and heavy construction."

Kirk looked straight ahead, no longer even trying to work out how he had reached this awful moment, this relinquishing of control.

"Judge," he said, forcing each word from his mouth, "I choose . . . to enlist in Starfleet."

Kirk caught the judge's flash of surprise. From the corner of his eye he could see his three tablemates staring at him.

"You've had an epiphany, have you?"

Kirk didn't dare say what he wanted to say, lifted a trick from Spock. "Indeed."

The judge hesitated for only a moment. "So ordered." She

tapped her gavel. "Same warning goes for you. You won't be given demerits or second warnings—you slip up even once, you're off to New Zealand, too."

Then the judge recorded something on her padd and addressed Kirk's legal officer. "Commander Bearden, I presume you and your colleague would like to appeal these sentences now."

Bearden pulled a file from a folder on the table. "Yes, Judge. We've prepared—"

"I'll save us all some time." Otago tapped her gavel again. "Appeals denied."

"Judge!" Norse protested. "You can't rule until we've made our presentation!"

"I can do whatever I damn well please, Ms. Norse. But look on the bright side—without wasting any of your time or this court's time, your appeals are now automatically bumped up to the review panel. Congratulations—you'll get to argue your case before six admirals, and not just one." The judge held her gavel over its stand. "Anything else?"

No one spoke.

"Very good." She tapped her gavel. "We're done here. Next case, Yeoman."

As everyone stood up from the table, the judge smiled at Kirk and Spock. "And Mr. Kirk, Mr. Spock—may I be the first to say welcome to Starfleet."

"Thank you, Judge," Spock said.

Kirk didn't respond. He had just surrendered his life and his freedom to the enemy.

And he didn't know why he wasn't as upset as he should be.

32

Mallory paused before the beat-up metal door. He could see four layers of different colored paint among the assorted dings and scratches. The security scanner above the frame was cracked and plainly not working. And the hallway with its sprayed-on carpet pattern didn't look convincing even in the dim lighting from the flickering overhead panels. Plus, since entering the building on the street level five stories down, everything reeked of stale vegetable steaks.

He could barely believe he was still on Earth. Almost two centuries since first contact with the Vulcans and the planet's emergence from the long shadows of war and poverty, and there was still reconstruction to be done in what were euphemistically called the "historic neighborhoods" of major cities.

He knocked.

A few moments later, he heard a deep voice call out, "Who is it?"

"Master Chief Joseph Kirk," Mallory shouted back, "I'm Eugene Mallory, Starfleet Command."

Mallory heard the buzz of the security lock switching off, then the door opened a few centimeters, enough for him to see the powerfully built man on the other side, in neat civilian clothes but still with his regulation haircut and service sideburns shaved to a point.

"ID," Joe said brusquely.

Mallory held up his case, activating it so his ID emerged. Then he waited because, unlike 99 percent of the people who ever saw that ID, Joe Kirk was actually examining it, and knew what to look for.

"Department of General Services?" he said. "Never heard of it."

"We're small," Mallory conceded. "Special projects, mostly."

Joe took a closer look at Mallory. " 'Special projects' could cover a lot of ground."

"Today, it covers your son, James. May I come in?"

Joe stepped back from the door and opened it.

Mallory was surprised when he crossed the threshold. Unlike the hallway, the apartment's interior smelled strongly of disinfectant and cleanser. And for such a run-down building, the room he had entered was in surprisingly good shape. The drab walls could use some paint, but everything was sparkling and squared away. It could have been a large suite on a starship. Mallory guessed that a few days earlier, before Master Chief Petty Officer Joseph Kirk came to town, the apartment had looked quite different, and had smelled different, too.

"I gather you've been busy," Mallory said.

"You have any kids?"

"Two. Boy and girl. Younger than your sons, but . . . I can only imagine what my boy's apartment will look like when he moves out."

Joe surveyed the apartment as if it still wasn't up to his standards. "That's what this one looked like, only worse."

Mallory saw the aquarium and the darting orange-and-white cloud of clown fish. "Nice aquarium. Are they James's?"

Joe went over to the tank, and the fish crowded close to him. "No, my other boy's. George, or Sam, now . . . He's decided he doesn't like the name everyone's been calling him since the day he was born."

Mallory heard the old anger in the man, yet watched how delicate his large hands were as he opened the aquarium's cover and carefully sprinkled a precise amount of fish food for his appreciative audience.

"Children get their own ideas," Mallory commented, one father to another.

Joe watched the fish. "Are you responsible for my Jimmy's getting a chance to enlist?"

Mallory debated breaking security on his plan. But Joe Kirk's record in the fleet spoke for itself. The list of commendations alone ran three pages.

Mallory asked the former Starfleet noncom a question he already knew the answer to. "You still have your security clearance?"

Joe shot him a sidelong glance. "Is this a test?"

Mallory didn't answer.

"If you're as good as you seem to think you are, then you know I don't," Joe said. "I don't do any consulting. I'm not in the reserves. I did my twenty, and I got out."

Mallory had no qualms about trusting the man. "Then let's talk off the record."

"If that's why you're here."

Mallory was beginning to see where Kirk's fierce independence had come from. "I'm the one who arranged for your son to be offered an opportunity to enlist."

Joe looked as if he still couldn't believe it. "I didn't think they did that anymore."

"Not in the civilian courts," Mallory agreed. "But every now and then when some youngster with promise interferes with Starfleet property . . . well, usually it's because they've got some interest in it. So instead of punishing them, we invite them in. Not every teenager has a clear idea of what he wants to do in life. Sometimes, all it takes is a little push in the right direction."

Joe put the container of fish food back on a tray of evenly arranged packages. "You think Jimmy has promise?"

"That's what I wanted to talk to you about."

"Grab a chair," Joe said. "I got some beer in the cooler."

Mallory sat in a threadbare armchair that had seen better

days, but had been realigned with a tightly folded blanket that served as an extra cushion.

Joe came back from the kitchen alcove with two pouches of a local beer, tapped them on the serving table to make the pouches change shape and harden into cylinders, then peeled them open and handed one to his guest.

Joe clinked his cylinder to Mallory's. "May rudders govern and ships obey."

Mallory appreciated the traditional toast, offered one back. "Ourselves—because no one else is likely to concern themselves with our welfare."

Joe understood. "What ship did you serve on?"

Mallory had served on a few. But there was only one that mattered at a time like this. "The *Constitution*. Before your day, though. I checked."

Joe approved, sat back on the couch. "How'd you get my boy to enlist?"

"I think it's something he's always wanted."

Joe's face darkened. "You don't know him."

"I think I do," Mallory said. "I've seen his files: from school, from the Riverside protectors, Star Cadets, Junior Explorers."

The mention of the children's group made Joe smile.

"And then something happened, didn't it?"

The smile faded, Joe said nothing, and just as Mahina Otago had recognized a particular kind of silence, so did Mallory. The topic he had just touched on was something Joe had sworn never to discuss.

"I have access to a great many files in my department," Mallory said easily. "So I think I've been able to fill in a few gaps in your son's history. But when Starfleet makes a promise, we keep it. And I give you my word there is absolutely no mention of Tarsus IV in any of James's records."

Joe put his beer on the table. There was no more friendliness or approval in him. "Then why mention it now?"

"He's one of the eyewitnesses, isn't he? One of the nine people who actually saw Kodos and can identify him."

Joe's eyes clouded. "That's not all he saw."

"Master Chief, I don't mean to bring up bad memories."

But it was too late for that. Mallory watched as the powerful man across from him seemed to shrink with age before his eyes. "It's just Joe. Those days are . . . It's just Joe."

"Joe, then. I need to know what your son can handle."

Joe Kirk looked up in alarm. "My son is under a death sentence! Word gets out that he's one of the nine—" Joe stopped to catch his breath, tried to calm down. "I never bought the story about them finding Kodos's body, not the way it was burned, no way to identify it. It's the sort of thing he'd do. Kill someone else to make it look as if *he* died, so no one would go looking for him.

"But if he's out there, then no one knows where. No one knows who he is or what he looks like now. So he could be anyone. Anywhere. And you can be damn sure that after what he did to those colonists, he won't hesitate to kill anyone who can identify him. Including my boy."

Mallory knew there had been more than four thousand casualties at Tarsus IV. He was looking at another right now.

"No one knows, Joe. I promise you that. I only put it together because of an anomaly in your boy's medical records—the inoculations he got before he left that summer. And the record of those inoculations has been deleted—I saw to that myself."

Joe wasn't convinced. "That's not enough intel to go on. You know more than that."

Mallory decided to trust the man even more. "One of my department's special projects is trying to track Kodos. So far . . . nothing. But we haven't given up. And we are keeping the names of the witnesses classified until we can be sure they're safe."

Joe accepted that, recovering. "Thank you for telling me."

Mallory moved on. "Tarsus IV changed your son."

"How couldn't it? He was fourteen, wanted to go out of the system so badly, ever since he was a kid." Joe stared past Mallory, and Mallory knew he was looking into the past. "One time, I was home on leave, and Jimmy, he was five. And this one night, we were out walking, out in the fields, the wheat coming up. And the stars, it was in the middle of nowhere back then, our farm, and the stars were like you see them in space, clear, and the Milky Way on fire across the sky. And Jimmy wanted to know which ones I'd been to, the ones I'd seen up close. So I started pointing them out, naming them, and the look . . ." Joe took a moment, caught up in this sweet, lost moment. ". . . the look in his eyes as he heard those names . . . I knew he had it then. The dream. You know?"

Mallory nodded. It was something everyone at Starfleet knew so well.

"And Jimmy said to me, he said to me, 'Daddy, I have to go there.' And he meant *all* of them. And I picked him up and I told him he would. I told him he would.

"And I sent him to Tarsus IV, Mr. Mallory. I sent him to Tarsus IV and I lost my boy . . ."

Mallory moved to sit beside the man until he had recovered. And then he made this promise: "I'll do everything I can to get him back for you."

Joe Kirk looked at Mallory like a man who desperately wanted to believe, but could not.

Mallory knew the feeling all too well.

33

His first day as a member of Starfleet wasn't as bad as Kirk had feared.

It was worse.

He and Spock were roused from their cells at Starfleet Headquarters at 0400 hours, given thirty minutes to shower, eat, and get into their civilian clothes. By 0440, they had been discharged from Starfleet custody, signed over to two Starfleet masters-at-arms, and marched onto a Starfleet air-shuttle.

The flight from HQ to the Starfleet Training Center took all of seven minutes. Kirk had watched the Academy pass by below, the lights lining the paths and roadways sparkling through the black silhouettes of the trees. Most of the room lights in Archer Hall were out, and anyway the angle was wrong to see Elissa's room.

Spock said nothing on the short trip. Kirk knew there was a lot they both had to say to each other, but they hadn't had a moment together without a guard or escort since they had been taken from the courtroom.

At least Spock had demonstrated he wasn't a complete uncaring alien lump—Kirk had caught him looking down at the Vulcan diplomatic compound as they had sailed over it. The assemblage of alien architecture was difficult to miss, especially at night, when its floodlit buildings glowed like rubies in a field of glittering blue-white diamonds.

The airshuttle touched down on a well-worn pad about one hundred meters from STC's main gates. Two white-and-blue Starfleet buses hovered by those gates. As he and Spock were escorted from the shuttle to a pedestrian walkway, Kirk could see that each bus was filled with eager young faces.

"Looks like you two'll have a lot of company," one of the escorts said.

Kirk didn't think of the kids in the buses as company. As far as he was concerned, they were the competition.

Spock, not surprisingly, said, "Indeed." Kirk was beginning to suspect the Vulcan was nervous.

Their paperwork—all on large, clunky padds that seemed to be fifty years old, at least—was waiting in the guard shack. They were given five minutes to complete it—all forty-seven pages and fifteen signature windows.

Given the time limit, Kirk signed without reading; enlistment document, dependency application, record of emergency data, medical waivers describing risk of accident, death, dismemberment, ebullism . . . he had to stop to read the definition of that term, cringed, signed, kept paging through.

He rolled his eyes when he signed the final window that affirmed he was voluntarily enlisting, then slid the padd back over the counter to the intake officer.

"Forty-seven pages in five minutes," Kirk said to Spock. "Starfleet planning at its best."

Spock put on his most bland expression. "I read them all."

Kirk frowned, and they were marched out of the office and onto the grounds of the STC.

At 0600 hours, with the sky brightening in the dawn, Kirk, Spock, and seventy other recruits were encouraged by uniformed personnel to stand at attention in a formation of four lines of eighteen.

A tall petty officer with a deeply lined face and a booming voice the recruits with a five-minute recitation of the history of the STC, with all the enthusiasm of someone who had given the same speech a thousand times.

As an institution, the training center had been operating

for well more than a century. The first crews to serve in the old United Earth Starfleet trained here, as did the scientific teams of the United Earth Space Probe Agency. MACO pilots, merchant marines, the first diplomatic exchange groups headed for Andoria, Tellar, and Denobula, all passed through these gates, enlisted personnel and officers alike.

Kirk guessed that's why the low buildings looked so old and so behind the times. He was not impressed.

The moment the history lesson was over, the recruits were marched—again—toward the quartermaster building. Inside, in controlled chaos, tables were laid out with standard Starfleet kit—clothes, boots, underwear, hygiene kits, and a large duffel in which to stuff everything.

The recruits had five minutes to find everything they needed. Kirk was beginning to see the pattern.

Then more marching: into another building where the males went through a door on one side and the females through the other, to shed their civilian clothes and give up their personal belongings. Kirk watched as Spock ingeniously argued his way into keeping some kind of Vulcan medallion that he wore around his neck. The Vulcan achieved this by calmly explaining to an exasperated clerk that it had deep cultural significance and that any attempt to force him to remove it would be a violation of his cultural rights as specified on page twenty-seven of the intake documents he had signed less than an hour ago. It seemed Spock *had* read all the paperwork, after all.

Dressed in ill-fitting recruit whites, including stiff-billed ball caps with a red Starfleet chevron, their next stop was the barbershop. Kirk looked in the mirror after his sixty-second makeover and all he saw was his crew-cut father staring back at him. The difference was that Kirk didn't yet have sideburns that could be cut to a point.

Spock ended up looking like a mythical elf. The long hair

that had covered his ears was now nothing more than dark stubble from which his ears stood out like dangerous weapons. Kirk had to give the Vulcan high marks for apparently not noticing how all the other recruits kept staring at him.

Less than ninety minutes after stepping through the center's gates, the transformation of the recruits was startling. Seventy-two civilians, male and female, in multicolored clothes, all shapes and sizes, had been roughly molded into a squad of identically dressed, flush-faced clones. Other than height, about the only difference among them that Kirk could make out was that the females had been allowed to keep more of their hair. Spock, of course, was the exception. He was noticeably different, and not just because he was one of the tallest recruits in the formation.

Then the gauntlet began.

Suddenly, eight petty officers appeared out of nowhere and started berating the recruits. This one's hat was at the wrong angle. That one's shirt wasn't aligned properly. What's that smudge doing on that boot, mister?! Don't call me sir, I work for a living!

If recruits tried to apologize, they were shouted at even more. Did I ask for an apology?! Are you giving me an excuse, mister?! Get those shoulders back! Eyes forward! Chin in! Not that far!

Kirk couldn't believe how transparent this show of domination was. Two petty officers decided to take on Spock, whose posture, attitude, and uniform were perfect. They couldn't even make him blink.

Then one of the two haranguing Spock noticed Kirk watching, and like predators sensing a weak member of the herd, they abandoned their uncooperative prey and swooped in on easier pickings with a barely concealed smirk.

"What are you looking at, Recruit?!" one shouted.

Kirk had heard what the others had answered, correctly

and incorrectly. It wasn't difficult to answer correctly. "Nothing, Chief."

"I *saw* you looking, Recruit! Are you calling me a liar?!"

"No, Chief. It won't happen again, Chief!"

"So you *were* looking!"

"If you say so, Chief!"

By now, Kirk had both chief petty officers a few centimeters from his face, screaming at ear-splitting volume, spraying spittle on him as they spoke in rapid-fire cadence.

"Are you mouthing off, Recruit?!"

"No, Chief!"

"Do you think you're a smart guy, Recruit?!"

Kirk knew it was wrong, *knew* it was wrong, but he couldn't stop himself. "No, Chief—I am a Starfleet recruit!"

For about half a second, Kirk had a taste of victory—the two petty officers actually paused in their assault as they processed his insult. Then they redoubled their efforts to get Kirk flustered.

"Do you think this is funny, Recruit?!"

Kirk thought, *This is too easy.* "Yes, Chief!"

Both petty officers sputtered. "What did you say?!"

"As a Starfleet recruit I am on my honor to tell the truth and ensure the full truth is known, Chief!"

Four petty officers swarmed around Kirk now, and he was ordered to the ground to do push-ups.

Kirk dropped as ordered and did as he was told. One petty officer squatted beside him while two others harangued the other recruits for watching. The fourth petty officer got on his hands and knees so he could shout into Kirk's ear with each push-up.

Everything blurred together. Not because any of it overwhelmed Kirk. But because none of it meant anything to someone who had gazed down the barrel of a laser rifle and realized he was going to die.

There was nothing even Starfleet petty officers could do that could come close to what he'd already survived.

Tarsus IV.

By the time fourteen-year-old Jimmy returned to his cabin with Matthew and the other boys, he was feeling warmer. The concentrate bars had settled his stomach, too, eased the hunger pangs. Though now he felt guilty for not having saved any for the others.

"Go get 'em out," Matthew told him.

"It's so cold," Jimmy said. "Maybe we should wait till morning?"

"They won't be cold for long. Get 'em out."

Jimmy walked up the three wooden steps to the cabin door, knocked on it. "Hey, guys, it's me!"

The door creaked open. Aki Kimura was there, very scared, very small. He was only eight years old, visiting his great-grandparents for the summer. Jimmy had liked meeting his great-grandmother. She'd been in Starfleet, fought the Xindi, had great stories to tell. And she made wonderful soba noodles.

"Hey, Aki, how are you?" Jimmy asked.

Aki bit his lip, looked past Jimmy, and gave a small whimper.

Jimmy turned to see Matthew and the others all aiming their rifles at the open door.

"C'mon, Jimmy," Matthew urged. "We gotta get back."

Jimmy felt as if he was watching himself on a viewscreen. The words wouldn't form in his mind, but he could see what was going to happen. The pressure to keep going without thinking, to do what he was told, was too much for him. It would be so easy just to open the door all the way, step back, call out the rest of the kids, and let Matthew and the boys in the red bandanas do what Jimmy feared they would do. So easy. Especially since Jimmy knew that if he didn't do that, if he resisted, if he argued, he'd be the first to be shot.

He wondered if they could run. Maybe that was the way. If he could get all the kids to suddenly run out in a stampede, like the transcattle, maybe Matthew would hesitate just a bit, just enough for the kids to race off across the field of withered grain and into the blighted forest and then they'd be okay. They could make it to another valley in the daytime. It would be warm enough. Maybe they could find a cave, and Jimmy even knew how to catch small animals and birds, because his father had taught him official Starfleet survival training when they went camping. If there were some birds left in the next valley, or the valley after that, then Kirk could catch them and all the kids would be okay until someone came to rescue them.

The plan flashed through Jimmy's mind in a second. He didn't know if it could work. But he did know that it had to.

"What's the holdup?" Matthew complained.

"Tell everyone to put on their shoes and slippers," Jimmy said quietly to Aki. "And wrap up in all the blankets, okay?"

But Aki shook his head and Jimmy saw tears in his eyes.

"What's wrong?" Jimmy asked.

"They're not here," Aki said. "They went after you."

Jimmy gently pushed the young boy aside, stepped into the cabin.

The bunks were stripped of blankets, even sheets. He called the names of the kids he knew. No answer.

He stepped back into the doorway. "Matthew, they're not here."

Matthew and the red-bandana boys pushed Jimmy back as they stormed into the cabin, using their rifles to pry up the mattresses, kicking open the bathroom door.

They swore like the older kids—language Jimmy would never use. His father was very strict about that.

"We're in so much trouble," Matthew said. Then he pushed Jimmy against the cabin wall. "Naw, you're the one in trouble. When Griffyn finds out everyone escaped because of you, you're off the list, Jimmy."

Jimmy saw his way out. "I'll find 'em, okay? They must've gone *off the road, tried a shortcut. I bet they're in the glade by the Leighton farm. That's the fast way back."*

Matthew nodded. "Okay, you go through the glade, we'll circle around on the road and be there when they come out. But if they make it back to the storehouses and Griffyn sees 'em, we're all off the list, get it? You ruined everything, so all of us have to pay for it."

The other boys glared at Jimmy. He had to get away. "I'll go now. I'll run." He held out his hand to Aki. "C'mon."

But Matthew grabbed Aki's shoulder, pulled him close. "We'll take care of the brat. You go and you run and I'll see you on the other side of the glade."

Jimmy couldn't argue. Not with four laser rifles pointed at him.

"Sure, Matthew," he said. "I'll run." He looked at Aki, knew he wouldn't see the child again. "I'll see you, Aki. We'll catch up with your bahn and oji-san, okay?"

Aki attempted a brave smile at the mention of his great-grandparents.

And then, hating himself, knowing that his father would never run from someone needing help, that's what Jimmy Kirk did.

And when he heard the laser rifles fire behind him, he ran faster, knowing what a failure he was, knowing how much he had let poor Aki down.

He didn't think it would ever be possible to feel worse.

He was wrong.

Kirk came out of his haze when he realized his face had just slammed into the paved parade ground.

"Give me *more*, Recruit!"

The order, loud as it was, came from a great distance, almost drowned out by the buzzing in Kirk's ears and the pounding of his heartbeat.

"I said, *give me more!*"

Kirk realized his arms wouldn't move. He knew they were there because he could feel them burning along with his chest. But they just lay beside him, useless.

Even in his haze, though, he knew he shouldn't offer an apology or an excuse—nothing to set the harriers after him again.

"Do you *hear* me?"

Kirk lay immobile on the ground. If he didn't play, they couldn't win.

Finally, he was aware of the petty officer getting up beside him. The next order was shouted at someone else. "You two—get this shirker on his feet!"

Kirk felt two pairs of hands grab him under the arms and lift.

He swayed, unsteady, arms on fire, dimly aware of the petty officers gathering around him again for more.

They wouldn't get the better of him, he vowed.

The first day went downhill from there.

34

At the end of that first day, Kirk and Spock had been assigned to the eighteen-member Gold Team, under the direct command of Master Chief Petty Officer Mary Elizabeth Gianni. Their leader was a formidable woman who claimed to hold the center's record for largest number of recruits to wash out before completing basic training. She also claimed she had never seen a group of recruits so ill-suited to the service.

Spock did not believe her. While marching past the Blue Team barracks, he had heard distinctly another petty officer make the same claim to his charges. In any event, there seemed to be no logic in an all-volunteer service that first strove to attract the best candidates possible, then tried to dissuade those candidates from completing their training. In fact, he had observed a great deal of posturing and dramatics in just his first few hours here.

Spock was not impressed.

Misleading training techniques aside, though, this first day had been an interesting experience.

The other recruits had gawked at him, especially after his long hair was shorn to half-centimeter stubble, but he was used to that level of attention from aliens. Something he was not used to was that no one had shown him any special treatment. The training staff had been as loud and disruptive toward him as they had been to the other recruits. Spock found that refreshingly satisfactory.

Not that they had been able to disrupt his concentration, of course. He recognized that was the purpose of the exercise: to desensitize recruits to noise, disorder, and confusion, so they could think clearly and act decisively in emergency situations on board a vessel in deep space, or when surrounded by hostile aliens on a distant world, or during any one of the hundreds of other unexpected disasters that could befall explorers. Vulcan children, however, learned to ignore noise, disorder, and confusion as toddlers. If a yowling *sehlat* demanding dinner were able to divert a Vulcan child from preparing that dinner, Spock doubted that any household would allow the pets—the consumption rate would be unacceptable.

Spock had had a *sehlat* and survived. Given just that one facet of Vulcan upbringing, he knew there was nothing that the Starfleet trainers today could have done or said, at any volume, to affect his concentration.

Interestingly enough, he had seen a similar unshakable mental focus in Jim Kirk. True, the trainers had been able to exhaust the human teenager physically after his 112 push-ups, but there was no real trick to that, Spock knew. Each species had its own physiological limits which no force of will could overcome. That was elementary biology. Even Vulcan muscles could be starved of energy after a thousand push-ups or so in Earth-normal gravity.

But despite forcing Jim Kirk into physical exhaustion, the Starfleet trainers had not been able to throw him off-balance mentally. Spock had been fascinated to watch that particular contest. It was almost as if, at some time in his past, the young human had faced a situation or situations exceeding any pressure the trainers could subject him to.

The other recruits, all human, most from Earth, had behaved as expected, reflecting their inexperience with the harsh realities of life away from their paradisiacal planet and colony worlds. As the trainers hoped, the young novices were flustered by the onslaught of shouted, overlapping commands and they lost the ability to concentrate effectively. Spock had no difficulty reading in their untutored conduct an explosion of emotional states, from anger to embarrassment to frustration. Admirably, though, no one had spoken back to the trainers or run off. Instead, they had accepted the confusion and fought to rise above it.

If their responses were common to all humans, and not just those predisposed to a Starfleet career, Spock could see how the human species, at some time in the future, might rise above its tendencies for erratic behavior.

Everything considered, he was looking forward to the days ahead. He anticipated that they were going to be even more interesting, and he hoped that soon they might also prove challenging. But for now, as far as he was concerned, Starfleet training was something to observe, not to take part in.

Spock's musing came to an end when Master Chief Gianni completed her barracks inspection, the last activity of the scheduled "night routine."

Spock, like the other eighteen recruits, stood at parade rest by his bunk in the common sleeping area. His footlocker was open with all items on display, arranged as indicated in the *Starfleet Recruits' Manual*, which was the one book the new recruits were currently allowed to have in their personal reading padds. He wore his recruit whites, boots gleaming, hat stowed in the locker, his bunk taut with precision, as demanded.

Gianni found fault with several other recruits, scolded them loudly, and stood over them as they realigned the items in their lockers or remade their bunks. When she came to Kirk, whose bunk was two down from Spock's, she found no fault with his preparations, but made cutting remarks about the dirt on the front of his uniform—he had not been allowed to change since the incident on the parade ground.

When Gianni came to Spock, she eyed all his preparations with deep suspicion, but in the end could find nothing to find fault with. Though it seemed to cause her some distress, she said, "Good work, Recruit."

Spock remained at parade rest, hands behind his back, eyes forward.

Gianni didn't walk on. "You're allowed to say 'thank you' when complimented, Recruit."

Spock immediately said, "Thank you," and Gianni launched her attack.

"Thank you, *what?*"

Spock considered her attempt to find at least one thing to correct about him a reach, but he gave her her due. "Thank you, Master Chief!"

Gianni walked on, completed her inspection, then stood at the front of the barracks precisely as a time alert chimed. "Twenty-two hundred hours is lights out. Feel free to cry yourself to sleep because you miss your mommies and daddies, and I will see you at oh five hundred. Good night, Gold Team!"

Almost in unison, the eighteen recruits shouted, "Good night, Master Chief!" And then the barracks plunged into darkness, the void penetrated only by a pale green lightstrip that ran along the center of the common area, apparently to guide new recruits to the latrine in the middle of the night.

Spock quickly undressed and got into his bunk in his underwear. Sleepwear was not part of their Starfleet kit at this time.

To relax before his evening's meditation, he resumed his ongoing calculations to prove the Riemann hypothesis for prime numbers. He perceived he was getting close, and with a few more years of calculations, he felt confident of achieving success. It was soothing work.

Within twenty minutes, even as he pictured the equations setting the pattern of trivial zeroes established by the Riemann zeta function, Spock could hear and identify sixteen different breathing patterns in the barracks, all indicative of exhausted sleep. For a few moments, he wondered about the identity of the one recruit, other than himself, who was not yet asleep, and then he heard surreptitious movement.

With his dark-adapted vision, Spock had no trouble seeing Jim Kirk rise from his bunk, already dressed. Silently, the human moved toward the barracks exit door and slipped out. No one else was disturbed—their sleeping patterns hadn't changed.

Spock weighed the pros and cons of going after him—they still needed to talk about Kirk's brother's involvement with a criminal organization that included a woman named Dala. Spock was unwilling to accept that the unwelcome name was a coincidence—real crime was too rare on this planet. But there was also the possibility that Kirk was planning on escaping from Starfleet as his brother had suggested. If that was the case, then the only logical course was to avoid further entanglements with Kirk.

That conclusion reached, Spock set aside his calculations and brought his hands together, fingertips joined, to begin his meditation. An hour of that, followed by a few minutes of sleep, and he would be ready to face a new day in Starfleet, with or without Jim Kirk.

He had little doubt it would be much easier without.

Whether it was because of the growing ache in his arms and chest, or his worry for Sam, or just that he was constitutionally unable to do what he was told by people he did not respect, Kirk left the barracks because he had to walk.

The damp night air off the bay was bracing, and the light fog swirled in misty streamers as it flowed past the floodlights and footpath markers that traced the low buildings and the many ways through the STC.

Kirk saw few other pedestrians around. As he crossed a

path between two large buildings, he glimpsed a large group of enlisted members jogging in the athletic field. They had backpacks, and two runners up front carried unit flags. Night maneuvers, he guessed. *That'll be something to look forward to*, he thought with a sigh.

Another building held the officers' club, and the windows flared with light. As personnel entered and exited the building, Kirk could hear raised voices in excited conversation, the clink of flatware and glasses. Since all Starfleet officers were trained at the Academy, he guessed everyone inside that particular club worked at STC. Looking from across a garden walkway, he could see into the building through its bright windows. He saw teams of white-jacketed servers bearing heaping plates to the officers at the tables.

Kirk thought back to the extruded food chunks he and the other recruits had been served *six* hours ago, in what was mockingly called the evening meal. It looked like the officers were eating steaks in there. The hypocrisy of the place astounded *and* annoyed him. He walked on, grateful, at least, for the fact that he wasn't hungry.

He rounded one building and there before him were three shuttle landing pads, well within the center's grounds. He decided they were probably for official Starfleet traffic, and not airshuttles bringing in new recruits. Beyond them, he saw the elevated monorail station. The trains there departed either for the Sloane Complex island or the Academy. He tried not to dwell on the thought that Elissa was only twenty minutes away. There was no use in torturing himself.

Kirk chose to skirt the well-lit pads and see if a train schedule was posted at the station. It was. Generally, it appeared he could count on a train leaving for the Academy every twenty-five minutes during the operational hours of 0500 to midnight. The headlight of an arriving monorail train stabbed the darkness as it silently approached the station, and Kirk ducked back into the shadows. By the time any passengers reached the ground, he was long gone.

Already feeling more settled by his unauthorized outing, Kirk circled back toward the Gold Team barracks and encountered a small observation tower, no doubt intended for some obscure and probably unnecessary training activity. It was only about fifteen meters tall, with a ladder running up the center support pylon. There were no lights on it. Ignoring the complaints from his arms, Kirk climbed the ladder, and his impulse was rewarded.

At the tower's top was an open-air platform that offered a view over the east side of the center, to the bay, the Golden Gate, and, almost invisible through the growing fog, a few pale lights that marked the old Presidio and the Academy.

But Kirk didn't care about that. He stared into the soft gray nothingness, willing the fog to part just enough for him to see a few of the lights of San Francisco.

But the fog did not obey him. Instead, it grew thicker, until even the lights of the bridge that offered a way out of this place and back to his life were swallowed.

Now the only lights were those of the center—his life's new boundaries.

Shutting out the despair that waited, always, to claim him, Kirk climbed down the ladder.

He reached the Gold Team barracks just before 2400 hours. The door opened quietly, and he had no trouble retracing his silent steps to his bunk.

This wasn't where he wanted to be, but at least now he felt he could sleep. He stripped off his clothes and slipped under the covers.

The lights blazed on.

"*Mister Kirk,*" Master Chief Gianni shouted.

35

This time, the punishment wasn't push-ups for Kirk. It was calisthenics.

For everyone.

Within five minutes of Kirk's return to the barracks, all eighteen members of Gold Team, groggy and stumbling, were up, changed into exercise gear, and jogging out to the athletics field.

Gianni put them through their paces for an hour—lunges, jumping jacks, Klingon squats, and push-ups. And she made certain every member of the team understood why they were out in the cold and the fog in the middle of the night.

"Starfleet is a *team*," she told them as she paced in front of the huffing and puffing teenagers. "*You* sorry lot are a *team!* Each one of you is responsible for team success! Do you hear me?!"

The wheezing, gasping voices answered: "Yes, Master Chief!"

"When you are in deep space and your ship's in distress, each *one* of you is responsible for protecting your *whole* crew from harm! Do you hear me?!"

"Yes, Master Chief!"

"If a crewmate dies, then it is *your* fault! And that will be *worse* than death for *you!* Do you understand?!"

"Yes, Master Chief!"

The exercises were so standard and Master Chief Gianni's rote exhortations so obvious that Spock found he could actually meditate during the activity, at the basic level, at least. Thus, at the end of an hour, he was the only member of Gold

Team not to have faltered, the only member not out of breath, the only member not even sweating. He felt refreshed.

The other members, complaining among themselves, red-faced, coughing, and walking slowly back to their barracks, took notice of the fact that what had been punishment for them was not punishment for Spock, and before they were halfway back from the athletics field, Spock found the only other member of his team he could walk with was Jim Kirk, who had been ostracized by the group just as thoroughly.

They said nothing as they walked beside each other. Spock couldn't ascertain what it was Kirk was feeling, and he didn't want to know.

Back in the barracks, five minutes after the second lights-out for the evening, Spock heard seventeen breathing patterns indicative of sleep. Expecting no other disturbances for the night, he fell asleep at once.

This time he dreamed of his *sehlat,* and the dry, hot, peaceful deserts of home.

For Kirk, his second day in Starfleet began in a blur. Reveille at 0500 hours. Then barracks inspection, during which he found everything in his locker had been jumbled about. The same had happened to Spock's. Then breakfast at 0545. The unappetizing extruded protein was delivered in the form of thick white slabs of pseudo-eggs and thin pink sheets of pseudo-ham.

Kirk and Spock ended up facing each other over their trays at the end of a table in the canteen. No one else would sit with them.

"Just fruit?" Kirk asked. He wasn't really interested, but he wanted to show the other members of his so-called team that he was capable of having a conversation.

"I prefer not to eat animal flesh," Spock said as he ate his apple with a knife and fork.

Kirk held up a strip of glistening pseudo-ham with his fingers. "I guarantee this has never been anywhere near a real pig."

"Of course not," Spock said. "It has been designed to last for years of storage as emergency shuttle rations."

Kirk stared at the dangling strip of pink substance. "Shuttle rations?"

"That is what recruits eat for the first two weeks of basic training. The information was in the documents we signed yesterday. As we gain in expertise and earn our ratings, we will be rewarded with improved rations. Starfleet advancement is based on competition."

Kirk dropped the extruded protein back on his tray. "They plan everything."

"Careful planning is essential to surviving in the unforgiving environment of space."

"You're actually enjoying this, aren't you?"

Spock couldn't understand how the human could ask him that question. Vulcans were the first alien species to make public contact with humans. They were the alien species humans had known the longest and interacted with the most. But humans still knew shockingly little about them, and Spock wondered if that ignorance arose from a general disinterest or some misguided belief that, in the end, all aliens were just like humans.

"I am a Vulcan," Spock said evenly. "Vulcans do not 'enjoy.' That is an emotional response to stimuli."

Kirk grinned. "Whatever you say, Stretch. But if that's the case, I'd sure like to know where all the little Vulcans come from."

Spock ignored him and his ignorance.

Then Kirk leaned forward, whispered, "We need to have that talk about what Sam and I were discussing in the cell."

Spock turned his attention to his orange. "At 0820 hours,

the first instruction period will commence. At that time, you and I are directed to go to the processing building to take our Starfleet Vocational Aptitude Tests." The other members of Gold Team had taken their tests prior to induction and most were already assigned to their specialty streams. "We will be able to talk then, without risk of being overheard."

Kirk nodded, went back to his extruded breakfast. "It's good to know that Vulcans know the importance of keeping a secret."

Spock methodically chewed his orange segment, with no intention of taking part in a conversation on that particular topic. He had far too many secrets of his own to protect, and could not begin to imagine ever sharing them with humans.

The SVA Tests were scheduled to take place over three hours. Spock completed his in thirty-four minutes, Kirk in two hours. The education petty officer skimmed through their test padds to be sure no sections had been missed, and seemed disappointed when he had to release the recruits early.

"Noon meal is at 1100 hours," Spock informed Kirk as they left the building. "That gives us thirty minutes."

"A 'noon' meal at eleven A.M." Kirk shook his head. "What kind of ranking does that give Starfleet on the old logic meter?"

Spock didn't know what kind of reply such a confused question warranted, and so disregarded it. He selected a path that would take the two of them approximately thirty minutes to traverse on their way to the canteen. He looked around and saw that no one was within earshot—at least, not within human earshot.

"If I understand what you and your brother discussed the other day, then it appears you are withholding evidence of a murder."

"You don't waste time, do you?"

Spock took a chance. "I believe that we each have information that might have a bearing on the difficulties each of us face. Therefore, logic suggests we should share what we know. Why would you not report a double murder to the authorities?"

Kirk stared at him for a moment, as if uncomfortable with what he was about to say. "Because I can't be sure it happened."

"Your brother is prone to stating untruths?"

Kirk's discomfort seemed to grow greater. "Sam gets confused sometimes. Anxious. And these people he's dealing with, they know it, and . . . they play games with him, to rattle him even more."

Spock tried to follow the rambling path of reason Kirk implied. "So, you believe there is a chance the murders did not take place as your brother claims?"

"Honestly, I don't know. But what gets me worried is that your two agents didn't show up in court."

The words came out of Spock so quickly, he had no chance to hide his regrettably emotional response of shock. "The consular agents? How are they involved with this matter?"

Kirk stopped walking, looked at Spock. "I thought you heard every word Sam and I said."

As much as Spock had enjoyed letting this human believe his auditory ability was indeed superhuman, he knew now he had to confess his limits. Just as he had to work on not enjoying being better than humans.

"Based on what I heard you whisper," Spock said, "I believe there were some words you did not voice, specifically when it came to identifying the victims."

Kirk thought, nodded. "You're right. We didn't say 'Vulcans' out loud."

Spock's mind raced as he tried to analyze all the permutations. "You believe the consular agents were the individuals Sam saw 'disintegrated'?"

"He said two Vulcans. The agents were always a pair. And they didn't turn up in court."

Spock stood still in thought, finally shaken out of his concentration when Kirk said, "Okay, there's obviously more going on here than I know about. We have to talk to someone, tell someone. What about Mallory?"

Spock shook his head. There were still more possibilities he had to work through. "You must answer a question for me first. Your brother mentioned someone's 'girlfriend.' The name he used was Dala. Do you know her?"

Kirk shook his head, then appeared to see through Spock's attempt at emotional control. "Do you?" he asked with interest.

Spock reluctantly said he did. "She is associated with a human called Abel Griffyn." Now Spock was startled by the effect the name had on Kirk. "I take it you know him."

Kirk appeared shaken, almost physically. "I never thought . . . but Matthew, of course. He's still working with Griffyn." He looked at Spock as if he'd been slapped. "How do you know him?"

Spock wasn't about to reveal the possibility that criminal activity might be under way at the Vulcan compound. "I know of him," he said, seeking and finding the line between lying and not telling the complete truth. "His name and Dala's are connected to what might be attempts to penetrate the security of the Vulcan diplomatic compound."

Fortunately, Kirk didn't press the matter, as if anything involving the Vulcan compound wasn't worthy of his interest. Instead, he seemed to come to a decision regarding what was of concern to *him*. "I take it back. Mallory isn't the person to tell this to. We can't trust anyone at Starfleet."

Now it was Spock's turn to be startled, though this time he did a better job of hiding his reaction. "Why?"

"You have to trust me, Stretch," Kirk said.

Spock wasn't inclined to do so, but he detected no obvious physiological sign that the human was speaking anything other than what he believed was the truth.

"I can't tell you how I know," Kirk continued, "but Starfleet claims that Griffyn is dead. That he died three years ago."

"If it is the same Griffyn, then Starfleet has made a mistake."

"Oh, yeah," Kirk said, and Spock could sense the young human's unease transforming into focused anger. "It's what they do best." Then, before Spock could object, he added, "Look, you're right. We have to tell the authorities, except not Starfleet. The thing is, they might be involved. Maybe not all of Starfleet, but some group who should know better."

"Involved in what way?" Spock asked.

Kirk gestured helplessly. "I don't know. But we're talking about humans, okay? We're weak, we're greedy, we look after ourselves before we look after others."

"Not in my experience."

Kirk frowned. "You're really not from around here, are you?"

In the interest of expediency, Spock conceded the point.

"Can you get in touch with Vulcan authorities through your embassy?"

"Certainly."

"Then do that," Kirk said. "Call them. Tell them about Griffyn and Dala. They're probably operating out of this robotic freighter at the docks. It's called the *Pacific Rome*. Got it?"

Spock listened with a practiced expression of bland indifference, struck by how much Kirk knew. "Yes," he said.

"Tell them you heard some prisoner talking in holding about seeing two Vulcans killed. Do your best to keep my brother's name out of it. I have to make sure he's somewhere safe before anyone can get word to Griffyn that the authorities are onto him. Otherwise, he's going to kill Sam." Kirk blew out a tense breath. "He'll probably come after me, too."

Spock still needed to know the reason for Kirk's suggested strategy. "Why do you believe it is better for me to tell Vulcan officials than for both of us to tell Starfleet authorities?"

"I already told you," Kirk said. "Right now, we don't know who we can trust in Starfleet. But you can trust your people, right?"

"Of course," Spock said, believing no such thing.

"Then they're the ones to tell. They can go right to the top. Leave Starfleet out of it and bring in Federation Security. When can you call them?"

"I believe I can receive permission to make a personal call during the noon meal."

"Good. Do that." Kirk looked off into the distance. "And I know what I have to do."

"What?"

"I have to get evidence. Physical evidence that I can hold in my hands and show to someone other than Mallory so none of this can get covered up."

"What kind of evidence?"

"In the warp lab at the Sloane Complex. Someone installed a device there to jam the security system on the dilithium vault. A couple of days ago, I almost got to it, but Mallory stopped me. That's why we can't trust him. He's stopped me from everything I've tried to do to find the real thieves—Griffyn and Matthew and Dala and . . . their whole gang."

Kirk paused, as if a major realization had just come to him. "Mallory's in on it! That's the only answer. So it's up to you, Stretch. You have to tell your people everything!"

Spock nodded calmly. At any other time, in any other circumstances, he would have guided Kirk through the strained chain of logic he had forged, to reveal the weak links and identify unsupported conclusions in order to arrive at a more robust and realistic approximation of the truth.

But in this case, at this moment, Spock didn't dare. Because the human's logic so closely mirrored his own.

Jim Kirk felt they could not take what they knew to Starfleet because there was no way to know who in that organization was actually involved with the criminals.

For the same reason, Spock knew that he could not possibly reveal any of these details to the security office at the Vulcan compound because to the best of his knowledge, they were already aware and involved.

It was most troubling that he and Kirk had each had a different piece of the puzzle that could explain the Vulcan Embassy theft ring and Sarek's involvement with it, and how Griffyn and Dala and Kirk and Kirk's brother were somehow further connected in what could be the same mystery.

Fortunately, though, Spock reassured himself, Jim Kirk had told him all that he knew before he had been required to tell Kirk anything. Certainly, then, he could control this situation and handle it himself, though there would definitely be an advantage to having the young human provide help—as long as Kirk didn't know any more details than absolutely necessary.

"I'll contact the embassy," Spock agreed. "In the meantime, if you believe there will be evidence available for you to find in the Sloane Complex, I can suggest a way for you to find it."

Kirk didn't look hopeful. "Is there anything we can do that fits in with the sacred Daily Routine?"

"Yes," Spock said. "There is a simple way for both of us to gain entrance to the lab, with the approval of the STC."

Spock knew that was the way to get Kirk's full attention. When it came right down to it, humans were a simple people, easily distracted.

So Spock told Kirk his plan.

36

At 1700 hours, Kirk gazed blankly at the supposedly inspirational display screens in the waiting area outside the office of Command Master Chief Alun Fifield, the senior noncom in charge of all STC recruits. Master Chief Gianni had taken pleasure in ordering Kirk to appear here at this time. Then she had taken even more pleasure in wishing him good luck in New Zealand.

Spock, however, had briefed Kirk well. For an alien, Kirk had to admit Spock had come up with a good plan, firmly based in the indoctrination papers Kirk had not had time to read. The Vulcan had not only read them, he remembered them, and had discovered loopholes, inconsistencies, and reason for hope.

Before the office chronometer had rolled over to 1701, the screen on the desk of the young yeoman serving as Fifield's clerk clicked on. Kirk heard a brusque voice order, *"Send him in."* Fifield had not bothered to ask if Kirk was present, and Kirk understood what that indicated about the man's character: He was just like Joe Kirk. So Kirk walked into Fifield's office with all the dread of a young boy about to be disciplined by his father. He was seventeen, but he still hadn't rid himself of that echo of apprehension from childhood.

As instructed by Gianni on the first day, when she had described the required procedure for reporting up the chain of command, Kirk snapped to attention before Fifield's desk. The CMC was raw-boned, with leathery skin, and appeared not to have smiled for the past decade. His hair, to no great surprise for Kirk, was trimmed to a crisp crew cut, again like Kirk's father.

"Recruit Kirk reporting as ordered, Command Master Chief," Kirk said. He kept his eyes locked dead ahead, looking over the CMC's seated form at a large painting on the office wall. It showed four figures in old-fashioned, bronze-colored environmental suits working inside a section of ripped-open hull plating on a Starfleet vessel. In the background, indistinct Romulan drone-ships took on a squadron of MACO fighters, all of space on fire with phase-cannon blasts and atomic detonations that dramatically lit the suited figures in the foreground.

Kirk recognized the event: the Battle of Upsilon Andromedae, one of the costliest of the Romulan War. The Coalition of Planets, precursor to the Federation, won that battle only because of the sacrifice of four engineers who reconnected a damaged power conduit on the *U.S.S. Columbia* by hand, all four then instantly perishing when the power surge brought their ship back to life to turn the tide of battle. Kirk even knew the names of the engineers—he'd had their pictures on his bedroom wall when he was a child. They had been his heroes then. Not now.

"You like that painting, Recruit?" Fifield barked.

"Yes, Command Master Chief."

"You know the story?"

Kirk wanted to get this over with. "No, Command Master Chief."

Fifield gave a snort of disgust. "At ease, Recruit."

Kirk stood at parade rest, hands behind his back.

"Do you know how many young men and women apply for Starfleet service each year?"

Kirk felt another lecture coming on. What was it about Starfleet personnel that made them want to turn everything into a lesson? Why couldn't they just get on with things? "No, Command Master Chief."

"In this system alone, forty thousand. Including the colonies, close to one hundred thousand."

Kirk had not been asked a question, and so he did not respond—another of Master Chief Gianni's first-day instructions.

"At the STC, we can take in a thousand a month. At the SCTC on New Montana, we can take seven hundred a month. Do the math, Recruit. That means Starfleet can accept fewer than twenty percent of the people who *want* to serve. But for reasons that are still not clear to me, I ended up with *you*."

Kirk remained silent. He would not give this typically overbearing Starfleet puppet an excuse to chew him out.

Fifield dropped a black, wedge-shaped padd on his desk. "I have a report from your team leader. Less than twenty-four hours at this center and you broke procedure. An unexplained absence. Do you know the punishment for that, Recruit?"

Spock had told him. "The recruit found to have left his barracks without permission and with no acceptable reason after lights-out is subject to five demerits and loss of liberty, Command Master Chief."

For a moment, Fifield paused, as if trying to reconcile the defiant recruit described in the report with the perfectly behaved recruit standing before him.

"Not quite," Fifield said. "For any other recruit, you'd be right. But you aren't any recruit." He held up a smaller, sleeker padd. "This order transferring you from the custody of Starfleet Security to this center has an interesting condition. *Any* breech of the rules of the STC that would normally result in demerits *automatically* transfers you to the custody of Starfleet Justice for *immediate* transport to the New Zealand penal colony."

Kirk said nothing. That was exactly what he had been prepared for the CMC to say.

"Is there any reason why I should not inform Starfleet Justice that you are now ready for transport?"

Kirk prepared to deliver his lines. "I have an acceptable reason for being out of my barracks, Command Master Chief. Therefore, I am not subject to demerits, and therefore I am not subject to being transferred to the custody of Starfleet Justice." *Stuff that up your impulse port,* Kirk thought.

Fifield took on an icy edge in his reply. "There is no mention of an acceptable reason in Master Chief Gianni's report."

"Master Chief Gianni did not ask me if I had a reason, Command Master Chief."

Just as Spock had predicted, Fifield had been backed into a corner. Gianni had erred in not asking Kirk to explain his actions. Now, Fifield *had* to. And he did.

Kirk poured it on just as Spock had instructed. Because of the unusual nature of his enlistment in Starfleet, he had been denied the opportunity to fully read the documents presented to him when he arrived at the STC. Thus, he had not been made aware of information necessary for him to make informed decisions about his service. In order not to interfere with the smooth operation of the Gold Team barracks, Kirk had waited until all activities for the day had been concluded. Then he had left the barracks and gone to the Aldrin Engineering Hall to read the newest course postings that, regrettably, were not included in the version of the *Starfleet Recruits' Manual* downloaded in his personal reading padd. Upon reading the course postings, he had immediately returned to his barracks.

"Command Master Chief," Kirk concluded crisply.

Fifield tapped a skeptical finger against his desk. "Aldrin Hall closes at 2200. How could you read any course postings?"

"They are listed on a display screen visible from the main doors, Command Master Chief." Kirk was sure of his answer—he and Spock had checked.

The finger tapped faster, as if the CMC knew he was being played, but couldn't find any evidence.

"What courses did you see listed that were of interest?"

Kirk named six courses all connected to warp engineering, only two of which were included in the latest *Manual*.

"Your school records don't show any advanced courses in multiphysics, Recruit."

"It's a personal interest, Command Master Chief."

"Personal." It was obvious Fifield didn't believe a word Kirk had said, and was ready to pounce. "What's the difference between a power transfer conduit and a power transfer grid?"

Kirk cleared his throat, buying a few seconds' time. Spock hadn't said the interview would get into details. Then again, starship technology *had* been a personal interest for Kirk, a long time ago, and he dredged his memory.

"Recruit?" Fifield asked with the pleasant tone of someone who had just won a large pot in a hand of poker.

"In a warp-capable vehicle, the power transfer conduit channels warp plasma from the warp core to the drive nacelles. In a typical dual-bubble Cochrane configuration, a single conduit runs from the core to an arbitrary division point where it undergoes a magnetically modulated bifurcation before the plasma stream is then physically split to follow two separate conduits to the appropriate nacelles." Kirk took a breath, as amazed at what had come out of him as, apparently, Fifield was. "To the best of my knowledge, a power transfer grid is not unique to warp technology but describes a generalized power distribution system that is used to direct power to various systems on demand in a vehicle, building, or even a city as needed, Command Master Chief."

Fifield stopped tapping. "Have you always been such a smartass, Recruit?"

Spock hadn't coached Kirk on that particular question,

either. "I don't understand the question, Command Master Chief."

"The hell you don't," Fifield muttered. He jabbed a finger against a control on the wedge-shaped padd, and Kirk saw the screen wink out, as if Gianni's report had been erased. "Tomorrow morning, I will have the results of your vocational tests. If they bear out this 'personal interest' you have in warp engineering, I'll recommend you for the Warp Field Qualification Tests, and if those results show merit, then you'll be eligible for advanced specialist training.

"But all of that is contingent on your not giving Master Chief Gianni a *single* excuse to write you up over the next four weeks of basic. Is that understood, Recruit?"

Kirk blanched at the idea of spending four more weeks in this hellhole, but kept that reaction to himself. "Understood, Command Master Chief."

"Dismissed."

Kirk stepped back once to show a respect he neither felt nor believed the CMC deserved, then spun around and left the office, not certain that he had exactly won in this encounter, but pleased that Starfleet, by being unable to ship him to New Zealand, had definitely lost.

And any day that Starfleet lost was a good day in his books.

In the CMC's adjacent study, Mallory heard Fifield call out, "Are you happy?"

Mallory switched off the screen he'd been using to watch Kirk's interview with the CMC and joined Fifield in his office.

"You didn't need me to bend the rules, after all," Fifield said.

Mallory stared at the closed door through which Kirk had just left. "I didn't expect that." He guessed Fifield's unspoken question. "That he'd pick up on Starfleet procedure so quickly."

"All I can say is that I'm glad I didn't have to give in to him the way you wanted." Mallory had instructed Fifield to berate Kirk as much as he wanted, but in the end the recruit was to remain at the STC and not to be transferred to New Zealand.

Fifield rearranged the padds on his desk. "Why's Command so interested in James Kirk, anyway? He doesn't belong here. He doesn't want to be here. Forget about this New Zealand threat. Just cut him loose. Everyone wins."

Mallory had no intention of getting drawn into a debate with the CMC, just as he made no attempt to explain his decisions to Judge Otago. When he had seen Gianni's report on Kirk's offense, he had immediately contacted Fifield and with the full weight of Starfleet Command had formally requested that the CMC not turn Kirk over to Starfleet Justice. As it turned out, though, the request had not been necessary. Mallory hadn't had the slightest indication that Kirk would be able to work within the system to ensure that result for himself. Now, having seen Kirk in action, Mallory realized it was time to move up his plans.

"We still need him," Mallory said.

"Mr. Mallory, if you want to do that kid some good by exposing him to discipline and an ordered way of life, then get him into UESPA or one of the military commands. Starfleet's not for him."

Mallory glanced past Fifield to the painting behind him, commemorating the last time Starfleet's primary mission of exploration had been set aside for an overtly military role. There was only one way to be certain that change in fundamental policy would never again be forced on Starfleet—constant vigilance against threats arising from entities that did not share the Federation's peaceful goals.

With that in mind, Mallory graciously thanked the CMC for his input. It was an easier way to end this discussion than by telling him how wrong he was. Then he began to dictate the new orders Fifield was to prepare for Recruit Kirk.

If the tragic events in that painting were truly to remain in the past, never to be repeated, Starfleet needed people like James Kirk as much as James Kirk needed Starfleet.

37

The next day, after instruction period, Kirk and Spock both were given new orders. This time, Master Chief Gianni was not in good humor as she passed over the printed documents. Kirk hoped that meant he'd scored another win.

He scanned the orders swiftly, then smiled, victorious. Both he and Spock had been transferred to an advanced engineering stream, which they were to join at once.

"It is not logical," Spock said as they walked to Aldrin Hall to report.

"It is for Starfleet."

"How did you come by this low opinion?"

Kirk felt no need to explain himself again. He changed the subject. "What makes our new orders so illogical to you? I mean, more than usual?"

"We are still due for three and a half weeks of basic training."

Kirk shot him a wry glance. "As if there's anything more Gianni can teach *you*. You get everything right the first time."

"That does make sense in my situation. But not for you. No offense intended."

"Yeah, right. More like they saw my test scores and, having seen my brilliance, realized basic stuff for me was a waste of time."

"Unlikely. I have observed that, at the recruit level, Starfleet is a large and complex organization that can only operate by adhering to strict routine. Breaking that routine is most probably something that occurs only under remarkable circumstances."

"Well, I'm a remarkable guy."

"Or," Spock continued as if Kirk hadn't spoken, "the situation is being manipulated."

Kirk halted in his tracks. "Run that one by me again."

Spock stopped, took up a position with his hands behind his back, as if speaking to someone of higher rank. "I merely point out that our new orders are not typical of how the STC operates."

Kirk gave him a skeptical look. "How would you know how things 'typically' operate around here?"

Spock seemed surprised by the question. "I have read the *Recruits' Manual*."

"We've been here three days, Stretch. That thing's eleven hundred pages."

"Eleven hundred and twenty. Including the index."

"Whatever." Kirk waved away the Vulcan's automatic elaboration. "You're suggesting that someone, for some reason, has plucked us out of the crowd to give us special treatment?"

"Different treatment," Spock amended.

"Yeah, yeah." Kirk regarded him with sharpened interest. "I know *I* don't qualify for different treatment because my engineering aptitude comes nowhere near yours. So why are we *both* assigned to an engineering specialty?"

Spock's face took on a thoughtful look, as if he found the back-and-forth inquiry engaging. "Rather than think of those characteristics by which we differ, it might be more illuminating if we think of those characteristics we share."

"Okay," Kirk said, impatient, "so that rules out ears, sense of humor, and speed-reading. How are we the same?"

"Most obviously," Spock began, "in the way we came to the STC. Though not unheard of, it is rare for offenders to be given a chance to enlist."

Kirk thought that point over, and concluded that the Vulcan might be onto something. Something that he himself had missed. "Okay, Stretch, here's something else that's the same for both of us—we got caught up in Griffyn's operation. At least I did. And I brought you along for the ride."

"Interesting," Spock said, and Kirk was sure the Vulcan had thought of another connection.

"You think that's it?" Kirk asked him. "Someone's moving us around because of something we know about Griffyn? These orders, they might've come out of nowhere because you stirred something up when you called the embassy."

Spock's face lost any discernible expression.

"You didn't call the embassy?"

"I was not given permission to make a personal call."

"Two *Vulcans* might have been murdered. That must mean *something* to you." Kirk studied Spock, wondering if a Vulcan— this Vulcan—was capable of lying after all, and then, almost at the same time, he wondered what could trigger him to do so.

"We should resume walking," Spock said, and did. So did Kirk. They were less than two hundred meters from Aldrin Hall. "Perhaps when we are established in our new specialty stream, I will have another chance to request a personal call."

Now Kirk was certain Spock was keeping something back. "Just tell them it's your father's birthday, or your parents' anniversary. Starfleet's a sucker for family togetherness."

"Sucker," Spock repeated, looking pleased. "Now I understand."

Kirk wished he could say the same.

An hour later, Spock gazed out the window of the monorail, contemplating the mystery before him.

A theft ring was operating within the Vulcan Embassy, and his father was implicated as the thief both stealing and selling stolen artifacts, though that was, of course, impossible. Yet Sarek *did* know of the theft ring's existence and even claimed that the compound's security agents knew about it as well, although he had not trusted his son enough to confide this to him.

What Spock had been able to determine on his own, first-hand, were the names of the criminals buying the stolen arti-facts and the location of their base of operations on the *Pacific Rome*.

To those details, he now added the information unwit-tingly provided by Jim Kirk, which implied it was likely the same criminals were also involved in the dilithium theft from the Academy—a theft for which Kirk claimed his female friend Elissa had been falsely accused.

But implication and secondhand data supported only sup-position. What if he had acted on uncertain logic?

Most troubling of all to Spock was Kirk's insistence that Elissa had been set up. It seemed the Academy honor board agreed. The charges against her had been dropped, appar-ently as a result of Kirk's efforts to clear her name.

As Spock continued his search for patterns, he arrived at one possible match, a disturbing possibility: Sarek was also being falsely accused.

Spock had no direct experience with criminal conspiracies. But in his studies of the classic literature of this world, espe-cially the masterful works of M. Spillane and E. McBain, he had learned that diverting suspicion through false evidence could be a successful strategy.

He took a moment to consider this new line of thought. If Elissa and Sarek both were set up to serve as *mis*direction, then what was the correct direction?

What was the link between the stolen Vulcan artifacts and the stolen dilithium?

And how did all the facts and suppositions he'd gathered fit into his suspicion that he and Kirk were both being steered into specific positions as recruits within Starfleet?

No matter how many ways he viewed this problem, all of Spock's logic invariably converged on only one possible conclusion: *Another, bigger* crime was being planned, and he and Kirk were being put into place to take the blame.

It would follow then that, if his own conclusion was true, Kirk's corollary was also true: Such powers of manipulation could be exercised only by a person or persons in Starfleet itself. What other way was there to explain how he and Kirk had received their offers to enlist, and their current change of orders?

Spock knew the situation, though clear, was dangerous to him personally. He was a lone teenager on an alien world, unable to trust anyone in his compound, not even his parents. And if whoever was behind this ominous conspiracy would not hesitate to murder two Vulcan consular agents, then they certainly would have no compunctions about killing him.

Or Kirk.

The two of them were pawns in some larger game, as surely as if they were ceramic pieces being moved among the levels of a chessboard. And when pawns came under attack, there was only one possible response.

Mount an offensive.

Spock's body pitched forward suddenly as the monorail car slowed with a jerk, then inclined sharply downward, plunging into what felt like an endless fall.

Completely taken by surprise, Spock did what no Vulcan child ever would—he cried out in alarm!

"I warned you about the force field," Kirk said. "Everything back where it should be? Stomach? Eyeballs?"

Spock sat ramrod upright on the bench seat, face as frozen as a statue's. If Kirk had to guess, he'd say the Vulcan was embarrassed by what had just happened.

"We are in a precarious situation," Spock said.

Kirk had come to understand a little about his Vulcan companion by now. Spock was probably not referring to being startled by the monorail maneuver. "Tell me about it."

Spock raised his eyebrows. "This is hardly the place to discuss—"

Kirk waved him to silence. "Another colloquialism, Stretch. I meant, I understand. I agree."

The monorail car slowed.

Kirk glanced at Spock, who'd regained his general-purpose equanimity. "By any chance, did you mean our position is even *more* precarious than you thought it was before?"

Spock nodded once. "We need to take action at once."

"Now you're talking." Kirk almost punched the Vulcan in the shoulder, but knew better by now.

The car stopped and the doors opened.

"Counterattack," Kirk said fiercely.

For once, Spock didn't question or protest.

As ordered, Kirk and Spock reported to a small lecture hall in Lily One—the main lab of the complex. They'd both been given advanced standing in an STC warp-propulsion specialty course already under way. But before they could attend the course, they would first need to complete a day-long orientation lecture and safety-training tour, then pass a follow-up examination.

Given that there were no lectures and tours for enlisted personnel scheduled, Kirk and Spock had been added to a group of Academy plebes—first-year mids—who'd just arrived for early orientation.

Kirk surveyed the five plebes clustered together, down at the lecturer's level, in the center of the hall. There were too few of them to bother with sitting in the banks of seats that ringed the small amphitheater. The plebes were all male, all fresh-faced and eager, with recruit-like stubble on their heads, and wearing immaculate midshipman gray uniforms, quite different from the baggy STC whites Kirk and Spock wore. All were the epitome of what Kirk had always termed "suckers."

He and Spock walked down the aisles and stood just behind the clustered plebes. Kirk shifted restlessly from one foot to another while an earnest orientation officer in a pale blue lab coat delivered a sanitized history lecture about Lily Sloane, leaving out the best parts of her stormy, on-again off-again relationship with Zefram Cochrane.

Next up was a safety officer, also in a lab coat. Her lecture topic was more interesting to Kirk: all the horrific ways careless mids could die in the warp lab should anything go wrong when they weren't prepared. At the end of her talk, the safety officer opened a case of delta-radiation monitors on the lectern beside her, then called out the first participant's name.

"Dedo, Andrew Jude."

Kirk didn't hide his disdainful smile as a dark-eyed young man with black bristles covering his freshly shorn scalp marched up to the lectern with all the bearing of someone who was about to receive a medal of valor.

"Dewhurst, Philip Peter."

Another eager young mid stepped forward proudly, this one as pale-skinned as the first had been tanned.

"Mubarak, Bish Salim." This mid was the tallest, and marched as if he had practiced for hours.

Kirk leaned over to Spock to whisper something sarcastic, but the Vulcan wasn't watching the parade of mids. He was holding one hand to his chest, apparently deep in thought.

"Something bothering you?" Kirk asked him quietly. Spock had seemed to recover from his monorail whiplash, but who knew with Vulcans?

"Why would they be giving us delta-radiation monitors?"

"So they can tell the difference between us being cooked

medium and well-done," Kirk said. "Why do you think they're giving them to us?"

"Silver, Charles Anthony," the safety officer called out. This blond and blue-eyed plebe was older than the others, and from the way he marched, Kirk guessed he had grown up on another world with slightly different gravity—he still didn't have his Earth legs.

"If the static warp core in this complex is not in operation," Spock said in a low voice, "then there is no chance of anyone being exposed to delta radiation. Therefore, assigning monitors is illogical."

Kirk watched Spock's hand at his chest. "You sure you're not hurt or anything?"

"Swarts, Phillip Frederick." The last plebe reported to the safety officer, green eyes intent, looking very serious.

"I am in excellent health," Spock said, almost petulantly.

"Then what's the problem?" Kirk asked. "They probably just want us to get used to wearing monitors."

"Kirk, James . . . Tiberius?"

Kirk chose to saunter, not march, to the safety officer, who pinned the thumb-sized monitor to his uniform, turned it on to make the green SAFE indicator light up, then pointed out to him the blue DANGER light. Kirk showed her he knew where the ALERT button was, then walked back to join Spock behind the plebes.

Except Spock wasn't there—until he reappeared a moment later.

He'd been on one knee, adjusting one of his boots.

"Spock . . . uh, Mr. Spock?"

Naturally, Spock attracted the attention of all five plebes as he received his delta-radiation monitor and had it demonstrated for him.

Back in his place with Kirk, Spock stood quietly as the safety officer then held up a small audio unit and played the lab's seven different alarm tones, defining each. She pointed out, quite unnecessarily, Kirk thought, that no one had ever actually heard the final, steady-tone alarm, because by the time that one sounded, every living thing inside the complex's force field would already be dead.

"Starfleet humor," Kirk whispered to Spock.

But Spock was lost in thought again, staring straight ahead.

Kirk sighed in relief when, after an interminable hour, the lecture part of the program came to a close and another orientation officer entered. This one, though, wore a full Starfleet uniform, complete with red shirt. No lab coat for him.

This officer looked over the seven members of his group, paying no more or less attention to Spock than to any other person. And then he said the words Kirk had been waiting for—the words that meant he and Spock could at last take action, fight back, find the evidence, and reveal the truth once and for all.

"Head out this door," the officer said, "turn left, and proceed across the plaza to the warp-core facility—what we like to call Ground Zero. Yeoman Bell will give you your tricorders at the main doors."

Tricorders, Kirk thought. *Yes!*

The rest of this was going to be easy.

38

It was the scene of the crime, and Kirk couldn't have been happier.

Ground Zero, also known as the warp-demonstration lab, was an austere industrial hall roughly the size of a tennis court. Half of it was given over to the traditional tiers of raised seats facing the other half—the lab area proper.

There, a fully operational, class-E shuttle warp core lay on a series of support pylons bolted to the floor. Five and a half meters long, half a meter in diameter, the core was a few years behind the latest class-F models used on modern shuttlecraft, but in basic design and function, it was little different from the first dual-nacelle cores handbuilt by Cochrane for use in the *Phoenix*, and later the *Bonaventure*.

Despite himself, Kirk whistled softly as he walked down the steep stairs that divided the tiered seats. "Two of those can do warp three for a week," he told Spock, "on less than five kilos of antimatter."

"Vulcan shuttles can achieve warp five," Spock remarked, ending the discussion.

As he made his way down the rest of the stairs and then across the lab area to stand by the core with the others, Kirk took careful note of the layout.

The floor in this lab was gray polyduranium, textured for traction. Though there was no need for that here, as the floor was quite unlikely to pitch and yaw, Kirk knew it was the decking of choice for most Starfleet engine rooms. He guessed that it had been installed in this lab simply to lend authenticity.

Since the banks of engineering computers were arranged about two meters away from the warp core, Kirk reckoned the test warp bubble it created was smaller than the cleared area. That area was clearly delineated by alternating hash marks of yellow and black. Blank for now, a large status board hung down from the high ceiling to the right of the core. The display board was angled for viewing both by any operators assigned to the control station to the left and by the students in the tiered seats.

There were no windows—the lab was underground. Some of its illumination came from worklights mounted over key computer stations, but mostly it came from bright lightstrips hanging from the ceiling. In the shadows above those fixtures, Kirk saw reinforced support beams and an intricate weaving of brightly painted pipes and conduits, carrying everything from fresh air to fire-suppression gases. Very few of the drab gray wall surfaces were finished to any extent.

Kirk had the sense the warp-core demonstration lab was in a constant state of change, perhaps to keep up with new developments in the technology.

Then he saw what he had come for—the dilithium vault.

It was in a far corner, though still visible from the student seats, a squat cube about chest height and, like the warp-core pylons, bolted directly into the polyduranium floor.

A security input panel was located beside the vault's door. Mounted below the door were two polished metal arms that could be swung up like rails to position the dilithium holding frame while it was being slid into or out of the vault interior once the door had been opened.

Overall, the vault was clearly not as secure as one that might be found in a civilian setting, so Kirk guessed it was like the floor here—a re-creation of the kind of security installation found on board a Starfleet vessel. *No wonder it was so easy to break into,* Kirk thought.

Of course, he reminded himself, on a vessel underway, the engine room would always be staffed, and there would be little opportunity for anyone to surreptitiously gain access to the vault. In this teaching lab, anyone who went to the vault would have to pass the operators, but if no operators were on duty and the lab wasn't in use, then there would be many times that there'd be no one here to be a witness.

To Kirk, that meant there had to be surveillance devices in place.

As the orientation officer began to identify the main parts of the core, Kirk looked around to locate the visual sensors he knew had to be present. They were easy to spot ringing the lab from wall mounts, and they were all standard. *Good,* he thought. They'd be as easy to fool with a sensor repeater as the ones he'd outwitted in the Starfleet parking lot last week.

"Mr. Kirk!"

Kirk started guiltily and shifted his full attention to the annoyed red-shirted officer.

"Since you are clearly so familiar with warp technology, perhaps you could tell the group why this grill is located in this position, and not where it would be easier to service?"

Kirk drew a blank, groaned inwardly. He'd heard nothing of the officer's lecture while he'd been scanning the room. If he were now sent from the lab in disgrace, that would be the end of any attempt to search the vault.

Beside him, Spock raised his hand to his mouth, coughed in such a way that it almost sounded as if he had said, "Plasma intercooler."

Kirk blinked and refocused his gaze on the officer. The man was standing near the raised grills of an intercooler access plate. That was all he needed to know. He began rattling off his answer to the challenge.

"The plasma intercooler provides plasma coolant to the

warp drive. In the event of overheating, emergency cooling can be manually initiated by a forced coolant dump. If the intercooler access grill was located in a position more convenient for servicing, that would also mean that in the event of a dump, superheated coolant would be directed toward the vehicle, instead of away from it, with the potential to cause a catastrophic hull breach and loss of vehicle."

The officer nodded, pleased. "Well done, Recruit. That's word for word. Is it your habit to memorize every textbook you read?"

"Just the interesting ones, sir."

The officer looked at the other mids. "That's how it's done, gentlemen." He patted the core. "You work with one of these, with two hundred fellow crew depending on it to get them home, and when something goes wrong, there's no time to look up procedures in the computer. *Everything* you need to know to save your ship and your crew has to be burned into permanent memory—" He tapped the side of his head. "—right here."

The officer then walked over to the nacelle cap and swung open the dome to reveal the photonic impeller blades. As he began to describe their operation, Kirk gave Spock the elbow.

Spock at once drew back, but nodded as Kirk whispered, "Thanks for protecting my back."

Kirk braced himself for the inevitable question, but Spock had a different question for him. "Have you actually memorized an entire warp-propulsion textbook?" the Vulcan whispered.

"Why?" Kirk asked. "Don't think we humans have it in us?"

But it was obvious that wasn't what Spock meant. "I was only curious to know when someone with your aversion to Starfleet would have had occasion to read such a text."

Kirk brushed off his interest. "Long space voyages." He

pointed to the dilithium vault in the corner. "Can you get a reading on that? See if you can pick up a carrier from a dormant jamming circuit?"

Spock examined the two parts of the tricorder he carried—the sensor wand in one hand, the main body hanging on a strap from his shoulder. He flicked the sensor on, checked the main unit's display. "In theory, yes. But I shall need to be closer." He looked apologetic. "This is marked as a training tricorder and its range has been severely restricted. Very illogical."

"Not really," Kirk said. "It's to avoid temptation."

Spock didn't understand.

"Tune it to the right frequencies and you can use it to see through clothes."

Spock was appalled.

Kirk suppressed a laugh. "We'll get closer," he said. Then, to avoid being asked a question about something he might *not* have memorized so many years ago, he paid attention to the rest of the officer's continuing lecture. Much as he hated to admit it, it *was* kind of interesting.

Forty-five minutes later, Kirk hadn't managed to get any closer to the dilithium vault, and the red-shirted officer was directing his group up the stairs, telling them how to proceed to the next point on their tour.

Kirk let the mids go first, then slipped his ball cap out of a utility pocket on his uniform trousers and moved to drop the cap along the side of his leg to land behind a seatback.

Spock was the only one to have seen what he did, but before he could say anything, Kirk shook his head no, and motioned for the Vulcan to start up the stairs.

Waiting at the lift in the corridor, Kirk suddenly raised his hand to get the officer's attention. "Sir, my cover must've fallen out of my pocket. May I go back to get it?"

All the mids looked at Kirk. Caps weren't part of *their* uniforms. Neither were pockets.

"In the lab?" the officer asked.

"I believe so, sir."

"You have two minutes—go!"

"Yes, sir!" Kirk ran back to the lab, counting seconds.

Outside the main doors, he set the tricorder to visual scan, opened one door a crack, slipped the sensor wand through, and captured a visual image of the empty lab beyond. Then, using a trick Joonie-Ben had showed him, he opened the back of the tricorder, removed the thumbnail-size range-delimiter card from the main sensor input, and reset the power output to maximum. Now the tricorder was capable of transmitting a sensor signal consisting of any pattern already stored in its memory. Kirk had turned the device into a crude sensor repeater.

As his count reached forty, Kirk pushed through the doors and charged down the stairs. With the tricorder transmitting the visual image of the empty lab, no visual sensor would record his presence—he hoped.

By a count of sixty-five, he was beside the dilithium vault, out of breath. He checked for the positions of the visual sensors, then slid down to the floor on the far side of the vault with his back to it. In this position, he couldn't be seen, and he changed the tricorder's function from transmit to scan. By seventy-five, he had begun to sweep up and down the translinear spectrum, trying to get an echo back from any nearby duotronic circuitry designed to dampen a security alarm.

He found it, focused . . . moved the sensor wand back and forth . . . and there it was! A clear signal coming from the door of the vault! Just as he'd suspected, the circuit that had protected the real thieves from discovery had been installed as part of the vault's upgrade.

The count was ninety, but Kirk didn't care. He'd estimated

that once he'd been gone for the two-minute mark, it would take another thirty seconds for the officer to reach the lab to search for him. If he was running up the stairs with his cap by then, everything would be fine.

Which meant he still had more than a minute to open the vault and grab the thieves' circuit, recording everything with his tricorder to show to Federation Security.

Kirk stood directly in front of the vault door, adjusted the tricorder to function as an override, then aimed the device at the vault, knowing he was now being recorded by the visual sensors. But that didn't matter anymore. He had nothing to hide. The authorities would *have* to listen to him.

He activated the jamming circuitry with a standard signal, then took a breath and, counting on Starfleet doing *everything* by the book, entered Elissa's security code into the tricorder's transmit function and pressed send.

Now that Elissa had been cleared of all wrongdoing, he anticipated that her codes had been restored. And they had.

Kirk almost whooped with relief as the vault door's lights blinked on, one by one, and he heard it click open.

He put the sensor wand on top of the vault, swung the thick door open, and—

There was nothing in the holding frame.

The dilithium that had replaced the stolen crystals was gone.

Kirk recovered swiftly, decided that couldn't be his problem now. He'd lost count of how much time he had, knew he had to hurry.

He checked the inner surface of the vault door, saw the access panel where the upgraded circuits had been installed.

And in the same instant that he realized he had nothing he could use to open that panel, a strange musical note rose up and the vault was washed by a flickering golden light.

Transporter.

With a sinking feeling, Kirk slowly turned just as three Starfleet Security officers with drawn laser pistols solidified around him.

Kirk raised his hands. "I can explain," he said.

No one was interested.

39

Fourteen-year-old Jimmy Kirk ran across the hard, frozen ground toward the glade that bordered the Leighton farm. The cold air burned his lungs, but he couldn't let that stop him. The kids were out here somewhere. His kids. His responsibility.

As the oldest in the cabin, he'd made sure their clothes were clean and they wrote notes back to their families and read the lessons about crop rotation and how to care for transcattle. But now he couldn't fool himself anymore about what was really happening. He couldn't look the other way and hope for the best. His job was to keep his kids alive.

He reached the edge of the glade, and the trees there rose up like a wave about to crash, a wall of black blocking the faint star glow of night. He paused to catch his breath before plunging into the utter darkness of the glade, searching desperately for any sign of the path the kids might have taken.

Then his eyes caught a red flicker to the left. Another. Two more after that. Laser fire in the glade. He flinched, apprehensive, afraid to call out. But he took off in the direction of the shots, running helter-skelter, banging into trees, stumbling over roots and fallen logs, catching his own laser rifle on low branches.

He was lost and on his own, and the only thing that kept him moving was his kids.

Up ahead he saw the flash and glow of palmlights moving in a clearing. At once, he forced himself to slow down and breathe quietly while he crept up to the clearing's edge, maintaining cover. He needed to see who held the palmlights and what they were doing.

Adults. Two of them. He thought he might have glimpsed other people in the clearing, maybe huddled or lying on the ground on the other side, but the palmlights no longer shone there, so he couldn't tell.

He held his position, unsure what to do, worried that Matthew and his followers would come crashing through from the other side. Then he'd never find the missing kids.

He thought quickly, frantically, then decided to let the adults go on their way, and dare crossing the clearing by himself. He tried not to think of what he might find on the other side. But if any of his kids were hiding there, then at least he'd see what had happened to them.

He concentrated on the two tall figures who stood together in the clearing, their palmlights spilling down, illuminating their legs and boots but nothing else. They appeared to be looking at something one of them held. Jimmy could see the pale blue glow that came up from it. It was just like the light from a small sensor display. Then —

Jimmy blinked. For just a moment, one of the adults had seemed to have two heads. He didn't think there were any aliens in this colony. He didn't know of any aliens with two heads. Would aliens be part of a rescue party?

The two figures turned in his direction, and Jimmy was pinned in the palmlights. The beams were so bright his eyes hurt and he couldn't see to run.

In his instant panic, he barely heard the voice calling out to him. "It's all right, child, come out. Nothing bad will happen."

Jimmy froze, conflicted. He knew that voice. It sounded kind.

"There's someone here who thinks he knows you."

"Jimmy?"

It was Donny Roy.

"Jimmy? I'm cold. Please help me."

Jimmy had no choice. He stood up and pushed through the last, crackling barricade of old dry branches and into the clearing, holding one hand to shield his eyes from the lights.

"Donny?"

He was close enough now to see the two adults clearly. One was an older teenager unknown to him. The other was a red-haired man with a high forehead and neatly trimmed beard and mustache. He looked familiar, maybe one of the farmers he had met this summer?

"Kirk?" the man asked, solving the mystery of why he'd appeared to have two heads. He was carrying Donny inside his cloak.

Now Jimmy knew why the red-haired man's voice was familiar. He'd heard it on the public-address announcement.

"I'm Jimmy Kirk. Are you the governor?"

"I am," the man confirmed. "Were you looking for your friend here?"

Kirk nodded. For no reason he could articulate, he knew he shouldn't mention he was looking for other kids, too.

"Well, there you go then." The governor gently let Donny to the ground and the little boy ran to Jimmy and wrapped his arms around his legs. Jimmy could feel his shivering.

"I've heard good things about you, Kirk. That's why you're on my list. You understand what it means to be on my list?"

Jimmy's fingers went to the red bandana he wore.

"That's right. It means you're working for me now. Helping our colony survive difficult times. Doing what we have to do. Do you agree?"

Jimmy could barely find his voice, but he managed to say, "Yes, sir."

"Good." The governor patted Donny's head. "Are you ready to help with this little fellow?"

Jimmy didn't know what was expected of him, so he repeated what he'd said before. "Yes, sir."

The governor looked down at Jimmy sternly. "I want you to take him back to the storehouses. Go to any of the big tables there." He pulled out a yellow card, handed it to Jimmy. "Give this to someone at the table—anyone with a red bandana—and tell them it's for your friend. They'll make sure he's reunited with his parents." The governor paused and gave Jimmy a piercing look. "It's important for children to be with their parents at a time like this. In difficult times, it's the best way. The only way."

Jimmy looked at the card. It said TARSUS IV EMERGENCY MEASURES ACT, GROUP 2. That was all.

"Questions?"

"N-no, sir."

"Next—" The governor reached into his pocket again, handed him another yellow card. "—you give them this card for you."

GROUP 2. Just like Donny's.

"I know you don't have parents here, but my people at the table will take care of you as well. Oh, and you won't need this anymore." The governor took Jimmy's rifle from him. "I'll take it back for you."

Jimmy fought to keep his thoughts from showing on his face. He knew to a certainty that the yellow cards meant he and Donny would be killed.

The governor hadn't finished his instructions. "If you find any more of your friends on your way back to the storehouses, those cards will work for them, too. Be sure to tell them that. If they go back to the storehouses with you, they'll join their parents or their guardians, somewhere nice and warm, and they won't have to worry about being hungry. Understand?"

Jimmy understood that the only reason the governor wasn't killing him right now was because other children needed to be rounded up. Like the ostriches and transcattle. "Yes, sir," he said in as strong a voice as he could muster.

The governor looked down at him, considering. His calm, measured breaths wreathed him in the spilled radiance of the palmlights, the glow like a nebula in deep space. Jimmy knew he would never, never, forget that face, that voice. If he lived.

"Off you go then. Do your part to help us all."

Jimmy reached down for Donny and lifted the small boy into his arms, willing himself to walk away, not flee in panic.

"Not that way," the governor said.

Jimmy had started for the clearing's far side where he thought he might have seen some other huddled children. Now he turned back. The governor was pointing to the dense bank of trees.

"That's the quickest way back."

"Yes, sir," Jimmy said. What he didn't say was what he knew now: The other kids were dead.

Holding Donny tight against him, he walked into shadow.

Jimmy wished with all his heart that his dad were here. His dad and his dad's starship and all his dad's friends in their uniforms beaming down with food and lasers and warm clothes. He wished that someone—anyone—would come to take this darkness from him.

Silently, in his mind, Jimmy sent out his call of distress. Over and over, calling for his dad and for Starfleet to save them all.

That cry still echoed in the mind of seventeen-year-old Jim Kirk when he woke in the darkness of his cell in the STC brig.

Three years on, and he still wished that someone would save him.

Spock was given fifteen minutes with the prisoner in the bright orange jumpsuit.

"Stretch. What's new?"

"Could you be more specific?"

Spock considered his question most reasonable. But Kirk frowned and leaned over the small, gray metal table where the guards had led them. "Okay, then—who's ahead in the lacrosse play-offs? What do you think I mean?"

Spock waited a moment before he spoke again. It was possible, he decided, that Kirk had been inquiring, in a very imprecise manner, about a general update. He edged his hard metal chair closer to the table, folded his hands, and leaned forward as well. Then he glanced to both sides to be certain the two guards weren't in position to overhear or read lips.

"I suspect Griffyn is within forty-eight hours of departing."

Kirk leaned even closer. "How do you know?"

"He is in the process of beaming freight containers from the *Pacific Rome* to an orbiting private cruiser."

Kirk grimaced as if in pain. Spock regarded him with some concern.

"I mean, *how* do you know? Did they let you off the center?"

"Ah," Spock said. "In addition to obtaining dilithium and staff cars, Griffyn has been purchasing rare artifacts stolen from the Vulcan Embassy, by Vulcan staff."

He'd already decided he could trust the human—at least that much.

This time Kirk looked confused. "Yeah, so?"

Spock leaned closer. "As I pursued the mystery of the embassy thefts, I presented myself as someone who could also supply Vulcan artifacts."

Kirk nodded, impatient. "Let's speed this along, Stretch. They only gave us fifteen minutes."

"I sold one to Dala. A small figurine. It was a forgery, of course. Undetectable by most methods because it contains a special transmitter that creates a false sensor image to make it appear authentic."

Kirk looked impressed. "Like a sensor repeater."

Spock knew that the transmitter he had designed was significantly better and more sophisticated than any sensor repeater Kirk had built, but decided this was not the time to remind the human of his inferiority. "The principles are somewhat the same," he allowed.

"But that still doesn't explain how you know what Griffyn's up to right now."

Spock idly brought a hand up to tap his chest, making certain the outline of his IDIC medallion could be seen through his white shirt. "The forged artifact contains a transmitter," he repeated.

Kirk's smile came more quickly than Spock had anticipated. "And that thing you're wearing is a receiver."

Spock folded his hands again.

"That's why you were worried about the delta radiation monitors," Kirk said. "You had to hide the receiver in your boot so you wouldn't set the monitor off when they pinned it right on top."

"As you said, we only have fifteen minutes," Spock reminded Kirk.

"What else do you know?"

But Spock had obtained few other facts through his listening device in Griffyn's office. So that the device would remain undetected, Spock had programmed it to record sound for hours at a time, then compress the data and transmit it at random intervals in microsecond-long, subspace bursts. Many times, it had simply recorded hours of silence when Griffyn's office was not in use.

He had, however, used his personal study time to access the Starfleet computer network from the STC's library.

"I did obtain a list of Starfleet material that has been stolen or reported missing in the past year, which is the period over which Griffyn's organization has been active. I believe he has assembled a collection of items which, if properly modified, will allow him to build a small vessel that will appear to all sensor scans as a legitimate Starfleet shuttlecraft."

Spock took Kirk's intent listening as the human's attempt to mentally re-create his logic. He was on the verge of telling him that they did not have enough time to complete such an exercise when Kirk held up a hand to suggest he not speak.

"Which would then give Griffyn a Starfleet shuttle that no one would suspect because no actual Starfleet shuttle will be known to have been stolen."

"Exactly," Spock agreed, surprised and impressed once again. "What particular use Griffyn intends for such a vessel, I do not know. The possibilities are many."

"Any theory why the Starfleet geniuses haven't figured this out?"

Spock blinked. "I believe that Starfleet analysts are not sufficiently devious to think as Griffyn does."

Kirk grinned. "And you are?"

"I have studied the literature quite extensively."

"Ah. And your conclusion, Sherlock?"

"Spock."

"Time's almost up . . ." Kirk warned.

"I believe that Starfleet analysts are aware of Griffyn's obtaining stolen Vulcan artifacts, and cannot reconcile those items with the other stolen goods. Their failure to do so prevents them from seeing how all the items fit the same pattern."

"You think the artifacts have something to do with building a fake Starfleet shuttlecraft."

Spock nodded, and just as he was about to guide the human through every step of his subtle, yet inexorable chain of logic, Kirk snapped his fingers and interrupted.

"Griffyn *knows* the artifacts are forgeries!"

Spock's eyebrows rose, beyond his conscious control. That was it, precisely.

"Griffyn knows *all* the Vulcan artifacts are forgeries! Yours and the ones from the embassy staff." Kirk's restless mood had changed completely. Now it was sharp, intense, focused. "But that's okay, because he only wants the circuits inside them that can fool sensors. He can use those to complete the illusion of the fake Starfleet vehicle he wants to build."

That conclusion was like a flash of lightning to Spock. Was it possible that there never was a criminal conspiracy *inside* the embassy? Could he have, instead, detected an official covert effort by embassy personnel to infiltrate an *outside* criminal conspiracy? If so, then the original artifacts had never been taken. They would still be safe, somewhere inside the embassy.

The logic of the plan unfolded with painful precision before Spock. Embassy personnel would have created two copies of each artifact they'd "stolen." One copy, with sensor-deceiving circuits, had been passed off to Griffyn. The second copy—what he had found in the embassy cabinet—would have been created as a safeguard against the possibility that Griffyn somehow tried to verify that the embassy thieves had left duplicates in place of the originals.

"You still there?" Kirk asked.

Spock wrenched his attention back to the present.

"One more question that needs your logic," Kirk said. "When you go through that list of things that Griffyn's stolen, is there anything he's missing? One last thing he needs to get—before he goes—so he can build his fake ship?"

Spock nodded. He had already run that exercise. "The dilithium Griffyn stole from the Academy is approximately half the amount he would need to operate a Starfleet-class warp drive suitable for a shuttlecraft."

Kirk's jaw tightened, an indication, Spock knew, that he was pursuing a thought with whatever baffling thought processes he used instead of logic.

"You know, I actually got as far as opening that dilithium vault before they arrested me."

That fact Spock hadn't known. The only information he'd been able to retrieve from the Starfleet computer system was that Recruit Kirk had been arrested and charged with attempted theft, and that Midshipman Corso had been implicated as his accomplice and was facing separation from the Academy. Additional details of the alleged crime were classified. Presumably that was to prevent others from identifying the security flaws that had allowed the attempted crime to take place.

"In other circumstances," Spock said, "I would offer congratulations."

"The thing is," Kirk said, "the maintenance log I accessed last week said that the stolen dilithium had been replaced with a new shipment. But when I opened the vault, it was empty. Is there any chance Griffyn managed to make off with the rest of it?"

Spock was pleased he knew the correct answer to that question. That he did so was one of the reasons his engineering course schedule had been rearranged this week.

"Dilithium is, as always, in short supply," he explained. "The replacement crystals that were shipped to the Sloane Complex have been requisitioned for more vital purposes."

"Which would be?"

"The *Starship Enterprise* is nearing the end of her refit, well ahead of schedule. The dilithium intended for her is still in transit from Delta Vega. Therefore, in order to expedite the calibration of her new engines, the dilithium from the Sloane Complex was transferred to Spacedock two days ago."

"And no one told me?" Kirk complained.

"You are not in the—" From the human's expression, Spock realized he should stop there. "Another colloquialism?"

"Sarcasm." Kirk hit his fist against his open palm. "So that's what we need to do."

Spock stared at him, concerned his concentration had faltered again and he had missed something significant Kirk had said.

"Think of it, Stretch. A starship undergoing refit. It won't have a full crew. Construction staff will be coming and going all the time. It's got to be a lot easier sneaking on board a vessel like that than getting into Ground Zero."

Spock didn't like the way the conversation was going. "Sneaking on board?"

"Griffyn's going to go after that dilithium," Kirk said. "And he's going to go after it in the next forty-eight hours."

Spock knew he wasn't keeping up with the human's rudimentary logic, and so did the human.

"That was your conclusion," Kirk reminded him. "He's getting set to go in forty-eight hours, and he needs that dilithium. All we have to do is get up on the *Enterprise* before him, wait for him to make his move, and we catch him in the act in the middle of Spacedock where he can't possibly get away."

Their time was up. The guards were walking toward the table.

Spock stood, regarding Kirk in Vulcan disbelief.

"What?" Kirk said. "That's logical, isn't it?"

"Except for one key point. You are in the brig."

"Just figure out how to get us on board that ship. Leave the details to me."

40

Even after centuries of war, disaster, and reconstruction, some traditions remained unchanged, and on Earth, the concept of the weekend still held sway.

For the mids of the Academy, the two-day break in routine that followed every five-day period of intensely scheduled activity was a time for independent study, private pursuits, and, for some, catch-up sleep. But for these two days in late August, for the recruits of the STC, it was also their first weekend liberty, and sleep was something that could be put off till early Monday morning.

As Spock prepared his bunk and locker for Saturday morning inspection, he was well aware of the plans the remaining members of Gold Team had made for their liberty. He was also well aware of their attempts to make it clear that none of their plans included him.

Even if he had been human, Spock doubted that exclusion would have troubled him. His own weekend plans were full, and they were certainly nothing he would share with any of his so-called teammates. He thought it unlikely that any of them would have the desire to risk spending the next two years in a penal colony, no matter how noble the cause.

In fact, the more Spock contemplated what he had planned, the more he thought it unlikely that until two weeks ago, *he* would have contemplated spending the next two years in a Starfleet penal colony.

But then, two weeks ago, he hadn't met Jim Kirk.

By 0800 hours, Gold Team had dispersed for the weekend, most going off in groups.

Spock walked by himself to the center's main gate where an embassy car awaited him, hovering in a holding area. As he got in the car and it soared away, he wondered if he'd be returning to Starfleet on Sunday night, or ever.

There were no weekend breaks in the brig.

Kirk was roused at 0500, and an extruded breakfast was passed to him through the security bars of his cell. He was given thirty minutes to prepare for the day's work detail.

It didn't matter that he had not yet been before a court-martial. Unlike his status at the time of his first brush with Starfleet authorities, he was no longer a civilian, and a different set of rules applied. Just by having lied to an officer about leaving his hat behind in order to gain unauthorized access to a secure facility—the Ground Zero lab—Kirk was enjoying ten days' incarceration at hard labor.

And, the guards promised him, those ten days would be a vacation compared to what was in store for him in New Zealand—the place he'd be going as soon as his court-martial was over.

The guards' cocky attitude set Kirk off, and he assured them in graphic detail that he had no intention of going to New Zealand *or* spending ten days at hard labor *or* remaining one hour longer than absolutely necessary in Starfleet.

The guards enjoyed his tirade, and an hour later Kirk was standing with a shovel, up to his knees with four other prisoners, in backed-up waste in the sub-subbasement of STC Building No. 5.

"Start shoveling," the crew boss told them.

"Join Starfleet, smell the worlds," one of the prisoners muttered.

Kirk just shoveled, knowing he wouldn't be here for long, though if asked, he couldn't have said exactly how he knew he would escape.

The *Kir'Shara* was the embodiment of Surak's teachings, which were in turn the foundation of Vulcan civilization. A replica of the ancient device, appearing to be nothing more than a narrow stone pyramid, scarcely a meter tall, stood in a place of honor in the meditation garden of the Vulcan compound.

It was there Spock found his father, contemplating the artifact that mirrored so well the conundrum faced by every modern Vulcan: How could it be that something so vital to the rule of logic had been lost by Vulcans, only to be found by a *human?*

For almost a century of Earth time, philosophers had contemplated that question. None, to date, had provided an answer.

"Have you had enough of this?" Sarek asked as Spock approached.

Spock's father wore a simple suit of brown cloth, devoid of any ceremonial gems or diplomatic markings. Spock was once again dressed in his dark civilian clothes and cloak. He saw his father raise an eyebrow as he noted his son's new hairstyle.

"Enough of what?" Spock asked. He stood near his father, hands behind his back. Both kept their attention on the *Kir'Shara* now.

"I believe humans would call it a 'game.'" Sarek did not bother to hide his disdain for the term from his son, though none but a Vulcan would recognize any change in Sarek's demeanor.

"You mean my enlistment in Starfleet."

"Of course, that is what I mean." Sarek was being short with Spock.

Spock felt he was ten years old again, being reprimanded for showing his dislike of being taunted by the other Vulcan children. "I find it an interesting experience."

"So is fasting for twelve days, but that does not mean one should fast for a year."

"My enlistment term is two years. I expect that time to be enlightening, and educational."

"It will be a waste of your time."

Spock had never heard his father speak so harshly.

"Father, by virtually all standards, I am an adult. I have the right to choose the direction of my education."

Sarek turned his attention from Spock to the alien blue sky above. Except for that glaring anomaly, because of the garden's design, only Vulcan vegetation and Vulcan buildings could be seen surrounding it. This was a place of refuge for those too long from their homeworld. Even the air here was scented with the dust and dried grasses of Vulcan's deserts.

"You have been confused by this world," Sarek said.

"I assure you, I have not."

Sarek cleared his throat. Spock often heard him do that when delivering a speech he did not entirely agree with. "Very well. If you wish to be treated as an adult, then I will arrange for you to receive a diplomatic security clearance. That will allow you to be told the details of what you believe to be a criminal enterprise operating within these walls."

"I know all the details."

Sarek gave him a skeptical look.

"The artifacts," Spock began, "that are being sold to a criminal organization run by a human known as Abel Griffyn are forgeries equipped with devices that return false sensor readings. In this manner, our embassy is cooperating with Earth authorities to learn the secrets of the organization, with emphasis on determining the reason for the unusual items it apparently is stealing."

Sarek looked at Spock as if he couldn't be certain it really was his son before him.

"You deduced this?" Sarek asked. "Through logic?"

"And investigation."

"Impressive."

Spock tried not to blush. Now he couldn't remember his father ever praising him so unreservedly. "Thank you."

"Do you wish to know the rest?" Sarek asked.

"Yes."

"Then you will need a security clearance."

Spock sensed his father was setting a logic trap. "Have I not already demonstrated that I deserve one?"

"Not by the little you managed to uncover on your own."

Spock knew he was stepping into the trap, but he had to know what his father was up to. "Very well. How will I obtain the clearance?"

"Resign from Starfleet. Accept your admission to the Science Academy." Sarek fixed his unblinking gaze on his son. "Then I will know you are an adult."

"And if I do not do as you suggest?"

"Spock, it would be illogical of you not to do as I suggest."

Spock was unable to control the flush of shame those cruel words sparked in him.

"I regret the need to be so blunt," Sarek said, though it was too late to cushion the shock of his insult. "But it is true."

Spock had never been so furious with his father. Calmly, he escalated their confrontation. "The consular agents, Strad and Kest, have been murdered by Abel Griffyn."

Sarek was so startled he took a step back from Spock before recovering. "We thought that might be a possibility. How do you know it to be true?"

"From an eyewitness."

"Who? The human boy who embroiled you in this?"

"No," Spock said. "And I involved myself when I discovered you did not trust me enough to tell me the truth."

"Spock, use your logic. Two of our consular agents have been murdered. Do you not understand the danger you face by your actions? My decision was not based on any measurement of my trust in you. It was based on my desire to protect you from harm."

"Why would you not tell me that at the time?"

Sarek gave Spock a look of subtle amusement. "Imagine the questions that admission would have unleashed from you. In that, you are much like your mother. Against all logic, it sometimes seems as if she is drawn to danger and . . . excitement."

"Interesting," Spock said. He had never considered that aspect of his mother's personality before, but he suddenly saw the logic in it. From a human perspective, how else to account for the desire to wed an alien and spend one's life on an alien world, if not, in at least some small part, for the excitement?

"'Interesting' is not an answer," Sarek said.

"I will not resign from Starfleet at this time."

"May I ask why?"

"The fact that you requested my resignation as a condition of telling me more about the theft ring suggests that the theft ring and Starfleet are connected. That confirms my assessment of what it is the theft ring wants."

Sarek was intrigued. "And what is your assessment?"

But Spock saw no reason for answering. If his own father, perhaps one of the most brilliant minds on Earth at this time, had not been able to deduce that Griffyn was intent on stealing the material needed to build a Starfleet shuttlecraft, then it could only mean that vital information had been withheld from him. And since the Vulcan Embassy was merely *assisting* the investigation, that implied that the vital information was being withheld by Starfleet itself.

Spock was suddenly struck by the realization that Jim Kirk might be right, and that at some level of command, Starfleet itself could not be trusted.

"Spock?" Sarek asked again. "Will you tell me your assessment?"

Spock followed through the likely chain of events that would be set in motion if his father was given data that the conspirators did not want him to have. None of the outcomes was acceptable.

"No," Spock said, because it was the only answer he could give.

Sarek lifted his head in affront. "For what reason?"

Because I wish to keep you from harm, Spock thought. But he could not voice that concern to his father. It would only inspire Sarek to redouble his efforts and bring him closer to the truth the conspirators did not want him to have.

"I regret that I cannot tell you at this time," Spock said. He checked the angle of the sun, calculated the time. There was still a great deal more for him to do. "I must go now."

"Where?"

"I have things to do."

"Related to this investigation of yours?"

"I would rather not say." Spock held up his hand, moved his fingers apart in the ancient gesture. "Peace and long life." Then he turned away.

But Sarek followed, almost as if he intended to block his son's way.

"Spock, you are an alien on an alien world. What can you do?"

Spock turned to face his father, so many things becoming clear to him. "You are mistaken, Father. On Earth, you are an alien. But like my mother, I am not."

41

Kirk could understand being shunned by his fellow members of Gold Team. They all had stars in their eyes, convinced they were part of some elite club of right-thinking do-gooders, none of them capable of accepting reality: that Starfleet was just another imperfect organization, imperfectly run by imperfect humans. History was littered with similar attempts at well-meaning grandeur, all of them praised at the beginning, then sent to the scrap heap in disgrace.

But what Kirk didn't understand was his being shunned by his four fellow prisoners.

They were all of them, him included, in the same position: each of them STC recruits in the STC brig, wearing the same garish Starfleet prisoner jumpsuit. As they'd set out for their morning work detail, he'd expected a certain level of camaraderie. After all, they were all "bad boys" who had fought back against the bureaucracy.

But apparently, that's not how the other four looked at it.

For some reason unknown to him, the other four were accepting of their incarceration and their punishment. Yet Kirk couldn't figure out why they were even being punished.

Paisley, a communications specialist from West Virginia, had committed the unspeakable offense of returning late from liberty, though he had missed no duty time. The soft-spoken Hamilton, within a month of shipping out as a security noncom on the *Enterprise*, had been caught "liberating" the flag of the visiting UESPA hockey team after the Starfleet hockey team he coached had beaten the visitors 18 to 2. Horn, a communications engineer, had apparently fallen behind his fellow conspirators during the commission of a prank and was the only recruit found in the commandant's office with a dozen squawking black chickens from the Colonial Agricultural Support Hall. And Rollins, covered with intricate Maori tattoos, had supposedly broken the chain of command by complaining about a lack of safety equipment in the engine lab to someone other than his direct superior—despite the fact that the safety equipment *had* been deficient.

Kirk had been stunned to hear how trivial the offenses had been, all of them resulting in one or two weekends of lost liberty and hard labor.

And yet, none of these hardened criminals—the most hardened Starfleet could come up with, it seemed—wanted anything to do with Kirk. When the others found out that *he* was the recruit caught tampering with the dilithium vault, they all kept their distance.

For his part, Kirk couldn't understand how people so dedicated to the system could ever survive at the cutting edge of exploration. Starfleet, as always, remained a mystery to him, and one he saw no way to solve.

By 0200 hours, Kirk's team had dredged away enough backed-up waste that a team of engineers could deploy a robotic probe to check the rest of the waste pipe leading to the main sewer system. For their efforts, the crew boss awarded them a fifteen-minute rest break before they'd have to move on to the next trouble spot on a lower level. His crewmates made quick work of their ration packs and water pouches, but Kirk did not. The smell of the place made the thought of food and drink impossible. But not the thought of escape.

So, while the other prisoners sat together and laughed and planned their next weekend liberty, Kirk sat to one side on a raised conduit pipe, tossing flecks of fallen insulation into the few pools of dark standing water that remained.

Fortunately, he knew, he would not be burdened by the

necessity of having to take the other prisoners with him. All he had to do was choose a time when the crew boss had left the work area, then he'd . . .

He looked up as a swath of light fell over him from the opening door of a utility closet in the stained, plasticrete block wall. A silhouette stood in the doorway—someone in the gray uniform of an Academy plebe. A very scrawny plebe with big ears.

Kirk eased off the conduit. As his boots hit ground, they splashed in a small puddle. But the other prisoners didn't look over or show they heard—the less they had to do with him, the better.

The silhouette held his finger to his lips, motioned Kirk forward.

Kirk called out that he had to use the head. His work crew kept talking, still not acknowledging him. So Kirk stepped through the door Spock had opened, and the door clicked shut behind him.

A few moments later, if Kirk's four fellow workmates had been looking, they'd have seen the thin band of flickering golden light that momentarily shone out from beneath the door, played over the wet surfaces, then faded from sight.

It was almost an hour before anyone realized Kirk was gone.

"Where are we?" Kirk asked. He was on a transporter pad somewhere, he knew. That much was obvious. But it wasn't at all like the one he'd glimpsed when Mallory had beamed him from the Sloane Complex to the plaza outside Starfleet Head-quarters.

"The Vulcan diplomatic compound."

Spock jumped down from the raised platform—large enough to transport ten people at a time, Kirk counted—and ran over to a control console.

"They just let anyone use this thing?"

"There is an elusive radiation leak that is defying the technicians' ability to detect." Spock was at the console, rapidly swapping data cards in and out of the input slots. "You will find your uniform and transporter pass over there." He nodded to a neatly folded pile of clothing on the floor by some kind of engineering display board covered with Vulcan script and flashing lights. "Leave your boots and coveralls on the pad."

Kirk kicked off his ruined workclothes. "No sonic shower?"

"I have set the transporter to exclude those aromatics."

Kirk sniffed the air as he climbed into his new uniform. Spock was right. He couldn't smell any of the sludge. "Nice trick."

"There is no trick. Vulcan transporter systems contain a database of the molecular frequencies of offensive odors."

Kirk tugged on his new boots. "Really? Then I'm surprised humans can use them."

"Vulcan transporter circuits did require considerable modification after first con—" Spock stopped and looked up, as if he had been caught revealing top-secret Vulcan intelligence.

"Are you ready?" he asked Kirk.

"Always. For what?"

Spock left the console, ran over to Kirk with two ID wafers. "These are Academy liberty passes. They will gain us access to Spacedock."

Kirk looked at Spock with surprise. "You have been busy."

A pounding noise suddenly came from a pair of sliding doors that remained closed.

"Unfortunately," Spock said, "I have also been forced to work quickly, with little time to 'cover my tracks,' I believe the colloquialism goes."

Now voices, calm but loud, called out from behind the

doors. Kirk guessed they were speaking a Vulcan dialect—he didn't understand a word.

"What're they saying?"

Spock handed Kirk one of the IDs, then ran back to the transporter platform. "They are attempting to offer support to the technicians they believe are trapped in here, being subjected to deadly radiation."

Kirk took his position on the transporter lens Spock indicated. Beside him, he noticed that Spock had donned an environmental modulator headband that covered his eyes with dark amber lenses, and his ears with acoustic baffles. Kirk was aware they were the type of device worn by colonists who had acclimated to, or had been genetically modified for, worlds with thin atmospheres. Since a few Academy mids might reasonably wear them, they were a good choice to cover up Spock's more prominent Vulcan features, without looking like a disguise.

"Should we say something to the guys at the door?" Kirk asked.

"That would only encourage their efforts to enter. According to the readings they're picking up, any Vulcan in here at this time would already be beyond saving."

A series of electronic tones came from the unattended control console.

"Is that right?" Kirk asked. "Are you beyond saving?"

"I believe that is likely," Spock answered. "But it shall be an interesting hypothesis to put to the test."

"I like your style, Stretch."

Spock flipped up his modulator lenses to see Kirk more clearly. "Indeed," was all he said.

"Indeed," Kirk replied with a smile.

Spock tapped his headband, and the lenses snapped down.

And then the transporter took them.

Elissa Corso stared at her empty closet, unwilling to close it yet. Reflexively, she untangled two hangers so even in its emptiness, the closet would reflect Starfleet standards of order. Only then did she close the door and turn for one last look at her dorm room.

Zee's padds and study guides and computer screen were neatly arranged on her desk. Elissa's desk was empty.

Her mattress was rolled up, linens folded neatly. Beside them, a laundry services bag and a Starfleet duffel contained her uniforms, exercise clothes, class supplies . . . anything and everything that would ever remind her of this place where her childhood dream had come true, and then had been crushed.

Her personal communicator chirped. The identifier display told her who it was.

Why not? Elissa thought. At least she was leaving Archer Hall with one good friend.

She flipped the communicator open. "Hi, Zee."

"You still there?"

"Just leaving. Are you around?"

"No, I . . . Look, I'm so sorry, but I've got an engineering seminar to help out with. I won't be able to get back for a couple of hours at least."

Elissa didn't question Zee, didn't ask for details. She understood completely. She was being separated for an honors violation—no sane mid would dare to have anything to do with her.

"It's okay. I gotta go."

"But it's so fast, Corso. I mean, they gave you a couple of days to prepare last time. They were going to hold an honor board. You had a chance to fight back."

Elissa didn't want to revisit the events of the last twenty-four hours. There was nothing more to think or feel. She was dead inside.

"They gave me a deal," she said flatly. "I signed a confession and agreed to accept separation for an honors violation, and Starfleet agreed not to come after me with criminal charges. As long as I go now, and go fast, that's the end of it."

"Criminal?" Zee sounded truly surprised. *"Your boyfriend tried to steal the dilithium, not you!"*

"Jim used my codes again. I was so stupid. And he knew it. He was only using me. And if I'm that easy to get to, I don't belong here. It's as simple as that."

"I wish you could fight it. I wish I was there and I wish you could go to the Commandant and tell him who really deserves to pay for this, and it isn't you."

"No. It's over. I'll go back to Risa. You . . . you go be an admiral or something."

"I'll come visit you on break."

Elissa knew Zee wouldn't, but appreciated the lie. "I'll see you then. Hot jets, huh?"

Zee didn't laugh at the old spaceman's greeting. *"You, too. Happy landings."* Then the circuit clicked off.

Elissa was finally alone with all that she'd lost. She hadn't told Zee, but she agreed with her on something.

Jim Kirk deserved to pay for what he'd done to her.

Zee snapped her communicator shut and cheered. "It worked!" She hugged Griffyn, pleased that Dala was down on the cargo deck with the boys. "You're brilliant."

Griffyn gave her a playful tap on her backside, then pushed her away—not the response she'd wanted. "She's really gone?"

"They had her sign a confession. The end."

Griffyn sat back in his chair. His voice echoed in his office—there was little left in it but the old furniture. All the crates, carpets, and other accumulated goods of the past year were packed and gone, transported up to the orbiting *Random*

Wave, the sleek little private transport he'd hired. Not much in the way of passenger amenities, though he wouldn't need it for long. And it had a remarkably large payload bay with a recently upgraded cargo transporter certified for biological organisms.

"So that's it?" Zee asked. "It's over?" She was in her Academy uniform. The long cloak she had used to cover it was folded on the old couch. She tugged down her gray shirt and sat on the edge of his desk, putting herself in easy reach, if he'd ever come to his senses.

"Almost. But for you, it is."

She reached out, put a hand on his chest. "Then I can come with you."

He sat unmoving until she removed her hand. "You know that's not going to happen."

Zee stared at him, feeling somehow abused. "I've done everything you've told me. That was the deal."

He reached up and took her chin in his hand. His grip was almost painful. Zee couldn't twist away.

"The deal isn't over, little admiral. You're home free on this one. You got us the dilithium. You got your idiot roommate to take the blame. You're perfectly in place. Three years from now you'll graduate, be assigned to Starfleet Command with a spotless record. Do you have any idea how valuable that makes you to the general?"

"That wasn't our deal."

Griffyn tightened his grip on her chin. Zee felt tears of pain sting her eyes. "Your only other option is to be dead. And that includes your family. You want to think that one over?" He released her and she almost lost her balance.

Zee knew she had to respond, and do so quickly. Her options had run out when she had placed herself in the general's power. But Griffyn could act. The general listened to him. All she had to do was give him incentive.

"All I'm saying is I want to go with you, Griff. I want to be with you. Doing the general's work on the frontier."

For once, Griffyn looked at her as if she meant something to him. "You don't want to be out there. This is a good assignment. No one's shooting at you. You've got a really good chance of not dying tomorrow."

"What about you?"

The intensity of his gaze weakened Zee. She didn't care what the dangers were. She had to follow him.

"This went well. So when I get to base, I know the first thing the general's going to do is send me out to do it again. And when I come back here, I'm going to need you again."

"I need you now," she said, risking his ridicule, but incapable of hiding her feelings any longer.

Griffyn stood and put his arms around her. "I know," he said into her hair, the heat of his breath soothing and exciting at the same time. "When I come back. No Dala. We'll be a team."

He stepped away, and Zee felt fluttery. "How long?" she asked.

"Four months," Griffyn said. "Six at the most. You should be on the Commandant's List by then."

"Deal," she said, already counting the days. But if she wasn't leaving with him now, then she knew that to keep herself valuable, she'd have to leave the *Pacific Rome* soon to go to her seminar and continue the mind-numbing monotony of being a mid.

Griffyn smiled. "I've just got one more thing to do before I go." He tapped a control on his communicator. Zee heard running footsteps on the metal stairs outside the office, leading up from the cargo deck. A moment later, Matthew rushed in, sweating, stained with dirt and packing grease from the work he was overseeing below. "Yes, sir," he said.

"One last loose end to tie up. A family matter."

Griffyn looked at Zee, and winked. A trickle of fear ran through her suddenly, then just as quickly vanished as she knew whose time had come.

The Kirk brothers.

She'd kill them herself if Griffyn asked her.

42

Kirk decided he was getting used to this transporter business. He felt a slight lurch in his stomach as the system compensated for the change from Earth's natural gravity to the artificial field he materialized in. And then . . . then it was as if nothing had happened at all.

"You do this a lot?" he asked Spock.

But the Vulcan was already on his way out of the transporter alcove. An amplified voice said, *"Please clear the platform for incoming traffic."*

Kirk leaped down after Spock and abruptly found himself in a stream of pedestrians, all moving to the right. He spotted Spock's headgear through the shifting landscape of shoulders—civilian, uniformed, and even a few alien—and sprinted after him. To his right, he passed transporter alcove after alcove, and travelers who were in the process of disappearing or reappearing.

The overlapping musical notes of the multiple beam-ins and beam-outs was magical. The constant ebb and flow of transporter light, the background hum of a hundred conversations, some in languages Kirk had never heard, all blended with nonstop announcements of arrivals and departures. He felt his heart race, his breath quicken. And his rapid breathing delivered scents to him he'd never experienced before—the sweat of humans who ate food grown in other ecosystems, the sweat of aliens whose chemistry had evolved on worlds a thousand light-years from Earth . . . Kirk's pace slowed. He felt himself bumped to one side, then another. It was as if he'd been swept up in rapids of memory, and he had no desire to swim to clear waters.

And then he felt a strong hand grip his arm and pull him to the side, out of the way of all the others who knew where they were going.

"Are you quite all right?" Spock asked. He looked concerned.

Kirk nodded, out of breath. "It's just . . . I had forgotten, that's all."

"Forgotten what?" Spock asked.

The old United Earth Transportation Hub was a smaller orbiting platform, primarily for commercial traffic, but to thirteen-year-old Jimmy Kirk, it was a stepping-stone to the realm that filled his dreams and his heart.

They had arrived by shuttle, father and son, and Jimmy had clutched his duffel all the way from Earth into orbit, and then again as he and his father had been cleared through customs, medical, and immigration.

It was his father's duffel, scuffed and mended with a faded Starfleet chevron and the names of three ships: three wondrous names that Jimmy still whispered each night before he slept.

U.S.S. Atlantis. U.S.S. Ames. U.S.S. Constitution.

They were the incantations of his childhood, and they had worked. Because here he was, looking through a viewport at a starship, not as grand as the ones whose names he'd learned so long ago, before he could recite the alphabet, but his starship—the one he would ride past all the planets and a thousand other stars, just like his father.

"There she is, son," his father said.

And Jimmy gazed out at the craft, little more than a blunt cylinder with twin nacelles: the Mariner Princess.

"She's a good ship," his father said, and put his arm around him, one last hug before the long absence and the missed birthday.

"Tarsus is going to be quite an adventure for you. A lot of fun, a lot of hard work, and if I know you, the second you get back, you won't be able to wait to go out there again."

Jimmy hung on every word, because what thirteen-year-old expects his father to lie to him?

"Nothing," Kirk told Spock. "I thought we were going to beam straight to the *Enterprise*."

Spock didn't seemed convinced, but pointed to a large main exit. "We must proceed to the Starfleet levels first."

"Always a catch," Kirk said, but he didn't hesitate.

Sam Kirk had run out of time and money. His brother was unreachable. His father's last message had come from Iowa, which meant he'd returned to the farm. That left him on his own again, alone in the city, with only Griffyn's gang for company.

Sam knew they would come for him. He knew Griffyn ruled his particular slice of Earth's fading, almost nonexistent underworld by fear. If a weak underling defied him by not doing as he was told and got away with that, others would start ignoring him as well.

I'll become his example.

Sam didn't doubt for a moment that that was the fate Griffyn had planned for him. His mind filled with a gruesome image: His body would be found with a hundred shallow laser burns crisscrossing it, hung upside down beneath some pier. Somewhere where the type of people who had dealings with Griffyn and his kind would be the first to see it.

The protectors wouldn't find his body for days. By then, the word would have spread, and Griffyn's lesson would have been communicated.

Defy Griffyn, and *this* is what you can expect.

But for all the time that Sam had worked for the gang

leader, endured his insults and his threats, knowing that those who failed to do as ordered met foul ends, he had never actually planned a personal escape.

His little brother would have, Sam knew. Of course, Jimmy never would have become involved with anyone like Griffyn, but show that kid a potentially dangerous situation, and his mind went to work on it, coming up with at least five different ways to backtrack or get out or simply avoid it. He was always figuring out the rules, Jimmy was, because when you knew all the rules, he'd say, then you'd know how to break them the right way.

Sam could only break the rules the wrong way.

And the rule he was breaking now was: Don't return to a known location.

He knew he was taking a terrible risk, but what else could he do? Hidden in his apartment was the thousand-credit wafer Griffyn had given him—the down payment for delivering Jimmy to the *Pacific Rome.* Sam had been afraid to carry it around with him. What if Griffyn asked for it back and he'd lost it when he blacked out in one of the establishments he liked to visit where the doors had no signs?

But now Sam needed that money himself. He'd worked out a half-formed plan to travel to New Zealand, to the Starfleet penal colony. He was guessing Jimmy might turn up there.

He pictured the look on Jimmy's face when he saw that his first visitor at the colony was him. It would be great. They'd be able to make plans again. They'd both get another chance. Sam clung to the reassuring thought. It gave him something to look forward to.

And then Sam reached the top of the emergency stairwell of his apartment building. He took a moment to steady his nerves, preparing to do one of the most dangerous things he'd ever done—enter his own apartment.

• • •

The first thing Sam noticed was the smell. There really wasn't one. Not a bad one, at least. Instead, his apartment smelled the way home had, years ago. *Dad,* he thought. The old man was obsessive when it came to keeping things ship-shape.

Sam knew enough not to turn on any lights. Not until he'd checked things out. So he waited inside the shuttered apartment, letting his eyes adjust to aquarium light and the faint glow of daylight coming through the slatted metal blinds. Gradually, he began to see the signs of his father's handi-work—everything *had* been cleaned up and straightened out.

At least he knew his fish had been cared for when he'd been hiding out. Joe Kirk would have seen to that.

That thought brought another swiftly to his mind. Sam stopped, uncertain, sorry he'd used the block inhaler before starting up the stairs. The block made life feel easier, but it kept him from thinking straight.

Who would look after his fish for him now?

He couldn't leave them. Jimmy would be in some place like New Zealand. *Maybe,* Sam thought, *I should call Dad again. Better yet, Mom. She could talk Dad into coming back for my aquarium. They could probably arrange the money for a transporter trip, at least on the way back. That'd be easier on my fish.*

Sam felt better. He'd figured out a plan himself. He'd get the cee-wafer, pack a bag, then, when he was back on the street and out of danger, he'd call home, tell his parents about the fish. Everything would work out fine.

He patted his jacket, felt the inhaler there. Maybe he should use it again, now that the problem with the fish was settled. That'd make packing easier. He pulled it out of his pocket.

That's when the hallway door behind him smashed open and he was thrown to the side.

Before he could get up by himself, he was dragged to his feet. Two kids he'd never seen before. But they smelled like packing grease and the bay, so he could guess where they'd come from.

One of them slapped his hand against a wall control, and the apartment filled with light as a third person entered.

Matthew stopped in front of him. No laser rifle. He had the alien weapon, and he was pointing it at him.

"Georgie."

Sam gave up then, as if a switch had been thrown or a circuit cut. "Just kill me now," he said.

"Aww, you're not going to snivel? Beg? Try to cut a deal?"

Sam shook his head. Without his brother or his dad, he had no way out of this, so why even bother.

"Where's the fun in that, Georgie? Griffyn told me we could have fun with you."

"I messed up, okay?" Sam said tonelessly. He was so tired. He felt the inhaler still in his hand, even though his hands were being held tight behind his back. He wondered if Matthew would let him use it one more time before they started to do whatever it was they were going to do to him. "I always mess up."

Matthew seemed disappointed. "You trying to become an honest man or something?"

"No, I'm nothing."

Matthew looked at his two soldiers. "Well, this is going to be a dull afternoon." He made an adjustment on the alien weapon. "Let's liven things up." He fired at the wall beside the kitchen alcove, scorching a framed poster for an exhibition of Tellarite mudsketches at the Exploratorium. The poster was ten years old. It had been there when Sam moved in.

Matthew frowned at Sam's lack of reaction. He fired into the couch, and a cushion exploded as the foam inside the fabric was released. Then he aimed at the aquarium.

"Not the fish," Sam said. His pulse fluttered. "C'mon."

Matthew brightened. "So you do care about something."

Sam tried to pull free from the kids but failed. "Matthew! You got me! That's all Griffyn wants! Leave 'em alone!"

"Gotta make you hurt somehow, Georgie. Griffyn's orders."

He fired the weapon and a lance of energy shattered the tank, spraying sparks where the mechanics of the pump and the light were disrupted. A cloud of steam hissed, and superheated water erupted from the jagged hole. Quick flashes of shivering orange and white cascaded to the floor.

Sam Kirk lost the capacity of rational thought.

Using strength his captors had not suspected, Sam wrenched his arms free and with an inarticulate cry of rage, brought his elbow up to smash the nose of one kid and spun to lodge his fist in the gut of the other.

Matthew just had time to lose his sneer as Sam lunged at him, using one arm to deflect the alien weapon as it swung toward its new target and the other hand to switch on the inhaler and spray its contents directly into Matthew's face.

Sam's mindless charge took him forward, barreling Matthew over until they fell, Sam landing solidly on top of his would-be assassin, spraying even more of the block as Matthew desperately gulped for air, stunned by the unexpected impact and fall.

Then Matthew's flailing arms flopped unsteadily to the floor as the block took effect. He moaned, unhurt but incapable of coordinated movement.

Sam heard movement behind him, spun around to see the two kids charge him, ready to take him down by themselves.

But Sam had the alien weapon now and he fired it, sweeping back and forth, stunning his attackers and dropping them instantly.

Still not thinking anything coherent, weapon in hand, Sam rushed to the ruin of the tank. His fish lay motionless on the floor. Dead. Because of him. Because of what he'd let his life become.

He couldn't leave them there like that, so he emptied out a cylinder of fish food and carefully laid the tiny forms inside together. He put the container back in the aquarium, on the damp gravel, and rearranged a few of the rocks that had been their favorite places for hide and seek.

A part of Sam knew that his fish had lasted this long only because Jimmy or Joe Kirk had taken care of them, just as they'd tried to take care of him. But he wasn't a kid anymore, and his family couldn't take care of his whole life.

Grieving, Sam lifted his inhaler in his hand, shook it. He heard the liquid slosh inside, enough block for another dose or two. Enough to ease his pain for now.

He knew Jimmy wouldn't use the block. Jimmy would already be making plans to be sure that nothing bad like this ever happened again.

It was a hard decision, and it surprised Sam that he could reach it without assistance. He put the inhaler in the damp gravel beside the container and said good-bye to both.

A few minutes later, he had stuffed his bag with clothes, put the thousand-cee wafer in his pocket.

The two kids were unconscious, breathing slowly. Matthew was singing some kind of song to himself, waving his fingers back and forth in front of his nose, oblivious to where he was and to the fact that Sam stood over him with a deadly alien weapon.

It would be so easy, Sam knew, as easy as using the inhaler, to fire the weapon at Matthew and keep firing until the stun effect stopped his heart or paralyzed his lungs. That would pay him back for a year of abuse.

But then, Sam thought, *I'd really be the same as him. And what would Jimmy think of me?*

He dropped the weapon on the floor, drove his heel into its barrel until it snapped and released a small puff of smoke.

He was finished here. It was time to make a real plan.

43

Reaching the Starfleet levels of Spacedock was deceptively simple. Kirk and Spock merely walked up a sloping pedestrian ramp and held their IDs at shoulder level as they passed through two of twenty-one sensor stations. To Kirk, the sensor stations looked like nothing more than empty doorframes.

"That's it?" he asked as he saw Spock attach his ID back on the equipment belt he wore under his gray midshipman's shirt.

"Yes," Spock said. He looked ahead, pointed to the left. "The viewing levels lead to the airlock decks."

Kirk attached his own ID to his belt. All around them, walking purposefully, were uniformed men and women in a surprising variety of Starfleet uniforms and civilian clothes. Kirk saw none of the crowding and pushing of the exotic public levels of Spacedock, yet the sense of charged excitement here was even more intense than it had been below.

"Can I ask how you managed to collect all this?" Kirk gestured so Spock would know he meant the uniforms and the passes and the IDs.

Spock began walking forward quickly, moving just as decisively as everyone else on this level. "Apparently, there are times when Vulcan diplomatic staff and political appointees need to travel to various Starfleet facilities, yet, because of security issues, do not wish their visit to be part of the public record. To aid such classified visits, Starfleet provides the embassy with documents and uniforms."

Kirk kept his eyes front as he matched Spock's pace. "So what you're saying is, you stole these disguises?"

Spock risked a glance at Kirk, broke stride. "I am an employee of the embassy. Therefore, I have the full right to use its facilities. Admittedly, I might have erred when I submitted my request for these items to the office of a clerk who has since returned to Vulcan. However, I am certain that the request will be forwarded to the proper clerk by tomorrow afternoon."

"And they'll turn it down, right?"

"Who can know the future?"

They passed through a large doorway and had just turned the corner when Kirk glanced ahead. He almost stumbled, caught himself. "Oh . . ." he said, or thought he said. He was vaguely aware that his voice sounded hoarse, but not much else registered as he stared at what lay before him.

An unending row of viewports, three decks high, looking into the vast technological cavern of Spacedock's largest berthing area.

And just outside those viewports, the spotlit, blue-white majesty of a legend. She was almost 300 meters long, almost 75 meters tall. Her saucer-shaped primary hull racing forward even at rest, exquisitely balanced by her soaring warp nacelles that rose up to either side like outspread wings. To carry her through the infinities.

She was beautiful.

He knew her shape intimately, from countless images, but never—*never*—had he seen her like this, alive, in person, so close he could almost touch her.

"The *Enterprise*," he breathed. And somewhere in the distant reaches of his memory, he heard Joe Kirk proclaiming the names of the stars in just such a voice, as an old dream he had all but forgotten reawakened within him.

Kirk heard Spock's voice as if from afar. "We should hurry. There is much we must do."

"I know," Kirk said, and together they rushed on.

• • •

The main personnel umbilical tunnel from the first airlock level of the drydock facility joined the *Enterprise* at an airlock in the lower aft section of her primary hull. And whatever majesty the ship possessed as seen from her exterior, on the interior there was none. At least, not in the cargo bay beyond that airlock.

A red-shirted security officer stood at the open pressure door, arms folded imposingly. Kirk noticed at once that he had one of the newest tricorder models with the sensor apparatus further miniaturized and now part of a single main unit. One good thing about Starfleet—it always gave its people the best toys.

Spock came to a stop at the ridge of the docking-collar pressure seal marking the line where the umbilical tunnel ended and the starship began. "Midshipmen Newman and Jones request permission to come aboard, Lieutenant," he said.

The officer took Kirk's and Spock's IDs, activated them. "Here for the seminars?" he asked.

Kirk didn't know what to reply. *What seminars?* he thought. But Spock seemed to know what to expect and said, "Yes, sir."

The lieutenant clearly approved of the way Spock had responded, as snappy and crisp as any new recruit.

"Which one?"

Kirk saw Spock blink behind his lenses. Apparently, that was a question he wasn't expecting.

Fortunately, it appeared the officer had had some experience with confused midshipmen. "Leadership or Engineering?"

"Engineering!" Kirk and Spock said it together. Main engineering was where the dilithium was stored, so that's where they'd wait for Griffyn to make his move.

The officer nodded, handed back the IDs. "Midshipman

Newman, Midshipman Jones, welcome aboard the *U.S.S. Enterprise.*" He pointed past a forest of scaffolding where workers were installing conduits in the exposed overhead, two decks up. Welding sparks cascaded down to bounce off the polyduranium decking and stacks of tarp-covered hex crates. "The turbolift's outside the main doors over there—look for the silver doors. Get in, tell the computer to take you to Deck Eighteen. You'll want Briefing Room Seven, halfway along the corridor on the left."

Then Kirk took his first step aboard the *Enterprise.*

The tunnel had had a bit of a bounce to it, as the artificial gravity field of Spacedock overlapped that of the starship, but once Kirk took that first step, the gravity that held him was solid and certain.

Kirk felt his chest relax. It felt like home.

The new turbolift control panel was smaller than the old one, and so was kept in place by gray tape. Handwritten notations were scrawled on the wall, indicating where new mounting holes were to be drilled.

"This ship isn't even five years old," Kirk said wonderingly.

"Starfleet policy," Spock explained. "No starship is ever completely finished. Upgrades are constant as technologies are refined."

Kirk considered that statement as Spock told the computer which deck they wanted. He'd always thought of Starfleet as a hopelessly moribund organization, mired in the past. It appeared their starships weren't.

There was a slight sway as the lift car began moving to the side, then another as it began to drop. Kirk visualized their location based on his mental picture of the exterior. He reckoned the car had taken them directly aft through the saucer section, and that they were now traveling straight down the angled support pylon connecting the primary and secondary hulls. Somewhere in his mind's memory files, he retrieved the information that Deck 18 was one of the uppermost ones in the secondary hull. That could pose a problem. "I don't think Eighteen's the engineering deck," he told Spock.

"Correct. Main engineering is one deck down. There will be ladders."

"Ladders," Kirk said as the turbolift hummed to a stop and the doors puffed open. "Advanced technology. Of course."

Kirk's attention was on full alert as they stepped into the corridor. He noted that this section of the vessel, at least, looked as if the refit had been completed. The walls and traction carpet were new and unworn in an artfully blended range of monochromatic grays. The corridor felt slightly cramped to him, with its series of narrow, A-frame emergency pressure seals every few meters. But considering that the ship could carry a crew of two hundred, he conceded that space, even in a vessel as large as this, had to be at a premium.

Spock started walking to the left.

"Wait," Kirk said. "We're not really going to the seminar, are we?"

Spock's serious expression indicated he had no intention of wasting any additional time. "There will be an interdeck ladder at the end of this corridor. We will use it to descend to Deck Nineteen."

"How do you know so much about this ship?"

"I studied the deck map."

Kirk had seen a deck map posted outside the umbilical tunnel entrance, but they had passed it in seconds. "When?" he asked.

"When we passed it at the entrance to the umbilical tunnel," Spock answered.

Kirk walked the rest of the way beside Spock in silence, telling himself he had to stop underestimating the Vulcan. Probably, *all* Vulcans.

The corridor took them past Briefing Room 7, where some sort of engineering seminar was being held for mids. But Kirk and Spock kept eyes front. Neither slowed down or looked in.

Which is why they didn't notice the seminar leader notice them.

Midshipman Zee Bayloff was on her personal communicator in seconds.

44

The curving corridor on Deck 19 looked like a war zone—the refit here was still in progress. There was no carpet. Kirk's and Spock's boots rang on the only deck surface: gleaming bare antigrav plates of splotchy anodized blue-gray. The corridor's starboard bulkhead was missing for most of its length, revealing an impenetrable wall of densely packed pipes and wires that Kirk never would have suspected existed. And the corridor's uneven lighting issued from a string of plasma globes haphazardly hanging from overhead supports. A few of the globes were flickering, their charges running out.

"This is no way to treat this ship," Kirk said as he stepped around antigrav work platforms and equipment carts.

"I am sure the *Enterprise* is not aware of how she is being treated," Spock countered.

"That's not the point." Kirk straightened a work order sheet that was clipped to a cable that'd been pulled out of a conduit. Then he had the jarring realization that that was something his father might have done. He made a mental note not to repeat his action. It was bad enough he had his father's haircut.

The silver door to engineering was not much larger than any of the others they'd passed, so Kirk guessed there must be other ways into it—how else to install the equipment that must be inside? Then he wondered if the fact that it was closed meant that he and Spock would need some kind of additional clearance to enter.

"Do we just walk up to it?" Kirk asked.

"I am aware of no special security measures in effect," Spock said.

Kirk walked up to the closed door, and at the last moment, it slipped open and he stepped into the heart of the *Enterprise.*

The first thing that struck him about the facility, other than its double height overhead, was that it was staffed. In a manner of speaking.

Two plebes were working at a section of the long, black control console that ran along the starboard side of the room. From the tense way they spoke to each other, they had a problem to solve and weren't solving it. But as if in counterpoint to the tension between them, a second classman with the metallic shirt and longer hair that marked his year, leaned against a nearby stair rail, arms folded, with a delighted grin plastered across his face.

That grin widened as he saw Kirk and Spock. "Ah," he said in a lilting Irish brogue that Kirk suspected was not how the mid usually spoke. "Fresh victims!"

Kirk and Spock exchanged a look. They had expected workers to be present, not trainees.

"Shaun Finnegan," the smiling mid announced as he approached the newcomers. "And you would be . . . ?"

Spock stood at attention and Kirk realized he should follow suit: They were wearing third-classman uniforms, indicating they were about to begin their second year in the Academy. But Finnegan was a second classman, beginning his third year, so according to the Academy's code of conduct, they should report to him as they would any superior officer.

"Midshipman Newman," Spock said.

"Midshipman Jones," Kirk said.

Finnegan made a face, disappointed. "Newman and Jones? You're not scheduled for any tests here."

"Our scheduled seminar has been delayed," Spock said

promptly, and Kirk was impressed with how easily he concocted that story on the fly. "So we have elected to undertake an orientation tour."

"On your own? That's not quite Starfleet procedure. Which company would you be with?"

Kirk took up the explanation, ignoring the question. "A ship in this kind of shape, there's a lot of confusion."

Before Finnegan could repeat himself, one of the plebes at the console called to him in a voice of despair. "Mr. Finnegan, we can't rectify the input signals." The plebe was at least a head taller than Spock and had auburn stubble and broad features. In centuries past, his soft accent could only have been labeled Russian, but Kirk heard the slightly clipped compression of his vowels. The plebe was someone who had grown up in the Martian Colonies.

The second plebe turned from the console. Her strong but balanced features conveyed strength more than beauty, but only slightly more. Her eyes were the same gray as her uniform, and her stark black hair had been cut stylishly like a skin-tight cap with delicately feathered bangs. It was well within regulation length, but it most certainly was not the work of a Starfleet barber. She was holding up a single-unit tricorder. "But this says we've done everything right and the circuit is perfect."

Finnegan made a show of rubbing his chin in thought. "Hmm, y'don't say. Then might I make a tiny suggestion?"

"Please," the martian plebe said.

"In a case like this," Finnegan continued with utmost sincerity, "you'll find it's vital to double-check the interior connections of the duotronic ports."

The Martian and the striking young woman looked at each other as if Finnegan had just given them instructions in Klingon. The Martian spoke first. "We don't know how to do that on this equipment."

"Ah," Finnegan said, as if the mystery of the universe had just been revealed to him. "What you'll need to do first is to unlatch the M-4 module to the right, there, then swing it open, and that's where you'll see it, sure as I'm standing here."

The plebes nodded, turned back to the console. Kirk heard several clicks as contact points were released, and then both plebes jumped back with cries of startled shock as giant alien worms erupted from the console to attack them.

Kirk reflexively started forward to help the plebes fight the creatures, but Spock's hand gripped his shoulder and kept him from making a fool of himself.

As peals of Finnegan's laughter echoed in the engineering hold, the alien worms bounced and skittered across the deck, revealed as nothing more than springs wrapped in brightly colored cloth.

The plebes were embarrassed and, Kirk could easily see, angered. But they said nothing, and even attempted good-natured smiles as Finnegan extolled the virtues of always expecting the unexpected in space.

Finnegan picked up one of the spring snakes, a particularly lurid purple and pink monster. He admired the way it flopped around as he came back to Kirk and Spock. "Now, where were we?" he asked. "Ah, yes, you were avoiding my very simple question. Which company would you be with?"

Kirk waited to hear what story Spock was going to come up with this time when the main door puffed open behind them. At first, Kirk was thankful for the interruption. Then he saw who had entered and realized the time for stories was over.

"Jimmy," Zee said from the open doorway, almost purring, "what a surprise." She looked at Spock. "Who's the alien?"

"Alien, is it?" Finnegan asked. He walked around Kirk and

Spock to stand near Zee as she stepped forward and the door behind her closed.

Kirk could see that Spock understood there was no more reason to remain in disguise. He took off his modulator headpiece.

"A Vulcan?" Finnegan said in surprise. Then he smiled. "In a midshipman's uniform when the Academy has no Vulcans at all, at all." He turned to Zee with no attempt to conceal his pleasure. "Would you happen to be knowing these two, then? Newman and Jones they called themselves."

"Meet Jimmy Kirk and Mr. Spock," Zee said. She seemed just as pleased as Finnegan.

Kirk stepped forward. "I can explain. The people who stole the dilithium from the Academy—they're going to try to steal the dilithium here."

Zee shook her head. "Nice try, Jimmy, but Elissa confessed. She's left the Academy, and last I heard she was buying a ticket back to Risa."

"She left . . . ? But she didn't do anything." Kirk had an idea and acted on it swiftly. He pointed to the two confused plebes who hadn't budged from the booby-trapped console. "You two, what're your names?"

"Naderi," the Martian told him.

The young woman said, "Del Mar."

"Okay," Kirk said, "Naderi, Del Mar, use your tricorders on . . ." He looked around the engine room, saw the accelerator chamber stretching into the distance behind its wall of safety screen, the modular power converters lined up on the port side, then found what he was looking for in the forward section. "That!"

"Dilithium storage?" Naderi asked.

"Check the security function. Look for a signal-jamming circuit."

"No!" Zee ordered. "Don't listen to him."

Kirk saw the plebes automatically respond to the chain of command. Zee wore her third-year uniform and on that basis outranked them.

Zee gave Kirk a smug smile of triumph, pulled out her communicator.

But Finnegan interrupted. "Close that thing for a moment, would you. There's something not right here."

Zee hesitated. Finnegan's Irish brogue faded a bit as he took control of the situation. "I gave you an order, Midshipman. Your uniform tells me you're a third classman—" He waggled a finger at Kirk and Spock. "—just like these two imposters, it seems."

Kirk could see that Zee disliked being compared to him and Spock. "I'm Zee Bayloff. Company Twelve." She held out her communicator. "You can call administration and confirm."

Finnegan took the communicator, kept it shut. "Now that that's settled, may I ask a question?"

"Call administration," Zee urged.

Finnegan's smile disappeared completely. "I'm the ranking mid here, so I'll give the orders. Now why don't you want the dilithium vault scanned? Seems suspicious to me."

Zee stayed silent. But her face revealed frustration.

"All right, then," Finnegan said. "Mr. Naderi, Ms. Del Mar, scan the vault as Mr. Kirk suggested."

Kirk looked at Spock, wondering if he'd have to change his opinion of Academy midshipmen, as well. This Finnegan seemed to be a reasonable guy, giant spring-loaded alien worms notwithstanding.

The plebes weren't yet proficient with their tricorders, so Finnegan let Kirk help them with the settings. Both got the same results—the security system in the vault was defective.

"Is there dilithium in the vault?" Kirk asked Finnegan.

Finnegan looked concerned by the tricorder results. "The warp core's cold and not due for calibration till next week," he said. "So I'd say yes." He took another look at one of the tricorders, adjusted a few settings, then handed it back to Naderi.

"For a moment there," Finnegan said to the group, "with all this funny business going on, I was thinking to myself that maybe a few of my friends were trying to play a small prank on me. Though why, I couldn't tell you. But now, I think we've gone a little too far and it's time to move this up the line." He opened Zee's communicator.

"You can't do that!" Zee protested.

Finnegan narrowed his eyes. "And why is that?"

Zee sighed as if giving up. "Because it is a prank. Not on you." She pointed to Kirk and Spock. "On them. Classmates." She gave a sheepish grin. "Guess I played it too seriously."

An uncertain smile played over Finnegan. "Now I like a good joke as much as the next mid, but . . ." He trailed off as Spock moved to stand before him, head cocked, eyes questioning.

"Mr. Finnegan," Spock said, "do I *look* like an Academy midshipman?"

That was when Kirk put the final piece of the puzzle in place. "It was you!" he said to Zee.

Finnegan looked at Kirk, puzzled. But he didn't stop him from talking.

"You're part of Griffyn's gang," Kirk said to Zee. *"You* got him Elissa's codes to steal the Academy dilithium." Kirk pointed to the vault. "And *you're* here to steal that dilithium, too! How?" he demanded. "What's the plan?"

Zee stared at him like someone trapped before a stampede. But before she could defend herself or confess or simply argue that he was mistaken, a blaring alarm rang out, reverberating in the oversize engineering compartment.

"What's that?" Naderi asked.

"It is the alarm code for an escape-pod drill," Spock said loudly.

Finnegan frowned. "But we're in Spacedock."

And then, the ship's computer voice joined the alarm, and to Kirk, everything became clear.

"This is an emergency evacuation order," the measured, mechanistic voice calmly intoned. *"All personnel must abandon ship at once. This is not a drill. Repeat: This is not a drill."*

Kirk knew exactly how Zee planned to steal the dilithium. He just didn't know how to stop her. Yet.

45

The *Random Wave* was a small ship by most standards, and could easily fit within the saucer section of Starfleet's *Enterprise*. Her flattened warp nacelles lay tight to her single, crescent-shaped hull. The configuration meant that her overlapping warp bubbles could be smaller and thus required less energy, though at the same time it restricted her top speed to slightly more than factor 4.5.

In short, she was a commercial vessel intended for local voyages: the Alpha Centauri colonies, Vulcan, an occasional vacation run to Risa. To reach the Federation's frontiers would take her almost a year, and yet, she was the ship Abel Griffyn hired to carry his illegal cargo to the general at the frontlines of the great struggle.

The Starfleet analysts had not been able to calculate the reason for Griffyn's decision, nor the connection between the stolen Vulcan artifacts and the disassembled components of Starfleet technology that Griffyn's operation had amassed. When it came to finding a common pattern underlying that operation's goals, nothing seemed to fit, which is why Starfleet had made the difficult decision to observe, rather than act.

Griffyn, however, knew exactly what he was doing. And, unaware of how minutely each of his decisions had been studied and debated by those unused to true criminal behavior, he had taken all but the last few steps he needed to leave Earth.

In less than twenty hours, the operation would be over, and he would return to the general, victorious.

At the same time that Kirk and Spock were watching spring-loaded snakes burst from an engineering console on the *Enterprise*, Griffyn stood in the empty cargo hold of the *Pacific Rome* and took one final look at the safest home he had ever had. He felt no regret. His capacity to feel that and most other emotions had long since been beaten from him by the harsh conditions of the life he'd led in the general's camps. His constant and relentless exposure to life and death, brutal punishment and sublime reward, had taught him to give the highest value to survival.

Satisfied that no trace of his operation remained on the freighter, Griffyn took out his subspace communicator and gave the order for transport. The hold dissolved around him and, a timeless instant later, he stepped off the transporter platform in the crammed cargo hold of the orbiting *Random Wave*.

Dala was there to greet him, dressed in working clothes for a change: green overalls and brown boots, with her hair tucked into a cap. It seemed strange to see her without her usual shimmer of bold facial color, but she honored him with her usual insincere smile. It was a shame they wouldn't be spending more time on this ship. He knew many ways to change that smile.

Dala held up her own subspace communicator for Griffyn. "Right on schedule," she reported.

Even over the communicator's small speaker, Griffyn could hear she was right. He recognized the blare of a Starfleet evacuation alarm. It had to be coming from one of the acoustical bugs his little admiral had placed on the *Enterprise.*

"Has Zee checked in?" Griffyn asked. He walked with Dala toward the low cargo-bay entrance that led to the corridor.

"Twenty minutes ago," Dala said. "And get this—Jimmy Kirk and the Vulcan are on board."

Griffyn's eyes lit up as he considered the new possibilities available to him. Since Elissa Corso had been separated from the Academy, she was no longer a candidate for taking the blame for a second dilithium theft. Kirk and Spock, though, could definitely be the new front-runners. Perhaps he wouldn't have to sacrifice Zee after all.

He hurried along the narrow corridor, turning sideways to fit through the pressure-seal frames. Dala followed close behind.

"Has she opened the vault yet?" he asked over his shoulder.

"Haven't heard a thing since her last report."

Griffyn's mood changed abruptly. The plan had called for Zee to place her open-link communicator on the dilithium holding frame once she had opened the vault. That should have occurred within forty seconds of the evacuation drill.

"How long has the alarm been active?" he asked sharply.

Dala checked the communicator readout. "Almost two minutes."

Griffyn slapped his hand against the wall control that called the small ship's only turbolift. "Something's gone wrong."

Dala tapped the communicator against her chin. "Aww, poor Zee."

Griffyn didn't have time for any of this. He wasn't about to waste a year of effort because of a last-minute foul-up. "Tell the others we're breaking orbit. We're going right now."

Dala widened her eyes ingenuously. "You're not going to try to rescue Zee?"

"What do you think?" Griffyn growled.

Dala smiled. "Just what you're thinking." She kissed him until the turbolift arrived.

In the main engineering compartment of the *Enterprise*, Finnegan ran for the main doors and they slid open before him. Then he turned back as he realized no one was following. "Can't you hear the alarm?! Abandon ship!" The alarm grew in volume. Finnegan raised his voice to be heard. "That's an order!"

The two plebes, Naderi and Del Mar, indoctrinated in Starfleet procedure, bolted forward, heading for Finnegan, but Kirk blocked their way—to do what he had to do, he'd need all the help he could get.

"No!" he shouted. "This isn't a real emergency!"

"Then what is it, for bloody sake?" Finnegan shouted back.

"It's to cover for a theft!" Kirk knew he was right because Spock nodded in agreement. "We have to stay here to protect the dilithium!"

"Mr. Finnegan, what do we do?" Del Mar called out.

All eyes went to Finnegan, including Kirk's and Spock's. The plebe's question was correct. Finnegan was the ranking member of Starfleet. What he decided would determine if Del Mar and Naderi stayed or went.

"You saw the tricorder readings!" Kirk urged. "The vault's been tampered with."

Finnegan hesitated, then stepped away from the doors and they closed. "Right you are, then. Tell me what you know."

Though Kirk could tell the upperclassman wasn't happy with his decision, he'd made the right one.

But before Kirk could explain, Zee launched herself at Finnegan from behind, and with three quick blows to his side, his neck, and his head, she dropped him to the deck before he even realized he was under attack.

Now flushed, breathless, she faced Kirk, Spock, and the two plebes.

Kirk felt sure she'd acted from desperation, because she had no options. "You can't fight us all," he said loudly as he motioned to the others to fan out and surround her.

But Zee held out her communicator as if it was a weapon. Warily, she began to edge toward the dilithium vault. "I don't have to fight you," she shouted. "I just have to tag the dilithium and I will be out of here."

A new electronic chime joined the evacuation alarm.

"What's *that* one?!" Naderi exclaimed, addressing no one in particular.

Out of the corner of his eye, Kirk saw Spock reach into his shirt, pull out his Vulcan medallion. The chime got louder when the medallion was free. Kirk understood.

"Stretch, that transmitter—is it working like a tracking module?"

Spock snapped open the medallion and Kirk saw a small, glowing display inside. "Yes," Spock confirmed. "But not for long."

Kirk kept his attention on Zee, moving between her and the vault. "Why not? The power cell's running down?"

"No," Spock answered, his voice clear and loud. "This tone means Griffyn's ship has left Earth orbit. Once he leaves the system, he will be out of range."

"No . . . ," Zee cried.

Kirk and Spock both stared at her.

"He doesn't have the rest of the dilithium!" she shouted. "He wouldn't leave without that! He wouldn't leave me to take the blame!"

Kirk understood exactly what had happened. Zee cared for Griffyn. But Griffyn had only used Zee.

"Zee, listen." Kirk tried to be kind even though he still had to yell over the alarm. "You didn't get him the dilithium, so that's why he's cut you loose. You were just another one of his gang, no one special."

Zee, overcome, stared at the communicator in her hand, then suddenly threw it to the deck where it cracked into pieces.

The alarm cut out. The computer voice announced, *"Evacuation complete."*

Del Mar was already kneeling by Finnegan, taking his pulse with two fingers on his neck. She didn't look worried, and Kirk took that as a good sign. "So . . . Ms. Bayloff," Del Mar said, "what do we do now?"

Kirk groaned as the implications of her question struck him. Zee was still the ranking member of Starfleet. The plebes had to look to her. She could even order them to take Spock and him into custody.

But Kirk wasn't about to give control of this situation to anyone else, not when there was still a chance to salvage it.

"Zee," he said urgently, "look at what we've got here." He gestured to include all of engineering. "A *starship.* Let's go catch him!"

Zee looked at him in open disbelief. "You think *you* can run this thing?"

Kirk glanced at Spock. "I've read some operations manuals. How about you?"

Spock swallowed. "Three," he said.

That was good enough for Kirk. He turned back to Zee. "We can at least try."

Zee stared at him in indecision until the other plebe prompted her again. "We need orders, Miss," Naderi said.

Kirk considered Zee's shrug as her indication of defeat. He was right. She *was* out of options. Wild elation rose in him.

Zee pointed at Kirk. "Do what he says."

The plebes had their orders and looked to Kirk expectantly.

For his part, Kirk fought down his excitement and tried to look composed. He glanced at Spock. "You think you can find the bridge?"

46

The silver turbolift doors swept open and without a moment's hesitation, Kirk rushed out.

The bridge of the *Enterprise* was pristine, each surface newly refinished. The lenses of the optical controls at the science station gleamed like jewels. The gray safety rail that ringed the upper deck shone like a sculptor's polished stone. The white duty chairs were spotless; the small hooded viewers on their flexible necks were perfectly aligned at helm and navigation; and the almost square main viewscreen displayed a close-up of a Spacedock brace with brilliant clarity.

Against the subdued gray tones of the bulkheads and deck, and the pure black of the surrounding consoles, the myriad status displays of the ship seemed alive with intense and shifting colors.

Kirk absorbed all of this in just a heartbeat, and the sensation of it, the sight and sound and even the crisp smell of it, burned into his mind as a permanent, unalterable memory.

But even in that moment, there was no time to savor it.

Kirk ran to the helm station, started to sit.

Spock stopped him. "I can operate the maneuvering thrusters." Spock pointed to the center of the bridge. "This is your mission, that is your place."

Kirk stared at the command chair, made no move toward it.

"Even if we succeed in bringing the ship's systems online," Spock said, "Spacedock Control will not let us leave unless we can provide a sufficient explanation."

Kirk raised his empty hands. "I don't have one." *So close,* he thought, intensely frustrated, disappointed. Without that explanation there was nothing to do except wait for security to come back on board and then spend the next two years in New Zealand trying to get someone to believe him.

Then Midshipman Del Mar said, "We were scheduled for a training cruise tomorrow." She and Naderi were gently positioning Finnegan's unconscious form on the upper deck by the engineering station.

"That's perfect!" Kirk said. He worked out a new plan in a second. "We'll go a day early." He turned to Spock. "Can you call up the cruise details on the computer?"

Spock entered some basic codes at the helm station. "Already programmed," he said, sounding surprised.

Kirk looked past the command chair at the communications station. "Who knows how to run comm?"

Zee took the position. "I guess that's me," she said.

Kirk went to her, put an encouraging hand on her shoulder. "Let them know you're a mid on a training cruise. The evac drill is over, and now we're ready to go on our cruise a day ahead of schedule."

Zee found the controls for programmed hailing frequencies. "I'll give it a try."

Kirk felt adrenaline begin to flood him. He spoke faster, moved more quickly. "Naderi, Del Mar—who can handle engineering? We'll need propulsion."

Naderi stepped carefully over Finnegan. "I know the station, but I'd never be able to control thrust in such a small volume."

"Don't worry about Spacedock," Kirk said. "If they buy our story, they'll use tractor beams to get us out of here. Once we're in open space, can you give the helm what it needs?"

Naderi nodded, still somewhat less than confident.

Kirk pointed to Del Mar. "Tell me you can navigate."

She snapped to attention. "Sort of."

"Close enough," Kirk said.

She took her position beside Spock.

Kirk looked back at Zee. "What's the word?"

Zee appeared shocked. "Uh, they gave us clearance to go on the cruise."

"Really?" Kirk asked.

Spock turned in his chair. "I would suggest we not allow them the time to reconsider."

"Good point," Kirk said. He looked at the comm controls on the arm of the command chair. "Is it this white one?" he asked Zee.

She pressed a control on her console. "Go," she said.

Kirk thought back to his cruise on the *Mariner Princess.* The captain had allowed him on the bridge for departure from the United Earth Transportation Hub. *How different could it be?*

Kirk pressed the white button. "Spacedock Control, this is the *Enterprise,* ready to depart."

Kirk looked around the bridge, saw that everyone else was looking at him. Then a voice came over the bridge speakers.

"Enterprise, *this is Spacedock Control. You are cleared for departure. Stand by for umbilical detach."*

From far distant places in the vast ship came the sounds of airlocks being sealed and the thump of umbilical tunnels and restraining clamps releasing.

"Umbilical detach confirm. Sit back, Enterprise, *and enjoy the ride."*

Kirk directed everyone's attention to the viewscreen. The Spacedock frame grew smaller as the ship's optical sensor backed up from it.

"I don't believe it," Kirk said.

Spock turned back to him again. "Tell me about it."

The viewscreen in Mallory's office showed an image of the *Enterprise* slowly pivoting in the berthing area.

Mallory thought about what Kirk must be feeling and tried not to smile. His guest wasn't as amused as he was.

"This has gone far enough," SCIS Special Agent in Charge Luis Hamer said. If he had been annoyed at Mallory before, now he was furious. "You're letting them steal a *starship!*"

"I'm letting them borrow it."

"Why?!"

Mallory didn't reply, and eventually Hamer seemed to realize he wouldn't for a very good reason.

The answer was classified.

The lead flight controller from Spacedock contacted Mallory again. His voice came from the deskscreen that now showed the *Enterprise* aligned with Spacedock's main doors.

"This is it, Mr. Mallory. Are you sure we should open the doors?"

Mallory knew what a gamble this was. But he had also read the preliminary report from the experts on his steering committee.

They had suggested a plan that would give Starfleet a different way to confront the general's threat. The cost would be high, but not as high as sending security forces to slaughter children.

Mallory didn't know whether or not the tactic would work. But to him, what was transpiring in Spacedock right now was the dry run.

Project Echion would go forward or would be rejected, based on what happened when he gave his next order.

"This is Mallory at Starfleet Command," he said into his communicator. "Open the doors. Let's see what happens."

47

"They're opening the doors." Kirk stared at the image on the viewscreen as if in a dream.

The *Enterprise* slipped forward, under the control of Spacedock's tractor beams.

"They still have thirty seconds to realize their mistake," Spock pointed out.

"Thank you for those encouraging words."

Kirk was still standing beside the center chair, and though he glanced at it from time to time, he made no move to sit in it.

Then the thirty seconds had passed, and all the viewscreen showed was space and stars.

"Um, what do we do now?" Del Mar asked.

"Spock," Kirk said, "can you get a heading from your tracker?"

Spock opened the Vulcan medallion and placed it on the helm console. He read off coordinates from the display and Del Mar entered them. "This isn't looking good," she said, worried.

"Where's he going?" Kirk asked.

"Out of the main traffic lanes. I'd say he was getting ready to go to— Oh no. He did."

Kirk tried to see what Del Mar had seen on the medallion's display, but the display was blank.

"It would appear that Griffyn has gone to warp," Spock announced.

Kirk asked a question he already knew the answer to. "Anyone know how to start a warp engine?"

"I know it takes about a day," Naderi said. "Um, if the dilithium crystals are already installed. Which ours aren't. Because they're still in the vault."

Kirk gave the plebe a tight smile. "I can only come up with one thing to do," he told his erstwhile crew.

"Go back?" Del Mar asked.

Kirk shook his head, insulted. "No. Set a course to follow Griffyn's initial heading. Maybe . . . maybe his warp engine will blow or something and we can catch up." He looked toward the engineering station. "Hey, Naderi. We do have full impulse, right?"

"Aye, sir."

"Aye?" Kirk repeated, then let it go. "Just give the helm and navigation all the power you can give them."

Naderi seemed not to know how to reply, so he just nodded once, forcefully, and went back to his board.

"Course laid in," Del Mar said. Then she added, "No! Wait . . . wait . . ." She readjusted her board settings. "Okay . . . okay, that's right. Now the course is laid in."

Kirk waved his hand forward. "Then . . . uh, full speed ahead, Mr. Spock."

They all froze in place as a strange rumbling filled the bridge, but then the stars on the viewscreen shifted to the side as the ship changed heading and began to accelerate.

"Pursuing at one-half impulse," Spock called out.

Kirk leaned against the chair. There was nothing to do now except wait to be caught.

Then he heard a distinctive chime again, and saw Spock pick up the medallion.

"Fascinating," the Vulcan said.

"What is?" Kirk asked.

"The tracker is working again."

Kirk felt the thrill of exhilaration. "He dropped out of warp?"

Spock nodded as he studied the medallion's display. "And he appears to have entered orbit of Neptune."

Kirk did the math swiftly. "Average distance to Neptune is . . . what? Four point one, four point two billion kilometers?"

Del Mar entered something on her board. "Right now, the nav database shows it at four billion, two million, eight hundred thousand . . . and the rest just keeps changing."

"Okay," Kirk said, "at half impulse, that puts us there in . . . just under five hours. Let's go. Lay in a course. Full speed. Whatever it takes."

With those stirring words, the *Enterprise* raced for Neptune.

"Neptune?" Hamer repeated. "Why Neptune?"

Mallory checked a data readout on his deskscreen. "That's where Griffyn's ship is."

Hamer looked over Mallory's shoulder. "All that material he stole during the past year, and he's taken it to *Neptune?*"

"It can't be his final destination," Mallory said. "He could be refueling at Triton Station, checking to see if he's being pursued, or . . . he's identified another source of dilithium."

"Are there any warp facilities in near-Neptune space?"

Mallory input more search strings, read out the results. "Two ships have been lost at Neptune, but decades ago. They both burned up in the upper atmosphere. If any wreckage survived, it looks like Griffyn would have to retrieve it from the bottom of eighteen thousand kilometers of nitrogen, water, and ice—at pressures that would have fractured any dilithium crystals within days."

"Has anything crashed on the moons?"

Mallory checked. Neptune had nine classic moons and twenty-seven moonlets. There had been a few crash landings and failed launches from them over the years, but according to Starfleet records, no significant wrecks remained unsalvaged. "Nothing."

He tapped the control that turned off the screen and stood up from his desk.

"What now?" Hamer asked.

"I'd say Kirk and Spock have the right idea," Mallory answered. "We're going to Neptune."

48

"I don't think I can do this," Del Mar said.

On the main viewscreen, Kirk saw the blue dot of Neptune growing perceptibly larger. "That's a planet," he said. "This is a starship. Isn't there an automated setting for standard orbit?"

"Not for Neptune."

Spock turned from the helm. "It is not a standard planet. Its magnetosphere is dramatically misaligned to its axis of rotation, resulting in severe electromagnetic distortions for the instruments of orbiting vehicles. It has four rings and more than thirty moons and moonlets, even the least of which could cause considerable damage to this vessel."

Kirk didn't want to hear about obstacles. "There's got to be some way to figure out how to orbit it."

"There is," Spock said. "Four years of advanced astro-navigation studies."

Neptune was growing ever larger. Now Kirk could make out delicate white swirls of clouds against a soft background haze of sky blue. The planet looked welcoming, though intellectually he knew the temperature of that appealing blue haze was more than 200 Celsius degrees below zero.

"We didn't come all this way just to do a flyby," Kirk said. All he could think was that if Griffyn knew how to orbit this planet, then— The idea came to him that fast. "Stretch! Use the ship's sensors to find Griffyn's ship, then *match his orbit!*"

Spock looked around the bridge, saw what he was looking for. "I will need to use the science station."

"Go," Kirk said, and as Spock got up from the helm, Kirk took his place.

Neptune filled almost half the viewscreen now. Del Mar gave Kirk a hopeful smile. "I got us here. Now it's up to you."

Kirk checked the layout of the controls. They were nothing like the flyers he had flown.

Del Mar seemed to realize what was happening. "Any of those look familiar?"

Kirk laced his fingers, cracked his knuckles. "Lots of computers on this ship. How hard can it be?"

Del Mar's faint smile remained frozen in place as Kirk took the *Enterprise* off her programmed flight path and began to fly her manually.

Griffyn sat back in the command chair of the *Random Wave*, enjoying the shoulder rub Dala was giving him, ignoring Matthew.

Matthew, with a bandaged broken nose from Sam Kirk's attack, sat in tense disgrace at the sensor control station, under no illusion what the general's reaction would be to his failure.

When Matthew had reported to Griffyn after his humiliating defeat, Griffyn had arranged to have Matthew and his two bloodied soldiers beamed directly up to the *Random Wave*. But when Matthew had stepped off the transporter platform, his two soldiers were no longer with him. At Griffyn's order, their matter streams had not been collected—instead, they had simply been beamed into nothingness, their disassociated molecules becoming an expanding cloud that rapidly faded from sight.

Griffyn relished the peace and quiet that kind of punishment brought to his ship. He doubted anyone would be complaining for weeks to come.

For now, then, the only sound on the small ship's flight deck was the occasional ping from the navigational shields and sensor array, as various particles of ring and moon debris were contacted in the orbital path. The contacts were so infrequent and small, to Griffyn the sound was like the white noise of running water. He found it quite soothing.

Until a loud buzz jerked him upright. "What was that?!"

"Collision alarm," Matthew said. His fingers flew over his input board. "I don't get it. It's some kind of meteoroid."

"Avoid it!" Griffyn said.

"The auto system's been trying," Matthew told him. "But it keeps changing course to . . ." He looked over at Griffyn. "It keeps changing course."

"On-screen!"

And there it was.

The *Starship Enterprise*.

Closing erratically, but closing all the same.

On the *Enterprise*, the collision alarms sounded.

"Too close! Too close!" Del Mar said.

Kirk adjusted the ship's rate of descent. He had wanted to bring her in at a slightly higher orbit directly behind and above Griffyn's vessel. He had heard that proximity sensors usually had the weakest coverage in that area—not in a Starfleet vessel, of course, but civilian ships were another matter. "Are the shields up?" Kirk called out.

"Yeah! Got 'em!" Naderi answered.

Kirk risked looking up from his board for a few seconds to see what was on the screen.

The half-crescent shape of Griffyn's ship was ahead, and it was slowly listing into a 360-degree roll.

"Why's he rolling like that?" Kirk asked.

"He is not," Spock said from the science station. "We are."

"I want to know why the sensors didn't see that coming," Griffyn demanded.

Matthew worked furiously, checked all the sensor settings. "They did! They did! But Griffyn, look at the readings—there's no crew on that thing! There's no warp engine! The power signature's flat! I can't even tell if it has shields!"He looked up at Griffyn like a fearful child expecting to be beaten."So many readings are below the threshold, the sensors didn't recognize it as a ship!"

Griffyn glared at the viewscreen. "It's a Starfleet starship! How can the sensors not recognize *that?!*"

In the middle of the commotion, Dala remained by the command chair, leaning on one elbow that rested on the chair's tall back."I wonder why it's rolling like that."

Then a signal chime sounded.

"We're being hailed,"Matthew said.

Griffyn snapped his fingers, and Dala ran to the comm station to answer.

A deep voice growled out of the flight deck's speakers. *"Unidentified civilian cruiser, this is the, uh, captain of the* U.S.S. Enterprise. *You are in, uh, restricted Starfleet space. Drop your shields and prepare to be taken in tow."*

Griffyn put both hands to his head in absolute fury. "How?!"He slapped Matthew across the side of his head."We were on full alert and—"

"Shh!"Dala hissed."Listen!"

The flight deck speakers were still picking up the transmission from the *Enterprise,* only now the captain's gruff voice was missing from the mix. Instead, someone who sounded more familiar said, *"I think they bought it. Are their shields down yet?"*

And someone else said, *"Which one of these is the tractor control?"*

And someone else said, *"Can the tractor beam work through our shields, or do we have to shut down, too?"*

And the oh-so-familiar voice of Griffyn's little admiral said, *"Oh, crap. Guys, this is still on."*

Click. The transmission ended.

Griffyn couldn't contain his relief or his shout of triumph.

"Maybe they didn't hear the rest of it," Zee said.

Kirk, Spock, Naderi, and Del Mar stared at her accusingly. Finnegan still lay mute and motionless on the upper deck.

"I didn't do it on purpose!" Zee protested. "I want to get him as much as you do!"

Kirk raised his hands like a referee sending fighters back into their corners. "It's okay. He's not responding. He probably turned off his—"

Griffyn's gleeful voice boomed over the bridge speakers. *"Captain Jimmy of the U.S.S. Enterprise, I don't know how you managed to steal a starship, but I've got to thank you for delivering it to me."*

"He heard it," Zee said dejectedly.

"If you can figure out how to use your sensors, you might want to check our weapons status."

Kirk looked at Spock. The Vulcan was waving his hands over the optical switches, changing the displays above the science station until a schematic of Griffyn's ship appeared with flashing red lights at the weapons nodes. The Vulcan couldn't hide his apprehension. "Two phase cannons. Old-fashioned, but powered up and effective."

"That should've been enough time," Griffyn continued. *"So now that you see what you're up against, play it smart, Jimmy. Drop your shields and prepare to be boarded. Or wait for us to shoot your bridge full of holes, and then prepare to be boarded."*

"What's our weapons status?" Kirk asked Del Mar.

The plebe moved to the helm seat Kirk had vacated. "Fully charged phaser banks!"

"Phasers?! That's state of the art!" Naderi said excitedly.

"Can you fire them?" Kirk asked.

Del Mar nodded. "In simulations."

"Let's see how good they were. Fire a warning shot . . . across their bow!" Kirk glanced over at Spock. "Always wanted to say that."

Del Mar made adjustments to her board, pressed a large control, and a powerful capacitor discharge echoed in the bridge.

At the same instant, a flare of scintillating light burst from the viewscreen as a shaft of phased energy hit Griffyn's ship dead center!

"I said across the bow!"

Del Mar spun around and shrugged apologetically. "I told you I've never fired these things!"

Kirk looked back to the viewscreen—Griffyn's ship was missing. "Where'd he go?!"

"He has dropped below us," Spock said calmly, "and now is rising behind us. Ah, he is on an attack run."

"Shields!"

"They're already on!" Naderi told Kirk.

"Those are navigation shields," Spock pointed out. "We will need protection from weapons fire."

Naderi looked as if he was in pain. "I . . . I haven't had that class yet."

"Stretch—find the shield controls!" Kirk shouted, then he launched himself back to the helm station, reached over Del Mar, who sank into her chair, and jammed all the controls to port.

"Fire!" Griffyn shouted.

Matthew hit the controls, and just as a pulse of phase-cannon fire shot into the range of the viewscreen, the *Enterprise* spun out of sight.

"What?!"

Then the *Random Wave*'s collision warning sirens screamed as the viewscreen was blocked by a rapidly moving warp nacelle that was completing its roll and—

Above the peaceful blue clouds of Neptune, the small half-crescent of the *Random Wave* spun away from the collision like a badminton bird slammed by a baseball bat.

Both vessels were traveling at almost the same orbital velocities, so the overall force of the impact didn't overwhelm their shields and structural integrity fields.

But from both ships, gouts of transtator current flared from shattered conduits, and streamers of venting atmospheric gases made crazy pinwheel patterns that slowly and silently expanded, like smoke plumes on an ancient battlefield.

The *Random Wave* was the first to steady its orientation, through hundreds of computer-controlled bursts from its reaction control system. It came about again to charge at its enemy: the still spinning *Enterprise.*

Another alarm pinged on the bridge, and Kirk turned to Spock and asked which one it was this time.

"Weapons lock," Spock said. "We are being targeted."

"Fire phasers!" Kirk told Del Mar. "And this time—miss!"

"Fire!" Griffyn ordered, and a heartbeat later, the *Enterprise*'s phaser blast hit his ship's primary sensor array, and the viewscreen went dark as the flight deck controls arced with seething energy.

• • •

"Direct hit!" Del Mar exclaimed. "Sorry," she added.

And then the bridge of the *Enterprise* shuddered as the ship absorbed a phase-cannon blast.

"How's she doing?" Kirk asked Zee. The midshipman had gone to engineering so Naderi could go to the shields station.

"No venting," Zee said as she read her damage displays. "Structural integrity is holding. We're okay!"

"Not really," Spock added.

Kirk spun to him.

"Griffyn's ship is about to—"

The *Random Wave* spun like a boomerang, edge over edge, directly for the spinning *Enterprise*, until one flattened nacelle hooked around the central support pylon joining the primary hull to the secondary one.

The smaller ship wedged there, caught between the pylon and the starship's starboard nacelle, transferring its kinetic energy into momentum that the bigger ship picked up.

Viewport lights flickered, then went dark on the *Enterprise* as its power systems failed. The *Random Wave* was already without any running or propulsion lights.

Like wadded-up refuse, the two ships spun over Neptune, neither one with an operative reaction control system to stabilize their motion. And as both crews were quick to discover, the energy lost to their collision meant their overall velocity had diminished to below what was required for Neptune orbit, standard or otherwise.

The ships were locked in a death spiral, slowly descending to the giant planet below. And as cold as its atmosphere was, at the speed the ships would hit it, there would be hellfire.

49

Kirk pulled himself up from the deck, feeling dizzy. The once bright bridge was darkly shadowed, lit only by emergency battery lights.

"Sound off!" Kirk shouted over some mechanical whine.

Everyone answered but one. "How's Finnegan?" Kirk called out.

"Still unconscious," Spock reported. "But no new injuries."

A flash of blue light suddenly strobed through the bridge. A few seconds later, it happened again.

The viewscreen had reset itself and now showed flashes of Neptune as the *Enterprise* whirled over it.

Kirk went to the helm, but the controls were unresponsive. "I can't stop the spinning." He looked back at Spock, who had returned to the science station. "Any sign of Griffyn?"

"Unfortunately, yes." Spock waved his hand over a switch, and on the displays above him, views from the *Enterprise*'s other optical sensors took shape.

They revealed Griffyn's ship clamped around the middle of the *Enterprise* like a giant set of jaws. And the elongated dome of one nacelle was jammed up against the saucer's main impulse port. If that port fired, the explosion would tear apart both ships.

"Well, we stopped him, all right," Kirk said. "And he stopped us." He found Zee in the gloom and flashing blue light. "Zee, it's time to call Starfleet. It's time to call anyone."

But Zee was already at the comm station, resetting controls. "We've lost all channels. Communications are gone."

Kirk blinked, thinking. Each time the blue of Neptune

flashed across the bridge, it seemed brighter. He went to Spock. "Our orbit's decaying, isn't it?"

"It is," Spock confirmed.

"Do our lifepods have enough thrust to boost us to a higher orbit?"

Spock shook his head. "We passed that point ten minutes ago."

"Is there anything on this ship that's still working?"

Spock passed his hands over the sensors, making screen after screen of technical readout appear on the overhead displays. Then one screen remained, and some of the numbers on it were green.

"Transporters," Spock said. "One installation is still online and operational."

"Then you know what we have to do, right?"

Spock didn't look any happier than Kirk felt. "I do."

They left the bridge together.

Kirk staggered to the side as soon as he had resolved from the matter stream in the cargo hold of Griffyn's ship.

Spock had warned him the transport could be rough. Station-to-station or even lens-to-lens transport within a single station was one thing, but it was extremely difficult to beam to an open location that was less than half a kilometer away.

Kirk essayed a deep breath. *Good.* He could still breathe. He checked his hands—five fingers on each. All of that plus the fact that he was standing and thinking convinced him Spock had known what he was doing. Now it was up to him. Spock was certain that the *Enterprise*'s impulse engine could lift both ships into a more stable orbit, but not until the port was clear. Kirk had to get to Griffyn's flight deck and figure out some way to move this ship.

The other thing Spock was certain about was that they had

less than thirty minutes for Kirk to accomplish his mission. By then, Spock said, the first tenuous wisps of Neptune's atmosphere would be thick enough to tear both ships to splinters.

Kirk turned slowly in the cargo bay, using a tricorder to build a map of the ship's layout. Knowing Griffyn was somewhere on this ship, he would have liked to have brought a weapon, but the *Enterprise*'s armory had been empty.

He heard a quiet shuffling sound behind him, but he kept turning in a slow circle. He did, however, carefully adjust the tricorder to scan for life-forms.

But he didn't need a tricorder for what he found.

An eight-year-old boy. He wore coveralls that were too big for him, the sleeves cut down and the legs rolled up with a black equipment belt tightly cinching his waist. The boy's face was pale and hollow-cheeked, and his black hair was flattened to his forehead, long unwashed. A crust of blood was under his nose, and Kirk guessed he'd been hurt in the collision.

"Can you help me?" the boy asked Kirk.

Kirk felt a wave of fear course through him, but fought it down.

This wasn't Tarsus IV.

"What's your name?" he asked quietly.

"Bohrom."

"Do you have parents?"

"The bad guy hurt them."

Kirk stared at the child. How could this boy have been on Earth and ended up this way?

"What bad guy?"

"Gwiffyn." The boy's lips trembled.

"Do you know where your parents are?"

The boy snuffled, shook his head, wiped his nose with the back of his hand. "Will you help me?" he asked again.

Kirk crouched down, remembering all the ones he'd failed.

"I will. C'mere." He waved the boy closer and reached for his communicator. Spock could beam the boy back to the *Enterprise* and he'd—

The boy slashed Kirk's side with a flashdriver! The acid pain was startling.

Kirk toppled over, kicked out instinctively, but the boy laughed and danced around him, waving the sharp-pointed tool over his head. "Ha, ha—I get the pwize!" the boy sang.

Kirk rolled to meet his next attack, and Bohrom jumped back. But as soon as Kirk put his hand on the deck to push himself up, the boy darted in and struck again, slicing across Kirk's sleeves and into his arm.

Kirk had a sudden image of what would happen if he grabbed his arm and rolled back to the deck. The boy would be there to slit his throat.

So he reached to his side, offering himself up for another attack. Bohrom hooted in delight and ran at him!

And Kirk swung his arm back around with the tricorder and caught the boy under the chin, sending him flying. The flashdriver skittered across the metal deck.

Kirk was by the stunned boy in an instant. He used the child's own equipment belt to tie Bohrom's arms and hands behind his back. He ripped the shoulder strap off the tricorder and used it to tie his legs.

He thought of gagging him, then just as quickly decided not to. The boy's nose was so clogged from crying or dirt, there was a chance he'd suffocate.

That moment of hesitation was all it took.

Bohrom's eyes cleared, and for a moment panic set in as he realized his arms and legs were immobilized.

He shrieked then, the sound more cutting than any alarm on the *Enterprise*.

Kirk knelt by him, thinking quickly. He couldn't put his hand over the boy's mouth because he *knew* he'd be bitten.

He wouldn't hit him again because that had been wrong and he didn't want to know where that violence had come from.

So as the boy thrashed and struggled and tried to break free of his bonds, Kirk grabbed a fistful of Bohrom's T-shirt and stretched it over his mouth, at least muffling the sound.

Too aware of the time limit he faced to save his ship and his friends, Kirk rapidly scanned the cargo bay, trying to find someplace he could safely stash the boy.

That was when he realized the boy's alarm had been heard.

Three teenagers were in the cargo bay doorway, two of them holding laser rifles.

The third was Matthew.

And all three wore red bandanas.

50

*Four days after the revolution, four days after fourteen-year-old
Jimmy had been given his red bandana and his yellow card all on
the same night, he knew it was over. He'd failed the younger ones
he was supposed to protect. And he was going to die now.*

*Of the twenty-four who had been in his cabin, four were left.
The governor himself gave him Donny because everyone knew
Jimmy Kirk always followed the rules: He'd take Donny back to the
storehouses and then just give himself up because that's what he'd
been told to do.*

*Donny Roy was four. Billy Clute, seven. Edith Zaglada, eight.
Tay Hébert, nine. They'd survived long enough for him to lead them
to safety under the arena stands. But now Matthew was coming
and he'd kill them all.*

Four days after the revolution, it was over.

*Approaching footsteps crunched heavily over frosty ground,
over rubble, over bodies.*

"We've got a sensor, Jimmy! We're gonna find you!"

"They know where we are," Tay whimpered.

*A tall figure jumped down beside them, boots grinding on de-
bris. Edith and Billy both screamed. Tay cried. Donny hugged
Jimmy, shaking silently.*

*"Get up." It was Griffyn, from the storehouse table, wearing his
parka and the red bandana that said he was on the governor's list.*

He pointed his laser rifle at Jimmy.

"Get up, kid!"

*Jimmy stood up, but his legs were exhausted, no longer under
full control. He almost lost his balance.*

Griffyn grabbed Donny's arm and yanked him away from

Jimmy, throwing the child out from under the stands. "All of you! Up!"

Tay, Edith, and Billy got to their feet, huddled together, crying, sobbing.

Jimmy felt powerless. He knew he should be doing something. He had to do something.

But he was just a kid and he didn't know what.

"Move!"

Jimmy felt Griffyn's hand on his back as he was shoved forward. The four children stumbled after him until they were in the arena, by the bodies, encircled by the smoking ruins of wooden seats lit by laser fire days ago. Jimmy gathered the children close to him, trying to shield them as long as he could.

Griffyn held his rifle on them, thumbed a communicator. "This is Griff. I got that last pack of kids by the depot."

"Names."

It was just one word over a comm link, but Jimmy recognized the governor's voice.

"It's Kirk like we thought, Hébert, Zaglada, Clute . . ." *Griffyn glared at Jimmy, pointed his rifle at Donny.* "Who's the brat?"

Jimmy didn't recognize his own voice as he answered reflexively. "Donny . . . Donny Roy."

"Roy," *Griffyn repeated.*

"The records have been updated," *the governor replied.* "Have Matthew take care of this."

"Done." *Griffyn thumbed the communicator shut, glanced away from his captives for a moment.* "Matty! Time to earn your rations!"

Matthew came out from the shadows then, his face blank and unreadable, so different from four days ago.

Jimmy didn't want to know what his best friend had seen in the last four days. How many more he had killed.

Matthew didn't look at him or any of the kids.

"Griff . . . Jimmy's my friend. . . ."

Griffyn placed a hand on his shoulder. "You've done this before. You're on the list, they're not. You know what that means."

"Yeah, but maybe I don't want to do this anymore."

Griffyn grasped Matthew's jaw hard, forced him to look up at him. "The governor saved your life. He offered to save Jimmy's, too. You can't get much fairer than that."

Jimmy saw the cold, hard look in Griffyn's eyes that said if Matthew didn't kill the children, then Griffyn was going to kill Matthew.

"You want to make the governor proud? Let him know he made the right choice?"

Matthew nodded.

Griffyn released his grip on Matthew. "Then do Jimmy first. It'll be easier."

Jimmy watched, incredulous, as Matthew raised his laser rifle, activated it, then awkwardly swung the heavy weapon around to him.

"Remember, you're on the list," Griffyn said. "He's not."

Matthew took aim. Jimmy saw his friend's lip tremble.

Jimmy was frozen in place, unable to think, unable to move, unable to breathe.

But then Edith screamed and ran and before Jimmy could do anything, Matthew jerked around and fired and a red lance of light punched through Edith's torso in two puffs of vaporized blood front and back, instantly silencing her as her body went limp and she fell facedown on the other bodies, arms and legs waving like blowing grain. As her flimsy shirt burned, small flames flickered around the blackened hole in her spine.

In shocked silence, Jimmy heard only the sizzle of flesh, smelled only the sharp tang of ionized air. Then the frightened cries reached him. Donny was curled up on the ground. Billy and Tay clutched each other, weeping.

"Good shot," Griffyn said to Matthew. "Shut the rest up and we're done."

This time, when Matthew turned his rifle on Jimmy, his lip didn't tremble. And there was nothing awkward in the way he raised the weapon.

He said, "Fair's fair, Jimmy. You had your chance."

Even before Matthew fired the laser, Jimmy felt himself die.

Then the wall behind Griffyn and Matthew exploded into light and Jimmy felt himself lifted through the air in a silent blast of heat.

For a moment, he was glad that being killed by a laser wasn't painful, then he landed on the hard broken flooring and felt enough pain to wake him to the reality of the situation.

Soldiers.

They wore helmets and goggles and sleek uniforms that swam with ever-changing patterns of adaptive camouflage.

Fire pulsed from their weapons—not ordinary lasers, Jimmy recognized, but blasts of phased energy that stunned, not killed.

He knew then they weren't soldiers. Starfleet had arrived.

Four days too late.

He didn't hear the shouts of the security forces or the hum of their phased weapons. The roar of the antimatter charge that'd blown open the arena wall still hissed in his ears.

He didn't see what happened to Matthew or Griffyn. He got to his feet while the battle raged, careless of the possibility of being shot. His fear of death had been lost in the moment Matthew aimed his weapon, finger pressing on the stud. Now he felt only rage.

At some point, the firefight ended and a Starfleet security officer found him. The large man twisted something the size of a communicator in his gloved hands and a thick, warm blanket unfurled. He peeled back a tab on a silver packet and Jimmy smelled the first hot food—the first real food—he had seen for more than a month.

The officer spoke to him, but Jimmy still could not hear. Nor did he want to.

The officer put his hand on Jimmy's shoulder, just like his father had done. Just like Griffyn had put his hand on Matthew's shoulder. The hand that said everything was going to be all right.

Jimmy struck that hand away with all his strength.

The officer stepped back, startled.

"Where were you?" Jimmy cried, and as if a dam had burst, the tears came, along with every emotion, every chord of fear, every pang of loss he had not permitted himself to feel for the past four days.

"Hey, kid . . . it's okay. We're here now."

"No!" Jimmy pummeled the officer and didn't care that the combat armor protectively hardened at the impact of his fists. "You were supposed to save us! You were supposed to be here when we needed you!"

"Kid . . . kid . . ." The officer tried to ward off his attack.

Jimmy lost the power of words. Only a hoarse cry of despairing fury escaped him, something so powerful, so basic, born so deep in his unformed mind that speech was impossible.

The officer reached out to—

Jimmy screamed and punched and kicked and saw again the blood vaporize from Edith's back, and Donny curled up on the ground, and Tay and Billy weeping, and he knew—he knew—this was all someone's fault. It had to be.

Jimmy's fingers felt a patch on the officer's shoulder, tore it free from its adaptive camouflage connector so that it resolved in color in his hand.

Ad astra per aspera, the patch read—words Jimmy knew by heart, cradling a golden arrowhead rushing against the stars.

He crushed the patch in his fist and stumbled back, tormented.

The officer held out his hand to the boy. "Kid . . . let me help . . ."

Jimmy threw the crumpled emblem of Starfleet on the smoldering ruins and ran, escaping into the gray storm and chilling wind that flashed snow past him like stars at warp.

But inside, he was burning with shame, with fear, and with

*hatred for the only answer he could grasp at to explain the horror
he had seen. Starfleet had failed here. Starfleet had failed him and
Edith and everyone.*

Jimmy ran and ran and ran.

And three years later, he was still running.

Kirk stood still in the middle of the cargo bay, held in place
by two laser rifles jammed under his chin.

The third teenager untied Bohrom.

"I should've done this the first time you came to the docks,"
Matthew said.

"You'd better listen to me," Kirk said.

Matthew looked at his fellow teenage soldier, and both of
them gaped in mock surprise.

"We're in a decaying orbit. The *Enterprise* can get us out of
it, but your ship's blocking the impulse port. We have to move
it."

Matthew nodded in agreement. "I think you're absolutely
right, Jimmy. Since our transporter's shot, you *should* use your
communicator to have that Vulcan beam us back to the *Enterprise* to get her dilithium. Glad to see you're thinking."

"We have twenty minutes," Kirk said. "Then we die."

Matthew spun his rifle around and drove the butt into
Kirk's stomach, making him double over, gasping for air.

"Maybe you die," Matthew said. "Maybe other people die.
But me, I live forever." He reached to Kirk's equipment belt,
tore off the communicator, pushed it into Kirk's face. "Call the
Vulcan."

"No," Kirk said.

Matthew nodded to his soldier and the teenager dug the
muzzle of his rifle into Kirk's side where the flashdriver had
sliced into him. Viciously.

Kirk winced but pushed the rifle aside, stared defiantly at
Matthew.

"You *want* to die?" Matthew asked.

"That's not much of a threat," Kirk said. "In twenty minutes, we're all going to die. Even you."

Matthew nodded at his soldier again, and as the laser barrel pushed in, Kirk swept his hand down to deflect it, then spun around to clip the teenager on the side of his head with his fist.

In the two seconds it took for Matthew to swing his own rifle up to cover Kirk, Kirk had the second soldier's rifle aimed at Matthew.

"I can save us all," Kirk said.

"Too bad you're outnumbered." Matthew jerked his head to the side.

From the corner of his eye, Kirk saw the third teenager, rifle raised and aimed. Bohrom was beside him, clapping his hands with excitement.

Kirk began to lower his rifle. "Guess you got me."

"Some things never change, Jimmy. You're still a loser."

Kirk shrugged, then swung up his rifle in a blur and fired at the third teenager's weapon to make it explode.

Then Matthew fired before Kirk could turn, the laser beam slicing into Kirk's rifle, making the power cell erupt in flames.

But before Matthew could fire again, Kirk threw his blazing rifle at him, making him duck. Kirk seized the opening to slam into him and drive him to the deck.

Matthew fought for his life, because that's all he had been trained to do.

But Kirk was fighting for Spock and Zee and Naderi and Del Mar and unconscious Finnegan and the *U.S.S. Enterprise* and every one of his kids that he'd lost on Tarsus IV.

It wasn't even close.

The two wounded teenagers and the boy stared nervously at him as he stood over his fallen enemy. Kirk *knew* it would take just one more blow to crush Matthew's neck and put paid to the horror of what happened three years ago.

"Do it," Matthew croaked. His eyes were swollen, but Kirk knew he could see.

Kirk shook his head.

"I killed your brother."

Kirk reached down, grabbed Matthew by the collar, pushed in close to his face.

"That's right," Matthew spat past broken teeth. "In his apartment. He cried and he cried and begged for you to save him and you weren't there."

"Liar," Kirk said. "He'd have begged for our dad. He's the one who taught me how to fight." He let Matthew fall back to the floor. He turned to the two teenagers and the boy. They flinched away from him.

Kirk took a step forward. "I won't hurt you. I only want to—"

Three laser beams sliced the air beside Kirk and killed the three children.

Kirk wheeled around to see a man standing over Matthew, aiming a laser pistol at his head. He fired once, and Matthew died, too.

The man looked up at Kirk.

"Jimmy," Griffyn said. "It's about time."

51

The bridge of the *Enterprise* was a study in controlled chaos.

Zee had found a critical-equipment locker that held actual printed operations manuals, presumably to be used at times like these when the computer systems were down.

Naderi was paging through one on antigravity systems, trying to see if there was some way to shake loose Griffyn's ship by reversing gravitational polarity.

Zee was trying to find the sections that described emergency communications. She was convinced there had to be a battery-powered back-up system on the bridge, even if it just used ordinary radio waves.

Del Mar was doing calculations to determine how much thrust she could get out of the ship's reaction control thrusters. If they were all fired at once along the same velocity vector, she was certain she could buy them at least another orbit.

Finnegan was wrapped in a blanket with a first-aid pack serving as a pillow. Del Mar had told the others he was in some kind of coma, and when they had time, there was probably something in sickbay that could repair the damage. Provided it came with instructions.

But of the skeleton crew that was conscious and capable of doing something, no matter how desperate, only Spock remained still, sitting in the chair at the science station, staring with rapt attention at the flickering blue and black that marked each revolution of the locked-together, dying ships.

"Is there a reason you're not doing anything?" Zee finally asked, her voice thin with frustration.

"I am doing something," Spock said pleasantly. "I am trying to determine the logic behind Griffyn's decision to come to Neptune."

All three mids looked at him in shock.

"And that is going to help us figure a way out of this situation how?" Zee asked.

"I believe that is the point," Spock said. "We do not have to 'figure a way out.'"

Now they all stared at him in confusion.

"There is only one reason for Griffyn to have come here. And that means the way out will present itself shortly."

The mids exchanged looks, then returned to their manuals. Their search became a touch more frantic.

When Griffyn shoved Kirk onto the flight deck of the *Random Wave*, only one young woman was at the helm. Kirk was puzzled that none of the other flight stations was staffed.

"I'm Dala," the woman said. Griffyn handed her his laser pistol, and she smiled sweetly as she kept it aimed at Kirk.

"Where're all your other kids?" Kirk asked. "I saw at least ten more in the freighter."

Griffyn shrugged. "When their jobs were over, I took them off the list."

Kirk felt himself turn to stone, but not from fear. "You're still working for Kodos."

Griffyn sat down at the communications console, glanced back at him. "The governor died on T-IV. Didn't you hear? They found his body."

"*A* body," Kirk said. "Too badly burned to be positively identified."

Dala shivered. "Ick."

Griffyn worked some communications controls. "Kodos tried to be a hero, save the colony. If you're still looking for him, I suggest you try Starfleet. They're all heroes, right?"

Kirk studied the spinning stars on the viewscreen. The

angle it showed didn't include Neptune. "We've got maybe ten minutes before our ships start to burn up."

"I don't think so," Griffyn said. Whatever he'd been doing at the console, he was finished. A blue light flashed there.

A signal, Kirk thought. And then he realized why Griffyn wasn't worried about being destroyed in a handful of minutes.

"You're expecting company."

"Always knew you were a smart one, Jimmy." Griffyn got up, took the laser pistol from Dala. "That's why I'm offering you a job. Whether you want it or not."

"A rendezvous?" Zee asked.

"It is the only logical explanation," Spock said. "Griffyn is expecting to offload his stolen cargo. He'll need a vessel more suitable for traversing a high-velocity smuggling route out of Federation space."

"I might have to argue with you about that," Del Mar said from the navigation console.

"Indeed?" Spock replied. "You do not believe Griffyn expects to rendezvous with another vessel?"

"How about *three* other vessels?"

Spock turned to the science displays, activated a scanning circuit, and saw what Del Mar referred to.

Three new ships were rising out of Neptune's depths.

And even with the crude resolution of the science scanner, Spock knew what kind of ships they were.

As they slipped through the last layers of Neptune's frigid atmosphere, the three ships could be glimpsed in the flickering light from the incandescent streamers of plasma shed by their shields.

They were all of the same class: compact, shaped like closed mollusk shells, all propulsion units and sensor pods and weapons arrays curved and blended into the arcs of their single hulls, with the forward bridge resembling a warrior's helmet.

The silhouette of these ships was known to every Starfleet crew, especially to those who had last served on the *Enterprise* and successfully repulsed a boarding effort by the aliens who flew them.

Their hulls were green, so all would know their masters.

Deep within the heart of the Federation, deep within the peaceful home system that had given birth to Starfleet, three Orion corsairs rose to do battle.

"Pirates," Spock said.

Of the three mids on the bridge, Naderi was the most perplexed. "How did *Orion* corsairs get this close to Earth? How did they even get past the frontier?"

"Excellent questions," Spock observed.

The praise didn't help Naderi. "How about some excellent answers?"

"I have none," Spock admitted.

Del Mar sighed. "Well, then it gives us something to look forward to when you do have some."

Spock gave Del Mar a curious look, but she was already flipping hurriedly through a weapons manual. "We've got no torpedoes. We have no idea how to recharge those new phaser banks. We can't raise shields. And we can't call for reinforcements. So here's *my* excellent question: How do we blast those nasty green clamshells out of space?"

"Even if we knew how," Spock cautioned, "it would not be prudent."

Del Mar put her hands on her hips. "Keep going, Mr. Spock. By now we've all sort've figured out that if we just stare at you long enough, you'll eventually get around to explaining whatever it is you're talking about."

As Spock replied, it was almost as if he had to struggle to keep the barest flicker of a smile from appearing on his lips. "Midshipman Del Mar, those 'nasty green clamshells' are what will save us."

Del Mar grinned but didn't give way. "You can't stop there. . . ."

Kirk lurched back as the Orions' tractor beams engaged the *Random Wave* and the small ship's flight deck tilted.

He saw Dala stumble, too, and quickly checked out Griffyn.

But Griffyn had anticipated the contact and had braced himself. His weapon was still pointing directly at Kirk. "Don't even think about it," he warned.

"Think about what?"

Griffyn wasn't so easily distracted. "Seriously, don't spoil a good thing. My friends out there will stabilize our orbit long enough to beam over the cargo, then we go, too."

"You can't make me do anything," Kirk said.

"Kid, I remember you back on T-IV, before the fungus hit. You rode my horse."

Kirk nodded. That was one memory of Tarsus IV he didn't have to block out.

"You didn't know what you were doing," Griffyn said, "but you wouldn't let anyone tell you what to do, either. Stubbornest kid I ever saw. That's what I told Kodos. That's why he chose you."

Kirk held on to the side of the empty command chair as the flight deck creaked. "Why did Kodos choose you?"

"Simple. I wanted to live."

"Everyone wanted to live."

"Not everyone could."

"We had months of food in the storehouses."

"And the next cargo fleet wasn't due for a year."

"A year's a long time. A lot of things could've happened."

Anger flashed in Griffyn's eyes. "What does it matter, kid? It's over and done with."

And with those words, as simply as that, Kirk understood what he never had. Once again he heard Mallory's voice from that first night they met. *Patterns*, he had said. *You've heard that old saying: Those who don't remember the past are doomed to repeat it?*

Kirk had, but had never comprehended what it really meant.

For seven thousand years or so, humans appear to have lived in a permanent state of forgetfulness . . . not one generation free of war or famine or injustice. And then . . . we woke up. It took the worst war we'd ever experienced, but out of all that came Cochrane and a new generation that for the first time wouldn't forget. Because the pattern was broken. So no more wars. No more need. No more injustice. The world, our world, is the way it is today because we remember the patterns of history and we do not repeat them.

"We woke up," Kirk said quietly.

"What?" Griffyn asked.

"The pattern was broken," Kirk said, his voice gaining strength.

"What pattern? What are you talking about?"

Kirk looked into the face of the beast from his past and knew why Kodos had chosen Griffyn; knew why Tarsus IV was over for him.

The children who had fought for Kodos, committed atrocities, killed their own friends and families, they didn't know what they were doing. They were innocent, unformed, and trusting.

But the puppet masters—Kodos and Griffyn and, eventually, Matthew, all those who should have known better, who should have known the patterns of the past and should have

woken up and should have refused to repeat those patterns—
they were already dead, if not in body, then in spirit.

For three years, Kirk had tried to forget the nightmare
world he had seen and been part of. And that's what had
trapped him in his past. But if he remembered the pattern of
what had gone so horribly wrong, he would not repeat it—he
could break it.

That knowledge freed him like nothing he had ever experienced before. And in the midst of that release, he remembered something else that Mallory had told him. Something
else important that he'd not understood.

Until this moment.

"If *we* remember the patterns of history, *we* do not repeat
them."

Griffyn stared at him. "What do you mean by 'we'?"

"Starfleet," Kirk said.

52

"The Orions are beaming cargo from Griffyn's ship."

Zee looked up from the auxiliary tactical station where she had managed to bring more sensors on line. "At the rate they're going, I'd say they'll be finished in five, maybe six minutes."

"Then they're going to drop us again, aren't they?" Del Mar said. "Push us back into the atmosphere to burn us up, along with all the evidence."

Naderi suddenly jumped up from his chair at the helm. "Shuttlecraft! There should be at least two down on the hangar deck!"

"There will be," Spock said, "once the hangar deck refit has been completed."

Naderi frowned. "No shuttlecraft?"

Spock shook his head. "A worthy suggestion, however."

Naderi jumped up again. "Saucer separation!"

"We would need the impulse ports to be clear."

Naderi sat down again, dejected. "I know, another worthy suggestion."

"C'mon, people," Del Mar said. "We've got *most* of a starship here. There's got to be something it can do to take out those pirates. Or at least slow them down."

"Slow them down . . ." Spock said, deep in thought.

Del Mar ran up to him, motioning with her hands as if to coax a few more words out of him. "I like the way you said that. Keep going."

Spock stood. "*Our* transporters work. As they beam the cargo over to their ships, we will beam it back to ours."

Del Mar leaned in, paused, asked, "That's a fake uniform, right? You're not really a mid?"

Spock shook his head.

"Good. Then the fraternization rules don't apply." With that, Del Mar hugged him. Then she said to the others, "Naderi, stay at the helm. Zee, keep trying to restore communications." She patted Spock on the shoulder, and he was proud that he controlled himself and did not flinch. "The great imposter and I will be in the transporter room, making life miserable for our friends out there." Del Mar grabbed Spock by the arm and dragged him to the turbolift. "Let's go, handsome. You're on!"

Spock wasn't quite certain what had just happened, but it was fascinating nonetheless.

Griffyn spun around in his chair and punched a comm switch.

"What do you mean they're stealing our cargo?"

The reply was in the Orion traders' tongue. Kirk couldn't understand it, but he recognized the cadence because it was so often used in holo-entertainments featuring Orion villains and, inevitably, Orion dancing girls.

"Then raise your shields!" Griffyn shouted.

Kirk thought he knew what was going on. It sounded as if the people on the *Enterprise* were doing what the Orions were doing—beaming cargo off Griffyn's ship.

An irate Orion tirade came over the comm link.

Whatever was said, Griffyn had had enough. "Forget the cargo then! Lock on to any life signs you can find and beam the *crew* over! Beam them into space for all I care. Just stop their interference!"

Griffyn's frustration was the equal of the unintelligible Orion's at the other end of the comm link. He angrily flicked a switch on and off several times, which Kirk knew would cause an annoying screech for the receiver.

"Acknowledge, will you?" Griffyn demanded, and by doing so left himself wide open.

As Kirk leapt into action, he had the thought that there was at least some justice playing out today. Griffyn was so preoccupied by the threat outside his ship, he'd forgotten the threat inside.

Kirk's first punch from behind caught Griffyn on the side of his head.

Griffyn twisted with a savage shout, and Kirk easily caught his hand to block him from aiming his laser pistol.

Griffyn fired anyway, and the crimson beam slashed across the overhead, exploding lights and scorching the bulkhead in a sizzling arc until Kirk slammed Griffyn's hand down so hard on the console that the pistol dropped to the floor.

By now Griffyn had turned completely in his chair and he jumped up, trying to butt his head into Kirk's face. But Kirk sidestepped and threw Griffyn over his shoulder, then leapt on top of him, wrapped his arms around his neck, and began to put pressure on his carotid artery to drive him into unconsciousness.

"I think you'd better stop now," Dala said.

Kirk looked up even as Griffyn struggled beneath him, clawing at his arms.

Dala was aiming the dropped laser pistol at Kirk. "*Right now,*" she said.

"He killed Matthew!" Kirk told her.

"I never liked him," Dala said.

"And his crew of kids. That boy, Bohrom!"

"All damaged goods. The general saw to that."

Kirk didn't know who the general was, had no time to ask. "You won't shoot me."

"Yes, I will."

"No, you won't. Because once I've taken care of Griffyn,

you and I are in charge of this ship. We can go anywhere . . . do anything . . ."

Kirk felt Griffyn go limp. He had kept Dala talking long enough for the choke hold to work.

He stood up, but Dala didn't change her aim. She licked a corner of her lip. "Aren't you kind of young?"

Kirk tried to look at her as if they were already alone in a honeymoon suite on Risa. He had heard the stories. "Some women would think that's an advantage."

Dala pointed the gun away. "Just get me out of this system."

"I'll do more than that," Kirk promised with what he hoped was a seductive leer. Then he swept her up in his arms, and in the same movement, slapped the laser pistol from her hand, spun her around, and in less than ten seconds had her hands tied with her own equipment belt.

He pushed her down into the command chair, told her not to move, scooped up the laser pistol just to be sure, and rushed to the helm to raise shields and block the Orions' transporter before his fellow crewmates could be captured or killed.

Fellow crewmates, Kirk thought. That didn't sound so bad.

In the *Enterprise*'s one working transporter room, a feedback alarm chimed.

"Okay, now what?" Del Mar asked Spock.

She was up on the platform, soaked in sweat from throwing crates and other transported cargo to the floor as quickly as Spock could beam it in.

At the console, Spock checked the readings. "Griffyn's ship has raised shields to maximum, which means they encompass the *Enterprise* as well."

Del Mar jumped down to join Spock. "So we can't transport anything, but neither can the Orions! That's great news, right?"

"Apparently, the Orions do not share your opinion. They are powering up their weapons."

Zee and Naderi sat at the conn, staring at the tactical status display that showed the Orions locking weapons.

"Are the shields from Griffyn's ship going to help us?" Zee asked.

"They won't last more than a couple of salvos," Naderi answered. He brought up more tactical displays. "We've got to have something we can fight back with. There's— Whoa!"

"Whoa what?"

"The phaser banks have recharged!"

"By themselves?"

"Must be an automated system. We've got at least two more shots!"

"Better make 'em count."

Naderi frowned at Zee. "You think?"

Kirk saw the flight deck's tactical display light up. It was never intended for battle, but he could see the Orions were locking weapons.

Over the comm link, a deep Orion voice spoke in short, clipped words, with a regular pause between each one.

"Is that a countdown?" Kirk asked Dala.

"I don't know," Dala said petulantly. "I don't speak green."

Kirk put all the power the ship could generate into its shields. As the lights dimmed on the flight deck, he told himself it was the best he could do.

But as always, he wished he could do more.

Spock and Del Mar charged out of the turbolift onto the bridge.

Zee turned to them while Naderi remained hunched over his console.

"We've got phasers!" she said. "Two shots at least!"

"And I am going to make them count." Naderi held his finger over the weapons control.

On the screen, Spock saw that the three Orion corsairs had aligned themselves so all their weapons pods pointed in the same direction—directly at the *Enterprise.*

"Three . . . ," Naderi said. "Two . . ."

The weapons pod on the center corsair suddenly flared in a silent explosion. Arcs of energy leapfrogged over its hull, sending geysers of venting gas into space at each contact point.

Then the starboard corsair lost a propulsion nacelle to an even larger explosion. It spun, spewing vapor and sparks, to collide with the middle corsair. Just as both weapons pods on the port corsair blew up in a spectacular double explosion.

"Fantastic shooting!" Zee said.

"You're an ace!" Del Mar exclaimed.

But Naderi turned slowly from the helm, still holding up his finger. "It wasn't me."

"Ah, of course," Spock said. "It is the only logical explanation."

The three mids turned to him, Del Mar with her hands on her hips, and they waited.

53

There were ten Starfleet vessels in the emergency flotilla, including the newest *Constitution*-class starship, the *U.S.S. Potemkin*. The *Potemkin* had carried out the successful pinpoint attack on the Orion corsairs, disabling them without any loss of their crew.

In the five hours it had taken the hobbled *Enterprise* to make her impulse-power voyage to Neptune, those ten other Starfleet ships had arrived at warp and secreted themselves among the planet's moons and rings. There, with tractor beams, photon torpedoes, and fully charged phaser banks at the ready, they had waited to defend the *Enterprise* and the remarkable midshipmen and two recruits who had embarked on their foolhardy mission without ever once considering that they couldn't possibly have enough knowledge or experience to complete it.

The commander of the flotilla had allowed events to play out, in order to force all involved parties into the open. And it was safe to say that as much as the mids were surprised by the presence of Orion pirates in Earth's home system, Starfleet personnel were shaken to their core. The incident was undeniable evidence that there was an unsuspected weak link in the Federation's defenses. No effort would be spared to determine what it was and how it could be fixed.

But for now, the immediate mission had been accomplished, and the flotilla's flagship, carrying the commander, led the others back to Spacedock, all ten ships' combined tractor beams safely conveying the *Enterprise* and the four captured enemy vessels.

On the small, cramped bridge of the flagship—the battered science vessel, *Endurance*—Mallory watched the main screen where the *Enterprise* proudly flew.

"See," Mallory said as he sipped his mug of ginger tea, "as I promised, not a scratch."

Beside him, Captain Christopher Pike scowled. "At least on the outside." Despite the successful completion of the mission, he was no happier now than when Mallory had told him his precious ship was being used as bait in a criminal investigation.

"Now will you tell me why she was taken?"

"Probably not," Mallory said, though he softened his refusal with a smile.

Pike wasn't willing to let it go at that. "What if we had lost her? Are you certain the risk was worth that?"

Mallory had already considered that question and had no doubt as to the answer.

In his office safe, the Project Echion report waited for his decision. After what he had witnessed today, he knew he could approve it.

"For that crew," Mallory said, "yes. Even for the *Enterprise*."

Pike had a reputation for being driven, sometimes prone to dark moods. The possible loss of his ship, before he'd ever had a chance to command her, was obviously something that would haunt him for a long time to come.

"For that crew," Pike repeated. "Will you at least tell me who took it?"

"Again, probably not."

Pike hated not knowing, and didn't hide his frustration. "Why?"

Mallory thought of Tarsus IV, and a teenage boy who might be killed if his identity were ever revealed and his true story told.

"Because Starfleet made a promise," Mallory said quietly.

For Captain Pike, that simple explanation brought peace. His questions ended.

But Mallory felt no such peace.

There was still a promise he had yet to keep. One he had made to a master chief petty officer, to find his lost boy, and bring him back.

54

It was just a formality, they were told, but even with his new-found insight, Kirk was nervous sitting in the corridor outside the courtroom in Starfleet Headquarters. And he wasn't alone.

Beside him in the row of old-fashioned oak chairs sat Spock, and Midshipmen Finnegan, Naderi, and Del Mar. The mids were in dress uniforms with subdued metallic flashing. He and Spock were both in recruit whites—they hadn't been in Starfleet long enough to earn the privilege of owning a dress uniform. Kirk, much to his surprise, felt regret at the thought that day might not be in his future.

Kirk and his impromptu crew had been told they faced no charges, that this hearing was just to establish the events that had led to the unauthorized removal of Starfleet equipment from a Starfleet facility. Deciphering the euphemistic phrasing had not been difficult for anyone involved. The topic of discussion would be the theft of a Starfleet starship.

Everyone had turned up on time. Everyone waited. And nobody talked to anybody else.

Finally, about an hour after the proceedings had begun, the main doors to the courtroom opened once again.

Two red-shirted security officers escorted Dala from the room. Her face had been scrubbed clean and she was in a loose-fitting yellow jumpsuit labeled PRISONER. Her hands were bound by induction cuffs. She did not look up as she was led away.

The next out was Elissa, and although she was in her civilian clothes, she had no escort, which Kirk hoped was a good sign. He went up to her at once.

"Did it go okay?" he asked.

Elissa looked at him as if he was something on display in a museum. "All the charges have been dropped. The honor board records have been purged. I've been reinstated with a clean record."

Kirk tried to understand the reason for her disinterested attitude. "That's fantastic. So why aren't you happy?"

"Do you know how much faster all of this could've been dealt with, how much easier it would've been, if we had just . . . just trusted the system?"

"Isn't that how you got separated in the first place?" Kirk asked.

"The system works, Jim. But you didn't let me give it a chance."

"Next time, I will."

"No more 'next times,' " Elissa said. Then she walked off down the corridor. She did not look back.

Kirk returned to his chair beside Spock and sat down heavily. "Any of your Vulcan logic have anything useful to say about women?"

Spock remained noncommittal. "I could not help overhearing your conversation."

"Tell me something I don't know."

"Elissa is right to distance herself from you."

"*Et tu*, Stretch?"

"*Gesundheit*," Spock said.

Kirk grimaced. "Oh, we've really got to work on your sense of humor. I don't think I can take two more years of this."

"Two more years of what?" Mallory asked.

Kirk hadn't heard the man approach and instantly jumped to attention. Why? He didn't know. But there was something about Mallory that commanded respect, and as a Starfleet recruit, Kirk now had a way to express it.

Spock stood beside him, equally attentive.

"At ease, boys," Mallory said. "Your testimony won't be needed."

Kirk exchanged a puzzled glance with Spock, then they both looked down to Finnegan, Naderi, and Del Mar. A court clerk had just finished speaking to them, and they walked off together. They didn't look back, either.

"That's it?" Kirk asked.

"The records are sealed," Mallory said. "And the events you participated in are classified. So you are ordered not to discuss them with anyone except with express written permission of Command."

Spock inclined his head, giving his assent. Kirk thought about it for a moment, then decided he had no argument with that.

"We're free to go?" he asked.

Mallory did not reply for what seemed like a long time to Kirk. When he spoke, he did so in a serious manner. "Just so I'm certain you understand what's been going on, you do realize that you were forced into enlisting in Starfleet?"

Kirk and Spock both nodded.

"And you understand that it wasn't a fair sentence? Wasn't even legal?"

They nodded again.

"So you're under no obligation to continue your service."

"I would prefer to continue," Spock said simply.

As if he were watching himself in a dream, Kirk heard his voice say, "Yeah. Me too."

"Well, if that's the case, and you really feel that way, I have another offer you might want to consider."

Spock looked at Kirk, then faced Mallory again. "I believe I speak for both of us. We are all ears," he said with satisfaction.

• • •

Kirk had positioned himself before one of the tall viewports in the 511 Lounge on Spacedock. He stared out at the *Enterprise,* safely back in her berth.

"I don't know if I feel comfortable with this," he said.

Mallory was beside him, his eyes also fixed on the magnificent craft. "Why do you say that?"

"Because I know what Elissa went through to get in. The extra courses she took to get her marks up. The letters she got from her Federation council rep. From her uncle in the service. She killed herself. Took every interview. Did everything she could to get in. And now . . . you're just *giving* it to me." He shot a sideways glance at Mallory. "It doesn't seem fair."

"I could point out," Mallory said, "that each year there are approximately eighty-five slots available for 'special' appointments. Most of them are for serving noncoms, but there are always a few people that we go out to get. Why can't you accept that you're one of those?"

"It feels too easy."

Mallory laughed. "Well, I can promise you it won't be that. You're two weeks behind on prep courses already, so you'll have to make them up on your own time. You'll also have to take placement tests. And makeup classes will not be an option if you're deficient in any subject. By the time the first exams roll around, you'll be a walking stack of books or you'll be gone. That I guarantee you."

Kirk watched as the workers in environmental suits flew around the *Enterprise* with thruster packs. "Sounds positively grim."

"I won't kid you. It is."

So many thoughts raced through Kirk's mind that he gave up even trying to make sense of them.

Mallory broke the silence. "I have a question for you."

"Shoot," Kirk said.

"I watched the bridge recordings of what you did on the *Enterprise.*"

Kirk steeled himself not to overreact to criticism, knowing he must have done more than one thing wrong by the book.

"You spent five hours on the bridge before you got to Neptune. Another twenty minutes or so when you arrived. For all intents and purposes, you were the commanding officer, which made you the captain of the ship."

"Yeah . . . so what's the question?" Kirk had no idea where this was going.

"You never took the center chair, James. Why is that?"

Kirk didn't even have to think back to the journey. He knew exactly why he hadn't sat in the captain's chair.

"That's something you have to earn."

"Then accept my offer."

Kirk stared out the viewport at the *Enterprise*.

55

"It is called a special admissions appointment," Spock said. "And I have accepted."

It was night in the meditation garden of the Vulcan compound, and the script of the *Kir'Shara* shone with a gentle green glow. The words of Surak were meant to calm the mind, but for this night, they were not effective.

Sarek kept his attention on the artifact, as if he couldn't bear to see his son while they argued. "Spock, the Vulcan Science Academy is—"

"An institution I can attend at any time," Spock interrupted. "Once I graduate from Starfleet Academy, there is no end to the advanced courses and degrees I can study for."

"Study, yes," Sarek said. "But how can you *attend* the Science Academy when you are serving on a starship a thousand light-years from home?"

"There are many ways to serve, Father. On a starship, yes. But there are also starbases. Research centers on dozens of worlds."

Sarek was dismissive—a shocking breach of familial relations that ratcheted the tension in the garden even higher.

"It is illogical to delude yourself," he said. "If you attend the Starfleet Academy, you *will* accept a posting to a ship. It is in your nature."

Spock felt threatened, under attack. He pulled his dark cloak more tightly around him, as if donning armor. "It is illogical of *you* to predict what I might or might not do four years from now."

Sarek turned from the artifact, took a step toward his son,

disregarding his preference for maintaining a nonconfrontational distance. "There is a proposal before a Starfleet planning committee suggesting that a starship should be commissioned for an all-Vulcan crew. Would that satisfy your need for . . . for excitement?"

"I do not need excitement."

"Then why do you persist in this illogical dream that makes a mockery of everything your mother and I have planned for you?"

"Father—what about *my* plans?"

"You raise your voice to me?"

"If it is the only way to ensure you hear me, yes."

Sarek walked around the narrow stone pyramid, his pacing suggesting he found it difficult to keep still. "How can your plans include being surrounded by humans at the Academy for four years? They will ridicule you. Distract you. Erode your logic and your emotional control."

"But Father, they do not. On board the *Enterprise,* the midshipmen I worked with did not treat me as a Vulcan, or as an alien. I was accepted for what I could offer the crew and the mission. For what I could do. They accepted me without labels and without preconceptions. I was not Vulcan. I was not human. I was just Spock. And I wish to experience that again."

"What you are telling me is that you are turning your back not just on me, but on your heritage."

"My heritage is different from yours."

"Are you not Vulcan?"

"I want to be Vulcan. I have tried to be Vulcan. But . . . perhaps it is time that I look to the other half of my heritage."

"Spock, use your logic. If you are my son, then you *are* Vulcan. No other option is available."

"Then, Father, perhaps I am not your son."

Spock left the garden.

56

The door to the apartment flew open and Kirk rushed in.

"Sam!" he shouted. "Wake up!"

It was noon. He figured his brother had slept long enough. He ran to the bedroom door, pounded on it. "You're not gonna believe what happened!"

He listened. Nothing. He opened the door. "Hey . . ."

The bed was empty. The built-in wall drawers were pulled out. Kirk checked them. Sam's clothes were gone.

He stood in the bedroom doorway, bewildered. Then he saw the aquarium. Its gravel was dry.

"Sam . . ."

Kirk picked up the cylinder of fish food, could guess what was inside. He saw the block inhaler beside it, picked it up, shook it, heard sloshing. Why had his brother left it there?

"Well, Sam," Kirk said to the empty apartment. "Wherever you've gone, you're not gonna believe it."

He went back to the main door where he'd dropped his Starfleet duffel. He bent down and rummaged in it for his personal communicator.

He had to tell someone, so he took a breath to steady himself, flipped open the communicator: "Mom and Dad."

He waited in silence for the call to go through. He heard the click of a connected circuit. "Mom . . . Dad . . . It's Jim! You're not gonna be—" He stopped then, to let the recorded message play through to the end. A computer voice politely asked if he wished to leave a message for the Kirks.

He snapped the communicator shut and looked around the apartment once more, registering and dismissing the scorch marks on the wall and the framed poster. Sam's things were gone, so whatever happened, he told himself, his brother had had time to pack. His brother had had time to get away.

He just didn't know where.

He looked at the communicator. *Why not?* he thought.

He flipped it open: "Elissa."

But her communicator rejected the call. He didn't even reach a computer voice.

He was seventeen years old and this should have been the best day of his life. But it wasn't. There was no one he could share his news with.

Jim Kirk was alone, and he didn't like it.

57

It was morning, the fog was gone, and the Presidio Gate of Starfleet Academy was open.

A cab pulled up to a stand on the sidewalk just outside the gate, and Kirk got out, Starfleet duffel in hand. As the cab flew off, another car landed. Its passenger windows were too dark to see through, but Kirk recognized the diplomatic plates.

Spock got out. The car returned to the airlanes. Kirk went to him.

"How'd it go with your parents?" Kirk asked.

"Satisfactory," Spock said. "And your family?"

"Really excited." Kirk smiled brightly. "It's not a very Vulcan reaction, but it's good for humans."

"Yes," Spock agreed.

Kirk looked up at the stone and metal of the gate. The scene was surreal to him. He still had a picture in his mind of what that gate had looked like two weeks ago, late at night, with the fog rolling through and a Starfleet staff car just sitting in the lot across the street, waiting.

The ironwork had been a barrier then. But now . . . it signified an entrance. He decided to share this insight with Spock, but when he looked away from the gate, the Vulcan was already gone.

He was walking along the Presidio Road that led to the main buildings.

"Hey, Stretch!" Kirk shouted. "Wait for me!"

The Vulcan turned and dutifully waited as Kirk jogged up to him.

"I just wanted to, you know, wish you luck and everything.

I don't think we'll be having any classes together, and I'm sure not going out for any sport you're going out for."

"Thank you," Spock agreed. "Good luck to you as well."

"Luck?" Kirk said. "That's not very logical, is it?"

"Not really," Spock said. "But when in Rome . . ."

Kirk grinned. "Very good. You've been practicing."

Kirk shot out his hand just as Spock raised his and held his second and third fingers apart.

"Ah," Kirk said. He guessed Spock was giving him some kind of Vulcan salute. So he raised his own hand and attempted to separate his fingers just as Spock reached out to shake.

"We're never going to get this right," Kirk said.

"Indeed."

They resumed walking along the side of the road, and when they came to the main circuit path, they stopped.

Kirk asked where Spock was headed.

"I must report to the science adviser in Burke Hall."

"I'm heading over to pilot training in the Mayweather Building."

They stood in silence for a few moments, then Kirk shrugged. "I guess this is it, then."

"Most likely," Spock said.

"Remember that night we met?"

"I am unlikely to forget it."

"I said it was going to be fun. And it was, wasn't it?"

Spock gave Kirk's question considerable thought, then surprised him by concluding, "Yes. It was."

Kirk hefted his bag onto his shoulder. "Well, see you around, Spock."

"See you around, Jim."

Then each went off in a different direction, going their separate ways.

For now.

Midshipman Jim Kirk will return in

STAR TREK®
ACADEMY
Trial Run

For further information about William Shatner,
science fiction, new technologies, and upcoming
William Shatner books and other projects, log on to
www.williamshatner.com